"Are you s   back?"

Quavell replie
by Baron Coba
betraying his own kind. He vowed to oppose
the Imperator even if it meant warring with his
brother barons." She paused, and the tip of
her tongue touched her pale lips nervously.
"That apparently is happening. This installation
will be under full assault by dawn, and we
need to know where you stand."

"I stand where I always stand. Against your
kind. If the baronies are factionalizing, it's best
for the rest of us—humanity—to sit back and
let you fight it out."

She shook her head. "That will not do this
time, Kane. You must choose a faction in this
war, a war your actions have brought about."

Kane suppressed a profane comeback. "I
didn't create the barons or the villes, Quavell."

Maddock stepped forward, stating impatiently,
"It doesn't matter who created who or started
what. We've got a war brewing and those of us
here have already chosen the side they will
fight on. And so will you."

Other titles in this series:

JAMES AXLER

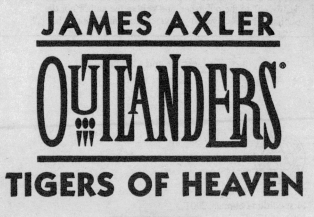

OUTLANDERS®

TIGERS OF HEAVEN

THE
IMPERATOR
WARS

BOOK 2

A GOLD EAGLE BOOK FROM

WORLDWIDE.

TORONTO • NEW YORK • LONDON
AMSTERDAM • PARIS • SYDNEY • HAMBURG
STOCKHOLM • ATHENS • TOKYO • MILAN
MADRID • WARSAW • BUDAPEST • AUCKLAND

To Deirdre and Chesley—
Kangei suru!

First edition February 2001
ISBN 0-373-63829-9

TIGERS OF HEAVEN

Special thanks to Mark Ellis for his contribution to the
Outlanders concept, developed for Gold Eagle.

Copyright © 2001 by Worldwide Library.

But when the blast of war blows in our ears,
Then imitate the action of the tiger.
—William Shakespeare, *Henry V*

The Road to Outlands—
From Secret Government Files to the Future

Almost two hundred years after the global holocaust, Kane, a former Magistrate of Cobaltville, often thought the world had been lucky to survive at all after a nuclear device detonated in the Russian embassy in Washington, D.C. The aftermath—forever known as skydark—reshaped continents and turned civilization into ashes.

Nearly depopulated, America became the Deathlands—poisoned by radiation, home to chaos and mutated life forms. Feudal rule reappeared in the form of baronies, while remote outposts clung to a brutish existence.

What eventually helped shape this wasteland were the redoubts, the secret preholocaust military installations with stores of weapons, and the home of gateways, the locational matter-transfer facilities. Some of the redoubts hid clues that had once fed wild theories of government cover-ups and alien visitations.

Rearmed from redoubt stockpiles, the barons consolidated their power and reclaimed technology for the villes. Their power, supported by some invisible authority, extended beyond their fortified walls to what was now called the Outlands. It was here that the rootstock of humanity survived, living with hellzones and chemical storms, hounded by Magistrates.

In the villes, rigid laws were enforced—to atone for the sins of the past and prepare the way for a better future. That was the barons' public credo and their right-to-rule.

Kane, along with friend and fellow Magistrate Grant, had upheld that claim until a fateful Outlands expedition. A displaced piece of technology...a question to a keeper of the archives...a vague clue about alien masters—and their world shifted radically. Suddenly, Brigid Baptiste, the archivist, faced summary execution, and

Grant a quick termination. For Kane there was forgiveness if he pledged his unquestioning allegiance to Baron Cobalt and his unknown masters and abandoned his friends.

But that allegiance would make him support a mysterious and alien power and deny loyalty and friends. Then what else was there?

Kane had been brought up solely to serve the ville. Brigid's only link with her family was her mother's red-gold hair, green eyes and supple form. Grant's clues to his lineage were his ebony skin and powerful physique. But Domi, she of the white hair, was an Outlander pressed into sexual servitude in Cobaltville. She at least knew her roots and was a reminder to the exiles that the outcasts belonged in the human family.

Parents, friends, community—the very rootedness of humanity was denied. With no continuity, there was no forward momentum to the future. And that was the crux—when Kane began to wonder if there *was* a future.

For Kane, it wouldn't do. So the only way was out—way, way out.

After their escape, they found shelter at the forgotten Cerberus redoubt headed by Lakesh, a scientist, Cobaltville's head archivist, and secret opponent of the barons.

With their past turned into a lie, their future threatened, only one thing was left to give meaning to the outcasts. The hunger for freedom, the will to resist the hostile influences. And perhaps, by opposing, end them.

Chapter 1

Kane sat in the corner of the cell, his teeth chattering. Even crouched on the bunk with the heavy blanket tucked around him, he felt that he would freeze to death in a matter of minutes. He knew he wouldn't, despite the violent shudders that shook his body from toe-tip to nose-tip. The bone-deep, marrow-freezing cold was by now familiar.

For a long time, he just sat hunched over, his teeth clenched so tightly his jaw muscles ached. He listened to the slow steady beat of his heart and he imagined he felt the last bit of the drug creeping through his veins and circulating through his body. Shortly, it would be fully metabolized and the somatic aftereffects would kick in. Absorbed through the skin, the aphrodisiac gel always gave him a serious chill before utter exhaustion settled over him like chains. He doubted his cell was less than sixty degrees Fahrenheit, but he still shook and trembled as if the temperature were on the low side of zero. He fought against the growing drowsiness.

Eventually, he would fall asleep, and when he awoke his body temperature would be back to normal and his hunger ravenous. He would awaken to find a tray of food in the corner, near the cell door. It was always there after his slumber, but he never saw who put it there. This time, he was determined find out.

The food was always the same—a bowl of warm gruel resembling oatmeal, two small plastic jugs of milk and water, a sugary substance in a paper envelope, a plastic spoon and a slice of dark bread. The only way he could measure how long he had been in custody was by how many times he had eaten. He no longer had any idea of how many days he'd spent locked away in the vast complex beneath the Nevada desert, in the sprawling installation known two centuries ago as Area 51 and Dreamland.

Kane forced himself to smile as he tugged the blanket up around his ears. If he had dreamed since his imprisonment, he couldn't remember any of them. In fact, memories of a life preceding his imprisonment in Dreamland were fading, becoming little more than half-remembered dreams themselves.

Kane knew all about the techniques of disorientation. It was a common enough procedure with the Magistrates of the Intel section back in Cobaltville. But the purpose behind his confinement had nothing to do with keeping him confused and dull-witted. He was allowed to leave his small cell at least once every two days, or at least he thought it was every two days. There was no time in his cell, no daylight, no dawn or darkness; there was only a routine eternally lit by a single yellow neon strip inset into the ceiling.

The room that he called home measured hardly twelve paces by ten. Only the small spy-eye vid lens bolted in an upper corner relieved the monotony of the smooth, white blocks and mortared seams of each wall.

Kane's existence seemed like perpetual twilight. His reality was blurred, all the sharp edges blunted. For a while he tried to reckon the passage of time by periods of work and rest, but he lost count and it did not greatly matter anyway. Still, he clung to his old habit of thought, thinking of the sleep periods as nights and his work periods as days. Kane left his cell only to work, to be put out to stud. There was no other word, term or euphemism for it. His life had been spared by Baron Cobalt only so he could father children, plant his seed in the female hybrids in the installation.

He shivered again, and he forced himself to remember the first time he had awakened in his cell. After sleeping off the gel-triggered exertions, the first thing he saw was the tray of food on the floor beside the door. Ravenous, he snatched it up and mindlessly began stuffing himself. Then the memories of what he had been forced to do and with whom wheeled through his mind in a kaleidoscope of broken, humiliating pictures. Roaring with rage and shame, he hurled the bowl of porridge at the spy-eye bracketed in the corner on the opposite wall.

He recollected how he laughed when the thick gruel smeared over the lens. He was still laughing when the door opened and six men rushed in. They wore crisp, multipocketed gray jumpsuits and rubber-soled shoes identical to the articles of clothing he had been given. The two guards in the lead were armed with long, black batons with thready skeins of electricity crackling between the double-pronged tips. The Shocksticks were devices used by ville Magistrates for crowd control. A little under three feet in length, the batons delivered six-thousand-volt localized shocks.

None of the men spoke as they closed in on him from all sides. Kane bloodied his knuckles and the nose of one man before the rest of them grappled with him, bearing him down by sheer weight of numbers. One of the guards reeled away, disabled by a vicious foot to the groin. Kane caved in the front teeth of another man with the crown of his head a split second before he glimpsed the tip of a descending Shockstick. When it touched the side of his neck, all of his muscles convulsed and spasmed. Streaks of agony lanced through his body, and he went down writhing, curling up in a fetal position.

There were more blows, both with feet and Shocksticks, and darkness claimed him. When the light returned, the mess of oatmeal had been cleaned up and two new guards stood over him. He lay on the bunk, aching and angry. One of the men deigned to speak to him.

"Wake up, little Nemo," he said, thrusting a new tray of food toward him. He was a young man with short-cropped blond hair. "Welcome to Dreamland."

Biting back groans of pain, Kane sat up and took the tray. Although his stomach growled and hunger pangs stabbed through him, he made no motion to touch the food. He asked, "How long?"

"How long what?" the second guard asked. He was a seam-faced, wire-muscled man, his dark hair gleaming with pomade. "How long you've been unconscious?"

"That'll do for starters."

"About three hours."

"How long have I been here in Dreamland?" Kane inquired.

The young man answered the question. "About three months. Shortly after you blew the mesa."

Kane's lips quirked in a cold smile. "Heard about that, did you?"

Flatly, the man retorted, "I was there, Kane. I guess you don't remember me."

Kane studied the guard's face for a long moment, searching his memory for a match. "Your name is Maddock?"

The man nodded curtly. "That's right. I was on the hover-tank crew."

Kane arched an eyebrow at him. "I let you go."

"Only so I could deliver a message." Maddock's expression and voice were completely dispassionate. "I still remember it. 'The revolution has officially started.' I delivered it. And now here you are and here I am."

Kane's smile broadened. "Then you should thank me."

"For what?"

"For getting you reassigned to a detail this soft."

Maddock's face suddenly showed emotion, twisting in a grimace. "I'm not part of that. I don't have the qualifications."

Kane's eyebrows rose. "What kind of qualifications do you need for this kind of work?"

"For one thing—"

"Shut up, dipshit," the other man snapped. "He doesn't need to hear your life story."

The man stepped forward, putting the tip of a Shockstick close to Kane's head. "Our orders are to make sure you eat. So eat."

Kane shrugged, lifted the lid of the tray, picked up his spoon and dug into the oatmeal. He said nothing else to Maddock, remembering the night when he, Grant, Brigid Baptiste and Domi inadvertently destroyed the medical facility beneath the Archuleta Mesa in New Mexico. The barons depended on the facility, and though its destruction had been the accidental by-product of shooting down an aircraft, Kane wasn't about to tell the guards that.

At the end of the twentieth century, the Aurora aircraft had been the pinnacle of avionic achievement. Before the nukecaust, the Aurora enjoyed the status of the most closely guarded of military secrets. Supremely maneuverable, it was capable of astonishingly swift ascent and descent, could take off vertically and hover absolutely motionless.

Powered by pulsating integrated gravity-wave engines and magnetohydrodynamic air spikes, the Aurora was a true marauder of the skies, and as such, the baronial hierarchy relied upon it to locate sources of raw genetic material in the Outlands, kill the donors, harvest their organs and tissues, and deliver them to the mesa to be processed.

The mission that brought Kane and his companions to the New Mexican desert was to eliminate the barons' method of harvesting fresh material—merchandise, as they referred to it. Grant shot down the Aurora with a rocket launcher while it hovered above its underground hangar. The impact of the crash breached the magnetic-field container of the two-tiered fusion generator—or at least that was Brigid Baptiste's theory. Whatever happened, Kane couldn't argue with the cataclysmic aftermath, akin to unleashing the energy of the sun inside a cellar. Although much of the kinetic force and heat were channeled upward and out through the hangar doors, a scorching, smashing wave of destruction swept through the installation. As he learned later, if not for the series of vanadium blast-shield bulkheads, the entire mesa could have come tumbling down.

Kane blinked, biting back a yawn, trying to focus not only on the memory of the night at the mesa but also on his reintroduction to Maddock. He wondered if the young man felt any gratitude toward him. Apparently, his partner Gifford wondered the same thing, so after that brief meeting, he never saw Maddock again. Only Gifford came thereafter, using a magnetic card to open the cell door and make sure he always ate the oatmeal served to him three times a day. Three times a day a smirking Gifford inspected the toilet and tiny sink to make sure he hadn't dumped the food.

It took Kane several servings of the bland food to figure out why his diet never varied. The porridge was high in protein and probably laced with both a stimulant and blood-building enzyme. The stimulant was more than likely of the catecholamine family, drugs the Magistrate Divisions used to counteract shock and exhaustion. He dredged his memory for the details of how it worked on the renal blood supply, increasing cardiac output without increasing the need for oxygen consumption.

Combined with the food loaded with protein to speed sperm production, the stimulant provided him with hours of high energy. Since he was forced to achieve erection and ejaculation six times a day every two days, his energy and sperm count had to be preternaturally high, even higher than was normal for him.

Kane knew he was supposed to be special, for a variety of reasons—or at least that was the story he had been told by Mohandas Lakesh Singh who had founded the group of exiles at Cerberus redoubt. The qualities that made him unique sprang from the Totality Concept's Overproject Excalibur. One of its subdivisions, Scenario Joshua, had its roots in the twentieth century's Genome Project, which mapped human genomes to specific chromosomal functions and locations. The end result had been in vitro genetic samples of the best of the best. In the vernacular of the time, it was referred to as purity control.

Everyone who enjoyed full ville citizenship was the descendant of the Genome Project. Sometimes, a particular gene carrying a desirable trait was spliced into an unrelated egg, or an undesirable gene removed. Despite many failures, when there was a success, it was replicated over and over, occasionally with variations. Even the baronial oligarchy was bred from this system.

Some forty years before, when Lakesh had determined to build a resistance movement against the baronies, he rifled Scenario Joshua's genetic records for the most desirable traits to breed into potential warriors in his cause.

According to Lakesh, Kane's family line possessed the qualities of high intelligence, superior adaptive traits, resistance to disease and exceptionally potent sperm.

Kane wasn't a superhuman, but he was superior. Baron Cobalt knew that. He had access to the same records as Lakesh, and he took full advantage of them. There was more to the process than insuring Kane's superior traits. With the destruction of the Archuleta Mesa medical facilities, the barons no longer had access to the ectogenesis techniques of fetal development outside the womb. The conventional means of procreation was the only option for keeping the hybrid race alive.

Lakesh speculated that since Area 51's history was intertwined with rumors of alien involvement, Baron Cobalt was using its medical facilities as a substitute for those destroyed in New Mexico. Of course, he couldn't be sure if the aliens referred to by the predark conspiracy theorists were the Archons. If so, the medical facilities in Area 51 would be of great use to the hybrid barons since it would already be designed for their metabolisms. Lakesh suspected Baron Cobalt could have reactivated them, turned them into a processing and treatment center without having to rebuild from scratch, and transferred the medical personnel from the Dulce facility.

Baron Cobalt's occupation of Area 51 was still a matter of wonder to Kane. As far as he remembered from old Magistrate Intel reports, most of Nevada was considered Outlands. It wasn't a part of official baronial territory, certainly not Baron Cobalt's. The nearest ville was that of Snakefish in California.

Kane couldn't even hazard a guess as to how much of the Area 51 installation was still intact. The few scraps of intel that Lakesh had found in the Cerberus database were nearly two hundred years old, and had to be assembled like a jigsaw puzzle with most of the pieces missing.

Baron Cobalt might be able to provide some of the missing pieces if he felt generous, but generosity was not part of his personality. For that matter, Kane hadn't seen the baron since the day of his capture and his inauguration into stud service. He hadn't seen Domi or heard anything about her, and he wasn't inclined to ask questions. If she had escaped apprehension and was still free and undetected in the enormous installation, he didn't want one of his questions to spur a search for her. If the albino girl had somehow managed to escape, then so much the better.

For reasons he couldn't name, he knew Domi

wasn't dead. Even if Gifford told him she was, he wouldn't believe it until he viewed her corpse. His certainty she still lived derived less from faith in her survival skills than his own instincts. But, he reminded himself darkly, if his instincts were everything he purported them to be, he wouldn't be penned up and treated as a prize bull.

Very little interest had been evinced toward him, other than his capacity to plant his seed in the females. For that matter, Kane had no idea how long he would be allowed to live. He assumed it would be until the first pregnancy was carried to full term, but he didn't know how many months comprised a hybrid's gestation period. Nor did he know if a hybrid female could even conceive a child by a human male. All he knew was what Baron Cobalt had told him upon his capture, accusing him of perpetrating an act of genocide. Rather than kill him outright, the baron had promised, ''I won't let you die.'' The vow became a mantra, not of mercy but of condemnation and punishment.

However, Kane did know the male hybrids were incapable of engaging in conventional acts of procreation, at least physically. As he had seen, their organs of reproduction were so undeveloped as to be vestigial. Before his capture, he had actually shied from wondering if the females were similarly underequipped, but as he discovered many times since arriving at the complex, they were not.

Sleep suddenly washed over Kane in waves. He swallowed a yawn, the effort making his ears pop.

His eyes began to water. He realized he was no longer cold. In fact, he was warm, comfortably, wonderfully warm. Snuggled in the blanket, he tried to remain upright, but it took all of his strength to keep his eyes open. Dimly, he became aware of his body falling over to one side. He was deep asleep before his head touched the pillow.

Chapter 2

A small sound, so faint and indistinct as to be sublimal, gently pierced the black cloak of slumber swathing Kane's mind. With an effort that seemed to take hours and concentration so single-minded it was an obsession, he managed to crack open one eyelid.

He saw a square panel in the wall where it joined with the floor closing almost silently. He spied his tray of food next to the door, and he smothered a laugh of triumph. He remained motionless on the bunk. It wouldn't do for him to act as if the sound of the panel opening and closing had roused him. For the benefit of the spy-eye monitor, he maintained steady deep breathing, as if he were still fast asleep.

He lay unmoving for what seemed like an hour, then slowly he stirred, rolling over, shifting position and finally sitting up. He knuckled his eyes and yawned. He shuffled across the cell and bent over to pick up the tray. As he did so, he glanced surreptitiously at the wall. Now that he knew what to look for, he just barely discerned a square outline barely thicker than human hair.

Kane sat on the edge of the bunk and obediently ate the inevitable oatmeal. He had gone to great lengths to seem docile, but always he waited for an opportunity, for an edge, for an opening.

He wasn't used to waiting. He had been a poor student of the waiting game, but he'd forced himself to learn it. He also forced himself to accept the fact no rescue would be forthcoming. Minutes after his and Domi's arrival in Area 51's mat-trans gateway, the unit had been shut down and the jump lines cut. Grant, Brigid, Lakesh and anyone else back at the Cerberus redoubt in Montana interested in their fates would have to travel cross-country to find out what had happened.

Kane seriously doubted he and Domi could be traced by the signals transmitted by their biolink transponders. Everyone in the Cerberus redoubt had been injected with a subcutaneous transponder that transmitted heart rate, respiration, blood count and brainwave patterns. Based on organic nanotechnology, the transponder was a nonharmful radioactive chemical that bound itself to an individual's glucose and the middle layers of the epidermis. The signal was relayed to the redoubt by the Comsat, one of the two satellites to which the installation was uplinked.

The Cerberus computer systems recorded every byte of data sent to the Comsat and bounced it down to the redoubt's hidden antenna array. Sophisticated scanning filters combed through the telemetry using special human biological encoding. The digital data stream was then routed through a locational program to precisely isolate an individual's present position.

As far as Kane knew, his present position could be

under half a mile of vanadium-shielded rock through which the telemetric signal couldn't penetrate. The Cerberus personnel knew to where he and Domi had jumped, but he was certain they had no idea if the two were alive, dead or otherwise. So Kane resigned himself to do what was expected of him, at least for the foreseeable future.

Only Kane's sense of humor, his appreciation of the ridiculous vagaries of life, kept him sane. When he reflected on his many celibate months after his escape from Cobaltville, the irony of now having more female flesh than he cared to deal with sometimes made him laugh. Of course, the amusement value had begun to pall as of late. He couldn't help but wonder about Baptiste's reaction when—not if, he reminded himself fiercely—he told her of Baron Cobalt's concept of penance.

When he finished his meal, he returned the tray to its place on the floor and went back to his bunk. As soon as he lay down, he heard the click as a magnetic card was swiped through the electronic lock. The door swung inward.

"Kane!" Gifford barked.

Kane sat up as the man stepped into the doorway, Shockstick in one hand, a set of chrome-plated swivel cuffs in the other. Gifford never entered the cell alone, but always waited just a single step out into the corridor.

"I haven't been asleep two days," Kane said.

Gifford chuckled snidely and made an exaggerated show of checking his wrist chron. "More like sixteen hours. Poor fella, I guess those bitches wore you out. Get ready to be worn down to a nub. You're pulling a double shift, you lucky bastard you.''

Kane stiffened in surprise. The routine had never varied before. ''On whose orders?''

The guard scowled. ''It doesn't matter to me and it sure as shit doesn't matter to you. The deal is simple enough, ain't it?''

Kane didn't answer, but he silently agreed with Gifford. If he performed, he lived. If he didn't, he died. The mantra Baron Cobalt crooned into his ear upon his capture still echoed in his mind: ''I won't let you die.''

''Up,'' Gifford snapped.

Levering himself to his feet, Kane stood in front of his bunk, wrists together. He was unshaved, and his thick dark hair lay against the base of his neck in unwashed strands. No fear showed in his gray-blue eyes or in the set of his long, lean-muscled body, but a spasm of vertigo caused him to totter briefly. The dizziness was a side effect of the drug-laced food.

The guard shifted his weight from one booted foot to the other and grasped the molded plastic grip of the Shockstick tightly. In a suspicious tone, he demanded, ''Are you all right?''

Kane smiled thinly, showing the edges of his teeth. ''I didn't think it mattered.''

Gifford's eyes narrowed, and he gestured with the baton. ''It might to some. It doesn't to me. Now move, slagger.''

Kane moved, trying to step jauntily despite the

weakness in his legs. As cold as he had felt a few hours ago, his hopes of escape or rescue were even frostier.

As he entered the corridor, the guard pointed at his chest with the Shockstick. "Stop. Hands."

In an almost involuntarily motion, Kane extended both hands, wrists pressing against each other. The guard slapped the shackles in place and locked them with a loud, final click. Kane didn't resist. He had learned already that any attempt to do so earned a touch of the Shockstick and unendurable agony.

He preceded Gifford down the featureless corridor for a hundred paces, his rubber-soled shoes occasionally squeaking on the floor tiles. He had seen very little of the legendary Area 51 complex, and what he had seen of it was no more dramatic than hallways and offices.

The corridor ended at a T junction. Beyond it an arched tunnel stretched in either direction as far as the eye could see. A small, burnished-metal shifter engine and passenger car rested in perfect balance atop a narrow-gauge monorail track. It disappeared into the darkness to the left and to the right.

Gifford unclipped a small trans-comm unit from his belt and spoke into it. "This is Gifford in section 47-12a. I've got the donor at station three."

Kane had heard himself referred to as such many times, so he no longer took offense at being objectified.

The voice filtering from the comm sounded bored. "Code."

Gifford tried to subvocalize so Kane couldn't hear, but days—or weeks—ago he had read the man's lips. He said lowly, "Jimmy six January."

"Roger," responded the voice from the comm. "Powering up."

The engine suddenly emitted a soft electric hum. At a gesture from the Shockstick, Kane climbed into the passenger car. The monorail system appeared to be the only way to move around the many and widely separated sections of the installation. Except for a cargo train he had seen in the warehouse area on the day he arrived, the cars carried only two people. Without the proper code words, power wouldn't be fed to the rail.

Sitting beside him, Gifford said into the comm, "Green. Go."

The hum rose in pitch and with a slight lurch, the train slid almost silently along the rail. It swiftly built up speed. Overhead light fixtures flicked by so rapidly that they combined with the intervals of darkness between them to acquire a strobing pattern. Neither man spoke as the train sped down the shaft.

The rail curved lazily to the right, plunging almost noiselessly into a side chute. Lights shone intermittently on the smooth walls, small drops of illumination that did little to alleviate the deep shadows. The trains slowed, then hissed to a halt beside a broad platform.

Gifford climbed out first, then gestured for Kane to step onto the platform and walk down the corridor ahead of him. Kane did so and after a few yards stopped automatically in front of an open cubicle.

"Hands."

Kane extended his arms and Gifford deftly unlocked the shackles. The first few times Kane performed the drill, the urge to deliver a *teisho* blow to the man's nose and spear his brain with fractured shards of nasal bones had been almost overwhelming.

"Strip."

Kane unzipped his jumpsuit, kicked out of his shoes and stepped naked into the cubicle. A door slid shut behind him. Kane stood in the small dark room hardly larger than a closet—or a coffin. A red ceiling light winked on, and hard sprays of liquid hit him from every direction. Grime, caked sweat and even dead skin cells slid off his body. The jet sprays reeked of disinfectant. The decontamination booth was a prelude to copulation. The hybrids didn't want him spreading any nasty diseases among their numbers. It was certainly a valid fear. Despite their enormous intellects, the hybrids were susceptible to an entire range of congenital immune-deficiency diseases, so he was periodically subjected to a cleansing process that sterilized even his thoughts.

Kane moved about in the spray, working it even into his hair like a shampoo. The streams ended, replaced by warm air gusting down from a ceiling vent. His very clean, sterilized body was dried within a minute. A light bulb flashed green on the wall and a drawer slid out. From it Kane removed a small battery-powered shaver, which he ran over his face, removing the stubble. The skin of the hybrids was thin and sensitive, and the females were particularly susceptible to beard burn.

A panel on the opposite side of the cubicle slid aside, and Kane stepped into the Spartanly furnished chamber where he would spend the next eight to ten hours. Despite the muted lighting, he saw the bed and the small table holding a carafe of water and a pair of folded towels. He went to the side of the bed and stood, waiting for his first partner of the shift to come through the door.

At first the females selected for the process donned wigs and wore cosmetics in order to appear more human to the trapped sperm donors. Kane had overheard snatches of conversation about how a number of men pressed into stud service were so terrified of the hybrid females they had difficulty achieving erection, the aphrodisiac gel notwithstanding. They had to be strapped down, and for the first couple of sessions, so had Kane. He was never sure if the restraints were designed to keep him from attacking his partners or simply controlling him so he wouldn't injure the fragile females in a blind rutting fever when the gel took effect.

Lately, the restraints hadn't been employed, either. He wasn't sure if the reason was an acknowledgment of his ability to control himself during the sessions or his apparent lack of fear of the hybrids. He knew that not all of the human men regarded the females with terror. Right before his capture, Kane killed a guard and was so stunned by the grief displayed by a female hybrid he had nearly been shot in the back.

He still didn't know who the other men in the installation were, their numbers or where they came from. He assumed most of them were Magistrates, probably survivors of the sec force assigned to guard the Archuleta Mesa complex. Since the clam-mouthed Gifford was his only human contact and therefore his only source of information, it was still a mystery how many men were donors like himself.

The door opened and a female stepped in, moving with the bizarrely beautiful danceresque grace all hybrids seemed to possess. He recognized her immediately. Her name was Quavell, and during his escape from the Archuleta Mesa, he had kept Domi from killing her. He had never let on he knew her, and she behaved as if the encounter had never happened. He knew, however, the hybrids forgot nothing, no matter how trivial. And there was something more—although his memories of seeding sessions were often cloudy, tending to blur into one another, he was fairly sure this was at least the third time Quavell had come to him, perhaps even the fourth.

She was excessively slender and small of stature, less than five feet tall. Her compact, tiny-breasted form was encased in a silver-gray skintight bodysuit. Silky blond hair topped her high, domed skull. The texture seemed to be a cross between feathery down and thread. Above prominent cheekbones, huge, up-slanting eyes of a clear crystal blue regarded him in a silent appraisal. They looked haunted, gleaming with a flicker of emotion that was not characteristic of her kind.

As he gazed at her, Kane recalled other ways in which Quavell was different from the other females he had serviced. Almost all of them mounted him and rode him mechanically, not looking at him at all. It was obvious they would have never engaged in intercourse with any human male but for the baron's orders.

Quavell, he recollected, writhed and moaned a time or two. Although his memories were fragmented, he thought she had orgasmed at least once during their previous couplings.

They gazed at each other dispassionately for a long moment, neither one speaking. Long ago Kane had come to terms with the hybrids' unusual physical appearance, their gracile builds, their inhumanly long fingers, fine-pored skin, and small ears set low on the sides of their heads. Grudgingly he admitted they were by and large a beautiful folk. They weren't ugly; they were just different. In fact, he had yet to see an ugly hybrid, male or female. They were so delicate, so elfin, so self-possessed, he understood why many of them referred to his kind—the old shambling, anarchic humans—as apekin. Yet even as he physically responded to the sexual challenge of her beauty, he felt a moment's repulsion for her alienness. He knew from experience the revulsion was transient and easily remedied.

Following procedure, Kane lay down on the bed, linking his fingers and putting them behind his head.

He stared up at the ceiling, at the light strip shedding a suffused illumination into the room. Mood lighting, he thought wryly.

Wordlessly, Quavell stepped beside him, removing a small squeeze tube from a pocket of her bodysuit. She uncapped it and, gazing down at him with solemn eyes, spread a thin film of colorless gel over his chest and in a line down his stomach.

Within seconds the familiar warmth began to spread over his skin as the substance seeped into his pores and caressed his nerve endings. Gently massaging and kneading, Quavell's long fingers smoothed the gel over his rib cage and down his lower abdomen to just above his pelvic bone. In a voice so faint, so distant it sounded like the rustle of faraway wings, she whispered, "We must speak."

"Why?" Kane asked gruffly.

A flicker of fear appeared in her eyes, but was quickly veiled. Swiftly she placed a forefinger on his lips. "Say nothing. Just listen."

Kane's respiration deepened, his pulse quickening, his blood beginning to burn with a flame that first warmed then threatened to scorch his nervous system and consume his reason. His vision clouded, fogging at the edges as the aphrodisiac began to take effect. He knew from bitter experience fighting it was futile. The best he'd ever been able to achieve was a temporary balance between a horrified realization that his body's reactions were out of his conscious control and primordial lust. Always lust won out over horror.

Quavell's face hovered over his, and she was suddenly transmogrified from an inhuman succubus to a sensuously beautiful vixen. He felt his penis engorge and rise. She self-consciously averted her gaze from the rigid, jutting evidence of his arousal. She unzipped her suit and peeled out of it, revealing a slim, pale body with a wispy suggestion of silk threads between the juncture of her thighs. Her breasts were very small, but very well formed with a great deal of point.

Quavell leaned forward, her face pressing against his. She breathed into his ear, "Things are not what they seem. We need your help."

Kane could have easily encircled her waist with his two hands or her throat with one, but he did neither. Although sweat gathered at his hairline and blood pounded in his temples, he realized with a distant wonder that he was still rational, not blind with rutting fever like all the times before.

His tongue felt thick and clumsy, but he was able to retort in a husky whisper, "I thought that's what I was doing."

Quavell hissed sharply into his ear. "Do not speak, damn you. Concentrate on my words so you will remember later and be able to take the appropriate action. We are being monitored so you must perform, but remember what I say."

Her firm, berry-tipped breasts pushed against his hard chest, and her hand went between them. Her fingers plucked then curled around his erection. "I have given you a diluted mixture of the stimulant so you will be able to think. But you can't let on."

Quavell squirmed on top of him, Kane cupping her tiny muscular rear end. Straddling his hips, she reached down with her right hand and grasped his hard length. "Not all of us here are in service to Baron Cobalt. He brings war to our people—he breaks unity."

She positioned the crown of his swollen member between her moist labial lips and groaned through her clenched, perfect teeth. Like all hybrid females, she was excruciatingly small but she worked herself down on him gradually. "The baron believes he can use you to father a new race, one under his sole dominion."

Clutching at her hips, Kane growled a question, trying to make it sound like a vocalization of bestial lust. "Just me?"

Quavell bent forward and replied in a trembling, whispery contralto, "Just you. The baron feels that putting you in such harness is both a punishment and a salvation. He is…deluded."

She began rocking back and forth, taking more of him inside her. She moaned into his ear, "We will help you. You'll know when. Now be silent and do as you are supposed to do."

Kane did so and for the first time since his imprisonment actually enjoyed it.

Chapter 3

Grant studied the vast blue canopy of the sky where it met the horizon. He squinted, trying to see beyond the shimmer of heat waves. He kept his Copperhead subgun pointed in the general direction of a clump of mesquite, but with one eye he monitored the readouts on the electronic sextant-compass held in his other hand. He glanced all around at the parched terrain as if expecting to see something other than a dead land stretching away in drifting dunes of ocher and saffron.

"Hell," he rumbled in disgust. "If we cut cross-country, we'll be heading miles out of our way. And we've done enough of that already."

"That's what I told you yesterday, after that last detour we took. We've got no choice in the matter," Brigid Baptiste said crisply.

Grant didn't respond. Half the time he never responded to anything except danger anyway, but Brigid noted how he had become even more taciturn over the past couple of days. He consulted the compass again and then looked up at the position of the sun, squinting despite the dark glasses over his eyes.

"Long nights and short days. Less time for safe traveling," he muttered peevishly.

"That's what happens in late fall," said Sky Dog,

approaching with two self-heat MRE packages in his
hands. "That's what I told you ten days ago when
you arrived at my village."

"Has it been that long?" Grant asked with a sour
sarcasm. "Time passes like nothing when you're having this much fun."

Grant's long, heavy-jawed face momentarily
twisted into an expression of barely leashed anger.
Droplets of heat and tension-induced perspiration reflected the sunlight, causing them to sparkle against
his ebony skin like stars. His tan khaki shirt sported
dark half moons of perspiration under the arms. He
sweated profusely, globes of perspiration springing to
his brow and body. Even the usually placid Brigid
Baptiste blinked against the glare and grimaced at the
unseasonably high temperatures.

Standing six feet five in his thick-soled jump boots,
Grant was exceptionally broad across the shoulders
and thick through the chest. Gray threaded the short
hair at his temples, but the down-sweeping mustache
showed coal-black against his coffee-brown skin.

Brigid wasn't offended by his dismissive comment.
She understood his short temper sprang from worry,
guilt and Magistrate-bred impatience with forestalling
preemptive action. She shared his emotions, though
her face was expressionless. During her years as an
archivist in Cobaltville's Historical Division, Brigid
had perfected a poker face. Because historians were
always watched, it didn't do for them to show emotional reaction to a scrap of knowledge that may have
escaped the censor's notice.

She was dressed similarly in clothes of tough khaki, but she had unbuttoned her shirt and tied the tails beneath her full breasts. Despite the season, the hardpan of the Nevada desert reflected heat like an open oven.

Brigid's red-gold mane of thick, wavy hair fell artlessly over her shoulders and upper back. Her complexion, usually fair and lightly dusted with freckles across her nose and cheeks, was a colored deep pink from the merciless glare of the sun. Her eyes beneath the dark lenses of the sunglasses weren't just green; they were a deep, clear emerald. Her willowy body was slender but rounded and taut, long in the leg, her bare stomach showing hard and flat.

Sky Dog extended one of the MREs toward Grant, but he refused it with a shake of his head, returning his attention to the compass-sextant.

"No matter how long you stare at that thing," Sky Dog told him, "it's not going to tell you anything different. Following the road is the most direct route."

Sky Dog's face was lean and sharply planed with wide cheekbones and narrow eyes the color of obsidian. Shiny black hair plaited in two braids fell almost to his waist. Behind his right ear dangled a single feather, as white as the snow-covered peaks of Montana's Bitterroot Range they had left nearly twelve days before.

He wore a loose vest of smoked leather, fringed buckskin leggings and a pair of boot moccasins.

Around his waist was a heavy, brass-studded belt that carried, in loops, a knife, a set of pliers and a polished chunk of turquoise. His erect carriage exuded the quiet dignity of his shaman's position in his tribe.

Grant didn't answer. From a clip on his web belt he took a set of microbinoculars. Pushing his sunglasses back, he brought them to his eyes, peering through the ruby-coated lenses. He swept them over the gently rolling, sandy terrain, then fixed them to a black ribbon of ancient roadway stretching out to the horizon, where Interstate 15 disappeared into a sprawling jumble of rubble eight miles in the distance.

The binoculars' 8x12 magnifying power brought into sharp relief the broken buildings jutting from the desert floor and shattered colors scattered across the parched ground.

"What did the predarkers call that place—Sin City?" he asked quietly.

"That was one name for it," Brigid answered.

Grant continued studying the wreckage of Las Vegas, noting the absence of bomb craters or signs of direct strikes. Several multistoried buildings still stood, hotels and gambling casinos. But unlike the ruins of Newyork, most of the structures weren't very tall. He saw gaping cracks in the earth and through the highway where nuke-triggered quakes had set the tectonic plates to shifting and colliding.

There were no signs of habitation, temporary or otherwise. He spotted no smoke from cookfires or dust raised by movement. Still, the upthrusting collection of buildings reminded him of sharpened stakes planted at the bottom of a pit, a tiger trap. He told himself he and his party would be safe inside the steel belly of the war wag, since it was like riding inside a mobile fortress.

Lowering the binoculars, he glanced behind him at the huge dark shape bulking up from the ground. The massive war wag rested on its double tracks like a dozing prehistoric beast of prey. The armor plate sheathing the huge vehicle was rust pitted, but its dark hull bristled with rocket pods and machine-gun blisters, and was perforated all around by weapons ports.

Nearly forty feet long and probably weighing in at fifty tons, the wag was an MCP, a mobile army command post of predark manufacture. The double thickness of steel planking showed deep scoring in places where AP rounds had almost penetrated.

The Cerberus redoubt database yielded the likelihood that the wag had started life as a C2VI automated tactical command post for mobile armored operations. State-of-the-art two centuries previous, it provided mobility, power and intravehicular data connectivity with other armored vehicles. The controls had been electrically powered from an onboard primary generator unit, as well as offering mounting provisions for onboard and ancillary equipment.

Powered by a six-hundred-horsepower drive train, the C2VI was designed to survive nuclear, biological and chemical threats, not to mention electromagnetic environmental effects. Its armor provided protection against 7.62 mm ball ammunition at two hundred meters, and against 155 mm high-explosive artillery rounds at thirty meters. The wag had been playfully christened Titano by Kane some months back.

A burst of laughter commanded Grant's attention to the left of the MCP. A canvas lean-to had been erected at the starboard door of the mammoth machine. Sheltered from the blaze of the sun beneath it were half a dozen copper-colored, bare-chested men. Their long black hair was braided, and most of them wore breechclouts and deerskin leggings. They were tossing handfuls of small animal bones daubed with spots of paint.

The name of the game was *arcahey,* the Sioux game of bone casting. *Arcahey* wasn't too different from dice, except color combinations were counted, not numbers. Sky Dog's warriors played it every time they stopped for more than fifteen minutes, but Grant had never joined in the games because he didn't see they had anything worth winning. He had no idea what stakes the Indians used for gambling. For all he knew, it could have been the war wag.

Strictly speaking, Titano belonged to the Amerindians. They were the Cerberus redoubt's nearest neighbors—its only neighbors for that matter. Recently, direct contact had been established between the redoubt's personnel and the tribespeople when Kane had managed to turn a potentially tragic misunderstanding into a budding alliance with Sky Dog. Not so much a chief as a shaman, a warrior priest, Sky Dog was Cobaltville bred like they were. Unlike them, he had been exiled from the ville while still a youth due to his Lakota ancestry. He joined a band of Cheyenne and Sioux living in the foothills of the Bitterroot Range and eventually earned a position of high authority and respect among them. Part of that position was to serve as the keeper of his people's great secret—the war wag.

According to tribal lore, nearly a century before, a group of *wasicun* adventurers had ridden inside its iron belly up the single treacherous road wending its way around deep ravines to the mountain plateau. When the vehicle made its return journey, it ran out of fuel, and the Amerindians had set upon the people inside of it. After killing them all, they had hidden the huge machine and removed all of its weapons except the fixed emplacements.

When a set of circumstances brought Grant, Brigid and Kane into first conflict, then alliance with the Indians, Sky Dog proposed the people living on the mountain plateau make the vehicle operational again. They had agreed, since a fully restored and armed war wag would make a solid first line of defense against a possible incursion from Cobaltville. The task to bring a machine back to life after it had lain dormant for at least a hundred years entailed far more effort and time than any of them had foreseen.

First the engine had to be taken apart piece by piece, and then put back together again. All of the instrument panels needed to be rewired. The control systems, designed to be operated and linked by computers, had to be rerouted to manual-override boards.

Periodically over the past couple of months, Grant

and Kane visited the Indian settlement to complete the refitting of the MCP. The front-mounted 20 mm cannons had been repaired, the side and rear rocket pods made fully functional and a drum-fed RPK light machine gun reinstalled in the roof turret. Once the huge vehicle was completely operational with all of its weaponry in perfect working order, it became a true dreadnought, a mobile skirmish line, far superior to the ville Sandcats. Although the war wag was not as maneuverable or as fast as the smaller Cats, it was essentially unstoppable, as all of them had reason to know. It had completely routed a Magistrate assault force a short time before, disabling the two Sandcats that had ferried the force from Cobaltville.

Grant's eyes ran over the war wag's unlovely exterior, but he appreciated its functional form nonetheless. All of the ordnance came from the Cerberus armory, an arsenal literally stacked from floor to ceiling with predark weaponry. It in turn had been supplied from caches of matériel stored in a hermetically sealed Continuity of Government installation. Protected from the ravages of time and the nuke-outraged environment, all the ordnance and munitions were as pristine as the day they rolled off the assembly line.

Grant turned away, swallowing a sigh. All of the blasters, grens and LAW rockets in the armory hadn't proved of any use over the past two weeks. When Kane and Domi stepped into the Cerberus gateway unit to jump to Area 51, they might as well have jumped to another planet or dimension. The telemetric signals transmitted by their biolink transponders vanished from the tracking screen like candle flames snuffed out by a sudden breeze. Nor did their successful transit register on the huge Mercator relief map that displayed all the known working mat-trans units in the Cerberus network.

At the time, no one panicked. Any number of reasons presented themselves for the cessation of the transponder's transmissions, from sunspots interfering with the Comsat's uplink to the signals being blocked by either vanadium shielding or iron ore.

Lakesh told them Area 51 was, in the latter years of the twentieth century, a place as fabulous to Americans as Avalon had been to Britons a thousand years earlier. This particular Avalon, however, was very real and financed by the government. Also known as Dreamland and Groom Lake, Area 51 was a secret military facility about ninety miles north of Las Vegas. The number referred to a six-by-ten-mile block of land, at the center of which was located a large air base the predark government only reluctantly admitted even existed.

Lakesh claimed the site was selected in the mid-1950s for testing of the U-2 spy plane and later, due to its remoteness, Groom Lake became America's traditional testing ground for experimental ''black budget'' aircraft. The sprawling facility and surrounding areas were also associated with UFO and conspiracy stories regarding retrofitting of alien technology. According to Lakesh, Area 51 was a popular symbol for the alleged U.S. government UFO cover-up.

Grant had no reason to doubt Lakesh's history, since one of the experimental aircraft that rolled from the hidden hangars of the Area 51 complex was the Aurora. In New Mexico, he had downed a small, prototypical version of the stealth plane and later Kane, Brigid and Lakesh had seen to the destruction of a far larger and more deadly Aurora aircraft that had been kept in deep storage beneath Mount Rushmore.

Since the Dreamland complex was alleged to be mainly underground, Lakesh opined Kane and Domi materialized in a subterranean section where the biolink signals were blocked. As for the mat-trans materialization not registering on the map of mat-trans units, Lakesh had an explanation for that, too. The unit in Area 51 was not part of the indexed gateways.

Grant and Brigid knew that the Cerberus redoubt had served as a manufacturing facility where the gateway units were mass-produced in modular form. Most of the mat-trans units were buried in subterranean military complexes, known as redoubts, in the United States. Only a handful of people knew the gateways even existed, and only half a handful knew all their locations. The knowledge had been lost after the nukecaust, rediscovered a century later and then jealously, ruthlessly guarded. There were, however, units in other countries—Japan, England, South America and Mongolia to name a few. The exact purpose of the mat-trans units had vanished when the ultimate nuclear megacull had destroyed civilization all over the world.

After a full twenty-four hours passed without so

much as a squirt of a signal from the transponders, Grant and Brigid decided to go after them. When the gateway's auto sequencer couldn't achieve a coordinate lock with the target unit, their dread turned to fear. An active transit lock couldn't be established, so there was no way to tell if the jump line had been cut from the other end or if Kane and Domi were speeding madly through the entire Cerberus network in the form of disembodied digital information.

The decision about the next course of action was reached very quickly. They would travel overland, from Montana to Nevada and either rescue Domi and Kane or discover their fates. Nearly two weeks later, they stood on a crumbling road, wondering whether to forge on through the ruins at night.

Brigid's quiet, uninflected voice drew Grant back to the present. "If we start now, we may be able to navigate our way through the place before nightfall."

Grant eyed the position of the sun again, noting how it seemed to sink swiftly toward the flat westward horizon, aswim in a lurid sea of variegated reds and purples.

"We might," he replied at length. "But that doesn't give us time for a recce beforehand. We'll just have to push on through, no matter what we find there."

A faint smile ghosted over Brigid's lips. "Isn't that the Mag way? Just smash on through, meeting anything out there head-on?"

Grant favored her with a scowl, then he turned it into a bleak smile. "That's the Mag way, all right.

But as you keep pointing out, me and Kane aren't Mags anymore.''

She kicked at a loose stone, stirring up a sifting of dust. "Sometimes," she admitted, "the Mag way has its advantages."

Grant understood she was just as consumed with anxiety and impatience as he. He went back to scanning the panorama of desolation with the binoculars again, sweeping his gaze from left to right. He saw pockets of ruins scattered all around the vicinity of Las Vegas—houses leaning in on themselves, roofs cocked sideways, the burned-out shells of old service stations and fast-food restaurants rising from the arid landscape like headstones.

"Sometimes it feels like we spend half our damn lives crossing one desert or another," he murmured.

Brigid nodded. "That's because half the damn world is a desert now."

Someone who didn't know her wouldn't have caught the hint of bitterness in her matter-of-fact tone. Grant lowered the binoculars, glanced from her face to Sky Dog's and declared decisively, "We're burning daylight. Saddle up."

Brigid ran a hand through her mane of hair and drawled with dry sarcasm, "Viva Las Vegas."

Only Sky Dog laughed.

Chapter 4

In the Lakota tongue, Sky Dog instructed his warriors to stop gambling and strike the canvas lean-to. As they worked, he explained how they were going to penetrate an old *wasicun* center of evil, and so they had to be exceptionally alert.

All of their good humor and relaxed demeanors vanished, replaced by a grim fatalism. Since the nuke-caust, many Indian tribes had reasserted their ancient claims over ancestral lands stolen from them by the predark government. By that measure, almost every square foot of America belonged to the native peo-ples, so they tended to view not only the forces of the villes as interlopers but all non-Indians. Fortunately, Sky Dog's band gave the inhabitants of the Cerberus redoubt a special dispensation.

Grant and Brigid remained outside until the war-riors climbed aboard the battle wagon. As they took their stations at the weapons emplacements, Grant noted how their speech became clipped monosylla-bles, their movements swift and tense. They were like soldiers preparing to enter a war zone.

After they were aboard, Grant made sure the star-board door was sealed, and he walked along the side of the war wag. He and Brigid climbed up into the open hatch at the rear of the wag and strode up the long, narrow passage that led to the pilot's cockpit. Their boots clanged softly on the grillwork of the floor as they walked past the tiny, cramped sleeping quarters. The cargo compartments holding handblasters and jerricans of fuel took up most of the interior space. Small side alcoves led to the fixed weapons emplacements.

Grant hoped the time for their use wouldn't come, since he doubted the Indian warriors abilities to handle them efficiently. When he'd trained them with the handblasters appropriated from the Mag force, he never could completely change their tendencies to hose ammo around indiscriminately.

That was the main reason he and Kane had taken the Magistrates' Sin Eaters back with them to the Cerberus redoubt. The Sin Eater was a Mag's assigned weapon, almost a badge of office, so when the Mag survivors of the engagement were disarmed and allowed to go on their way, Kane and Grant laid claim to their discarded handblasters. They were murderous weapons, and almost impossible for a novice to manage. Even Mag Division recruits were never allowed live ammunition until a tedious six-month training period was successfully completed.

Grant and Kane feared the Indian warriors, unaccustomed to blasters of any sort, would wreak fatal havoc by experimenting with them.

Grant sat in the pilot's chair, the gimbel squealing. Brigid joined him, taking the copilot's position. After Grant keyed on the battery power, they went through the systems checklist, a task they performed at least twice a day, despite its tedium. Both of them knew if a minor problem was overlooked, it could swiftly become major and leave them stranded in the Outlands with no way to alert Cerberus to their situation.

One of the many frustrations of this particular trek was being completely out of touch with the redoubt and the intel it could provide. Bry, the installation's resident tech-head and Lakesh's apprentice, had recently concocted a way to establish a long-range comm channel using the redoubt's satellite uplinks. However, the link depended on the Sandcat's onboard wireless transceiver and computer system. The C2VI wasn't equipped with either, so they were deaf and dumb to anything happening not only at Cerberus but in the villes. For that matter, the only way Lakesh knew Grant and Brigid were still among the living was by the transponder telemetry. And for all Grant knew, Domi and Kane had escaped and were even now safe and snug back in the redoubt. He never allowed himself to dwell for long on another possibility.

Brigid flicked switches on the instrument panel, and needle gauges twitched and indicator lights flashed. The rad counter wavered between green and yellow. The oil level showed nominal, but that was acceptable. The engine temperature was well below the danger zone, too, so Grant turned the ignition key and the wag's engine roared into life.

Smoke puffed from the double exhaust pipes, and the entire vehicle vibrated with such building power.

Grant cautiously released the clutch, and Titano lurched forward. He carefully shifted through the gears, and, wrestling with the steering wheel, Grant guided the wag in a lumbering course down the center of the interstate.

Now that they traveled on a road, even one as rutted and furrowed as I-15, the ride was much smoother than any during the past week. The big engine throbbed steadily without missing a beat, and the suspension didn't squeak or creak.

Brigid unfolded the map and spread it open on her lap. Blessed with an eidetic memory, she really didn't have to consult it, since she'd already memorized the route before they left Cerberus. Still, as they found out to their sorrow and frustration, there was a vast divide between what predark topographers printed on paper and the ruined reality.

"We'll be hitting the Strip," she announced.

"The Strip?" Grant echoed, not removing his gaze from the ob port.

"The main drag, the primary thoroughfare, where all the major casinos and tourist traps were located."

He cut his gaze toward her. "Tourist traps?" he asked sharply.

"A figure of speech. Not traps in the conventional sense. Besides, we're not tourists. Anyway, the Strip is the straightest shot through Vegas. It's wide enough, so we should be able to navigate around obstacles without taking a detour."

Grant grunted, his hands flexing on the wheel. "Wouldn't that be a welcome change?"

Brigid smiled, not answering his sour question. In hindsight, almost since the first day of their journey, it seemed that all they encountered was one detour after another. It wasn't as if Lakesh hadn't warned them when they informed him of their plan to travel to Nevada.

He protested but not too vociferously, at least not after Grant told him how he planned to enlist the aid of Sky Dog and the war wag. The question of whether the Amerindians would help them never entered anyone's minds. The tribespeople owed them several debts, not the smallest of which was the virtual annihilation of a band of Roamers who had attacked their village and carried off a number of women and children.

Grant forbade the warriors to go out hunting or fishing or venture far from the nightly campsites. All of them ate the MRE packs, and though they contained all the minerals, vitamins and proteins a human needed to keep healthy, they all seemed to share one of two flavors—bland or repulsive. No middle ground seemed to exist, and even the most undiscriminating of palates eventually ended up in a form of shock.

The MCP carried a reservoir of fresh water but only to drink. Infrequently, they came across streams where the water was uncontaminated enough in which to bathe. So not only was the war wag's interior stuffy, but it stank, too. As with opinions about the food, no one complained, although Grant caught Brigid wrinkling her nose at his odor when he was in close proximity with her. It wasn't as if she were the paragon of hygiene, either. He knew she was embarrassed by her own disheveled appearance.

After the first five days, Grant stopped initiating conversation, speaking only when spoken to and then in a minimum of words. He concentrated on piloting the monstrous machine. He was the only one who could do it with any degree of expertise. Brigid wasn't strong enough to steer it around obstacles, and the Indians weren't experienced enough to handle shifting, braking and clutching.

As they traveled, Grant did not allow himself to dwell on the possibility Domi and Kane were dead. He kept their images, alive and vital, fixed firmly in the forefront of his mind. But as the short days and long nights wore on, it required more and more effort, more and more concentration to maintain the visualization.

If Brigid ever entertained any doubts the two people were dead, she never voiced them. At first Grant found her calm, unruffled composure a comforting bulwark against his own fears. Lately, he reacted with impatience and irritation not only to her cool facade but to Sky Dog's stoicism, as well.

The old interstate led through the outskirts of Las Vegas, through fields of devastation that stretched almost out of sight. The blacktop road ahead showed the characteristic ribbon effect of earthquakes. The few structures still recognizable as buildings rose only a few stories, then collapsed with ragged abruptness. The wag rolled past burned-out ruins and tumbledown condominiums. Some of the outlying areas were nothing but acres of shattered brick and concrete with rust-scabbed reinforcing bars twisting around the rubble like gnarled, skeletal fingers.

Weeds sprouted from cracks in the pavement and footpaths, sickly green growth with ropy stems that twined around streetlight poles and virtually covered bus-stop benches.

With every passing minute, the broken skyline of Las Vegas loomed larger in the ob port. A towering monolith dominated it. Grant read the huge letters near the top with difficulty. "MGM Them Par. What the hell is that?"

Brigid only shook her head as the vehicle entered the city proper, rumbling down the crumbling blacktop. As they passed a corroded street sign imprinted with the words South Las Vegas Blvd, Grant demanded, "Where's this Strip you were talking about?"

"We're on it," Brigid replied tensely.

Plucking a headset from the instrument panel, he slipped it on and announced into the microphone, "We're here, Sky Dog. Tell your warriors to go on triple red."

By now, all of Sky Dog's warriors knew what the last two words meant. They had heard them often enough over the past twelve days. For most of them, they were the only English words they knew.

"Acknowledged," came Sky Dog's response over the comm link.

The street, though rutted and deeply furrowed, was wide enough for the war wag to circumvent the heaps of rubble that had fallen from the ramparts of the taller buildings. Grant downshifted to get across a heap of shattered concrete, scattered shards of glass and twisted girders of steel.

The facades of the buildings, with their broken neon letters, crumbling masonry and peeling paint, all looked scabrous, as if they were afflicted with leprosy. Grant could still decipher the signage on some of the structures—Dunes, Circus Circus, Bally's. Although the city hadn't received any direct hits, it was obvious hot radioactive particle drift had blown in to kill off all organic life and act as a corrosive in the years that followed.

He steered the vehicle between double rows of rusted-out husks of automobiles, noting how they had been stripped of anything salvageable years, if not decades ago. A few large mesquite bushes sprouted among them, but otherwise the Strip was bare of vegetation. The buildings seemed empty of bird life, and none appeared winging through the sky, tinted now with the red-orange hues of approaching sunset. At least the oppressive heat was finally abating, and the shadows cast by the structures felt like touches of cool water.

As the wag approached the base of the towering monolith, Grant saw the massive statue of a lion toppled over in the street. The head was nowhere in sight, and the paws were chipped and cracked.

"MGM Theme Park," Brigid declared suddenly. "That's what that place used to be."

"What was it? Another gaudy palace?"

"Sort of. More of a family attraction, I think. A

place where the kids could play while the adults gambled away their college tuition money.''

''Oh,'' said Grant. He didn't bother to disguise his puzzlement.

Some of the huge building had collapsed under the weight of the years, and in the not too distant past. A great pile of rubble and broken stone spread out in a heap across the Strip. Grant drove over the outermost part of it, the C2VI jouncing and rocking as the treads crushed the brickwork and concrete blocks to powder. The wag passed into the long shadows of the shattered tower. Black windows and gaping rents in the ancient masonry leered down like caricatures of eyes and mouths.

He steered the vehicle into a narrow channel formed by the debris field. The right-hand treads rode up on the curb, causing it and the sidewalk to collapse and crumble. A row of tall buildings blocked the light of the setting sun, washing the street with the purple hues of dusk.

A prickling of dread began inching its way up Grant's spine to settle in a cold knot at his nape. His scalp felt as if it was pulling taut. Something was wrong. He could sense it the way a seasoned wolf sensed a trap. He looked out the ob port in both directions and saw no sign of danger. Between the buildings, the sky was a crimson-and-orange wash. Glancing over to Brigid, he saw she appeared unconcerned—her posture alert but not tense.

Grant exhaled a breath through his nostrils, hoping the knot of warning at the back of his neck would relax. He told himself he was only experiencing a bout of claustrophobia because of the way the close-packed antique structures hemmed the wag in on both sides. Las Vegas was like any number of ruined cities all over the Outlands. But he didn't like how the darkened lobbies of the casinos and hotels reminded him of shadowed caves where anything could be waiting to pounce. The statue of the lion put him in mind of beasts of prey crouching in their lairs.

As soon as the notion registered, a tiny pinprick of light flickered crimson against the black backdrop within a gaping hole in a building on the wag's right. His initial, adrenaline-fueled assumption was that it was the glinting eye of a mutie predator. A puff of powdery dust kicked up by the C2VI's passage was suddenly bisected by a pale violet thread of light. Instantly, Grant's Mag training kicked in, and almost instinctively he identified the pinpoint and thread of light as a photoelectric cell, a trigger for a proximity detonator.

Lips peeled away from his teeth in a silent snarl, Grant stamped hard on the accelerator and upshifted with a nerve-scratching grinding of gears. The war wag surged forward in a roaring rush, smoke pouring from the exhaust pipes.

Brigid blurted wordlessly in surprise as she was slammed hard against the back of the copilot's chair. Her voice was instantly drowned out by the ear-knocking concussion of a high-explosive charge.

Chapter 5

The night sky was filled with billowing clouds, completely blotting out the starlight. Lightning flared along the mountain peaks. A gale-force northern wind, heavy with Canadian cold, howled around the plateau, bringing with it swirling curtains of snow mixed in with particles of ice.

There was a flash of lightning, dazzlingly close, burning its afterimage into the retina, followed by a peal of thunder so loud it made the plateau quiver. At least, Mohandas Lakesh Singh thought it did.

He blinked at the monitor screen patched into the exterior sec spy-eye. The sensitive infrared filters had been overwhelmed by the lightning stroke, and the monitor showed nothing but shifting veils of gray and white. Not that it would have shown anything else anyway, he thought bleakly.

The weather in late fall at such a high altitude was always sudden and unpredictable, but it had become more so since the nuclear winter, the skydark of two centuries ago. A lightning storm combining sleet, snow and hail was like a return to those days, but at least it would abate in a few hours. It wouldn't last for weeks. Or Lakesh fervently hoped it wouldn't.

Sitting at the main ops station, he squinted through

the thick lenses of his eyeglasses to the environmental console in order to read the outside temperature. The thermometer showed minus thirty degrees Celsius. He winced when he added in the wind-chill factor. It was so cold, the blood would congeal in a human's veins and all the moisture in their bodies turn to frost. A person would die of hypothermia within minutes without state-of-the-art thermal garments.

Such garments were available in the Cerberus redoubt, but he had no inclination of testing them. Lakesh repressed a shiver at the very concept. He had been born in the tropical climate of Kashmir, India, and even after almost 250 years, his internal thermostat was still stuck there. Although he had spent a century and a half in a form of cryogenic suspension, and though it made no real scientific sense, he had been very susceptible to cold ever since.

Lakesh pushed himself back from the station, the casters on his chair squeaking. The noise seemed strangely loud in the high-ceilinged, vault-walled central control complex, like a plaintive wail for help. He repressed another shiver, but not from imagined cold. Sometimes the control complex, the very redoubt itself, seemed haunted.

He was alone in the softly lit center at 1900 hours. It was still fairly early for the big room to be so deserted, and so everything seemed strange. Inside the Cerberus installation, time was measured by the controlled dimming and brightening of lights to simulate sunrise and sunset, and even the hum of power units and disk drives from all the computer stations carried an eerie note.

Lakesh caught a reflection of himself in a blank monitor screen, and not for the first time he experienced a faint jolt of dismayed surprise at his appearance. He looked as if he'd been given a ticket to his own funeral but had yet to attend. His short, ash-gray hair was disheveled, and the thick glasses with the hearing aid attached to the right earpiece lent him a resemblance to a startled bird. Nor was his appearance improved by the magnifying effect the lens had on his rheumy blue eyes.

For the first few years after his resurrection from cryonic stasis, he was always discomfited by the sight of blue eyes rather than brown staring out at him from his own face. The eye transplant was only the first of many reconstructive surgeries he underwent, first in the Anthill, then in the Dulce installation. Although the transplanted eyes were free of disease, they had grown weak over the past fifty years.

For that matter, when any part of his body began to fail, it was either corrected or replaced. His malfunctioning heart was exchanged for a sound new one, his lungs changed out and calcified knee joints removed and traded with polyethylene.

Although the operations had definitely prolonged his life, they had not been performed out of Samaritan impulses. They were done to extend his usefulness to the baronial oligarchy, to serve the Program of Unification and, by proxy, the Archon Directorate.

From a technical, strictly moral point of view, Lakesh had betrayed both, but he found no true sin in betraying betrayers or stealing from thieves. He could not think of the hybrid barons in any other way, despite their own preference for the term *new human*.

New perhaps they were, but whether they deserved the appellation of human was still open to debate. However, if their numbers continued to grow, his own personal definition of humanity would vanish and the self-proclaimed new humanity would take its place.

Swallowing a sigh, Lakesh switched the toggles to route the security vid signals through the main VGA monitor, a four-foot screen of ground glass. He transferred the vid network to the exterior cameras. Despite the night-vision system, it was very dark, appropriately enough since the redoubt was built into a Montana mountain range known colloquially as the Darks. Once, in the centuries before America became the Deathlands, they had been known as the Bitterroot Range. In the generations since the nukecaust, a sinister mythology had been ascribed to the mountains, with their mysteriously shadowed forests and hell-deep, dangerous ravines.

Cerberus was built in the mid-1990s, and no expense had been spared to make the installation a masterpiece of impenetrability. The trilevel, thirty-acre facility had come through the nukecaust in good condition. Its radiation shielding was still intact, and an elaborate system of heat-sensing warning devices, night-vision vid cameras and motion-trigger alarms surrounded the plateau that concealed it.

The road leading from Cerberus to the foothills was

little more than a cracked and twisted asphalt ribbon, skirting yawning chasms and cliffs. Acres of the surrounding mountainsides had collapsed during the nuke-triggered earthquakes nearly two centuries ago. It was almost impossible for anyone to reach the plateau by foot or by vehicle; therefore Lakesh had seen to it that the facility was listed as irretrievably unsalvageable on all ville records. The installation had been built as the seat of Project Cerberus, a subdivision of Overproject Whisper, which in turn had been a primary component of the Totality Concept. At its height, the Cerberus redoubt had housed well over a hundred people, from civilian scientists to military personnel. Now it was full of shadowed corridors and empty rooms, where most of the time silence ruled in absolute sovereignty.

Lakesh checked the immediate area around the closed sec doors, but saw nothing. The storm continued to dump soft, wet snow on the plateau, obscuring his view of where the flat-topped crag debouched into the higher slopes, and completely blanketed the grave sites of Cotta and Beth-Li Rouch.

He transferred the view to a camera just inside the main entrance. The massive sec door was closed, locked tight. Vanadium alloy gleamed dully beneath peeling paint. The multiton door opened like an accordion, folding to one side, operated by a punched-in code and a lever control. Nothing short of an antitank shell could even dent it.

A large illustration of a three-headed, froth-mouthed black hound was rendered on the wall near the control lever. Because the sec cameras transmitted in black and white and shades of gray, he couldn't see the lurid colors of the large illustration on the wall. But he'd so memorized the crimson eyes and yellow fangs that his mind supplied the garish pigment the artist had used. Underneath the image, in an ornately overdone Gothic script, was written a single word: Cerberus.

The artist had been one of the enlisted men assigned to the redoubt toward the end of the twentieth century. Lakesh hadn't bothered to remove the illustration, inasmuch as the ferocious guardian of the gateway to Hades seemed an appropriate totem and code name for the project devoted to ripping open gates in the quantum field.

He transferred the view to the main corridors. No one walked the twenty-foot-wide passageways made of softly gleaming vanadium alloy. Great curving arches of metal and massive girders supported the high rock roof. There was no point in checking the redoubt's well-equipped armory or the two dozen self-contained apartments. He knew four of them were vacant, and had been for days now.

In the two weeks since the disappearance of Kane and Domi, and the twelve days since Grant and Brigid Baptiste left the installation in search of them, Lakesh had found precious little to keep his mind occupied. To his consternation, he realized he experienced a great deal of difficulty adjusting to the absence of the four people. Despite the fact Cerberus had functioned longer without them than with them, they had become the focal points around which all events seemed to revolve. Of course, he reminded himself, the redoubt hadn't functioned as much more than a hideout, a bolt-hole for the various exiles from the baronies.

Only with the arrival of Kane, Grant, Brigid and Domi had the Cerberus resistance movement initiated action of any sort. There had been casualties since their recruitment—Adrian and Davis in Mongolia, Cotta in the Antarctic and Beth-Li Rouch right within the vanadium walls of the installation itself. All the deaths were unexpected, all sad, even Beth-Li's.

The prospect that Kane and Domi might be added to the casualty list was more than sad; it would be devastating. Lakesh felt too frightened by the possibility even to feel sad about it. If they were killed, if Grant and Brigid perished in the attempt to discover their fates, the work of Cerberus would end. He knew he wouldn't have the heart to recruit more people to compose—as Kane wryly put it—the enforcement arm of the operation.

And even if he had the heart, his access to qualified people was exceptionally limited now that he was an exile himself. His usual method of operation was to select likely candidates from the personnel records of all the villes, set them up, then frame them for crimes against their respective barons. He had used this ploy to recruit Brigid Baptiste, Reba DeFore, Donald Bry and Robert Wegmann, knowing all the while it was a cruel, heartless plan, with a barely acceptable risk factor. It was the only way to spirit them out of their villes, turn them against the barons and make them feel indebted to him. This bit of explosive and potentially fatal knowledge had not been shared with the exiles other than Kane, Grant and Brigid, and they had occasionally held it over his head as both a means of persuasion and outright blackmail.

It wasn't as if Lakesh hadn't undertaken enormous risks himself in his covert war against the barons. Before, as a trusted member of the Cobaltville Trust, he'd straddled the fence between collaborator and conspirator. Unfortunately, the suspicions of Salvo, a fellow Trust member and Magistrate Division commander, had been aroused by his activities. He pulled Lakesh off the fence and onto the side of a conspirator, because he suspected him of not only being a Preservationist, but of assisting Kane, Brigid and Grant in their escape from the ville.

Part of his suspicion was true, but the other part was a deliberately constructed falsehood. Salvo had bought into a piece of mole data that Lakesh himself had sent burrowing through the nine-ville network some twenty years before. Salvo was convinced of the existence of an underground resistance movement called the Preservationists, a group that allegedly followed a set of idealistic precepts to free humanity from the bondage of the barons by revealing the hidden history of Earth.

The Preservationists were an utter fiction, a straw adversary crafted for the barons to fear and chase after while Lakesh's true insurrectionist work proceeded elsewhere. He had learned the techniques of mis- and disinformation many, many years ago while working as Project Cerberus overseer for the Totality Concept.

Salvo believed him to be a Preservationist, and that he had recruited Kane into their traitorous rank and file. When Baron Cobalt had charged Salvo with the responsibility of apprehending Kane by any means necessary, the man mistakenly presumed those means included the abduction and torture of Lakesh, one of the baron's favorites.

Lakesh had been rescued and taken back to Cerberus, but the retrieval increased the odds the redoubt would be found. Although the installation was listed on all ville records as utterly inoperable, Lakesh extrapolated that Baron Cobalt would leave no redoubt unopened in his search for him.

Now something else was happening, and Lakesh sensed momentous events moving toward either a violent climax or a terrifying synthesis. Many times over the past couple of weeks, he had tried to work out a provisional hypothesis of its nature, but without hard data he could only guess.

Employing the communications link devised by Bry, he had patched into the Cobaltville wireless systems in order to find weak areas in ville defenses and baron-ordered operations in the Outlands that could be exploited. The process was far from perfect; the electronic eavesdropping could be adversely affected by anything from weather fronts to sunspots.

The last thing any of them expected to overhear was a plan to covertly dispatch Mags from Cobaltville into the territory of Baron Snakefish in California.

Such an act was not only unprecedented, but it was also strictly forbidden by the nonaggression terms established by the Program of Unification more than ninety years before.

When Kane, Brigid, Grant and Domi investigated the incursion, the trail led to the semimythical Area 51. Kane and Domi volunteered to conduct a recce, but had never returned.

Lakesh switched the view on the screen again. He didn't bother glancing in at the room that had served as Balam's holding facility for three years. Just like the apartments of Kane, Domi, Brigid and Grant, it was empty, his glass-walled cell dark and vacant. Balam, the sole representative of the so-called Archon Directorate, and therefore the masters of the baronial oligarchy and the entire hybrid dynasty, hadn't escaped—he had been set free.

In the months since the entity's departure, Lakesh had toyed with the notion that Balam had chosen to remain a prisoner in Cerberus for more than three years until the resistance group was strong enough to actually make a difference in the war to cast off the harness of slavery.

Two centuries before, Lakesh was told that the entirety of human history was intertwined with the activities of the entities called Archons, though they had been referred to by many names over many centuries—angels, demons, extraterrestrials, and the ubiquitous gray aliens who figured so prominently in UFO abduction literature of the twentieth century.

Balam claimed that Archons was a code word first

applied to his people in the twentieth century, and referred to an ancient force that acted as a spiritual jailer, imprisoning the spark of the divine within human souls.

His folk's involvement with humanity stretched back to the dawn of history. In order to survive, Balam's people conspired with willing human pawns to control Man through political chaos, staged wars, famines, plagues and natural disasters.

But the tale of the Archons was all a ruse, bits of truth mixed in with outrageous fiction. The Archon Directorate did not exist except as a vast cover story, created two centuries ago, and grown larger with each succeeding generation. Only one so-called Archon lived on Earth, and that was Balam, the last of an extinct race.

Even more shocking was Balam's revelation that he and his folk were humans, not alien but alienated. Lakesh still didn't know how much to believe of that story. When he attempted to solve the mystery of the so-called Archon Directorate and its agenda the morass of complex and broad legends made him give up in despair. The little he had learned, supplemented by the intelligence Kane, Grant and Brigid had gathered, was still the most shallow, imperceptible scratch on the surface of a vast tapestry of secrecy.

Repressing a shudder, Lakesh switched the view to the dispensary. To his dismay, he saw Banks sitting on the edge of an examination bed with DeFore, the resident medic, timing his pulse. He couldn't hear what they were saying, so after a moment of watching, he decided to check it out himself. He wasn't particularly anxious to go anywhere, but he was tired of sitting and brooding in the ops center. It could be left unmanned for a little while, since the complex had five dedicated and eight shared subprocessors that continued standard operations automatically.

Lakesh walked down the wide corridor and turned left at the T junction. He heard the murmur of voices wafting from the open door of the infirmary. When he entered, he saw DeFore shining a penlight into Banks's right eye.

DeFore glanced his way when he came in, but said nothing. Buxom and stocky, she wore the one-piece white bodysuit common among the redoubt's personnel. Her ash-blond hair was tied in intricate braids at the back of her head, the color contrasting sharply with the deep bronze coloration of her skin.

"Are you all right, friend Banks?" Lakesh asked.

The slender young black man with the neatly trimmed beard jerked in reaction to Lakesh's voice. Lifting his head to peer over DeFore's shoulder, he said, "I don't know. That's what I'm here to find out."

Unlike Bry, Wegmann and Farrell, Banks was not a tech-head. He was currently in training to serve as one, but computers and electronics were not his field of expertise. Lakesh had arranged for his exile from Samariumville for two reasons—one was his training in biochemistry. The second, and by far the most important, was the strong latent psionic talents that had shown up on his career placement tests. Both attributes had proved invaluable during the three-plus years he had served as the warder for Balam. His telepathic ability was strong enough to screen out Balam's attempts at psychic influence, except for the one instance when he was able to insinuate himself into Banks's sleeping mind.

But now that Balam was gone, Banks needed to be trained in another area, several if possible. He was also under the tutelage of DeFore, learning the basics of medicine.

DeFore straightened, turning off the pen-flash. A slight frown tugged at the corners of her full lips. "He's been complaining of difficulty in sleeping and head pain."

"For how long?" Lakesh inquired.

Banks lifted a shoulder in a negligent shrug as if the matter were of little importance. "A few days now."

DeFore snorted. "More like a week. You told me it had been going on for a few days before you asked me for something to help you sleep."

Banks smiled abashedly and rubbed his forehead. "The headaches have only been going on for a few days. Or nights, since they only happen at night when I'm trying to sleep."

Lakesh eyed Banks keenly, then DeFore. "You can't find anything wrong with him?"

She shook her head. "His blood pressure is a little high, and so is his pulse rate. If he wasn't so generally laid back, my prognosis would be that he's suffering from anxiety."

"Anxiety about what?" Lakesh inquired.

"You might ask me," Banks interjected peevishly. "I'm the patient, remember?"

Even such a minor display of asperity was out of character for the normally easygoing young man. Lakesh nodded to him apologetically. "Sorry. Are you anxious about something in particular?"

"No more than usual."

"Then why are you having trouble sleeping?"

Banks's brow wrinkled in thought. "I don't know. I'm restless, as if I'm supposed to do something important, but I've forgotten it. I have insomnia most of the night. When I do manage to drop off, dreams wake me up."

"Are you prone to nightmares?" DeFore asked. "Night terrors?"

"I didn't say they were nightmares," Banks retorted a little defensively. "Just dreams...but strange ones, though. And they've been getting stranger."

Lakesh pursed his lips contemplatively. "Do you remember them?"

Banks made a feeble attempt to smile. "That's the problem. I can't forget them. They're always on my mind. That's why I've been wondering..."

His words trailed off, and he wet his lips nervously with the tip of his tongue.

"Wondering what?" DeFore pressed.

"Wondering if they're dreams at all. They're more like messages so strongly imparted in my mind, I can't forget them like an ordinary dream. But I can't make sense of them, either."

"What makes them so unforgettable?" Lakesh asked suspiciously.

Banks inhaled a deep breath, held it and exhaled noisily. "Because Balam is in them."

The short hairs on the back of Lakesh's neck tingled, even though he had half expected the response.

His eyes narrowed, DeFore declared matter-of-factly, "According to Brigid and Kane, Balam is thousands of miles away in Tibet."

Distractedly, Lakesh said, "Distance means nothing when telepathic communication is involved. Thought transmissions don't have range limitations like radio waves."

"That's what you think I'm experiencing?" Banks's voice held a note of apprehension.

Lakesh didn't immediately reply. Because of his long association with Balam and his latent psionic abilities, Banks had empathically melded with the entity to facilitate a verbal dialogue between warder and prisoner. It was possible, even probable, that the link hadn't been as temporary or as one-way as they had initially believed.

"What's the nature of your dreams?" asked Lakesh.

Eyes growing preoccupied, his voice distant, Banks answered, "A lot of different kinds of imagery, different scenery and settings."

"Give us an example," DeFore suggested, sounding interested in spite of herself.

"Apocalyptic, primarily. Rivers running with water

the color of blood, dead fish floating on the surface, deserts on fire, people dead of disease and famine.''

The young man straightened his slouching posture. ''Then, all those images go into reverse, like when you rewind a vid tape. Then everything is all cleaned up—the water is clear and blue, the deserts turn into forests, people are healthy and happy.

''Balam is always there, walking around like a tour guide, giving me the impression that I'm seeing the past and present, but not necessarily the future. But he imparts the message that it can be—if we allow it and work toward it.''

'' 'We'?'' DeFore echoed dubiously. ''You mean the humanity his plans helped to obliterate?''

Lakesh was surprised when Banks shook his head. ''No,'' the young man declared firmly. He gestured to Lakesh, to the infirmary, to the redoubt at large. ''Those of us here, in Cerberus. And there's another thing—when I see Balam in my dreams, he always casts a shadow.''

Both DeFore and Lakesh favored him with slightly perplexed looks. Lakesh ventured, ''How is that significant?''

Banks shook his head in frustration. ''It's hard to explain, but it seems an odd and small detail to always remember. In whatever scene I see him, Balam has a shadow right beside him, but it's not like a real shadow—it's more like someone else that I can't really see.''

''As if someone is hiding from you?'' DeFore inquired.

"No," Banks answered musingly. "More like I'm supposed to see him but not recognize him until the time is right."

"The time is right?" Lakesh demanded. "For what?"

"I don't know, I really don't. All I get is the feeling that Balam is becoming frustrated with me because I'm not reacting to his messages the way he thinks I should."

He forced a grin. "Good thing they're all just dreams, right?"

Lakesh tugged absently at his long nose. He exchanged a questioning look with DeFore. When she shrugged, he turned back to Banks. "Perhaps I can help clear up the confusion of whether you're dreaming or experiencing a communication. And if the latter is the case, we may end Balam's frustration and permit you to enjoy a restful night's sleep."

Banks shifted uncomfortably on the edge of the bed. "What have you got in mind?"

"Hypnosis." Seeing the fleeting glint of fear in the young man's eyes, he added reassuringly, "Don't worry. I'm fully accredited—not that a two-hundred-year-old certificate would mean much to you—and I've done it before to Kane. He recovered sound of mind."

"That's a matter of opinion," DeFore remarked with a dour smile.

"Once I place you in a suggestible state," continued Lakesh, "you will be able to describe in greater detail these dreams or messages."

"Do you really think it's that important?" Banks asked.

"You tell us," replied DeFore. "You're the one suffering from headaches and insomnia. I can't find an organic cause, and prescribing sleeping pills or antidepressants treats only the symptoms."

"And," interjected Lakesh, "we definitely should determine if Balam is psionically contacting you. I don't think it's a coincidence that this began to happen shortly after two of our people disappeared into Area 51."

"Why not?" Banks asked.

"According to Brigid, Lord Strongbow of New London claimed he interrogated Balam in Area 51 in the year or two preceding the holocaust. He was a former intelligence officer, and there's no reason he shouldn't be taken at his word. There must be a connection."

Banks nodded unhappily. "I suppose you're right. When do you want to do this?"

Lakesh consulted his wrist chron. "I'd judge now is the best time."

Chapter 6

The white-red flash of the explosion washed all the shadows from the man-made canyon, turning it from dusk to high noon. A roaring wall of flame belled out from the dark throat of the building's lobby like a fireball flung from a catapult.

The C2VI rocked violently as the wall of concussive force struck it broadside like a wrecking ball. The shock wave was so powerful, it sent the MCP veering up onto the layers of rubble on the left. Grant wrestled with the wheel, wincing at the eardrum-compressing gongs of debris raining onto the wag's heavy metal hull.

A black pattern of cracks spread swiftly over the building's foundation, huge flakes popping loose with loud snaps. Shards of flying stone fell all around, tons of masonry toppling only yards behind the wag. In the dim light, veiled by swirling clouds of dust, the building seemed to come apart in sections, tumbling and toppling and crashing down in a tempest of destruction. Flying fragments struck the C2VI, making a cacophony like a work gang pounding repeatedly on the armor with sledgehammers.

The tower swayed far out over the street. It tottered, seemed to suspend itself in midair for a long moment, then toppled. With a thunderous roar, the entire top half of the building collapsed in a torrent of stone, brickwork and masonry. Great slabs of concrete crashed into the street. The ground quaked beneath the vehicle's treads, as a seething avalanche of bouncing rock slabs and dust cascaded down. Huge chunks of concrete, cornices and bricks collided in a grinding rumble and crash.

The entire war wag trembled with a prolonged tremor, causing loose objects in the cockpit to fall and clatter. Grant opened the throttle wide, trying to outdistance the thick, whirling dust cloud sweeping toward them. Within seconds, it engulfed the vehicle. The pilot's compartment became as dark as midnight, illuminated feebly by the indicator lights on the instrument panel. They disappeared as a layer of grit and powder coated them.

Grant squeezed his eyes half-shut against the stinging particles of pulverized rock forced through every crack, seam and open ob port. A brick splinter coming in through the side window nicked his hand, but he crouched over the wheel. He kept his foot firmly pressed on the accelerator as the earth heaved and trembled around the wag. Faintly, he heard Sky Dog shouting in alarm over the comm link in his ear, but he couldn't make out the words.

The ringing echoes of stone shards pelting the C2VI tapered off to intermittent bongs, and by degrees the billowing dust cloud thinned, allowing more light to peep into the cockpit. The shuddering crash of tumbling, falling stone slowly faded.

Grant kept the gas pedal floored until they were free of the gray vapor. Then he slowly eased back on the pressure and downshifted. He carefully applied the brake, and the hull shivered and trembled as the vehicle shuddered down to a clanking halt.

"What happened?" Brigid demanded, her voice hitting a high note of both fear and anger.

Grant coughed, fanning the air in front of his face. He spit out grit and snarled, "Demolition charge—a fucking booby trap and I rolled us right into it."

Before Brigid could respond, Grant stripped off the headset and stamped out of the compartment. He met Sky Dog at the starboard side hatch. "Any of your men hurt?"

The shaman shook his head. "A few bruises, but that's all."

Undogging the hatch, Grant flung it open and jumped down, stumbling a bit on the debris-strewn ground. He looked back the way they had come. Settling stone and masonry continued to grate and grind. Peering through the thick pall of shifting dust and smoke, he saw a vast high wall of broken concrete, masonry and bricks completely blocking the Strip. When the building fell, it crushed a number of other structures on the opposite side of the boulevard. A vista of destruction lay before him, overhung by a rising umbrella of dust and smoke.

Brigid, who had followed Grant out of the wag, said matter-of-factly, "A whole building wasn't boobied just to take out a single vehicle."

"No," Grant said flatly, "it was rigged with the

idea of making Vegas impassable. A scout wag would trigger the explosive, and either flatten or block a convoy.''

Sky Dog stared at the vista of destruction, overhung by a rising pall of dust and smoke. ''You mean someone expected a convoy of wags to come down this road?''

Grant nodded curtly. ''And took measures to make the road impassable, and to cut off one part of a convoy from another.''

''Divide and conquer,'' murmured Brigid. ''The standard baronial philosophy.'' She cast a glance toward Grant. ''And only a baron would have access to the matériel to make a booby trap like this.''

''Bulk explosives,'' he said reflectively. ''Probably Astralight mixed with RDX. It's a safe bet no Roamer could get his hands on a photoelectric cell and a storage battery.''

''And even if one managed to,'' Brigid agreed, ''it's even more unlikely they'd have the know-how to put it all together, and know where to place the demolition charges to bring the whole building down.''

She sneezed, clearing her nasal passages of grit and added, ''I think we can safely assume it's a baron taking measures against other barons.''

''Which barons?'' asked Sky Dog.

''Baron Cobalt for one,'' Grant replied. He turned away, back toward the wag. ''If he's claimed Area 51, he may have a way to know if the trap was sprung. I want to be well away from here before anyone is sent to check it out.''

They performed a quick inspection of the grit-filmed exterior of the wag, and except for a couple of small dings, it was undamaged. By the time they were back aboard and rolling again, the sun had all but vanished. What little light shimmered above the horizon was blurred by the shifting haze of settling dust.

Grant guided the machine along the Strip, reaching an area with few buildings more than a couple of stories high. Their worry about tripping another demolition charge became less acute. What didn't fade was Brigid's mounting fear about the fate of Kane.

As she gazed through the front ob port, at the ruins of Las Vegas, she realized the closer they came to their objective, the sharper her fear became. It was as if every mile they clocked had an exponential correlation with her dread about Kane and Domi.

She ran an impatient hand through her heavy mounds of tangled, unwashed hair, and tugged at her grimy clothes. She was an orderly, dedicated, brilliant, almost compulsively tidy woman, and going for the past five days without bathing made her feel more than dirty; it made her feel out of control. Even the bath she had taken at the last stream had been little more than splashing water on her face and limbs.

For some reason, she associated her own feeling of being trapped in events over which she had no direct control with Kane's disappearance. As long as she'd known him, she could never predict what Kane would say or do. He had the tension, speed and power of a stalking wolf. But unlike a stalking wolf, he had almost no patience at all. More than once he had displayed a reckless disregard for not just common sense, but his own safety, particularly when her life was threatened.

But that recklessness wasn't just within his exclusive purview. During their nightmarish mission in the Black Gobi, she had risked her own life to save his, acting on purely instinctive, almost primal impulses. She had been tortured, incapacitated, in a state of shock. Yet, when she saw the Tushe Gun's saber at Kane's throat, only one emotion predominated in her, and motivated her—she would not watch him die again.

The vision she had experienced during the mattrans jump to Russia, then again in the subterranean chamber beneath Kharo-Khoto, floated through her mind, but it was more than a vision; it was a memory.

She was lashed to the stirrup of a saddle, lying in the muddy track of a road. Men in chain-mail armor laughed and jeered above her, and long black tongues of whips licked out with hisses and cracks. Callused hands fondled her breasts, forced themselves between her legs.

Then she saw a man rushing from a hedgerow lining the road. He was thin and hollow cheeked, perhaps nineteen or twenty years old. His gray-blue eyes burned with rage. She knew him, called out to him, shouting for him to go back. He knocked men aside to reach her, and a spiked mace rose above his head, poised there for a breathless second, then dropped straight down—

She knew the young man had been Kane, she knew it on a level so visceral and soul deep that the intellectual prowess she prided herself upon could never touch it.

As the former overseer of Project Cerberus, Lakesh presumably was familiar with all the side effects of mat-trans jumping. Brigid had never told him about her vision of a past life. She feared what he would tell her, not only about herself, but about Kane.

Brigid knew she had seen Kane die that day, even if he bore a different name, but she couldn't believe this Kane, the one she knew and quarreled with, was dead. The mat-trans jump he and Domi made felt like so many other gateway transits, she just assumed he'd be back in a while and they'd resume their argument of the day.

When it wasn't resumed, and Brigid finally accepted the possibility it might never be, she felt more alone than she had in her entire life, even on that day fourteen years ago when her mother vanished from her life. She felt so alone, even in the company of Grant, Sky Dog and his warriors, that she really didn't want to go back to the redoubt and mingle with the people there. Cerberus and the war against the barons seemed to have less and less to do with her life, with anybody's life. For her part, if she learned Kane was dead, she would just as soon walk around the Outlands alone until Roamers or muties jumped her.

It wasn't as if she even missed Kane all that much,

but she did feel resentment that if he was dead she would have to clean up the mess he left behind. Over the past few months, Brigid's resentment over the redoubt's reliance on Kane had become more difficult to keep in check.

After Lakesh abdicated his position of ultimate authority, most of the Cerberus personnel looked to Kane as the decision maker and arbiter of policy. Because he was perceived as the leader, she sometimes felt she had been forced into the role of Kane's sidekick, his yes-person, incapable of deciding her own course of action.

True enough, Kane was decisive, but his choices weren't always right. Not only had she suffered, but she had also watched people die due to his swift decisions. Making split-second, life-and-death choices was part of his training, as deeply ingrained in his identity as his wry sense of humor. And when he was wrong, he was usually very, very wrong. She feared he had wrongly assessed a threat in Area 51 and both he and Domi died because of it.

But frequently, at night, she dreamed of Kane and she woke up to hear his voice, so real she looked around expecting to see him standing off to one side, smoking one of his noxious-smelling cigars and getting ready to engage her in one of their eternal disagreements. In those half-lucid moments, she realized with a heart-stopping terror that if Kane was dead, she would lose her own sense of purpose. She would go on living from sheer habit and momentum.

But she did not let Grant or any of her traveling

companions see how easily the visions of Kane and her terrors invaded her thoughts. She masked it, not allowing them to know how her old sense of being analytical and logical had left her so completely that she wondered what contribution her intellect and font of knowledge had made to anyone.

Brigid was so preoccupied battling despair she didn't hear Grant speaking to her until he repeated her name, harshly and sharply. She swung her head toward him and saw him regarding her with stern eyes, the glow from the instrument casting eerie highlights on his dark, fierce face.

"Sorry," she said. "I was distracted."

"That's the last thing we need," he bit out.

Brigid managed to keep the profane retort from leaving her lips, but she asked coldly, "What were you saying?"

"I asked you about the route."

Brigid flipped through the card file of her eidetic memory. "We stay on I-15 for about twenty more miles, then turn left onto U.S. Highway 93."

"And then what?"

"We follow that for about eighty-five miles."

Grant hissed out a slow, frustrated breath between his teeth. "Shit. Too risky to make it an all-nighter. We'll have to make camp and get rolling again at daybreak."

He turned on the wire-encased, hooded headlights. Twin funnels of yellow-white washed the roadbed with a ghostly illumination. On both sides of the highway stretched extensive tumbles of gray rubble.

Looking to the left and the right, he said, "I'll find us a defensible place in this mess."

Brigid nodded. "If there is such a thing here. But according to the *Wyeth Codex*, it was inhabited over the past hundred years."

The *Codex* was a journal of sorts written by Mildred Winona Wyeth, one of the enduring legends of the Deathlands. Born in the twentieth century, Wyeth had slept through the nukecaust and skydark in cryonic suspension. She was revived after nearly a hundred years by another semimythical figure of the Deathlands, Ryan Cawdor. Wyeth joined Cawdor's band of survivalists who journeyed the length and breadth of postholocaust America.

At some point in her journeys, she found a working computer and recorded many of their experiences and adventures. In many ways, the *Wyeth Codex* began the sequence of events that led to Brigid's exile from Cobaltville.

"Yeah?" Grant inquired. "What'd she have to say about it?"

"Not too much, really," admitted Brigid. "The convention center was used for gladiatorial games by a group of self-styled barons. This was long before the Program of Unification and the oligarchy."

Grant grunted softly. Brigid knew that as far as he was concerned, Cawdor, Wyeth and others were just names from the wild old days before the united baronies were established. She glanced out the ob port at the lowering curtain of twilight, then stiffened as a flicker of orange caught her attention in the darkening sky. She leaned forward, her eyes narrowing.

Grant glanced toward her questioningly. "What?"

"Kill the lights," she said curtly.

Grant's brow furrowed but he did as she said, at the same time relaxing his foot's pressure on the gas pedal. Brigid reached beneath her seat and brought out the binoculars. Putting them to her eyes and propping her elbows on the dashboard, she peered through the dust-streaked polymer glaze of the ob port. She tried to focus on the flecks of tiny lights drifting across the westward sky, but the wag's vibration confused the image.

"Stop us," she said.

Grant braked carefully to a halt, and she managed to track and center the lights. She saw the distinctive waspish configuration of a Deathbird, riding the air in an oblique course toward Las Vegas. The fore and aft running lights of the black chopper glowed like embers against the indigo backdrop of the sky.

"A Deathbird," she said. "About six miles away and it's coming fast."

Wordlessly, Grant engaged the gears and turned the wheel of the C2VI sharply to the right. The wag left the road, bouncing over an embankment. Putting on the headset, he announced the situation to Sky Dog, so that he could alert his warriors.

Grant moved the machine into the mounds of silted-over rubble, slabs of tip-tilted concrete and thick copses of scraggly, thorny underbrush. Slowly the war wag lumbered through the ruins. The old

structures, once homes, restaurants and movie thea-
ters, were toppled and smashed with only a few
sheared-off support posts and pylons lifting toward
the sky. All around stood a maze of crumbling walls
made of wind-scoured brick and concrete block. Brigid felt as if they traveled through the skeleton of a
long-dead giant, rolling past huge, fossilized bones.

Grant expertly maneuvered the vehicle as close as
he could to one of the walls, and slid the gears into
neutral. The engine continued to idle. Brigid peered
through the binoculars, trying to get a fix on the chopper's position. The helicopter skimmed into view, and
she felt a chill touch the base of her spine.

Painted a matte, nonreflective black, the chopper's
sleek, streamlined contours were interrupted by only
the two ventral stub wings. Each wing carried a pod
of sixteen 57 mm missiles. The foreport of the black
chopper was tinted a smoky hue. She knew the Death-
birds were equipped with FLIR instruments—forward
looking infrared—and if they were on, they could
track people by the warmth of their footprints.

"Won't they pick up the heat signature of the engine?" Brigid asked.

"They'll pick it up whether the engine is running
or not." Grant's tone was quiet and uninflected. "If
they spot us, I don't want to risk an emergency restart
and mebbe stalling us out."

Brigid nodded, squinting through the eyepieces of
the binoculars. The Deathbird was closer, but swinging in a great circle at least two hundred yards away,
maintaining an altitude of about a thousand feet. Only

faintly could she hear the drone of the T700-701 turboshaft engines, and the swish of the steel vanes slicing through the air.

Body tense, breath coming with difficulty, Brigid kept expecting the chopper to dive toward their position, loosing missile after missile. After less than a minute, the chopper rotated and flew off back to the west. It gathered speed, and soon its running lights were swallowed by the deepening gloom.

Grant gusted out a sigh and ran a hand over his unshaved jaw. Softly, Brigid asked, "Where did it come from? Why didn't the crew spot us?"

He uttered a thoughtful grunt. "A lot of reasons. Mebbe their heat scanners weren't working. Mebbe they didn't get close enough to detect our signatures."

Grant didn't sound as if he believed his own words, so Brigid said, "The nearest barony is Snakefish, which is in northern California. A Deathbird's internal fuel range is what, around three hundred miles?"

"Give or take ten or so."

"There's no way it could have come from Snakefish unless there's a fuel depot nearby."

Grant swiveled his head toward her. "Couldn't it just as easily come from Area 51, to check out the explosion?"

She shook her head. "Not unless it was already in the air and halfway here. Area 51 is approximately ninety miles away."

Impatiently, Grant demanded, "What's your point?"

"My point," she answered tersely, "is there may be a garrison of soldiers, maybe even Magistrates, between here and where we're going."

"Are you saying we shouldn't stick around here?"

She nibbled her underlip nervously. "I find it hard to believe that Bird crew didn't spot us."

Grant's hands clenched around the steering wheel. He heaved a deep weary sigh before saying, "Me, too."

He engaged the clutch and the gears, pressing on the accelerator. "I'll find us another campsite."

The wag's treads crushed a portion of fallen wall to powder, then there was a streak of flame from the shadows on their left. A few yards ahead of the vehicle's bow, the night lit up with a hot orange flash, a fireball ballooning upward and outward. Stone shards and chunks of soil rattled against the hull.

"Son of a bitch!" Grant snarled, jerking on the wheel, sending the front end of the war wag through a wall. It cleaved through it like the prow of a ship through an ocean wave, sailing across the fields of rubble.

Between a split in a section of wall, Brigid glimpsed the bobbing of multiple headlights and silhouetted man-shapes flitting to and fro. A crumping detonation hammered at their ears, and a tall pillar cracked at the base amid a spray of rock chips and debris. It folded over like a jackknife, toppling directly in front of them. It landed with such an impact that they could feel the ground quake even in the MCP. Dust mushroomed in a heavy blanket.

Grant wrenched the wheel violently, and the wag inscribed a swerving, zigzagging course. Brigid fell against the bulkhead, banging the back of her head painfully on the metal wall. Pushing herself upright, blinking the pain haze from her eyes, she looked frantically to the left and right, trying to spot the origin of the fire. Even as she twisted in her seat, she glimpsed the fiery, sparking contrail of a projectile arrowing on a direct course with their starboard side.

Chapter 7

The first few times after a session, Kane felt terribly exposed and vulnerable as Gifford led him out of the chamber. He thought all eyes were upon him, on his nakedness, gauging the depth of his humiliation as he was paraded down a corridor. But then he realized no one wanted to see him, particularly the few hybrid males he passed. He figured he reminded them of how an inferior old human, one of the apekin, could accomplish things they couldn't.

So despite his weariness, Kane forced his head up, stiffened his spine and put a spring into his step. The hybrids looked away from him as he walked by, but he made it a point to wink at them and smile in cold superiority.

Near the monorail platform, Kane and his guard stopped at a cubicle where he donned a fresh coverall—or the same one, just recently laundered—and his rubber-soled slip-on shoes. Then Gifford shackled his wrists, and they returned to section 47-12a. By the time they reached it, Kane was already shivering from the aftereffects of the gel.

As Gifford escorted him down the corridor to his cell, the man asked, "How many does this make so far, Kane?"

With a distant quiver of surprise, Kane realized he couldn't remember. He no longer counted either the number of sessions, or the females involved in them. He tried to cover a shiver with a dismissive shrug. "I don't know. Four this time, I think."

Gifford snickered. "Keep at it, boy. You're bound to get it right one of these days."

"Very whimsical," Kane countered in mock approval. "You can make a funny. I'm impressed. Maybe I've misjudged you."

Gifford dropped back a pace, allowing Kane to move ahead of him, then he jabbed him hard in the small of the back with the Shockstick. Streaks of fire lanced up and down Kane's spine. He felt his lungs seize as he fell to all fours. It took every iota of his focused willpower to keep from curling up in a fetal position.

Gifford loomed over him, swishing the humming tip of the baton over his head. "I'm sick of your mouth, Kane, sick of nursemaiding your turncoat ass, sick of seeing you still alive when you should have been executed for treason."

Kane forced himself to one knee, gulping air. "You're more than welcome to take my place, Gifford."

The man's face flushed beet-red, and his eyes glinted with jealous malevolence. "I wouldn't be in your place for a baron's ransom, boy. Having to stick it in those half-human bitches—"

His shoulders heaved in an elaborate shudder. Kane knew his revulsion was feigned. Slowly, stiffly, he rose to his feet and said, "I know some of you full-blooded men have done more than stick it in the half-human bitches, Gifford. A guy named Hank comes to mind."

Gifford's lips writhed as if he were about to spit in his face. His hand clenched on the molded grip of the Shockstick, the knuckles standing out whitely.

"Secondarily," Kane continued in a monotone, "the baron decreed you don't have the right stuff to take my place. That's why you're my nursemaid and why you can't work me over."

With his bound hands, Kane gestured first to the Shockstick and then to the spy-eye cam on the ceiling. "You get spotted using that on me just because you feel like it, adversely affecting my sperm production, and your ass will be the one executed, not mine."

Making a growling sound deep in his throat, Gifford took a threatening half step forward. Kane held his ground, his gray-blue eyes boring unblinkingly into the guard's flushed face. "Think about it, Gifford," he advised quietly.

Some of the angry tension left the man's posture, but he still glared balefully. He gestured impatiently with the baton. "Go."

As they started walking again, Gifford asked, "You think I'm jealous of what you're getting, with what I have?"

"And what's that?" Kane inquired with a studied indifference.

"The finest little piece of albino ass that ever pulled a train."

It required all of Kane's willpower to keep himself from rocking to a halt and spinning. Instead, he forced himself to keep walking.

Gifford chuckled, an ugly, slobbery sound. "We use that fuck jelly on her, and she turns into a little white screwing machine. There's been some nights when she's taken the whole squad, and she still begged for more."

Kane clenched his teeth so hard he heard them squeak and grind. His heart began to pound in fury and a building horror.

"Stop," Gifford ordered.

Kane halted in front of the door to his cell, his stomach muscles spasming. The guard swiped his key card through the electronic lock, and the cell door swung open smoothly and silently.

"Hands."

Kane turned, extending his cuffed wrists. As Gifford unshackled him, he said in a conspiratorial whisper, "Just thought you'd like to know what happened to her. Damn shame you lost her, ain't it?"

"No," Kane replied in a similar soft whisper. "This is the damn shame."

With his hands still extended, he snatched a double fistful of Gifford's coverall and yanked him forward, at the same time butting him in the face with the crown of his head.

The man's nose flattened with a mushy crunch of cartilage, and both nostrils spewed twin scarlet streams as if they were the nozzles of hoses. As Gifford reeled across the width of the corridor, arms windmilling, Kane swiftly stepped back into his cell and the door closed automatically.

On the other side of the door he heard nasal, liquid snufflings and bursts of obscenities. Kane waited, assuming a combat posture just in case Gifford was so maddened he would charge in alone for some payback. Kane seriously doubted he would, now that he was unfettered. The guard might eventually incapacitate him with the Shockstick, but not before receiving injuries far more serious than a broken nose.

After a minute, the faint cursing died away, and Kane relaxed, then hugged himself as a shudder shook his frame. His knees felt weak and wobbly, and he dropped down on the edge of the bunk, reaching for his blanket. As he drew it around him, he tried to convince himself Gifford's sneering description of Domi was a cheap intimidation ploy. It didn't seem reasonable that if Domi had been apprehended at the same time as he was the guards wouldn't have apprised him of it.

Bleakly, he realized her capture very well might have been withheld from Baron Cobalt. The baron would not have allowed a subbreed Outlander to live, much less give the permission for her to be used as a sex toy.

Kane squeezed his eyes shut, not wanting to think about it. His only spark of hope—and a small, dim one at that—had been planted on the possibility of Domi's escape from the installation.

He lay down, huddling in a fetal position, waiting for the waves of sleep to overwhelm him. Although he felt weak and weary, slumber did not come. Drowsily, he mentally replayed Quavell's cryptic comments, trying to reason out their meaning now that his mind wasn't clouded by the aphrodisiac gel.

Things are not what they seem. We need your help.

Even if it were true that she had applied only a diluted mixture of the gel, and that others like her opposed Baron Cobalt's plan for him, he certainly didn't take her words at face value.

We will help you. You'll know when.

Presumably the hybrids, like the humans who lived in the villes, were conditioned to obey the barons without question, indoctrinated from birth to uphold the principles of unification. Even if Quavell felt Baron Cobalt threatened that unity, Kane couldn't accept the concept that she and other hybrids would turn against him.

He toyed with the notion that Quavell had fallen in love with him during their couplings, but he almost instantly dismissed it. Not so long ago he'd thought exploiting the attraction the Amazon Ambika had for him would make her willing to cater to his every whim. An hour later she'd tried to castrate him with a sword, so he reassessed his effect on women, even hybrid ones.

Also, visceral emotions did not seem to play a large part in the psychologies of the so-called new humans. Even the bursts of passion Kane had seen displayed by Barons Cobalt and Sharpe had been of the most rudimentary kind. Lakesh had theorized that although the tissue of their hybridized brains was of the same organic matter as the human brain, the millions of neurons operated a bit differently in the processing of information. Therefore, their thought processes were very structured, extremely linear. When they experienced emotions, they only did so in moments of stress, and then so intensely they were almost consumed by them. Kane had witnessed firsthand infantile temper tantrums staged by both Sharpe and Cobalt.

His stomach growled and a hunger pang accompanied it. He hitched around on his bunk, looking toward the wall, half-hoping his meal would be early. It wasn't, and he closed his eyes, drifting off into slumber.

Almost immediately it seemed, he awoke. For a few seconds he wasn't certain what had awakened him. Then he realized it wasn't a noise, but rather the fact that the overhead neon strips had flickered and gone out, leaving him in complete darkness. The disappearance of the sound had penetrated his sleeping mind and prodded his point man's sense into raising an alarm. His time sense told him he had been asleep only a few minutes. With a faint shock he realized he was no longer cold and his lassitude had left him. The diluted gel had also diluted the somatic side effects.

He continued to lie on the bunk motionless, casting his eyes toward the corner where the spy-cam was bolted. When he didn't see the green glow of the tiny power-indicator light, a surge of desperate energy galvanized him into rolling off the bunk.

For a moment, he crouched in the impenetrable

blackness, listening and looking. He heard nothing but the rapid beat of his excited heart and saw nothing, not even the faintest hint of light shining under his cell door. Instantly he knew there was no power to this section of the installation and his door couldn't be unlocked by a key card.

We will help you. You'll know when.

Unconsciously holding his breath, Kane crept across the cell to the wall next to the door, his fingers swiftly exploring it near the wall. For a few seconds he felt nothing but the cool, smooth expanse of sharply cut stone and the recessed seams.

He groped blindly for what felt like an interlocking chain of eternities, expecting at any second the lights to flash on and the door to open and Gifford to come in, laughing cruelly at how he had been tricked. Anger burned within him, and he snarled wordlessly, clawing at the wall, fingernails scraping over its surface.

When he touched a narrow slot, he almost laughed wildly with elation. He tugged at the square panel, swinging it open wide on tiny hinges. He felt a catch lock on the inside. Falling prone, he ran his hands around the opening, judging its dimensions by feel alone. The fit would be tight—Kane carried most of his muscle mass in his shoulders and upper body like a wolf, but he was positive he'd shed some pounds during his captivity.

Extending his arms as far as he could into the opening, Kane felt a square shaft dropping straight down vertically. His fingertips slipped over smooth metal sheeting. He figured his food was brought up to his cell by a dumbwaiter type of contrivance, probably operating automatically. The elevator had to be equipped with some kind of device to both unlock the wall panel and push the tray into his cell. He felt no mechanism, no winch or cables above the opening.

He struggled to control his almost frantic need to leap headfirst into the shaft, heedless of what lay at the bottom. He checked the impulses, angry at himself for allowing his captors to turn him into an animal, charging madly toward even the most unreliable avenue of escape.

Reversing position, Kane lay on his back and put his feet into the aperture and scooted forward. His flesh tingled at the prospect of climbing down into the yawning throat of blackness, but he half crawled, half slid into the duct. There was only darkness below him.

Kane placed both hands flat against the walls of the shaft and wriggled entirely in. The duct was about three inches wider than his shoulders, which helped him squirm down it. Expanding his shoulders until they pressed against the smooth metal, he jammed the sides of his feet tightly against the walls, for the first time glad for the rubber-soled shoes. They helped him achieve a degree of traction. By pushing with his feet and shoulders in unison, he gained the leverage he needed to keep from sliding uncontrollably down the chute.

Kane moved only a few inches at a time. At first he tried to estimate how many feet per minute he descended, but the muscle-straining process of contracting his shoulders, expanding them, and bracing with his feet required all of his concentration. After a few minutes, a cramping pain began to flow through his shoulder sockets and the arches of his feet. Because there were no welds or seams where the ductwork's sections joined together, he slipped a time or two. Once he slid for at least a dozen yards before he braked himself, hands and shoulders scalding with the friction.

Perspiration pebbled on his face and trickled beneath his clothes, but Kane maintained the steady downward progress, over and over with hands, shoulders and feet. He lost all track of how long he did it, or how far he descended. The ache in his shoulders became a bone-deep, boring pain. The confined space of the shaft threw back the echoes of his harsh, labored respiration until it filled his ears and he could hear nothing else, even if there were other sounds.

The sweat ran in runnels down his arms and onto the palms of his hands, causing them to slip. He expanded his shoulders, holding his body in place with them and the edges of his shoe soles to wipe his hands dry on his coverall. The movement dislodged him and he slipped from his position.

Kane tried to spread his shoulders wide and slap the flats of his hands against the shaft walls to slow himself, but the braking effect was negligible. He couldn't secure a grip, and his body plummeted straight down, the wet skin on the palms of his hands

making a protracted squeal as he plunged into a sepia
sea.

He didn't fall long or particularly far. Kane landed
flat-footed, the double impacts jacking both knees into
his lower belly and sending streaks of agony scorching through his ankles and into the Achilles tendons.
Over the explosion of air violently expelled from his
lungs, he heard the faint ring of metal and a noisy,
cracking clatter beneath his shoes.

He was only dimly aware of falling on his right
side against a hard surface. Kane didn't lose consciousness, but he hovered at its brink for what
seemed like a long time. He opened his eyes in utter
darkness. His head whirled, and there was dull throbbing in his belly and sharp pains in his ankles. Dragging air into his straining lungs, he forced himself to
his hands and knees, his limbs trembling.

Reaching out, he groped around in the blackness.
His hands touched the walls of the shaft, the floor,
then nothing but air. He felt rather than heard an insistent mechanical throb, overlaid with the faintest of
electronic hums. He ran his fingers around him and
realized he was kneeling on a square platform raised
less than a foot from the floor. The platform was the
elevator, probably propelled up the shaft by a tele-
scoping, pneumatic piston like the lift disks in the
Cobaltville Administrative Monolith.

A warm, semisolid substance squished beneath his
knees, and he caught the whiff of porridge. He had
landed on his tray of food, crushing the container of
milk, spilling the oatmeal and breaking the tray. Ap-

parently, the elevator was about to deliver his meal when the power went out.

He edged off the platform, sweeping his arms back and forth just above the floor. He felt as if he had been rendered blind as he crawled through the Stygian darkness, and imagined that cold, mocking eyes watched him fumbling along. Kane's breath came in harsh, ragged bursts as he struggled to control his mounting anxiety. Even if the little elevator operated by an automatic setting, someone had to have placed the tray there and he, she or they might still be in close proximity.

Kane's fingers brushed an object lying in his path, and he tentatively picked it up and examined it. He felt stiff fabric, a pair of slender, flexible, bulb-tipped rods about six inches in length and two large circular shapes that felt like glass. He recognized it as a night-vision headset he had seen worn by Dreamland sec forces when they pursued him in the warehouse section.

Swiftly, Kane slipped the skullcap over the top of his head. It didn't fit snugly, and he had to adjust it so it wouldn't slide askew. He figured it had been designed for a hybrid's oversize cranium. Running his fingertips along the rims of the goggles, he found tiny switches. He flicked them and heard a nearly inaudible whine of the batteries powering up. The two infrared projectors attached to the skullcap came to life. The room viewed through the lenses seemed eerie, but he couldn't suppress a sigh of relief that a form of vision had been restored to him.

The thermal-imaging goggles caught the heat radiating from a pair of horizontally mounted steel tanks in a far corner. They exuded a wavering, molten glow as if they were covered in white-hot lava. Kane climbed gingerly to his feet, grimacing as he put his weight on them. Despite the pain, he didn't think his ankles were broken or even sprained. Still, he walked slowly and carefully, as if he were treading on eggshells.

A network of pipes stretched out from the ends of the tanks with glass meters and valves attached to them at regular intervals. The pipes fed into a metal-walled upright disk, about six feet in diameter and three feet thick. As he drew closer, he saw the words Danger! High Voltage stenciled in red on its dull surface. Kane scanned the walls and ceiling for concealed spy-eyes and found none. He could only assume that he was in a maintenance room, probably a secondary power-generating station. However, the power it produced wasn't being fed to the lighting system.

Away from the heat shed by generators, the room acquired a strange, flat, unshadowed appearance, as if he were walking through a two-dimensional stage setting. He found an open doorway and eased out into a corridor, hugging the right-hand wall. The tiled floor acted as a heat damper, so despite the headset, much of the hallway was too dim to see beyond a few feet. Shadows took on various shades of gray and green.

Kane felt his way forward, step by step. The only sounds he heard were those of his own breathing and the faint scuff of his shoe soles on the floor. He had no idea where in the enormous base he was, or where he was supposed to go. Obviously, Quavell had arranged for both the blackout and the night-vision goggles, but he had no inclination to skulk from one stretch of empty corridor to another until he found someone—or someone found him.

He saw a right turn up ahead and as he approached it, he heard the steady squeaking of rubber footwear coming from around the corner. A rod of what appeared to be solid white incandescence pierced the gloom. Kane came to a halt, pressing his back against the wall. He stood stock-still, not even breathing. The light wavered, so bright Kane squinted against it as if it were a beam of condensed and compressed sunshine.

A stocky man strode rapidly around the corner, holding a flashlight in his right hand. He was sallow skinned with a dark blond crew cut. Judging by the fixed expression on his face, his concentration was totally occupied by reaching a destination or fulfilling a task.

He was so preoccupied he nearly stepped on Kane's toes before he glimpsed him. He did a violent double take, stumbling to a halt, voicing a gargling cry of shock when he saw the bug-headed figure looming in the shadows. His expression of open-mouthed astonishment was so comical, Kane nearly laughed. When he saw the man grab the trans-comm unit at his belt, all the amusement value vanished.

Kane stabbed him with a left-handed thumb-and-forefinger thrust to the larynx, crushing the man's windpipe and driving whatever alarm he was about to raise back into his throat.

He dropped the flashlight, and as it rolled it splashed the corridor with an unearthly, unreal illumination. Clutching at his neck, his eyes bugging out, the man dropped to his knees. A little spurt of blood spilled from his lips as he crumpled to the floor. He wheezed and gasped, and Kane quickly patted him down. He found no weapons, not even a Shockstick, but he relieved him of the trans-comm and a key card. By the time he had put both items in the pockets of his jumpsuit, the man was dead.

Kane felt a pang of pity for him, but it was distant, almost perfunctory. Grunts usually died unmourned and sometimes even unacknowledged. He knew that from spending most of his life as a grunt himself. Retrieving the flashlight, he thumbed it off and moved swiftly down the corridor, figuring the man had to have come from somewhere.

He found a door within the next ten yards and he approached it warily, risking the flashlight to locate the electronic lock. Pressing his ear against the door, he listened for sounds on the other side. There either was none or the material was simply too dense to allow any to leak through.

Standing to one side, he swiped the card through the lock's slit, but as he expected, nothing happened. The lock didn't have an internal power source. He tried the handle and wasn't surprised when it didn't budge.

Kane looked up and down the corridor. Not wanting to backtrack, he started walking farther into the gray-green gloom. He didn't use the flashlight for fear of alerting anyone who might be coming toward him. He passed several doors, but he didn't try the key card on any of them.

Because the features of the passageway didn't change, and he walked slowly, with one hand on the wall, he felt as if he were on a treadmill, not getting anywhere. Turning a corner, he began to wonder if there was any end to the stretch of hallway. Then he saw a faint glimmer of light piercing the darkness. It was small, irregularly shaped and it appeared to be a long way off. The headset showed it as a molten puddle, so the light put out a little heat at least.

Kane started forward quickly, almost breaking into a run. Then, to his astonishment, he found he'd reached the light after taking only a few long strides. Lying at the base of a door on the left-hand wall was a Nighthawk microlight, a standard piece of equipment he and Domi had carried with them from Cerberus. Though the Nighthawk emitted a powerful, concentrated beam, it was small enough to be fastened the wrist by a Velcro strap.

Kane picked it up and affixed it around his left wrist, unconsciously keeping his right hand, his gun hand, free. He missed the comforting weight of the Sin Eater. The 9 mm handblaster was the chief badge of office of the Magistrates. Normally, it was holstered to his right forearm where it could be drawn by tensing his wrist tendons.

He shone the microlight over the door, examined the electronic lock and then the handle. He decided not to bother using the card and gripped the handle, pushing it down. When a lock solenoid clicked aside, he felt the short hairs on his nape tingle.

Although the Nighthawk lying in front of the door was an obvious sign of the route he was supposed to take, his point man's sixth sense went on high, suspicious alert. Kane's senses were uncannily acute when something nasty lurked around a corner, and tension built in him like subtle electricity. Carefully, he eased the door open. Bent in a half crouch, he stepped cautiously over the threshold. The interior was just as dark as the corridor.

Kane walked stealthily, heel-to-toe as he always did in a potential killzone. After a dozen yards, he reached a short flight of stairs, and he walked up them on the balls of his feet. He experienced a bad second when a riser creaked beneath his weight. Keeping close to the handrail, he edged along to the next floor. From the little his headset showed, it appeared to be an exact duplicate of the one below, and he squashed a rise of angry impatience.

From up ahead he heard a murmur of male voices speaking in an angry garble, and he came to halt near the throat of the stairwell. When he turned off the Nighthawk, his heart jumped in an uncharacteristic spasm of fear. The prospect of being recaptured suddenly seemed far worse than dying. The voices of two men carried to him hollowly.

"How the fuck do I know how this place can have a power failure?"

"Blown fuses? I haven't seen a fuse box since I've been here. Have you?"

"No, but I haven't looked for one, either. Besides, the blackout is just in this section."

"What about emergency generators?"

"They're out, too."

From around a corner, the glare of a flashlight blinded Kane, the goggles magnifying the glow to dazzling brilliance. He threw himself back toward the stairwell, but he misjudged the distance. Grabbing the handrail, he stumbled and the headset slammed against the wall. One of the infrared projectors snapped off like the stem of a dried flower, and he was in the dark.

The two men saw him, and they apparently decided if he ran from them, he had no business in the base. Subscribers to the shoot-first-ask-questions-later school of internal security, they triggered handblasters in his general direction. Smears of orange flame stabbed out of the darkness. The sound of the shots were flat, almost lackluster cracks, and Kane guessed the calibers to be no greater than .38s, but he still wasn't going to expose himself to the fusillade.

Bullets smacked the wall over Kane's head, sprinkling him with plaster dust. The rounds ricocheted with whistling whines. Two more shots, coming so fast they sounded like a single report, shook the air. There was nothing lackluster about the reports. They were booming thunderclaps.

Then there was silence. Kane heard the echoes of the last two shots rolling down the corridor, like the crash of a distant surf. The sharp smell of cordite cut into his nostrils. He stayed where he was, crouched on the stairs, one hand on the rail. It wasn't heroic, but he figured it was certainly prudent. He stripped off the headset and peered around the corner.

The bright beam of the fallen flashlight danced over the corpses sprawled facedown on the floor. Pools of blood, black in the dim light, spread thickly around their bodies. Both men looked to have suffered head shots inflicted from behind.

Faint footsteps sounded from down the passageway and a funnel of light bisected the murk. Kane ducked back, listening to the footsteps grow louder with every passing second. The light shone full in his face, and he tensed to jump and fight and die.

Domi's childlike voice piped angrily, "'Bout time you got here!"

Chapter 8

The C2VI rocked back and forth like a ship caught in the embrace of typhoon-torn seas. The springs and shocks squealed a perpetual protest as Grant wrenched the machine on a lumbering, tangential course away from the streaking rocket. He doubted the warhead packed sufficient power to penetrate the armored hull, but the kinetic impact of the explosion could play hell with the onboard electrical systems.

The missile skimmed just beneath the war wag's chassis through the space between two track assemblies. It passed entirely beneath the vehicle, struck a metal flange a glancing blow and went spiraling on a crazy trajectory, its smoking contrail weaving a corkscrew pattern in the air. It exploded against a heap of rubble, the crump of the detonation only slightly muted by the wag's armor. A squall of gravel rattled against the undercarriage like hail.

"Whoever they are," Grant half shouted to Brigid, "they're trying to take out the tracks to disable us!"

The trip-hammer roar of the turret-mounted RPK filled the MCP with an eardrum-slamming stutter. A brass rain of empty cartridge cases tinkled down into the passageway, and the astringent stink of cordite cut into their nostrils.

"Cease-fire!" Grant roared into the transceiver. "We don't have targets! Cease-fire!"

Faintly over the din, they heard Sky Dog repeating Grant's order in Lakota. Another rocket scorched a path across the wag's prow, detonating on impact against a concrete pylon. The column exploded in a ball of fire and fist-sized chunks of stone. They struck gonging chimes on the hull, bouncing away from the double-glazed polymer of the ob port.

"Can you see anybody?" Grant demanded loudly.

The wag hit a deep rut in the ground, and only Brigid's safety harness kept her in her seat. "No," she replied breathlessly.

Despite the noise of the explosions, Grant was aware that all the fire seemed to be herding them, driving them in a certain direction. He also noticed a distinct lack of small-arms fire being directed at them, so their attackers knew nothing less than high-caliber AP rounds could hope to do more than nick the heavy metal planking.

He glimpsed a small object arcing out of the sky, and a few seconds later a red-yellow bouquet of flame bloomed nearly beneath the wag. The deck shuddered, and the dulled thunder of the detonation made both Brigid and him wince.

"Now the bastards are using grens!" Grant snapped. But the grenade did nothing to impede the massive vehicle's progress.

The wag's prow sideswiped a support post. Grant lurched violently in his seat, his chest slamming into the steering wheel with breath-robbing force, but he kept his foot on the gas pedal. Grant turned the wheel back and forth, causing the vehicle to yaw and careen and make an exceptionally difficult target. The treads scoured the ground, hurling sprays of gravel and pulverized dirt in arching plumes. The streams of dust and grit hung in the air, making a smoke screen of sorts.

Grant spun the wheel hard to the left. The C2VI rocketed through a wide break in a wall, shearing off jagged edges with nerve-scratching screeches. They found themselves in a wide courtyard, surrounded on all four sides by the crumbling remains of walls. None of them appeared too much over fifteen feet tall. Judging by the number of verdigris-eaten brass handrails scattered around, he figured they were in what was left of a casino's gaming room.

Cutting the wheel sharply to the right, he stomped hard on the brakes at the same time. The resulting skid wasn't controlled, so the rear end slewed around in a wide arc. A wave of gravelly soil crested from beneath it. The wag clanked to a halt facing the breach in the wall by which they had entered.

Grant felt the pressure of Brigid's eyes on him, and he curtly answered her unasked question. "This place is halfway defensible. Gives the roof blaster a 360 field of fire. Only one way in by foot." He nodded toward the split in the wall. "It's not wide enough to let more than three men in at a time."

To his mild surprise, Brigid said approvingly, "We'll make them come to us rather than cooperate with the way they wanted us to go, right?"

Grant gave her a wry, half smile. "Right. We'll make a Mag of you yet."

Her return smile was jittery and sour. "Not in this lifetime."

Grant gave orders over the comm link for the warriors to stand by their stations. They weren't to fire until they acquired definite targets and then they were to be circumspect with their ammo. He kept his attention focused on the breach in the wall, expecting a rocket or a gren to come through. Brigid watched the rift and the tops of the walls around them. With muscles tensed and pulses racing, they waited, but nothing happened.

Sky Dog appeared in the compartment, bending between the seats, peering through the ob port. "Red Quill in the turret has spotted movement all around on the other side of the walls. We're being surrounded. They may think we're boxed in."

Grant nodded brusquely. "What about wags?"

Sky Dog's reply was grim. "Three, maybe four on the outer perimeter. Red Quill is pretty sure they're Sandcats."

Grant released his breath in a profanity-seasoned sigh. "So am I. Only Mags have this kind of firepower."

"Mags from where, though?" Brigid asked.

"I don't think it matters where they hang their helmets," Sky Dog retorted bleakly. "They're all the same—butchering coldhearts."

When Grant swiveled his head to regard him with

a challenging stare, the shaman added hastily, "Present company excluded, of course."

Grant acknowledged the comment with a wry smile. "Thanks. Well, Titano can take the Cats if it comes down to a head-to-head. But the Mags are armed with LAWs and probably gren launchers. A lucky shot could knock us off our tracks."

Brigid opened her mouth to speak when, with a rattling roar, the RPK in the roof turret opened up. On the rim of a wall a little to their left they saw pulverized concrete explode, flinging up fountains of grit. She caught only the briefest glimpse of a dark figure falling back out of sight. The autoblaster fell silent.

"Good," Grant grunted. "He didn't have to be reminded not to hose ammo around like it was water."

"We're fast learners," Sky Dog remarked dryly. "We've had to be."

They waited in silence again. Because of the steady, full-throated throb of the engine, they could hear nothing from the outside.

After a few minutes, Brigid asked, "Do you think they'll wait us out, hope we'll run out of fuel?"

Grant considered the possibility for a thoughtful moment, then shook his head. "I doubt that's their strategy. As far as they know, we have a full tank. For them to camp out and wait for that to happen requires a hell of a lot more patience than Mags are trained to have." His big hands clenched and unclenched around the steering. "No, they'll make a move before very long. More than likely, they'll start with a gren barrage. While we're distracted by that, an assault force will—''

He broke off, leaning forward, gazing intently out the port. His ''What the fuck?'' was a hoarse whisper of incredulity.

Following his stare, Brigid and Sky Dog both uttered wordless murmurs of surprise. On the other side of the wall breach, a strip of white cloth waved up and down, back and forth. All three people gazed at the white flag, astonished into speechlessness.

Brigid was the first to recover her voice. ''Are they calling a truce? Or are they surrendering?'' Her tone was heavy with suspicion.

''They want to parley,'' Sky Dog interjected. ''Only Wankan Tankan, the Great Spirit, knows about what.''

Grant knuckled his chin contemplatively, staring with narrowed eyes at the flapping, makeshift flag. He sat completely still for a long, stretched-out tick of time. Then he unbuckled the seat harness and arose, saying in a deliberate tone, ''Let's find out.''

Although Brigid protested his leaving the safety of the war wag, Grant pointed out that Magistrates as a general rule didn't employ subterfuge to achieve an objective. If they wanted to chill him, they wouldn't try to lure him out in the open to do it in full view of the unknown opposition aboard the vehicle.

''Besides,'' he argued, ''with all the weapons trained on the wall, they'll know whatever happens to me will happen to them.''

Grant walked the length of the vehicle toward the

rear hatch, pausing only long enough to strap his holstered Sin Eater to his forearm. The big-bore handblaster was less than fourteen inches in length. The
magazine carried twenty 9 mm rounds, and the stock
folded down when it was holstered along his arm.
Actuators attached to the weapon popped the Sin
Eater down into Grant's waiting hand when he flexed
his tendons in the right sequence, putting it there in
an eyeblink. There was no trigger guard, and when
the firing stud came in contact with his finger, it
would fire immediately.

At Brigid's urging, he attached a trans-comm to a
shoulder epaulet on his shirt and opened the frequency so she could overhear what was said outside.
He walked along the side of the C2VI and took up
position directly in front of the vehicle, making sure
he stood between the forward mounted missile pods.

Arms folded across his broad chest, he kept his face
a neutral, expressionless ebony mask. Women sometimes confused him, muties and hybrids disturbed
him, but he knew how to deal with Magistrates. If
they saw even a glimmer of fear in his eyes, so much
as a twitch of apprehension on his face, the Mags
would react like predators scenting fresh-spilled
blood.

A black silhouette appeared in the breach, arms
held wide, the white flag gripped in the left hand. An
uninflected male voice called, "I'd like to come in."

Like Grant's expression, the man's tone was of
carefully calculated neutrality.

"Who's stopping you?" Grant called back.

The figure shifted between the edges of the split and then stepped into the courtyard. Illuminated by the C2VI's headlights, he resembled a statue sculpted from obsidian, somehow given life and movement. The light struck dim highlights on the molded chest piece and shoulder pad. His face was concealed by a black helmet except for his mouth and chin. A red-tinted visor masked his eyes. His tread was measured, deliberate and menacing.

Grant appeared to be unmoved by the man's appearance, but he felt a slight chill. Part of the effect of a Magistrate's polycarbonate body armor was psychological, to instill fear in not just the criminal but in everyone. Glinting dully on the molded left pectoral was the red duty badge, a stylized scales of justice, superimposed over a nine-spoked wheel. The badge symbolized the Magistrate oath of keeping the wheels of justice turning in the nine baronies. As Grant knew, more often than not the wheels ground over the innocent and the guilty alike.

The electrochemical polymer of the helmet's visor was connected to a passive night sight that intensified ambient light to permit one-color night vision. The tiny image enhancer sensor mounted on the forepart did not emit detectable rays, though its range was only twenty-five feet, even on a fairly clear night with strong moonlight.

Looking at the man, Grant realized again how the design of the Magistrate armor was more than functional; it was symbolic. The figure approaching him, though smaller than him, looked somehow strong, fierce and implacable.

When a man concealed his face and body beneath the Magistrate black, he became a fearsome figure, the anonymity adding to the mystique. There was another reason behind the helmet, the armor, and it was a reason all Magistrates knew but never spoke of openly. When a man put on the armor, he was symbolically surrendering his identity in order to serve a cause of greater import than a mere individual life.

Grant's father had chosen to smother his identity, as had his father before him. For that matter, all current Magistrates, the third generation, had exchanged personal hopes, dreams and desires for a life of service, in order to bring a degree of order to the anarchic madness of postnukecaust America.

The Mag marched fearlessly up to Grant and halted ten feet away. He spread his arms, and even though a Sin Eater was snugged in its holster, the gesture let Grant know he had no intention of unleathering it. The two men faced each other in silent surmise for a long moment. Finally, the black-armored man asked, "Mind if I take off this fucking helmet? I've been wearing it for the last three hours, and I'm sweating like a swampie slut in heat."

Grant hadn't heard the vulgar simile in a long time, not since his own early days in Cobaltville's Mag Division. He tried but was unable to completely repress a smile. "Go ahead," he said. "I used to get heat rash behind my ears myself."

Moving with slow deliberation, the man undid the

underjaw lock catch and tugged the helmet up and off his head. Grant felt a faint twinge of surprise. The Mag was much younger than he'd expected, probably less than twenty-five years old. His smooth, boyish face was clean-shaved and bore no scars. His short, crisp black hair was of regulation length, and was neatly parted on the right. His brown eyes didn't possess the gimlet hard glint of a man who had seen and participated in so much violence he couldn't conceive of solving a problem without a blaster or bludgeon.

"I'm Ramirez," the man stated matter-of-factly. "Commander of this unit."

"Unit from where?" asked Grant.

"We're a combined force, from Snakefish and Sharpeville. I'm from Snakefish."

Grant eyed him skeptically. "Sharpeville is way the hell and gone across the country, up around Delaware. What are Mags from Sharpeville doing in Nevada?"

In lieu of a shrug, Ramirez revolved his helmet between his black-gloved hands. "The same thing as you, I imagine—penetration of Area 51."

GRANT'S MIND WHEELED with conjecture, skepticism and a thick layer of outright suspicion. Ramirez seemed to know the kind of thoughts spinning through Grant's head and he said nothing more, as if allowing the big man time to process it all.

Grant gave the younger man a slit-eyed stare, and Ramirez met it unblinkingly. After a few moments of trying to stare each other down, the Mag said blandly, "Your turn."

"My turn for what?"

"To either confirm what I just said or waste my time denying it."

Grant crooked an eyebrow at him. "You're pretty sure of yourself, letting your mission slip to a stranger you just met in the Outlands."

A smile tugged at the corners of Ramirez's lips. "We've never met, but I know who you are, Grant. I've heard about you. Hell, every Mag in every division in every ville has heard about you and seen your pix."

He ran a finger over his upper lip. "Of course, the mustache is a new addition. I guess you decided to buck the personal-appearance code on top of turning renegade."

Grant's stomach muscles fluttered in barely leashed anger. Forcing a note of nonchalance into his voice, he replied, "You know, after hearing that term applied to me and my friends a time or two, I finally looked it up. A renegade is someone who betrays a cause or a faith or a group of people who trusted him. I don't figure that's me."

"Really?" Ramirez inquired, striving to imitate Grant's casual tone. "Then who would it be?"

"Off the top of my head, I guess it would be the barons."

Ramirez nodded as if he weren't at all surprised by the answer. "I didn't call this truce so we could hammer out our political differences. Especially not when our respective goals are so similar.''

"I'm listening, son.''

Ramirez finally displayed a flicker of emotion other than detached superiority. Anger glittered in his eyes at Grant's patronizing attitude and use of the word *son*. He said sternly, "I don't have the time to waste in a firefight with you. And to be honest, it looks like it would take more ordnance than we can spare to stop that juggernaut of yours. And even if we could spare it, we'd probably suffer casualties.''

"No 'probably' about it,'' Grant interjected.

"All right,'' Ramirez snapped. "I don't know why you're going to Area 51, but I'm told that's your destination. You don't know why we're going there. So instead of us standing around trying to piss on each other's feet, let's talk some truth.''

Grant made a studied show of pondering the young man's proposal. In reality, he was consumed with curiosity, and if Ramirez had shown any reluctance to come clean with him, Grant would have taken him prisoner and beaten the whys and wherefores out of him. But he didn't want to appear too eager.

"You said you were told Area 51 was our destination?'' he inquired.

Ramirez nodded. "Yeah, that's right.''

"Who told you?''

A lazy smile played over the young man's lips. "Let's talk about it.''

"Then do it.''

"Not here." Ramirez gestured toward the wall. "Out there."

Faintly, even over the steady rumble of the MCP's engine, Grant heard Brigid's voice raised in protest filter over the trans-comm. He didn't need to hear her objections; he had plenty of them himself. Grant snorted in derision and demanded, "When you heard I was going to Area 51, did you also hear I was stupe?"

Ramirez frowned. "If the object was to simply chill you, it would've been done by now. I don't have all the answers to the questions you're likely to ask. I'm just the messenger."

"Who has the answers?"

Wordlessly, Ramirez again waved toward the split in the wall and arched his eyebrows quizzically. Grant met his gaze and said into the trans-comm, "If you want to be part of this, come on out and join us."

Ramirez's eyes darted up toward the ob port of the C2VI, but the cockpit was darkened, and he couldn't see who might be there. Grant asked, "You don't mind if I bring someone else to evaluate your idea of truth, do you?"

"Hey, invite anybody you want. Your whole crew even. How many is that now?"

Grant smiled dourly. "You'll understand if I decline to answer."

Ramirez nodded in a mocking imitation of a gracious bow. In spite of himself, Grant felt a growing admiration for the young man. His easygoing, insouciant manner and ready wit was in marked contrast to most hard-contact Mag personalities. In some ways, Ramirez reminded him of Kane, especially when his friend was about the same age.

Within a minute Brigid came walking up with her characteristic mannish stride. A mini-Uzi hung from a strap on her right shoulder, and an Iver Johnson automatic handblaster was snugged in a cross-draw holster above her left hip. When she stood beside Grant, Ramirez's eyes flicked up and down her form appreciatively. "Are there any more like you inside?" he asked with a grin. "If so, I just may consider turning renegade myself."

Brigid regarded him dispassionately, her emerald eyes cold. "My name is Baptiste."

"Brigid Baptiste, isn't it? Former archivist in the Cobaltville Historical Division and presently a condemned criminal." Ramirez gestured grandly toward the wall. "It's a pleasure to meet you, Brigid. Now, if we may move this along..."

Grant imitated his gesture with an exaggerated sweep of his left arm. "After you...son."

Ramirez didn't appear to be offended. If anything, his grin widened. He sauntered casually toward the breach. Brigid murmured disdainfully, "He thinks he's quite the charmer, doesn't he?"

"Compared to most Mags," Grant side-mouthed in response, "he is."

As they followed the young man, Grant unclipped the trans-comm from his shirt. "You there, Sky Dog?"

"Here."

"You might as well shut down the engine. I think we're here for the night."

The shaman's reply was tense. "And how long are we supposed to wait for you, buttoned up in here?"

"If you don't hear from us in one hour," Grant said, "then get Titano moving and flatten anybody in your path."

"My sentiments exactly," retorted Sky Dog. Imitating Brigid's comment and cadence of speech of less than an hour before, he added in a sarcastic drawl, "Viva Las Vegas."

Not bothering to ask the meaning of the cryptic sign-off, Grant thumbed the plastic cover closed and slipped the comm unit into a pants pocket. He followed Ramirez through the rift in the wall, Brigid walking closely behind him. On the other side, arrayed in a semicircle, were four Sandcats and at least two dozen men in Magistrate black.

Less than half the size of the C2VI, the Sandcats had originally been built to serve as FAVs, Fast Attack Vehicles, rather than as a means of long-distance ground transportation. A pair of flat, retractable tracks supported the vehicle's low-slung, blunt-lined chassis. An armored topside gun turret concealed a pair of USMG-73 heavy machine guns. The Cat's armor was composed of a ceramic-armaglass bond, shielded against both intense and ambient radiation. It was therefore lighter in weight and mass than the C2VI's armor but did not offer the same degree of penetration protection. However, the lesser weight made the Cat faster and far more maneuverable than the war wag.

Ramirez strode past the Magistrates, saying, "Stand down, stand down."

Brigid and Grant affected to ignore the men in the black exoskeletons although their flesh prickled with tension. Grant closed the gap between himself and Ramirez. "You said you were told Area 51 was our destination?"

"That's what I was told," the man responded curtly.

"Who told you that?"

Ramirez didn't answer until he reached the rear end of a Cat. The hatch hung open, and bowing deferentially toward the interior, he said, "He did."

Brigid and Grant squinted toward the two figures within. One was lounging across a couple of the folded-down jump seats, head propped up on a hand. He had close-cropped blond hair, broad shoulders and chilling milky blue eyes the color of mountain meltwater. His eyes were very large, shadowed by the sweeping supraorbital ridges characteristic of hybrids. His cheekbones and chin were very prominent, his pursed mouth little more than a slit.

His hair possessed a feathery, duck-down texture. His cranium was very high and smooth, his ears small and set very low on his head. Despite the bulky camouflage jacket and pants he wore, the man's body was excessively slender, and he didn't look to be more than five and a half feet tall. A bright blue scarf was wound around his slim neck.

The figure on the deck stirred, lifted his shaved head from a satin pillow and gazed at them speculatively with dark eyes. He wore a leather harness and velvet loincloth. The harness displayed his exceptionally well developed upper body. His torso looked to be all muscle from the neck down to his hips.

Whereas the harness showed off his bulging biceps and platter-sized pectorals, the loincloth did nothing to disguise his shriveled, atrophied legs. They stretched out behind him like flaccid, flesh-colored stockings half-filled with mud.

In a musical contralto voice, the blond man said, "Mr. Grant, Miss Baptiste, I'm very happy to meet you. This is my high councillor, Crawler. I am Baron Sharpe. You may call me 'my lord.'"

Chapter 9

Banks lay on an examination bed, hands clasped over his stomach, his respiration steady and regular. The overhead lights in the infirmary had been dimmed to a comforting, intimate dusk.

"Just try to relax, friend Banks," Lakesh said, reaching into a pouch on his bodysuit and removing a silver fountain pen. He pitched his voice to a low, soothing level.

"I've never been sold on the concept of telepathic communication," DeFore said skeptically from her place near the foot of the bed.

"It's happened to us before," Lakesh retorted testily, annoyed by the interruption. "Balam used Banks as a channel of communication on two previous occasions. Kane received a psionic summons and a plea for help from Fand halfway across the world."

"So he told us," the medic replied with an edge in her voice. "But it was a purely subjective interpretation, like the time you hypnotized Kane to recall details of a parallel world. What did you call them—casements?"

"Actually," Lakesh corrected her, "Balam called them casements. As for Fand's contact with Kane, Grant pretty much corroborated what he reported."

DeFore's full lips pursed as if she tasted something exceptionally sour. "I don't see how you can put any stock in information derived from hypnotic regression."

"It's all information, isn't it?" Lakesh challenged. "Objective, subjective, secondhand, even third-party rumors floating in the subconscious. It's up to us to distill it all down and make some sense of it."

"You're making my point for me," DeFore shot back. "You're filtering all that information through individual perceptions. What you're left with is a diluted and contaminated subjective viewpoint."

"Contaminated?" Banks repeated in puzzlement, raising his head from the pillow.

DeFore nodded. "Exactly. You were in such close proximity with Balam for so long it's only natural your unconscious would provide dream imagery of him."

"But why now?" Banks demanded. "And why so many dreams?"

"You may have been dreaming about him for a long time. They just never penetrated your conscious mind. Once they did, it's only logical you'd experience serial dreams with him as the central character."

Banks frowned uncertainly. "You could be right. But what if they aren't dreams of Balam, but really him trying to tell me something? If I'm put in a trance, he might possess my mind again."

Lakesh smiled down at him encouragingly. "Parapsychologists did find that subjects tended to score higher on ESP tests when they were hypnotized, so if Balam is trying to communicate with you, you'll be more susceptible after I induce a hypnagogic state.''

"Somehow," Banks said dryly, "that doesn't make me feel a whole lot better."

"You never feared Balam when you believed he was an extraterrestrial, did you?" asked Lakesh. "Now that you know he's as much of a native Terran as you—if sprouted by a different branch on the evolutionary tree—you should feel even less trepidation.''

Banks had served as Balam's warder and keeper for more than three years. Over the course of the creature's captivity, the young man had developed a bond, even a fondness for him. All of them had been surprised to learn that not only had Balam understood Banks's feelings, but he also actually appreciated his kindnesses.

The initial reaction of almost everyone else in the redoubt who came in close contact with the entity was a primal, mindless urge to kill him. Lakesh had claimed at the time that the xenophobic response was quite natural and human, but Banks had always been secretly offended by that statement. He felt he was as human as anyone else in Cerberus, and he didn't experience those murderous impulses. He found Balam far more interesting than frightening, despite the creature's great psi powers.

Putting his head on the pillow, Banks said calmly, "I'm not really afraid. Just a little nervous, that's all.''

Lakesh nodded. "Completely understandable. But hypnosis—or to be precise, heterohypnosis—is nothing to be afraid of. The common belief that in heterohypnosis the subject falls under the control of the hypnotist is completely unfounded. I'll only be acting as your guide."

The old man held the pen by thumb and forefinger, moving it back and forth before Banks's face. "Now please follow the pen with your eyes and listen to the sound of my voice."

Lakesh slowly waved the pen as if it were the needle of a metronome. Banks flicked his eyes slowly from right to left.

"Concentrate on the pen," Lakesh said, his reedy voice softened to a whisper.

The dim light glinted off the pen, causing it to sparkle with silver highlights.

"You're relaxing, sinking into a pleasant state of mind. Listen to the sound of my voice. Don't think about anything else."

Slowly, Banks's eyelids fluttered, then closed.

"That's it, friend Banks. Relax and we'll learn what secrets your memory has been hiding from your conscious mind. We will make manifest what has been hidden."

Banks's breathing deepened, his chest rising and falling slowly.

"Be at ease," Lakesh whispered. "Remember, my friend."

The young man's face became slack and his lips parted slightly.

DeFore eyed him curiously. "Is he under?"

"He's under." Lakesh stepped back from Banks and put the pen back in his pocket.

"That seemed awfully fast," DeFore observed dubiously.

Lakesh shrugged. "He's susceptible. I expected that."

The old man leaned over the head of the bed and said, "Friend Banks, I want you tell me about your dreams...tell me what you see in them, what you hear, what you feel."

Banks's lips stirred and he murmured fitfully. "Dreams..."

"Yes, your dreams...those in which you see Balam."

In a hoarse, scratchy whisper, Banks said, "Dreams they not. Speak try him while sleep. Dreams not they."

Lakesh listened, feeling the short hairs on his nape tingle and lift. He straightened, his heart pounding hard in his chest, his throat constricting.

"What's wrong?" DeFore demanded. "Why is he talking like that?"

Banks's voice grew stronger, louder. "Not dreams they not are. Are not. They are not dreams."

He spoke slowly, as if he were groping his away around verbal communication, trying to understand the rules of grammar and syntax. Lakesh had witnessed the phenomenon before. Trying to control the frightened fascination rising in him, Lakesh said, "I don't believe we're hearing Banks. I think Balam is trying to speak through him."

DeFore elbowed Lakesh aside, reaching for Banks's hands. The young man did not react; the neutral expression on his face remained unaltered.

Lakesh said in an urgent whisper, "Friend Banks, allow Balam to come through. Let him speak."

Banks shivered uncontrollably, his hands clenching into fists. His legs jerked as if they had been subjected to a jolt of electrical current. His breath tore raggedly through his throat.

"Make yourself receptive," Lakesh crooned. "Welcome him."

Banks's lips compressed and his forehead acquired deep vertical creases. He uttered a faint groaning sound.

"You're pushing him too hard," DeFore protested.

"Perhaps so," Lakesh replied. "But if Balam is attempting to impart some information to us, it must be exceptionally important."

DeFore grimaced, obviously displeased.

"Friend Banks," continued Lakesh, "don't be afraid. Let Balam in, share your perceptions with him, your language resources."

A prolonged shudder shook the young man's body. A dew of perspiration filmed his forehead, and he uttered a faint, aspirated cry. Tendons stood out in sharp relief on his neck. His arms flailed, his feet kicked.

"He's having a seizure!" DeFore exclaimed.

Lakesh didn't reply. He watched as the medic

struggled to restrain the convulsing Banks, to hold him down on the bed. She cast a half fearful, half angry glance Lakesh's way. "Help me, goddammit!"

Lakesh didn't move. DeFore grabbed Banks by his chin, trying to prise his jaws apart. "Get me a towel," she snapped breathlessly. "Roll it up tight or he may swallow his tongue."

Clearing his throat, striving to sound calm and clinical, Lakesh said, "Dr. DeFore, your ministrations are unnecessary. This will pass."

Eyes bright with worry, she demanded impatiently, "How the hell do you know?"

"I've seen this before. It's not a new experience to friend Banks, either."

Banks's body abruptly went slack under DeFore's hands, all of the tension leaving his muscles at once. He sank back down on the bed, a heavy sigh issuing from between his lips.

Grasping his wrist, DeFore timed his pulse, then placed a forefinger at the base of his throat. "His heart rate is slowing, regulating," she said. Lines of stress deepening around her nose and mouth, DeFore released Banks and stepped away from him. "I don't know much about hypnosis, but I do know you're the only one who can bring him out of the state or trance or whatever he's in."

Lakesh leaned close to Banks. "Can you hear me? Can you understand me?"

The young man's hands made aimless, jerking motions. His eyes opened, wide and staring. His normally soft brown eyes now glittered with hard, almost inner light. He swept Lakesh with a dispassionate gaze.

"Mohandas Lakesh Singh," he said in a formal voice. "I have been attempting to reach you for some time now."

LAKESH MET those dark eyes and felt his flesh prickle despite having witnessed the phenomenon before. Banks sat up stiffly, stretching his arms out and then over his head. He examined his hands, wiggling the fingers as if his limbs were new and unfamiliar.

"Balam?" Lakesh finally managed to husk out.

Banks nodded, a single jerk of the head. Lakesh fancied he could glimpse Balam's huge, slanted black eyes superimposed over those of Banks.

In a mild tone, Banks-Balam said. "When you placed this man in a receptive mental state, I was finally able to achieve a clear channel of communication. Reaching out to his mind when he slept was not particularly efficient and much time was lost. I would have preferred to send emissaries rather than use this man in such a fashion."

Lakesh couldn't respond for a long moment, overwhelmed once again by the knowledge that with Balam almost anything was possible—even speaking to him through the lips of Banks and seeing him through his eyes. DeFore had drawn away from both men, staring in dumbfounded silence.

Nervously, Lakesh asked, "Are you in Tibet? Is that why you couldn't send someone?"

"No," replied Banks-Balam flatly. "The reason is

much more prosaic than that. I could not dispatch emissaries because of the way you have encrypted the quantum interphase inducer autosequence codes.''

Long ago Lakesh altered the modulations of the Cerberus mat-trans gateway so the transmissions were untraceable back to their point of origin. He had taken a further security precaution by adjusting the unit's matter-stream harmonics so they would be slightly out of phase with other gateways in other places. The admission that some things were beyond even Balam's abilities made Lakesh feel better.

DeFore coughed and ventured apprehensively, ''So, wherever you are you have access to a gateway?''

Banks-Balam gave her an expressionless, over-the-shoulder glance. ''That is contraindicated by my first statement.''

He returned his attention to Lakesh. ''This form of communication places a strain both on myself and this vessel, so I must by necessity be brief. Mohandas Lakesh Singh, your aid is required to complete a task that will change the destiny of humanity. To this end, you must join me.''

''Join you where? In Tibet?''

''You will learn where if you agree. You must provide me with your gateway's destination lock code so I may send emissaries. They will explain.''

Lakesh felt his eyebrows crawl toward his hairline, even above the rims of his spectacles. ''What you ask cannot be lightly done.''

''Neither is the task I have set for myself, Mohandas Lakesh Singh. If you mean to honor your vow of atoning for your sins, to devote what remains of your life to freeing your kind from the yoke of baronial slavery, then you will do as I bid. Otherwise—"

Banks's body suddenly bent in the middle as if he were suffering from a stomach cramp. Sweat rivered down his face. "The link is weakening, and it must break soon or I will risk damaging this vessel."

His voice became hoarse and husky. "I was content to remain a prisoner here for more than three years. I waited until events I had extrapolated finally occurred. Then I left your custody and was free to put my own plans into motion…plans to benefit not just humanity but the hybrids of my blood and yours."

Lakesh heard the sense of urgency and conviction behind the words. "What is it you want me to do?" he demanded.

Banks-Balam blinked and wiped at the perspiration on his face with a trembling hand. "Agree to help me."

"How do we know this isn't a trick?" DeFore asked sharply. "A trap? You've lied to us before. Your kind lied to the entire human race for thousands of years!" The last was an accusation, full of bitter anger.

"What you interpreted as falsehoods we saw as learning tools, tests of perception and intelligence." Banks-Balam's breath came in short, labored rasps. "But I am not here to debate my folk's interaction with yours. I must have your answer, Mohandas Lakesh Singh. Otherwise, events will proceed without you, and you will have forfeited your right to effect changes for the sake of humankind.

"Once you said, 'As history clearly shows, if you do not create your own reality, someone else is going to create it for you. I allowed that to happen, and I do not like the reality I got. Now, as the end of my life approaches, all I want is to enter the house of my deity justified.'"

Lakesh bit back a startled, profane remark. He had indeed spoken those words but not to anyone in the infirmary. He had addressed them to Brigid, Kane, Domi and Grant on the day of their arrival at the redoubt over a year before. They were in his private office at the time.

"Here now is your opportunity, Mohandas Lakesh Singh." Banks-Balam spoke in a barely audible, strained whisper. "Perhaps your final opportunity to create a new reality and to justify yourself to your deity."

Lakesh swallowed hard, knotted his fists, unknotted them and studiously avoided looking in DeFore's direction. He took a deep breath and blurted, "Six-eight-eight-two."

"Lakesh!" DeFore shrilled in a near panic.

Banks's body slumped, a harsh gasp tearing from his throat. He shook violently, then fell onto his side on the bed. DeFore went to him, putting a hand under the back of his head. His sweat-damp face glistened in the dim light, and his eyes stared around unfocusedly. His first word was a pained croak. "Water."

While DeFore helped Banks sit up, Lakesh went to the sink and filled a glass from the faucet. His extreme thirst did not come as a surprise to Lakesh, since it was a hallmark side effect of channeling or mediumship. Nor was he particularly surprised that Banks had come out of the hypnotic state on his own. Balam had wrested control of the session away from him from afar, and that dismayed him profoundly.

Lakesh handed the glass to Banks, who brought it to his lips, tilting his head back. He swallowed mouthful after mouthful, gulping noisily. DeFore glared at Lakesh, not only in reproach but outright fury. "You've compromised the security of Cerberus by what you did. An army of hybrids can jump in here every time the gateway's transit lines are open."

Banks lowered the glass, shaking his head. "I didn't sense any deceit on Balam's part." Wincing, he touched the left side of his head.

"Would you have been able to sense it?" DeFore challenged. "You've just been possessed. How you can be sure of anything?"

"I wasn't possessed," Banks said defensively. "Balam asked for my permission to speak through me and I gave it, just like the last time."

"The last time he was right here in the redoubt," DeFore argued, her voice rising, hitting a high pitch of anger. "God only knows where he is now or what he has planned!"

She fixed her dark gaze on Lakesh. "I used to think Kane was the untrustworthy one because of all the risks he took. You've done far more than put us at risk. You've betrayed us!"

Sudden rage fountained up in Lakesh, but he tried not to let it register either on his face or in his voice when he declared, "I'm taking action."

Before he could say anything else, Bry's agitated voice blared over the wall trans-comm. "Incoming jumper! There's no origin-point signature!"

The comm was voice activated, so Lakesh called, "Keep calm. I'll be right there."

As he turned to leave the infirmary, DeFore demanded, "What about a security detail?"

Lakesh waved her question away. "If all Balam said was subterfuge, part of a master plan to occupy Cerberus, then a handful of us standing around the jump chamber with blasters won't make much difference—not with the resources he can throw against us."

He went down the main corridor and into the ops center. From the main control console, Bry swung his copper-curled head in his direction. "It's cycling through a materialization."

Lakesh strode toward the anteroom that held the mat-trans chamber. He murmured, "Didn't take the emissaries long to be sent on their way."

He knew his comment was essentially irrelevant. Mat-trans jumping occasionally resulted in minor temporal anomalies like arriving at a destination three seconds before the origin jump-initiator had actually engaged. Since the nature of time could not be measured or accurately perceived in the quantum stream, the brief temporal dilation was the primary reason Overproject Whisper's Operation Chronos had used reconfigured gateway units in their time-traveling experiments.

Lakesh stood in the doorway to the anteroom, gazing at the six-sided jump chamber. It exuded a sound like a fierce rushing wind that grew louder and louder. Bright lights flashed behind the eight-foot-tall slabs of brown-hued armaglass, swelling in intensity and in tandem with the hurricane noise. Within seconds, both the light and sound faded.

Lakesh waited, listening to the muffled whining of the interphase transition coils cycling down. Within moments, he heard the clicking of solenoids, and the heavy chamber door swung open on its counterbalanced hinges. Mist swirled within the chamber, so thick he could see nothing. The vapor was a by-product of the process, a plasma wave form that only resembled fog. Thread-thin static-electricity discharges arced within the billowing mass.

Then two figures appeared in the open doorway, and Lakesh felt his neck muscles tighten and his eyes widen. He hadn't really imagined what Balam had meant by emissaries, but he had not expected the two people who stepped gracefully from the chamber. One was a small figure, about the size of a half-grown child. Since it was swathed in a hooded, satiny robe from toe to head, Lakesh couldn't be sure of the gender or even the species.

He experienced no such confusion about the second figure. The woman was tall and beautiful, with a flawless complexion the hue of fine honey. Her long, straight hair, swept back from a high forehead and pronounced widow's peak, tumbled artlessly about her shoulders. It was so black as to be blue when the light caught it. The large, feline-slanted eyes above high, regal cheekbones looked almost the same color, but glints of violet swam in them. The mark of an aristocrat showed in her delicate features, with the arch of brows and her thin-bridged nose. Her face looked vaguely familiar to Lakesh, but he couldn't place in his memory where he might have seen it before.

A graceful swanlike neck led to a slender body encased in a strange uniform—high black boots, jodhpurs of a shiny black fabric, with an ebony satin tunic tailored to conform to the thrust of her full breasts. Emblazoned on the left sleeve was a familiar symbol. A thick-walled pyramid was worked in red thread, enclosing and partially bisected by three elongated but reversed triangles. Small disks topped each one, lending them a resemblance to round-hilted daggers. Once it had served as the unifying insignia of the Archon Directorate, and then was adopted by Overproject Excalibur, the Totality Concept's division devoted to genetic engineering.

In a mild, melodious, beautiful voice that stroked his nerve endings and sent shivers down his spine and then up again, the woman said, "Dr. Singh, it's good to see you again."

Lakesh was barely able to muster enough presence

of mind to stammer, "A-again? We've met? I'm sure I'd remember you."

She smiled at him wanly. "The last time you saw me was at least twelve years ago, and then only from afar during a council of the nine barons at Front Royal. I was in a wheelchair."

Lakesh inhaled a sharp startled breath, dredging his memory and finally coming up with the only possible answer. The council the woman referred to was the only one he had ever attended, and other than Baron Beausoleil, he recalled only one other female there. Despising the tremor in his voice he asked, "Sloan? Not Dr. Erica van Sloan?"

The woman nodded. "One and the same. Before that meeting, we occasionally crossed paths in the Anthill…nearly two hundred years ago."

Lakesh didn't reel or gasp, but he was glad he leaned against the door frame. The most ambitious Continuity of Government facility was codenamed the Anthill, so named because of its similarity in layout to an ant colony. He and the majority of Totality Concept scientists had been taken there days before the nuclear war. Many of them had spent the following century or so in cryogenic stasis.

He barely remembered Erica van Sloan from the Anthill, but that wasn't unusual. There were many people there and all of them seemed to have their own concerns. He recalled she had been attached not just to Operation Chronos but to the project overseer, Dr. Torrence Silas Burr.

Like Lakesh, she had been revived when the Program of Unification had reached a certain stage. She was only one of several preholocaust humans, known as "freezies" in current vernacular, resurrected to serve the baronies. He tried but failed to reconcile the memory of the withered old hag hunched over in a wheelchair with the tall, vibrant, superbly built beauty who regarded him from the doorway.

Lakesh opened his mouth to speak, but nothing came out. He made another attempt and finally managed to stammer, "How can this be?"

Erica van Sloan's sensual lips widened in a prideful smile. Gently, she pulled the small, hooded figure forward and tugged down the cowl. "This is my son."

Lakesh started. "Your son?"

The boy looked to be about ten years of age with a smooth, alabaster complexion. His thick hair was pure warm silver, framing his full-cheeked face like the edges of a summertime cloud. His big, long-lashed eyes seemed to shift with all colors and they were old eyes, at once wise and sad. In a soft voice he said, "Hello. My name is Sam. I'm happy to meet you, Dr. Singh. I've heard all about you, of course."

Erica van Sloan bent and whispered something in his ear. The boy nodded and declared, "My mother says for me to tell you it's an honor. I truly hope you'll join with us in charting a fresh course for the evolution of both the new and old human races."

The sound of the boy's voice touched off sweet vibrations somewhere deep inside of Lakesh. He was hungry to hear more of it. When Sam stepped forward purposely and thrust out his right hand, Lakesh took it eagerly. He was so enthralled he didn't pay attention to the distinctly unchildlike strength in the clasp or the faint pattern of scales between his fingers.

Chapter 10

Rarely had Kane been surprised into speechlessness or paralyzed by shock. But his relief at hearing Domi's voice was so absolute, so overwhelming he couldn't move a muscle or utter a syllable. He remained in a crouch as Domi removed the flashlight beam from him and cast it on her face.

"It's me," she said simply.

Despite the eerie shadows cast by the light, there was no mistaking Domi's angular, hollow-cheeked face framed by a ragged mop of close-cut white hair. Her eyes gleamed like polished rubies on either side of her thin-bridged nose. Her skin was the color of porcelain. She wore a gray coverall like his, but it bagged on her diminutive figure. The light glinted dully from the blued barrel of the Detonics Combat Master in her small right fist.

Kane rose to his full height, towering nearly a foot over the top of her head. "About time I got here?" he demanded, trying sound offended instead of relieved. "I should be telling you that. Where the hell have you been?"

Domi's full lips pursed in a sullen pout, then widened in a grin. "That's what I'm going to show you. C'mon, we don't have a lot of time."

She turned away, but Kane bent over the bodies of the guards, noting how the .45-caliber rounds had punched them both in the occipital areas of their heads. He plucked their blasters from lifeless fingers, swiftly examining them. The weapons were a matched pair of nickel-plated Mustang .380s. They were pocket guns and weren't designed to take very hot loads, but they were better than Shocksticks.

As he checked the magazines, Domi said impatiently, "You don't need those. Let's go."

Kane slipped one of the blasters into a pocket and turned to face her. The first giddy surge of relief that Domi was alive and apparently well was replaced by a rising tide of suspicion. "I'll be the judge of that, Domi. And you'd know that if you're the same Domi I know."

Her eyes slitted, veiled by snow-white lashes. "Huh?"

Coldly he replied, "For the last time, I don't know how many days I've been drugged, used, abused and manipulated. The only thing I heard about you was that you were in custody. For all I know you've been brainwashed and reconditioned, sent out as a stalking horse as part of some sick psych-war game to break me."

Domi regarded him silently, gravely for a long moment. Then she opened her mouth and allowed a torrent of raging, obscene invective to pour out. She called him a stupe bastard, she compared his brain with scalie fecal matter, she shrilly reminded him of the time he nearly killed them all with a crazy stunt in New Mexico. Essentially she told him that if he expected her to prove herself to him, he'd have a long wait, especially with one of the .380s crammed sideways up his ass.

By the time she reached that stage in her tirade, Kane was convinced she was the Domi he knew. Stepping forward, he clapped a hand over her mouth, saying into her ear, "I stand corrected. I apologize."

Domi continued with her profane diatribe. Her lips writhed against the palm of his hand, and for a second he feared she might sink her teeth into the flesh. Instead she struggled to wrest away from his grasp. Kane held her tightly. "I'm sorry I doubted you, all right?"

The muffled rant stopped, and Kane carefully removed his hand. She glared up at him, crimson eyes seething. In a sibilant whisper, she spit, "I'm the one who should worry about you. I didn't spend the last two weeks fucking my brains out."

"That's not what I heard," he retorted. Before she could demand a clarification he said, "Two weeks? That's how long we've been here?"

She nodded stiffly, heeling around. "Talk as we go. I'm not waiting for you, so move fast, stud-boy."

Kane clenched his teeth at the term but fell into step beside her. They jogged down the corridor, the flashlight in Domi's hand illuminating their way. Her sensitive eyes were more efficient than Kane's in the gloom. She spoke as they ran, reverting to the abbreviated Outlands form of speech.

"Power in this place is comp controlled," she said

in a breathless whisper. "Shut down the circuit feed to this section but only for an hour. Lights come back on real soon."

Domi had never displayed any aptitude for technology more complicated than an on-off switch. "You arranged that?" Kane asked doubtfully.

She shook her head. "Friends did. They hid me, kept me safe."

Kane opened his mouth to voice another question, but Domi shushed him into silence. They came to a halt, and she cocked her head in an attitude of listening. Far down the black throat of the corridor came the murmur of voices, and a second later the bobbing, glowing dots of flashlights appeared.

"Shit!" Domi hissed, flicking off the flashlight. She took Kane's hand and broke into a run. "Hurry!"

Kane hated being rendered blind again. Skin crawling, he kept one hand on the wall as the girl dragged him through the impenetrable blackness. He had no idea how she knew where she was going, but she sprinted directly toward the lights. Kane counted four of them, shining like distant moons.

The fear of recapture rose in him again, and he started to slow, tugging on her hand. Domi halted so suddenly he nearly trod on her heels. "Here."

Cupping his hand over the Nighthawk microlight around his wrist, Kane turned it on and glimpsed the metal frame of an open ventilation grille about four feet over his head.

"You first," she whispered. "Be quiet."

He turned the light off, fixed the vent's position in

his mind and backed off a few feet. He ran forward on the balls of his feet and jumped. His outstretched hands caught the lip, and his fingers tried to secure a hold on the slick sheet-metal sheathing. He drew himself upward, inch by inch, his arms trembling. Silently he cursed the weakness his two weeks of captivity had inflicted on him.

Domi made a stirrup with her linked hands and boosted him up by his feet. He managed to squirm his way into the opening. The ductwork was larger than the lift shaft, but not by much. At least it was on the horizontal plane. After he crawled forward a yard or two, Domi leaped up and, with the effortless agility of a monkey, hauled her small body into the opening. Grant had commented once or twice on how nimble Domi could be, and Kane couldn't help but wonder about the variations to which she might have put her acrobatic prowess to use.

Groping behind her, Domi pulled the grille closed and they lay silently in the shaft, waiting for the people in the corridor to pass by. Inside of a minute, slits of light shone through the grille and they heard the padding of rubber-soled shoes.

"I swore I heard shots," a man's tense voice said.

The response was a mumble, and the men passed out of Kane's range of hearing. He started to crawl forward, but Domi laid a warning hand on his ankle. He didn't move for a count of thirty, then the girl whispered, "Let me take the lead."

Kane lay flat as Domi wriggled and crawled over his prone body, her head bumping the roof of the shaft once or twice. He repressed a bleak grin. Under other circumstances, he would have enjoyed her ophidian motions.

When she slid into the shaft ahead of him, she turned on the flashlight and said, "Follow me."

She pulled herself along on her elbows, and Kane followed suit. Within ten feet the access shaft angled straight up. Domi crawled up, bracing her back against the side with her elbows extended in front of her, shoving her way up with her feet. Taking a deep breath, Kane mimicked her movements. It didn't take long before his overworked muscles screamed with pain. His heart pounded and he was drenched in a sudden sweat. He found himself wishing the power would come back on so the air-conditioning system could kick in.

Domi's impatient voice floated down from above him. "Can't you climb any faster?"

Kane didn't have the breath to either answer her or swear at her, so he tried to divorce himself from the pain of kicking and elbowing his way up the ductwork, taking advantage of the adrenaline speeding through his system.

The shaft bent again twenty feet up, stretching out horizontally. It also narrowed and was barely passable even by Domi. Kane, with a panting curse, wormed his way up, kicked with both feet and jackknifed up into the opening. He collapsed facedown, his breath steaming against the metal.

Domi nudged him with a foot. "Rest later. Almost there."

Kane lifted his head, and by the glow of Domi's flashlight saw a mesh screen about six feet ahead. "We'd fucking well better be," he croaked.

Squirming forward, Domi pushed against the screen and it swung open on tiny hinges. Kane caught glimpses of hands reaching up to help her out of the shaft. He slithered after her, wheezing and panting, half blinded by the perspiration flowing into his eyes. He felt strong hands close around his wrists and forearms and tug him out of the ductwork, steadying him as they lowered him to the floor.

Clearing his vision with a swipe of his hand, he saw tables and chairs scattered around the room, and the looming bulk of old vending machines. He guessed he was in a galley. He smelled a tantalizing odor like bean-and-bacon soup, and his belly rumbled in reaction. At the same time, he became aware of a number of presences in the gloom, but because of the poor illumination, he could barely make them out.

"The revolution has officially started," a man's voice said quietly.

Kane turned, and by the glow of a flashlight saw Maddock standing behind him, beneath the vent. Then the lights came on, after a fashion.

THERE WAS NO NEED to squint or shade his eyes. The light strips in the ceiling shed a shadowed, diffuse light, as if he wore a cap with a long bill pulled down over his forehead. The illumination was barely brighter than that provided by the flashlights, and once his vision adjusted, Kane saw why.

He was aware of small, pale, graceful shapes shifting soundlessly in the shadows, and Kane caught glimpses of their overlarge craniums. The optic nerves of hybrids' eyes possessed a natural sensitivity to high light levels, and so their vision functioned more efficiently in a semigloom.

He experienced a brief, shuddery flashback to the hybrid horde he, Brigid and Grant had fought off more than a year ago inside the Archuleta Mesa installation. It was difficult in the uncertain light to assess the number and gender of hybrids, but he estimated there were about seven females and three males. A number of human men were in the room, too, but including Maddock he counted only four.

Kane turned to Domi. "These are your friends?" he asked tonelessly.

She nodded. "They saved me from capture, mebbe kept me from being chilled."

"We kept her from being more than chilled," declared a black man of medium height. "We kept her from being dissected."

A hybrid male said in the soft, lilting tones of his kind, "We tried to capture her in the warehouse section. We had no choice but to incapacitate her with a wand."

Kane had faced the deadly infrasound wands a number of times in the past. Miniaturized masers converted electric current to directional ultrasonic waves and turned innocuous silver rods into weapons that could kill or cripple.

"That must have been a case of the cure being almost as bad as the disease," Kane said to Domi.

She nodded, lips compressing. "No shit."

She unzipped the front of her coverall. Even in the poor light, Kane saw, outlined in blue and red against the bone whiteness of her skin, a spiderweb pattern of broken blood vessels and ruptured capillaries extending across her upper chest to between her breasts. "And this is after two weeks. Shoulda seen me after the first couple of days. Make a stickie puke. Still sore."

The hybrid intoned, "You killed the one who rendered you tractable. I would judge you still came out ahead."

Domi zipped up her jumpsuit and said angrily, "Told you I was sorry."

Kane shook his head in confusion, curiosity warring with hunger within him. Lifting his hands palm outward, he announced, "Somebody better give me the brief on what this is all about. While you're at it, is there anything to eat in here other than that goddamn oatmeal?"

Domi took him by the elbow and pulled him forward, parting the semicircle of humans and hybrids. She led him to a table where a steaming bowl of soup and a half loaf of freshly baked bread awaited him. "Figured you'd be hungry," she said.

"Somebody was thinking ahead." Kane sat, and without much surprise saw Quavell sitting across from him.

"That was me," she said. "I knew you would miss your evening meal."

As Kane spooned up a mouthful of the thick broth, he asked, "I suppose you're the ringleader?"

She surprised him by smiling, though it was hard to tell in the murk. She might have been grimacing at the way he slurped at the soup.

"Only temporarily," she replied. "I will abdicate that position to someone else."

"Who?"

"You." She inclined her head toward Domi. "And her. She has already proved herself an able instigator and strategist."

Kane's memory flew back several months to the night the Archuleta Mesa installation was destroyed. It was also his and Domi's first brief encounter with Quavell, and he easily recalled how Brigid had kept her from shooting the female hybrid. He decided not to raise the issue. The entire situation was surreal and bewildering enough already.

Tearing off a chunk of bread with his teeth, Kane demanded, "Just tell me what the hell is going on. You said not all of you here serve Baron Cobalt, and that he brings war to your people?"

"He breaks unity," Quavell stated with an almost serene detachment. "He has violated the articles of unification, and the baronies are in turmoil. Barons Sharpe and Snakefish have made a pact, and even now combined forces from their villes make their way here."

Kane stopped chewing, staring wide-eyed at Qua-

vell. He cut his eyes over to Domi, and she nodded
in confirmation. He swallowed the bread and asked,
"Why just Sharpe and Snakefish? What about all the
others?"

Quavell's smooth, masklike countenance finally
registered an emotion. "As you know, Ragnarville
has no baron. Due to you, I have heard."

Kane didn't bother correcting that misconception.
A computer-generated hologram had actually killed
Baron Ragnar, but the story was too convoluted to
tell at the moment.

"And the others," she continued, "are waiting to
learn what action the imperator undertakes to restore
order and unity."

Kane felt his eyebrows knit at the bridge of his
nose. "The imperator? Did I hear you right? The imperator?"

Quavell nodded, linking her inhumanly long, delicate fingers beneath her pointed chin. "Yes."

"What and who the hell is an imperator?"

Patronizingly, Quavell said, "I see you know very
little about your own race's history."

"True," Kane replied, an edge slipping into his
voice. "Thanks to your race."

If Quavell was offended by the comment, she
showed no sign of it. Kane assumed she was aware
how the educational systems of the villes were deliberately limited. It was one way the barons used to
control the herd.

She said, "The ancient Roman Empire was gov-
erned by a senate, but ruled by an emperor, some-

times known as an imperator. This person served as the final arbiter in matters pertaining to government. The villes act independently, unified in name only. A proposal was put forth to establish a central ruling consortium. In effect, the barons would become viceroys, plenipotentiaries in their own territories.''

"Who made this proposal?" asked Kane.

"Baron Cobalt."

"Who else?" Kane muttered. "And so you're waiting around to see what he does next?"

She shook her head. "Baron Cobalt's proposal was adopted by another."

"Another what? Another baron?"

"No. In truth I know little of the identity of the one who has claimed the title of imperator."

Kane shrugged and returned his attention to the soup. "Well, for nearly a hundred years the barons believed they were the viceroys of the Archon Directorate, so I can't see how this setup is much different. Except the imperator isn't a myth, a control mechanism like the directorate was."

"Perhaps," Quavell said quietly. "But from what I understand, neither is the directorate."

Kane's spoon froze midway to his mouth. "It might be the apekin knows a little more about the so-called Archon Directorate than you. It doesn't exist."

"Perhaps," the woman repeated. "But one Archon does. Balam by name, and it is he who has installed the imperator as the ruler of the nine villes."

For the second time in one day, Kane was too stupefied by shock to move or speak.

Chapter 11

Brigid Baptiste's response to Baron Sharpe's pronouncement was not typical of her. Perhaps it was impatience, the anger at being confronted with baronial arrogance, that caused her to forgo her usual cautious approach. Ordinarily, from of a position of weakness, she would have kept silent, keenly observing the nature of a potential adversary before deciding on a confrontation. This time, she did none of those things.

Brigid uttered a derisive laugh and sneered. "You'll have a long wait before either of us calls you 'my lord,' Sharpe. You're not the lord of anything unless it's a lunatic asylum."

It was nearly impossible for Baron Sharpe's eyes to widen, but his prim little mouth gaped open. It was with difficulty Grant kept his own jaw from dropping. Although he knew the baronial oligarchy was not semidivine, he had never been in the presence of a baron before, and it made him feel exceptionally nervous. Brigid's uncharacteristic disrespect, and the insult flung at the anointed god-king, didn't exactly relax him, either. Intellectually, Grant understood the barons were born of science, of bioengineering, not mysticism, but his ville breeding still caused him to hold them in superstitious regard. He managed to maintain his usual scowl, but he tensed his muscles, waiting for the reaction invoked by Brigid's disrespectful words and tone.

Baron Sharpe's big, slanted eyes glittered momentarily in anger, and he cast a glance toward the crippled creature he had introduced as Crawler. "What should I do with her?" he asked.

Crawler's lips stretched in a smile. "Reward her, perhaps. She certainly has you pegged correctly."

Sharpe sat up and laughed, a high-pitched musical titter that sounded like the stuttering chirp of a flock of birds. He fixed his gaze on Grant. "Do you have a tongue?"

The sudden question took Grant aback. "I have one, yes."

"Then I suggest you use it instead of trying to intimidate me with scowls and silence."

He turned toward the crippled man. "Tell me more about them, Crawler."

Brow furrowing, Crawler stared intently at Grant with shadow-pooled eyes. Grant sensed a wispy touch against his mind, and his heart began to pound. The crippled man was a psionic, a doom seer, a doomie, possessed of mutant telepathic and precognitive abilities.

Most of the mutie strains spawned after the nukecaust were extinct, either dying because of their mutations, or hunted and exterminated during the early years of the unification program. Stickies, scalies, scabbies and almost every other breed exhibiting warped genetics had all but vanished, except in isolated pockets. Grant had assumed even the muties who looked otherwise normal except for their psychic powers had pretty much died off, as well.

"A doomie," Grant said, trying to sound as if he were interested only to be polite. "Couldn't have been easy locating one in this day and age."

"Easier than you may think," Sharpe responded smoothly. "Part of my legacy from my great-grandfather, the first Baron Sharpe, was a small private zoo of creatures that had once scuttled all over the Deathlands. One of his last acquisitions was Crawler here."

"Nice name," Grant observed snidely. "A lot better than Bill or Philip."

"It was more of a title than a name," Sharpe replied. "My great-grandfather bestowed it upon him after his leg tendons had been severed. He kept escaping from the compound, see, employing his mental talents to find the most opportune time and means to do so."

Grant decided to let the matter drop. If Crawler had been around in the preunification days, then he was very old, probably on the order of 120 years. But he had heard some muties possessed remarkable longevity.

The cobwebby touch disappeared from his mind as Crawler focused his eyes on Brigid. She stiffened, drawing in her breath sharply. After a moment, the doomie spoke in a flat, matter-of-fact voice. "My initial percepts were sound, Lord Baron. Our destination coincides with theirs, but our purposes are not the same. They seek missing friends while we seek enemies."

"Missing friends?" Sharpe repeated quizzically. "Who?"

Crawler chuckled. "We have met one of them. He made quite an impression on us both, you in particular. His name is Kane."

Baron Sharpe bobbed his head and uttered a long "Ahhh" as if finally solving a puzzle. "Kane the traitor. Kane the killer. Kane the baron blaster."

With icy irony, Brigid said, "I understand he certainly blasted you."

Sharpe laughed and undid the top buttons of his camo jacket, and the shirt beneath. Pulling them aside, he revealed the pale flesh beneath. An angry red stellate scar surrounded a raised, puckered ring in his upper chest. "He did indeed. Here is his signature."

Although neither Brigid nor Grant had witnessed Kane's brief encounter with Baron Sharpe and Crawler in Redoubt Papa, he had told them about it. Apparently, Crawler had duped Sharpe into accompanying a squad of Magistrates to the installation near Washington Hole. Sensing Kane's presence there, the doomie conceived a plan whereby Sharpe would be assassinated and thus avenge himself for the wrongs done to him by his great-grandfather.

When Kane refused to cooperate and be used as a pawn, Sharpe attempted to kill Crawler. Kane shot the baron, assuming he had dealt him a mortal wound.

Apparently, his assumption was in error, but not Lakesh's description of the baron's mental state. Brigid clearly recalled him saying Baron Sharpe was mad "like Emperor Caligula was mad."

As he buttoned his shirt and jacket, a smirk twisted Sharpe's thin lips. "Your friend didn't believe me when I told him I cannot die. I guess I showed him."

Neither Grant nor Brigid could think of anything to say in response, so they opted to remain silent. Sharpe craned his neck, peering past the two people. "Ramirez, is the area secure?"

"It is, Lord Baron," the Mag answered.

"Then find proper seating for our guests and myself. I'm tired of being cooped up in here."

Within a few minutes, Ramirez found three canvas-backed camp chairs and set them up near the Sandcat. While he was doing so, the Deathbird landed nearby, the skids settling gently on the ground, the vanes agitating the dust into swirling eddies.

Sharpe, Brigid and Grant sat in a semicircle. Crawler dragged himself over to the baron's feet by arms callused an inch thick on the elbows. His sickeningly diminished legs trailed behind him. By the light of an electric lantern, Grant saw the raised weals of ancient scars on the backs of his knees.

Crawler looked up into Grant's face as if intercepting his thoughts. "Yes," he said. "It was terribly painful. I nearly bled to death."

"My great-grandfather performed the actual surgery himself," Sharpe offered helpfully. "Crawler held a grudge for the longest time."

"At least a century, my lord."

"But," Brigid said with a wry smile, "you worked out your differences?"

The doomie nodded. "I finally came to realize our destinies were intertwined. Especially after your friend nearly killed him."

Sharpe smiled down at him fondly and ran his fingers lightly over his shaven skull. "It's a great comfort."

Brigid and Grant gazed stolidly at the pair, not saying anything. Both were aware of Ramirez hovering behind them, just beyond their peripheral vision.

"Now," announced Baron Sharpe with a decisive handclap, "let's get down to it. We can be of great help to each other. My goal is to breach the Dreamland installation by tomorrow morning and to displace the occupying forces."

"Why?" asked Brigid.

Sharpe glanced questioningly at Crawler. "Should I?"

Crawler nodded. "You should. They are allies and should be treated as such, not as pawns. Besides, they are very clever and resourceful. If you try to manipulate them, it will be to your sorrow."

Sharpe grinned. "I thought as much."

Brigid asked, "Why are you staging an attack on Area 51? Who are your enemies there?"

"Only one enemy as far as I am aware," answered Sharpe. "One you are intimately familiar with. Baron Cobalt."

Grant grunted in surprise. "Why is he there?"

Crawler stated, "My lord, they may not have known your brother baron was there, but they suspected the reasons why. You should offer them confirmation."

Baron Sharpe beamed, his perfect little teeth gleaming in a grin. "Very well, then. The installation in New Mexico where my kind was first birthed, the installation upon which my kind relied to maintain our health and vitality, was destroyed. Obliterated, essentially. I should know—I toured it a short while ago and saw the extent of damage for myself."

The smile disappeared from the high planes of Sharpe's face as if it had been wiped away with a cloth. "I also saw quite possibly the last generation of my folk—diseased and dying infants, their immune systems failing, their blood turning toxic. So I don't blame brother Cobalt for taking action to save our race."

Brigid angled an eyebrow at him. "Then what do you blame him for?"

Little spots of color burned on the baron's cheeks. "For being so arrogant as to presume he can dole out the means of our survival as he sees fit. He vexed the barons with an ultimatum, you see—to place him in a position of final authority as the imperator or die."

Sharpe fluttered his hand in the general direction behind him. "Within the complex once known as Dreamland, brother Cobalt found the medical technology necessary to save us. His forces have occupied it. We intend to take it away from him."

"And open it up so the other barons can receive their treatments again?" asked Brigid.

Baron Sharpe hesitated a second before saying, "More or less. We have our own people inside, transferred there from Dulce. They've been supplying us with information about the place for the past few weeks."

"What kind of information?" Grant demanded.

"The strategic kind." Ramirez spoke for the first time since fetching them to the baron. "Didn't you wonder how we got through the city without touching off the demo charge in the building? We were warned in advance."

"What other things were you warned about in advance?" inquired Brigid.

A lazy smile played over the high planes of Baron Sharpe's face. With an inhumanly long thumb and forefinger, he pinched the air. "Before we tell you, there is a tiny codicil that you must agree to observe first."

"Which is?" Grant asked darkly.

"That you will not oppose me or my forces occupying Area 51. I am working in the best interests of the oligarchy and the imperator."

Both Grant and Brigid eyed the blond, slender man with equal measures of irritation and confusion. "You told us Baron Cobalt wanted to be invested with that title," Brigid pointed out.

Sharpe retorted dryly, "Oh, he did indeed. He was running quite the game on us...dangling the means of our survival before us like bait, not revealing to us its nature or the location of the installation he had found. He almost got away with it. Then the game was raided, the tables overturned and the cards scattered to the four winds.''

"Talk sense," Grant growled in frustration.

Baron Sharpe smiled beatifically, rolling his eyes heavenward. In a hushed reverent tone he said, "We were permitted to witness a historic event—the return of the Archons."

A LONG PERIOD OF SILENCE followed the baron's pronouncement. It required all of Brigid's and Grant's self-control to keep from leaping from the camp chairs in shock. Incredulity and fear warred for dominance in their minds. Her throat tight, Brigid had to make two attempts before she managed to husk out, "The Archons…you actually saw them?"

Sharpe nodded vehemently. "Oh, yes, yes…" Then he frowned and shook his head, just as vehemently. "No, no…"

"Which is it?" snapped Grant.

"We saw one of them. Balam, by name. He brought us a savior."

Grant swallowed hard and glanced at Brigid. She shook her head slightly, warning him not to put into words the thoughts careening through his mind. She was fairly certain the same thoughts whirled in her own head.

Months ago, during the mission to Ireland, she had been told that the race they knew as Archons were hybrids themselves. According to what had been imparted to her in the Priory of Awen's citadel, a reptilian race of beings known in ancient Sumerian texts as the Annunaki arrived on Earth. They inhabited much of the landmasses, exploiting the natural resources and even tinkering with the indigenous hominid life-forms to create a labor force, which eventually and perhaps mistakenly became Homo sapiens.

Over the span of millennia, the Annunaki gradually reduced their involvement in mining colonies on Earth, and triggered the global cataclysm known in all cultures as the Great Flood. After an absence of a thousand years or more, an expeditionary force of Annunaki returned and found another advanced race had established a foothold, the humanoid but not human Tuatha de Danaan.

The two races warred for centuries, the conflict extending even to the outer planets of the solar system. Finally, with both the Danaan and the Annunaki at the brink of extinction, they struck a pact whereby not only their cultures would mingle, but their genetic stock and bloodlines would mingle, as well.

From this union was born the progenitors of the race that would eventually be called the Archons. What was left of the Annunaki and the Danaan withdrew from Earth, leaving behind a wellspring of confusing myths about wars in heaven, serpent kings, demons and angels. But the root race, as Balam referred to them, left their knowledge behind, in the care of their offspring.

Balam's folk initially did not hide from humanity;

they coexisted with them as advisers to mighty princes, friends and high counselors of kings.

But a catastrophe rocked the world, most likely a pole shift that may have caused the sinking of Atlantis, and the blotting out of entire nations, whole civilizations.

Humanity was hurled back into a state of savagery and Balam's people fared little better, not escaping the common ruin that shattered the face of the Earth. Only his people's knowledge of hyperdimensional physics saved them from complete extinction.

Later Brigid had learned that Balam himself had provided the raw genetic material for the creation of the hybrids. His race's DNA was infinitely adaptable, its segments achieving a near seamless sequencing pattern with whatever biological material was spliced into it. It could be tinkered with to create endless variations, adjusted and fine-tuned.

Brigid recollected what Kane had learned about Balam's race during his telepathic communication with him. After the global catastrophe, in order to survive, his race's knowledge of genetics helped them adapt to the new environment. Muscle tissue became less dense, motor reflexes sharpened, optic capacities broadened. A new range of abilities emerged, which just barely allowed them to survive on a planet whose magnetic fields had changed, whose weather was now drastically unpredictable.

With effort, she brought her attention back to the present. "Who was this savior?"

Baron Sharpe's high, smooth forehead creased horizontally in consternation. "A human child…at least physically. His name is Sam."

"Sam?" echoed Grant in disbelief.

Sharpe nodded.

"A human child?" Brigid demanded. "Balam brought you a human child?"

Again Sharpe nodded. "We saw him perform an act of healing little short of miraculous. Perhaps it was miraculous. I have no standard by which to judge. He also told us about Area 51. However, only brother Snakefish and I decided to verify Sam's story."

Brigid shifted in her chair. "What was the miracle?"

The soft, awed light shining in Baron Sharpe's eyes suddenly became hard and cunning. "Why should I tell you anything more? You've yet to speak in detail of your own reasons."

Grant inclined his head toward Crawler. "Can't you get all the information you need from him?"

"I receive only impressions," Crawler declared blandly. "Emotions and intentions. I see colors that denote feelings."

"What colors do you see now?" Grant challenged.

The doomie narrowed his eyes. "Yellow for fear. You fear for the safety of your friends, yet I sense you fear far more than that. Your purpose here is far larger than simply a rescue."

Crawler gazed unblinkingly into Grant's face. He tried to think of nothing. "Blue," Crawler blurted. "Ocean blue. But it's associated with black. Black

for death. Black for armor. Red for blood, red for
badges. Blue for the sea, for a port. For a place called
Morninglight.''

Sharpe screwed up his face in irritated bewilderment. ''Morninglight? You mean something happened at sunrise, or something will happen?''

Ramirez declared, ''My lord, I believe your councillor refers to Port Morninglight, a seaside settlement
within Snakefish jurisdiction.''

Grant hitched around in his chair as the Mag intoned, ''It was attacked a couple of weeks ago. Almost every one was killed.''

''Attacked by whom?'' Baron Sharpe wanted to
know.

''Magistrates, my lord. We found a large number
of them dead, most of them killed by bladed weapons.
Several of them carried ville scrip. Baron Snakefish
is certain they were dispatched from Cobaltville.''

Sharpe fingered his chin contemplatively. ''Yes, I
recollect brother Snakefish levying an accusation
against brother Cobalt during the council. He charged
him with invading his territory to harvest Outlanders
for his own use.''

Grant and Brigid knew the term ''harvest'' was a
euphemism. It was standard baronial practice to seek
out raw genetic material in the Outlands, kill the donors, harvest their organs and tissues and return with
them to the Archuleta Mesa installation to be processed.

''Yes,'' Ramirez agreed. ''But the question of who
slaughtered twenty Magistrates wasn't answered.''

The man slid his gaze to Grant, staring at him hard. "Until a few days ago, that is."

Grant met his stare unblinkingly, not allowing the cold fear stealing through him to show on his face.

Ramirez continued, "One of the survivors of Port Morninglight named the responsible party."

"And?" prompted Baron Sharpe.

"Oddly, he claimed two men in Mag armor and two women—one an albino and one with red hair—were involved."

Sharpe scoffed. "Only four people? I can't accept that."

"Nobody else could either. So the questioning became a bit more...persuasive. Finally, he said those four were in league with another larger group. And he named them." Ramirez paused as if he were savoring the taste and texture of the words he was about to speak next. Slowly and deliberately, he said, "The Tigers of Heaven. I'm really interested in learning more about them."

Chapter 12

Kane really had no idea why the mention of Balam rendered him dumb and numb. On reflection there was no sound reason for him to believe that the last time he saw Balam would in fact be the last time. Even after leaving the entity in Agartha, the age-old subterranean refuge of his people, Kane had often suspected that Balam had orchestrated his own freedom. Certainly, he was well-versed in practicing the artful deception his people had directed against the human race for thousands of years. Some nights Kane couldn't even sleep, wondering if Balam was scheming and plotting anew, safe in his underground sanctuary, half a world away in Tibet.

He didn't need Brigid's eidetic memory to recall with crystal clarity, not only the place, but the final words they had exchanged with Balam. He told them their vigil had begun, as well as their search to find a way for their people to survive as his had done. When Brigid pointed out the only way was to displace the barons, Balam hadn't argued.

Kane asked him if he was betraying the barons, blood of his blood, and Balam's reply had chilled him to the bone: "They are blood of your blood, too, Kane. I no more betray them than you do."

"A state of war will exist between our two cultures again," Brigid pointed out. "Rivers of that mixed blood will be spilled."

Balam's reply was characteristically cryptic. "If that is the road chosen, then that is the road chosen. Blood is like a river. It flows through tributaries, channels, streams, refreshing and purifying itself during its journey. But sometimes it freezes and no longer flows. A glacier forms, containing detritus, impurities. The glacier must be dislodged to allow the purifying journey to begin anew."

Kane had presumed Balam would involve himself no longer in the affairs of humankind and hybrid. That didn't seem be the case, and anger built in him, not at Balam, but at himself for believing what the entity said. It was just another example of how Balam and those of his kind tricked and lied to their human allies—or pawns—throughout history.

Kane dry-scrubbed his hair in frustration. "Are you sure of this? Balam is back?"

Quavell replied, "That is what we were told by Baron Cobalt. He claimed that Balam was betraying his own kind. He vowed to oppose the imperator even if it meant warring with his brother barons." She paused, and the tip of her tongue touched her pale lips nervously. "That apparently is happening. This installation will be under full assault by dawn, and we need to know where you stand."

Kane's appetite, if not his hunger, disappeared. Pushing away the bowl of half-eaten soup, he said, "I stand where I always stand. Against your kind. If the baronies are factionalizing, it's best for the rest us—humanity—to sit back and let you fight it out.''

She shook her head. ''That will not do this time, Kane. You must choose a side in this war, a war your actions have brought about.'' Anger edged her tone as she added, ''In that, at least, I am in complete agreement with Baron Cobalt.''

Kane suppressed a profane comeback. ''I didn't create the barons or the villes, Quavell.''

Maddock stepped forward, stating impatiently, ''It doesn't matter who created who or started what. We've got a war brewing, and those of us here have already chosen the side they will fight on. And so will you.''

''Against Baron Cobalt? That's a given.''

''No,'' Maddock shot back. ''Not against, but for.''

Kane eyed him challengingly. ''Explain.''

Quavell sighed softly. ''You destroyed the installation beneath the Archuleta Mesa, Kane.''

''So I've heard. I was there, remember?'' He didn't try to blunt the pointed sarcasm.

She ignored the gibe. ''The mesa was more than just a medical treatment center for the barons. It was the centerpiece of our culture, our community. The hybrid heart, so to speak.''

Kane knew the six-level facility in New Mexico had originally been constructed to house two main divisions of the Totality Concept—Overproject Whisper and Overproject Excalibur. The former one dealt with finding new pathways across space and time, while the latter was exclusively involved in creating new forms of life. According to Lakesh, after the institution of the unification program, only Excalibur's biological section was revived.

"When the mesa was destroyed," Quavell continued, "so was our community. It became clear to those of us who survived the disaster that an ongoing conflict with humanity would avail both races nothing. Only mutual genocide lay in our futures. After the remnants of our community relocated here, we decided the old rules and old protocols were not productive or survival oriented. A new paradigm had to be implemented."

"Like what?" Kane asked, his tone heavy with suspicion.

As if in reply, Maddock walked around the table and took one of Quavell's slender, fragile hands in his own. "A new, redefined Program of Unification," he declared. "One where we share what's left of the planet's resources with each other, instead of dividing it up between the conquered and the conquerors."

Kane's belly turned a cold flip-flop. Although he had been forced to copulate with any number of hybrid females over the past two weeks, Quavell among them, seeing an overt display of affection between human and the so-called new human filled him with revulsion.

"Are you fused out?" he demanded, his eyes boring into Maddock's. Rising to his feet in such a rush that his chair fell over backward, he surveyed the people in the room, human and hybrid alike. "Are you people fucking insane?"

His voice thickening with fury, he savagely gestured to Quavell and then to the nearest male hybrid. "These inhuman bastards have been trying to make us extinct for the past century. They believe they're superior to us, they've been bred to inherit Earth as part of a genetic-engineering program that began before the nukecaust. They're players in a conspiracy against the human race itself, and you're throwing in with them?"

Clenching his fists, trying to keep from losing all control, he stated matter-of-factly, "Their goal is to unify the world under their control. All humans are to be reduced to an expendable minority, to be exploited as slave labor and as providers of genetic material. That's their idea of unity."

There was a heavy, awkward silence, then the black man coughed self-consciously. "We know all about the hybridization program. The stuff we learned did fuse some of us out. But none of it makes any difference when it comes down to the bare bones of survival. The barons are the enemies, not the people in this room."

Kane uttered a scornful, derisive laugh of incredulity. "People?" Reaching out, he snatched a fistful of coverall of the nearest male hybrid, and jerked him forward, nearly pulling him off his feet altogether. He spun him as if he weighed no more than a straw-filled dummy, shoving him first toward the black man, then in Maddock's direction. "Look at him. Look at him! Is this a person?"

The hybrid didn't struggle. His body went limp as

he allowed Kane to manhandle him. Planting his hand on the man's chin, he forced the head back so Maddock could see the inhumanly large eyes, the too smooth skin, the high forehead, the small ears set too low on the head.

In a voice so thick with barely restrained rage it sounded like an animal's guttural growl, he said, "As far as his kind is concerned, the humanity we know is dead. The new humanity is taking its place. They believe it's all a matter of natural selection. Nature taking its course."

Kane's hand moved to the short, slender column of the hybrid's throat. His thumb and forefinger nearly encircled it. "And you turncoat bastards want to cooperate with their idea of natural selection?"

Domi stood, laying a restraining hand on his arm. "That's enough, Kane. Stop it."

Quavell said calmly, "Because we don't fit your standard of true humanity, that makes us enemies until the death? Are you trying to convince yourself of that, to justify what your murderous actions wrought in Dulce?"

Kane released the hybrid, wheeling to face Quavell, his eyes blazing. His voice rose to a hoarse roar of fury. "That's supposed to make me question myself, make me feel guilty? You sanctimonious parasite! You can't live without feeding off of us. You think I give a damn that I cut off your supply of victims?"

He whirled on Domi. "How can you mix with them? Not too long ago you nearly popped a cap in Quavell's head."

Domi's ruby eyes glimmered with an emotion he had never seen her display before. It took him a moment to recognize it, and when he did he could scarcely believe. It was pity and compassion. In a low, measured voice she intoned, "I want to overthrow the barons. If the people in here can do that, that's good enough for me. And it should be good enough for you, too."

Kane gaped at her in astonishment, his mouth working as he tried to dredge up a response. Quavell arose from the table and beckoned to him. "I want to show you something, Kane, the same thing we showed your friend."

"Show me what?" he snapped.

"A vision of the future if a new form of unity isn't forged."

Kane hesitated. Domi pushed him toward Quavell. "Go with her, Kane. It may change things for you. It did for me."

"And if it doesn't?" he rasped.

The outlander girl shrugged. "Then it doesn't."

Kane swept his furious gaze over the humans in the room and then stepped toward Quavell, following her across the room, out a door and into a hallway. It was lit just as feebly as the commissary. "Where are we going?"

"You've earned a look at the future," Quavell replied. "Afterward you can decide if you prefer to live in the past."

Kane only grunted. The corridor was little more

than a low-ceilinged accessway and so narrow he had to trail behind Quavell, not walk at her shoulder.

"Humans at the heels of hybrids," he said bitterly. "That's your idea of unification."

She cast a cold glance over her shoulder. "You and I have enjoyed our own form of unity through action, though, haven't we?"

Kane ground his teeth in frustration at the reminder, but he didn't respond. It had never occurred to him hybrids might possess a sense of humor, much less one with a cruel but clever cutting edge.

Nearly a century before, Unity Through Action was the rallying cry of the early Program of Unification. It awakened the long-forgotten trust in a central government by offering a solution to the constant states of hardship and fear—join the unification program and never know want or fear again. Of course, any concept of liberty had to be forgotten in the exchange.

One of the basic tenets of the unification program was taking responsibility. Since humanity was responsible for the arrival of Judgment Day, it had to accept the blame before a truly utopian age could be ushered in. All humankind had to do to earn this utopia was to follow the rules, and be obedient to be fed and clothed—and accept the new order without question.

For most of the men and women who lived in the villes and the surrounding territories, this was enough, more than enough. Long sought-after dreams of peace and safety had at last been transformed into reality. Of course, fleeting dreams of personal freedom were

PLAY GOLD EAGLE'S

LUCKY HEARTS

GAME

AND YOU GET

FREE BOOKS!

A FREE GIFT!

YOURS TO KEEP!

TURN THE PAGE AND DEAL YOURSELF IN...

Play LUCKY HEARTS for this..

exciting FREE gift!
This surprise
mystery gift could
be yours FREE

when you play LUCKY HEARTS!
...then continue your lucky streak
with a sweetheart of a deal!

1. Play Lucky Hearts as instructed on the opposite page.

2. Send back this card and you'll receive 2 hot-off-the-press Gold Eagle® novels. These books have a cover price of $4.50 or more each in the U.S. and $5.25 or more each in Canada, but they are yours to keep absolutely free.

3. There's no catch. You're under no obligation to buy anything. We charge nothing—ZERO—for your first shipment. And you don't have to make any minimum number of purchases—not even one!

4. The fact is, thousands of readers enjoy receiving their books by mail from the Gold Eagle Reader Service™ months before they are available in stores. They like the convenience of home delivery and they love our discount prices!

5. We hope that after receiving your free books you'll want to remain a subscriber. But the choice is yours—to continue or cancel, any time at all! So why not take us up on our invitation, with no risk of any kind. You'll be glad you did!

- ◆ **Exciting Gold Eagle novels—FREE!**
- ◆ **Plus a great mystery gift—FREE!**
- ◆ **No cost! No obligation to buy!**

The Gold Eagle Reader Service™—Here's how it works:

Accepting your 2 free books and gift places you under no obligation to buy anything. You may keep the books and gift and return the shipping statement marked "cancel." If you do not cancel, about a month later we'll send you 6 additional novels and bill you just $26.70 — that's a saving of 15% off the cover price of all 6 books! And there's no extra charge for shipping! You may cancel at any time, but if you choose to continue, every other month we'll send you 6 more books, which you may either purchase at the discount price or return to us and cancel your subscription.

*Terms and prices subject to change without notice. Sales tax applicable in N.Y. Canadian residents will be charged applicable provincial taxes and GST.

If offer card is missing write to: Gold Eagle Reader Service, 3010 Walden Ave., P.O. Box 1867, Buffalo, NY 14240-1867

BUSINESS REPLY MAIL
FIRST-CLASS MAIL   PERMIT NO. 717   BUFFALO, NY

POSTAGE WILL BE PAID BY ADDRESSEE

GOLD EAGLE READER SERVICE
3010 WALDEN AVE
PO BOX 1867
BUFFALO NY 14240-9952

NO POSTAGE
NECESSARY
IF MAILED
IN THE
UNITED STATES

completely crushed, but such abstract aspirations were nothing but childish illusions.

In fact, almost every tradition of the predark world that survived the nukecaust, skydark and the anarchy of the Deathlands was dismissed as an illusion. Even the ancient social patterns that connected mother, father and child were broken. That break was a crucial one in order for the Program of Unification to succeed. The existence of the family as a unit of procreation and therefore as a social unit had to be eliminated.

The passage dead-ended, opening into a square room nearly twenty-by-twenty yards across. Because the overhead lighting was as dim as the hallway and the commissary, Kane at first wasn't sure what he was looking at. The room seemed to be filled with rows of little plastic boxes, transparent cubes with no tops to them. Quavell gestured for him to walk farther into the room.

Reluctantly he did so, peering into the boxes. What he saw caused his breath to seize in his lungs, adrenaline to flood his system and raised the short hairs on his nape. None of his previous missions, not even the most rad-drenched pits of horror, had prepared him for what he saw. In the cages were hybrid infants, ranging in age from four-month-olds to one year, and he knew they were dying.

All of them lay listlessly on stained foam pads. Most of them were connected to IV drips. Kane said nothing, but nausea leaped and rolled in his belly, and bile slid up his throat in an acidy column. For a moment he feared he would lose the soup in his stomach. Some of the children raised their huge dark eyes to him as he passed by, but the majority paid him no attention whatsoever. They were obviously too weak to move. Their little chests rose and fell fitfully.

"Twenty-three out of two thousand." Quavell spoke with no particular inflection or emphasis.

Kane placed a hand on one of the box edges to steady himself. He glanced toward her. "What?"

"Twenty-three are all that remain out of the two thousand in the incubation chambers of Dulce. No, they didn't perish all at once in the explosion of the Aurora and the generator. Over a thousand of them did, however. Without access to the medical technology and treatments, the rest have sickened and died in the intervening months. These few are in the last stages of malnutrition and suffering from a variety of infections."

Something touched Kane's hand. He looked down to see a hybrid infant who seemed all ribs and swollen belly, blindly groping for him with its tiny, spindly fingers. Its hand found and closed around his thumb. The touch was no more substantial than gossamer, than a cobweb.

As he gazed at its bald, overlarge and scabrous head, a pressure built in Kane's chest, then spread to this throat. He could not speak. He could barely breathe. He had witnessed and occasionally been forced to participate in many acts of cruelty as a Mag and after, but he had never felt so stricken with guilt.

"We will not be able to install the processing

equipment in time to save them," Quavell continued. "And even if we could, what little raw organic material in storage here is reserved exclusively for Baron Cobalt…and any other baron who might be swayed to join his cause. Therefore, what you see here is the last generation of your loathsome new human."

Kane said nothing.

"Here lies your despised enemies, Kane. Will it make you feel better if I concede defeat on the part of the hybrids? You have beaten us. We surrender. You won that victory not in battle, not with cleverness and not with the old-fashioned human ingenuity you value so much. You won by the simple dint of striking at our most vulnerable resources…our babies."

Kane squeezed his eyes shut, his temples pounding. He husked out, "Human babies die every day, Quavell. In the Tartarus Pits, in the Outlands, in the hellzones. Why should your race's children be spared the torments and mine damned to suffer them?"

"Who orchestrates that suffering?" she asked softly, her voice barely above a whisper. "These babies here? Or the ville governments that you once so faithfully served?"

Kane had known that the hybrids, the new humans, were the physical manifestations of Balam's last-ditch effort to save his folk's seed from extinction. He knew they could not be held personally responsible for the tyranny of the barons. And if they could be blamed, then he, who had spent most of his life supporting the baron's despotism, was just as guilty.

Even more so, since he had inflicted terror and death on his own kind.

Opening his eyes, Kane said faintly, "The barons aren't going to relinquish their power even if all the new and old humans turn against them."

Quavell nodded. "We realize that. But if they're divided, if they're torn between swearing allegiance to the imperator and maintaining the sovereignty of their individual territories, then the chain of unity is broken."

"And they'll be vulnerable." Kane cut his eyes toward her. "But without the treatments to reverse their physical deterioration, won't they just die off?"

"And their human subordinates will step into the power vacuum as has happened in Ragnarville since the death of the baron there. The dictatorship will continue as it has for the past ninety years—a small ruling majority wielding the power of life and death over the enslaved majority. Does it make any difference if the tyrants are old humans or new humans?"

Gently, carefully, Kane disengaged his thumb from the clasp of the infant. Its heavy lids closed over its glazed eyes. Kane faced Quavell, straightening his spine with effort. "So what are you—an underground revolutionary movement here in the underground? What the predarkers called a fifth column?"

She shook her head. "We're not numerous or well-armed enough to meet that criteria. Obviously, many of my kind here support Baron Cobalt, probably as many as your kind does."

"How many is that exactly?"

"Fifty-one consisting of thirty-eight men, nine hybrid males and fourteen females." She waved a hand in the general direction of the commissary. "You have already met the resistance movement."

Kane grimaced in exasperation. "You're barely a gang, Quavell."

"Quite true," she retorted, unperturbed. "However, this installation is far too vast to be adequately guarded by our opposition. And we have an advantage they do not—we know a large, well-equipped assault force is on route to displace Baron Cobalt."

"How do you know that?"

"Allies of ours have infiltrated the baronies of Sharpeville and Snakefish. They apprised us of the joint mission by an encrypted telemetric signal."

Although Kane was a little dubious, he wasn't disbelieving. After all, Ambika, the self-styled Lioness of the Isles, had told him she had spies placed in Cobaltville. He couldn't help it. He laughed.

Quavell cocked her head at him quizzically in a manner that reminded him of Balam.

"Something amuses you?"

"I always wondered if there were agents provocateur in the villes, secretly working against the barons, even if for their own ends. I never figured they'd be working with hybrids."

"There is probably much you never figured." Her tone was chiding.

Kane didn't dispute her. Taking a deep breath and then releasing it, he said, "So when the assault force arrives, you'll help them penetrate this place."

"That's the plan, yes. If nothing else, in the confusion, we will be able to access the organic materials in storage and begin the treatments to reverse the deterioration of the children."

Kane narrowed his eyes. "What about you? Won't you need the same treatments?"

Quavell gestured to the plastic cube-cribs. "They are in far more need than the adults here." She added, "I suppose the concept of self-sacrifice is something else you never figured about us."

"That's true," he replied earnestly. "I presume you have some idea where they'll make the attempt."

"We'll give them the idea of the most efficacious area of egress."

"Good. We'll need weapons. And I'll need my armor."

"We already have it, as well as all the weapons you and Domi brought with you."

"It's not much, but it might be enough to open a back door." He strode purposefully toward the door. "I'll need a layout of the zone you plan to open up."

This time Quavell followed him down the narrow hallway. Before they reached the commissary, Kane paused, turned and asked in a low voice, "Is Baron Cobalt's plan for me to impregnate the females here biologically possible?"

"It is. We are chromosomally compatible."

"So…" He trailed off, but Quavell knew what he was going to ask. "It's too soon to know, Kane. Although a couple of the men engaged in coitus with females before you were captured, keep in mind such acts were unprecedented. Once you arrived, the baron ordered that we were permitted to have intercourse only with you. As it is, this procedure is still experimental.''

Quavell suddenly smiled at him in a way he could only interpret as coquettish. One of her long fingers traced the faint scar on his left cheek. Dropping her voice to a croon, she said, ''But some of us here—me, at least—find the process of trial and error very enjoyable.''

Chapter 13

It was the kind of dawn seen only in the Outlands. The sky looked like a rising curtain of blues and grays, smeared with angry flame-red streaks. Mineral deposits in the rugged Timpahute mountain range glittered dully with the reflected radiance of the sun. The jagged peaks, much eroded by the ages, resembled the points of diamonds.

All around was basically flatland, with not even sproutings of desert scrub to relieve the monotony of the terrain. The lifeless and sere lake basin spread out like a vast bowl of desolation. Brigid stood at the mouth of a pass twisting between ridges of barren rock, and surveyed the dry sunken bed of Groom Lake. There was nothing left of the lake, not even a few ponds. It looked as though an impossibly huge animal had stomped a hoofprint into the center of the basin, sinking it well below the foothills of the mountain range.

Raising the microbinoculars, she squinted into the eyepieces, adjusting the focus to accommodate her own slightly astigmatic vision. The rectangular-lensed spectacles that had more or less been her badge of office as an archivist were tucked in her shirt pocket. The glasses weren't for appearance only. After years of sifting through nearly illegible predark documents, books and computer files, her vision had weakened. She refused to put them on, ignoring the ache that spread from her eye sockets up into her skull.

Brigid had only recently recovered from a serious head injury, and it seemed her vision had been further impaired by the wound that had laid her scalp open to the bone and put her in a coma for several days. The only sign of it was a faintly red horizontal line on her right temple that disappeared into the roots of her hair. Although her recovery time had been little short of phenomenal, she had noticed she needed her glasses more and more in the weeks following her release from the infirmary.

Slowly, Brigid scanned the bowl-shaped dead lake bottom. Groom Lake was surrounded on all sides by looming mountain chains, making it the ideal location for the predark military to conduct its experiments in secrecy. About five miles away, a scattered collection of structures, control and guard towers rose from the ground, reminding her of the broken-off stumps of teeth. She guessed it was at least a mile's worth of ruins, all laid out against the pale gray strip of what was allegedly the longest runway in the world. It stretched nearly the entire breadth of the lakebed.

The line of structures was completely dwarfed by a building so tremendous in size, it was easily seen without the aid of the binoculars. Lakesh had said the largest aircraft hangar of predark days was built in Area 51, but "large" didn't even begin to cover it. Brigid estimated it was more than three-quarters of a mile long, a quarter mile wide and at the very least a hundred feet tall. The cavernous hangar was probably gigantic enough to comfortably house the entire Cerberus redoubt, with room left over for Cobaltville's Tartarus Pits. The region exuded an atmosphere of abandonment, of not having seen a living soul in many, many years.

At the sound of stealthy footfalls behind her, she whirled swiftly, her right hand making a reflexive grab for the Iver Johnson automatic pistol holstered at her hip. She blew out a half relieved, half exasperated breath when she saw Sky Dog approaching. He affected not to notice her startled reaction. She realized he had deliberately made more noise than he usually did while walking.

"You're wanted back at Titano," the shaman said without preamble. "They're about ready to roll out."

"'They'?" she echoed a shade sardonically.

Sky Dog shrugged. "It's the baron's decision, he and that Mag Ramirez. Grant's too, I suppose. My warriors and I weren't consulted about strategy, since we're along only to help Kane. I suppose that doesn't give us any voting power."

Brigid nodded, not replying. Everything came down to the price of power, she thought bleakly. Those who sought it, those who possessed it and those who suffered under it. For the scattered survivors of the nukecaust and their descendants, the price of power was tragically high. Many of them were forced to live beyond any concept of law or morality. Many more willingly chose that path.

Rather than rebuilding a civilization around which a new, wiser human society could rally, it was far easier to lead the lives of scavengers and nomads, digging around in the ruins of the prenuke world. A fortunate few managed to build power bases on what was salvaged. Still, the true measure of power was measured in human blood—those who shed it and those who were more than willing to spill it.

When the Program of Unification was established, the anarchy and barbarism that had ruled the Deathlands for more than a century was curtailed, and power was no longer measured in human blood, but the human spirit, the seat of the soul. The nine barons knew—or they were taught—if the soul could be controlled, then humanity could be bound in heavy harness.

Power existed for its own sake, not to accrue wealth or luxury or long life or happiness, but only to gain more power. Everything else—love, honor, compassion—was irrelevant. Those who controlled its price controlled not just the world, but every human being who lived in it and was born into it. The atomic megacull made the planet the property of someone else, and humans like herself were exiles on the world of their birth.

Even Sky Dog's Amerindians, their lives deeply entwined with the Earth and its energies, were viewed as parasites by the forces of the villes.

Brigid followed Sky Dog up the pass. Once, two hundred years or more ago, it had been a two-lane blacktop road lined on either side by motion sensors and a high, chain-link fence. Nothing remained of the sensors, and only a few rust-stained metal poles showed where the fencing had stood.

The road pitched down over the top of the ridge. At its base, arranged in a single-column arrow formation, were the wags, with the C2VI as the arrowhead. Mags and Sky Dog's warriors milled around and between the vehicles, performing last-minute checks. The Deathbird sent by Baron Snakefish rested on its skids a few hundred feet down the road. It hadn't made a flyover over the site in case a radar tracking system might be in use.

Grant stood at the rear of the MCP, donning his Magistrate armor. He had already pulled on the Kevlar one-piece undergarment that covered him from ankles to wrists to neck. He struggled with the molded breast and back plates. When he saw Brigid, he said gruffly, "Help me with this damn thing."

Brigid hesitated, then stepped forward, closing the two pieces around his torso. She sealed the side locks, snapping shut all the seams. She always felt a chill finger stroke her spine whenever she saw Kane or Grant armor up. Even as well as she knew them, despite owing both men her life, when they concealed themselves beneath the polycarbonate exoskeltons, she always feared the black carapace would encase their souls, too.

Brigid knew her fear was a carryover from being ville bred. But whenever she saw the Magistrates in Cobaltville, she was always reminded of stalking tigers on loose leashes.

Grant put on the arm sheathings, locking them into place magnetically. He tugged on the leggings, then the long gauntlets. After he had secured the arm and shin guards, he pounded his shoulders and legs, testing the seals. Then he popped the Sin Eater into his hand and slid it back into the spring- and electric-powered holster.

Ramirez sauntered over to him, the visor of his helmet masking his gaze. "You look almost like a real Mag in that rig, Grant."

"Thanks," Grant intoned. "So do you."

Ramirez acted as if he hadn't heard the comeback. "We're about ready to roll. You take the point."

"Why?" Brigid asked.

"Minesweeper," he replied curtly. "Titano packs the heaviest armor, so it makes sense we go out ahead. We already discussed it."

"When?" she demanded.

"While you were making your recce."

Brigid eyed him reproachfully. "What makes you think we'll come across mines?"

"Stands to reason if whoever in the installation has the matériel and ability to plant a demo charge to bring down a building, they can sow a minefield."

Brigid cast a glance toward Sky Dog. "Did they ask you about this? I mean, the wag is your property."

Sky Dog smiled thinly. "No, they didn't. But I'm not going to stand on the rules of courtesy at this late date."

Ramirez suddenly tilted his head to one side, then

said into the transceiver grid on his helmet's jaw guard, "At once, my lord."

Addressing Grant, he declared, "The baron is getting antsy for some mayhem."

Grant turned toward the open hatch. "Let's try not to disappoint him."

He climbed aboard, striding fast down the narrow passageway. Brigid and Sky Dog followed him, and Grant announced, "Get your men to their stations, Sky Dog."

Brigid was more than a little annoyed by Grant's terse orders, but she attributed much of his rudeness to weariness. The convoy of four Sandcats and one MCP had traveled all night to reach the outer perimeter of Area 51 in the ghostly hours preceding daybreak. She knew Grant hadn't gotten any sleep, but she doubted Sky Dog had, either. Although she had managed to catch a nap, she did not feel rested. Allying themselves with Baron Sharpe and a force of Mags didn't make for restful slumber, even if it did make sound tactical sense.

The night before, when Ramirez pointedly mentioned the Tigers of Heaven and keenly observed their reactions, neither Grant's scowl nor Brigid's poker face had faltered. Still and all, she and Grant were deeply relieved when Baron Sharpe showed a distinct disinclination to discuss the Tigers of Heaven. Since the Port Morninglight incident had occurred in the territory claimed by Baron Snakefish, it might as well have happened on the moon as far as the capricious Sharpe was concerned.

He wanted only to complete the mission, and focused on persuading Grant and Brigid to enter an alliance of convenience. Not having much choice, they agreed to do so, but not without regret and suspicion, particularly of Ramirez. He was clever and ambitious, but wisely he hadn't pressed the subject of the Tigers of Heaven with Baron Sharpe, sparing Brigid and Grant the effort of offering up denials.

The Tigers of Heaven were samurai, the military arm of Lord Takaun, the daimyo of the House of Mashashige. If not for the aid rendered by Captain Kiyomasa and Shizuka, his female lieutenant, Brigid, Kane, Grant and Domi would have been overwhelmed by a horde of crazed snake worshipers out in the California badlands.

If the sudden appearance of the samurai wasn't astonishing enough, the story told by Kiyomasa was even more startling. Because of internecine struggles in Japan, Lord Takaun had no choice but to flee his homeland and go into exile. Taking with him as many family members, retainers, advisers and samurai as a small fleet of ships could hold, they set sail into the Cific. Their destination was the island chain once known as the Hawaiians, where in predark days the Japanese had established a foothold.

A storm drove the little fleet far off course, and they had no choice but to make landfall on the first halfway habitable piece of dry ground they came across.

This turned out to be a richly forested isle, the tip of a larger landmass that had been submerged during the nukecaust. Evidently, it had slowly risen from the waters over the past two centuries and supported a wide variety of animal and vegetable life. The exiles from Nippon claimed it as their own and named it New Edo, after the imperial city of feudal Japan.

New Edo was on one of the Western Islands, a region in the Cific Ocean of old and new landmasses. The tectonic shifts triggered by the nukecaust dropped most of California south of the San Andreas Fault into the sea. During the intervening two centuries, undersea quakes raised new volcanic islands. Because the soil was scraped up from the seabed, most of the islands became fertile very quickly, except for the Blight Belt—islands that were originally part of California but were still irradiated.

In the eight years since the establishment of the colony, New Edo made exploratory voyages to other islands and to the mainland. As Grant and Brigid had reason to know, many of the chain of islands were claimed by pirates and self-styled warlords. New Edo gave these a wide berth, keeping their existence a secret. They revealed themselves only to the coastal community of Port Morninglight, whose residents traded regularly with them and kept their word not to speak of the location of New Edo.

When Port Morninglight was virtually annihilated by a contingent of Cobaltville Mags and the survivors captured in order to provide raw genetic material for medical treatments, a squad of Tigers set out in pursuit. Their paths intersected with those of the people from Cerberus, and together they wiped out the Mags and set free the prisoners.

Kiyomasa had provided Brigid with the longitudinal and latitudinal coordinates of their island colony, and Shizuka had provided Grant with something else—a fierce attraction for the dignified warrior-woman who bore the name of a Japanese heroine.

Grant took his place in the pilot's chair, hanging his helmet from a hook on the bulkhead. Brigid sat beside him and buckled the safety harness around her. Putting on the headset, Grant barked, ''Button her up!''

The interior of the C2VI echoed with the clangor of hatches slamming shut and the clatter of locking levers. Brigid swiveled the gimballed chair, looking down the passageway. She saw Red Quill climbing up into the MG blister. Off the passageway, other warriors took their positions at the weapon ports and missile emplacements.

Keying the engine to rumbling life, Grant shifted through the gears and sent the machine rolling up the incline. The crew braced itself as the metal leviathan laboriously lumbered up the grade to the top of the ridge, then down. The machine jounced roughly between and over rock formations, then emerged from the pass onto the dry lakebed.

The sun hung a handbreadth over the mountain peaks, flooding the basin with lambent, variegated streamers of color. If Brigid hadn't been so tense, she might have been able to appreciate the raw beauty.

Grant kept both of his gloved hands on the wheel,

his foot applying a steady pressure on the accelerator. The MCP rolled forward with a clatter of treads and a squeal of return rollers at a steady thirty miles per hour. Brigid glanced into the side rearview mirror. Through the plumes of dust churned up by the wag's tracks, she glimpsed the four Sandcats trailing in the C2VI's wake like nervous children. About twenty feet separated each vehicle from the other. She assumed Baron Sharpe rode in the Cat last in line.

Grant's harsh voice commanded her attention. "Eyes front, Brigid."

She hitched around, facing the windscreen. "Why?"

"I need you to be my lookout...watch for anything unusual in the ground ahead."

"Like what?" she asked.

"I don't know," he replied impatiently, gruffly. "Anything unusual, like turned-over dirt or tracks. Whatever might be a minefield."

She leaned forward, lifting the binoculars to her eyes. Since she was farsighted, her glasses wouldn't do any good. "What kind of mines would be laid out here?"

Tightly, Grant replied, "There's no way to tell. Claymores, mebbe, detonated by remote control. They could be bar mines, laid down by plow. Those are the worst."

"Why?"

"For one thing, a bar mine is all plastic, making it tough to detect. It's like a six-foot-long piece of timber, but it's sculpted out of C-4. There's a pressure plate on top, and if one of our tracks rolls over it, the explosion will sure as hell cut the tread in two. At the very least, we'll throw a track shoe.''

Brigid said sourly, ''There's got be a better way to get across a minefield than how we're doing it.''

''There is,'' he told her, ''but it takes more time and equipment than we've got. The standard way to clear a minefield is to fit a Cat without front rollers to open a path—providing, of course, the mines aren't fitted with fuses that detonate only when touched twice. Personally, I prefer plows to push the mines aside, but even that's not a perfect solution. There are some mines equipped with secondary igniters, built to detonate with any attempt to dislodge them.''

Wryly, she commented, ''Sounds like quite the area of study.''

Grant forced a stitched-on smile to his lips. ''It can be.''

''How many minefields have you crossed?''

''Just one,'' he admitted. ''Twelve years or so ago. But the mines were homemade pieces of black-powder shit, put together by Roamers. It was in the Great Sand Dunes hellzone—''

Brigid was loath to cut off Grant's reminiscences, since he was behaving halfway civilly for the first time in days, but she said sharply, ''Wait!''

He reflexively eased his foot's pressure on the accelerator. ''What?''

She didn't reply for a moment, peering intently through the binoculars, her body tensed like a bowstring, propping her elbows on the instrument panel.

Near the monstrous looming bulk of the hangar, she caught a flicker of both movement and light. A magnesium-and-thermite flare smoked through the air, ascending higher and higher until it exploded in a flash of bright yellow above the hangar roof. It hung there in the dawn sky, shining with a brilliant glow.

By this time, Grant had seen the flare, as well. "A signal flare…but is it meant for us?"

"Who else?" Brigid answered, suppressing a note of hope in her voice.

"Who fired it?"

"Kane maybe. Domi even."

"Mebbe," Grant replied dubiously. Into the microphone, he said, "Follow my lead."

He turned the wheel, aiming the MCP on a direct course with the distant hangar. He tapped the earpiece of the headset and said, "Acknowledged."

To Brigid he commented, "Ramirez sees it, too. He doesn't sound too surprised."

Brigid's reply was lost in the roar of sound from beneath the war wag. Tongues of flame whipped up around the prow of the MCP, sending a geyser of sand spraying in the air, covering the windscreen and blinding them both.

Chapter 14

All the weapons that Quavell's little group of insurgents could lay their hands on were brought to the commissary. The four handblasters were of different calibers and though in good condition, the ammo was restricted to one clip apiece. Kane decided to keep the Mustang .380 for use as a hideout blaster.

None of the hybrids had any experience with firearms, so Kane and Domi distributed a few of the grens they had brought with them to the installation in a kit bag. Kane kept one high-ex V-60 mini and a flash-bang for himself. Domi claimed a CS and an incend, and the rest went to the hybrids. The blasters were given to Maddock and three other men—Brodeur, Fuller and Tavares. All of them had been conscripted into the Dulce security garrison from Mag Divisions in various villes, though none of them had Kane's years of experience.

Brodeur, the black man, explained the Dreamland installation did indeed possess an armory, but only the watch commander of the different shifts had access to it. A chain of command had to be climbed in order to even meet with the watch commanders. Besides, the armory was a three-mile monorail ride from their present position. He added the mat-trans unit was even farther away than that, and heavily guarded, so the gateway wasn't an option. Kane didn't voice his pessimism about their chances of pulling off a successful inside insurrection. He was too happy to be free of his cell and back in armor again. Once he strapped his fully loaded Sin Eater on his forearm, his spirits soared.

Domi, though once more attired in the padded bulletproof vest and black coveralls, seemed pensive. She patted the coverall's pouches, bulging with extra magazines for her Combat Master. The big blaster was strapped to her thigh. Normally, the prospect of combat keyed her up, made her bright-eyed and chirpy. But this time she broodily examined the long knife, thumbing the serrated blade over and over. The knife was her one memento from the six months she had spent in Cobaltville as Guana Teague's sex slave. She had used it to slit Teague's throat when the Cobaltville Pit boss was strangling the life out of Grant.

Quavell left to attend to the infants in the nursery, and Fuller brought out several cross-section blueprints of the installation sandwiched between layers of transparent Lucite. "This place is so damn big," he complained, "there isn't one comprehensive map of the layout. It's divided by sections and if you don't know your starting point, you can get lost real fast."

Kane squinted through the semigloom at the confusing network of vertical and horizontal lines and colored geometric forms. Brodeur tapped a tiny green square from which two horizontal lines sprouted. "This is where we are."

With a forefinger he traced one of the lines to the far edge of the map, then slid another one over it. The line fed into a large red square. "This is the hangar on the surface. The only way to reach it is by a cargo elevator, and the only way to reach the elevator is first by the monorail system to platform 32, and then by a passenger elevator to level ten. Once there, you'll take some stairs up to section Z-9." He extended two fingers. "There are two sets of stairways. Either one will get you to the elevator...eventually."

Kane shook his head in frustration. "I hope there are signs posted."

"Sorry," Maddock said with a half grin. "But me and Brodeur will meet you there and try to run interference to the cargo elevator."

"And the elevator is nonstop to the surface?"

Fuller shook his head. "No. It makes automatic stops on levels eight, seven and six. There's nothing we can do about it."

"I think I'd rather take the stairs all the way," Domi said softly.

Quaice retorted stiffly, "That method would require a minimum of six hours and forty-five minutes to reach the hangar area. And that's assuming all the stairwell doors are unlocked."

Maddock ignored the hybrid's observation and tapped the square symbolizing the hangar. "The attack will center on that."

"How can you be so sure?" Kane wanted to know.

"Simple," Maddock replied. He gestured to the

hybrid. "Quaice will be up there by dawn with a flare gun. He'll draw the assault force's attention."

"What kind of outer defenses does the base have?"

Fuller shrugged. "We've heard rumors of a minefield in the lakebed, but since we're not upper-echelon members of the garrison, we don't know for sure. I haven't been topside since I was transferred here from Dulce."

Kane murmured wordlessly in irritation. "Is there anything about this damn place you do know for sure?"

Quaice said waspishly, "There is a fleet of wheeled vehicles in the hangar outfitted with automatic weapons."

"How many?"

Quaice gestured diffidently. Kane had seen Balam perform the same motion as the equivalent of a shrug. "I have only seen six, but that doesn't preclude more in storage."

Crooking an eyebrow, Kane glanced toward Maddock. "There's nothing like a hover-tank in storage, is there?"

A fleeting smile crossed Maddock's face. "I doubt it."

Kane referred to the armored, fan-powered patrol vehicle he had hijacked during the penetration of the Archuleta Mesa site. Maddock had been a member of its crew.

"From what I was told," the young man continued, "the tank is still out there in the desert where you left it."

Tavares spoke up. "According to the last coded message we received, the force reached Las Vegas about eight hours ago. They intend to wait until 2200 hours before making the push to Dreamland. If everything goes according to plan, they should reach the Groom Lake perimeter a little before daybreak."

"How are you receiving and sending these messages undetected?" Kane asked.

Tavares, a dark-haired man of about Kane's age, tapped his chest. "I'm the comm man here. No one else knows shit about the equipment. I realigned it to receive and send digitally compressed messages on a hopping frequency sequence."

"Nobody here can decipher them?" Kane's tone was studiedly skeptical. "Nobody notices when the signals come in?"

Tavares grinned proudly. "Hey, if I say the signals are caused by sunspots, nobody knows enough to know they don't know enough. They take my word for it."

"Remember," said Maddock, "Baron Cobalt only reactivated this place about three months ago. The staff here are all survivors from the Dulce garrison, and most of them are grunts, not techs."

"After the mesa was blown, why weren't you recalled back to your respective villes?"

Fuller shrugged. "At first our orders were to stay at Dulce to salvage what we could and dispose of the dead. We were just a glorified cleanup detail. When Baron Cobalt's orders came through to relocate ourselves and everything we could to here, do you think anybody wanted to question him?''

Fuller's explanation made sense, at least to sufficiently quell Kane's suspicions, if not completely lay them to rest.

Maddock announced, ''We have to get back to our posts. You and Domi can stay here and try to get some sleep.'' He unpocketed a trans-comm unit and held it up. ''At 0500 hours, I'll signal you on this. When you leave here, take the first right and go to monorail station 20. At 0530, you'll call sec central so they'll power it up. Identify yourself as Phillipson. The code words are—''

''—Jimmy six January,'' Kane interposed smoothly. ''Who's Phillipson?''

''The guy you killed. He's assigned to this section of the base and you have his comm, so you should be able to pull it off.''

''He won't be missed between now and then?''

''The base is already on a second-degree alert,'' Brodeur said gloomily. ''They're probably looking for you, but we've already hidden the bodies of the men you and Domi chilled. So sec central won't know you're armed.''

''But they're assuming I'm loose and trying to reach the surface?'' Kane inquired.

''Wouldn't you?'' Maddock responded. ''But they'll figure you've gone to ground somewhere. Besides, if I know Gifford he'll want to hunt you down personally.''

A humorless smile creased Kane's face. ''That's

nice to know. I'd hate to leave without saying good-bye.''

Human and hybrid alike filed out of the commissary, leaving Kane and Domi alone in the dim room. He was far too keyed up to sleep, so he examined all of his equipment. He strapped the motion detector around his left wrist. It was a small device made of molded black plastic and stamped metal. A liquid crystal display window exuded a faint glow. He turned it off and on, sweeping it back and forth experimentally.

The silence between him and Domi became awkward. She seemed disinclined to talk, to do much of anything except sit at the dining table with her head propped up by her hands.

After several minutes, Kane asked, ''Are you sure you're all right?''

''Yeah.'' Her voice was dull and listless. ''Just fine. You?''

''Grand.''

Another period of silence settled over the room. ''When we move out,'' he said, ''we should probably split up and head for the hangar by different directions. That'll minimize the chances of both of us being recaptured.''

''Or chilled,'' she interjected.

''Or chilled,'' he agreed. ''Do you want to look at the layout, choose an alternate route?''

Domi pulled the blueprints toward her and scanned them slowly, without apparent interest. Kane waited for her to say more, but she didn't. Usually, Domi was forthright, forthcoming and very verbal. He had been on a number of missions with her, and she'd earned his trust and respect. However, her behavior had changed prior to and during the op to penetrate Area 51. She was taciturn, even insulting, particularly toward Grant. The short fuse of her temper seemed to have shrunk to little more than a wick. It took only a tiny spark to trigger an explosion of homicidal anger.

Right before he and Domi had jumped from Cerberus, Grant confided in him that he was the reason for Domi's confrontational attitude. For more than a year she'd claimed she loved Grant, but he was always reluctant to return that emotion for reasons even he couldn't articulate.

Kane guessed Domi represented a kind of innocence to Grant, and he didn't want to taint it with sex—despite the fact she was no stranger to it before being smuggled into Cobaltville to serve as Guana Teague's sex slave. He also figured Grant didn't want to do anything that might diminish the memory of Olivia, the only woman who'd ever truly claimed his heart.

So Grant always drew the line at physical intimacy with Domi, sometimes citing the age difference between them as the reason, even though not even Domi knew how old she was. Kane never thought that argument defensible. Waiflike in appearance she might be, but Domi had proved time and again she was anything but a child.

She hadn't reacted like a child when she came

across Grant and Shizuka, the female samurai, locked in a sweaty embrace. That Grant had even informed him of the incident was a matter of some surprise to Kane. Although they were friends, partners for more than a dozen years, the two men observed an unspoken agreement not to speak of personal matters unless specifically invited. Very rarely had Grant extended a specific invitation. Therefore, when he told Kane about Domi seeing him with Shizuka after the battle with the Mags who had abducted the citizens of Port Morninglight, his first reaction was to be amused. The amusement didn't last long.

Kane sat on the edge of the dining table, consciously assuming a higher posture than the seated Domi. It was a cheap psychological ploy, but he needed to get past the girl's uncharacteristic reticence, and he wasn't above gentle intimidation. Matter-of-factly he said, "I have to admit I'm surprised by you. I thought you hated hybrids with all your heart. You didn't consider them human."

Gazing at the layouts, Domi kept her reply studiedly dismissive. "I can change my mind, can't I?"

Kane nodded. "Sure you can. But I'd like to know why you did—and so radically."

She cast him an angry stare, her eyes gleaming like drops of freshly spilt blood. "You don't trust me?"

"I didn't say that. But you can't deny the reversal in your attitude is pretty goddamn dramatic. Pretty much of a one-eighty from what it was. As you recall, you accused me, Grant, Lakesh and Brigid of being 'pussy-hearted' when we wanted to scout out this place before lighting it up. That was only two weeks ago.''

''Two weeks can be a lifetime,'' Domi retorted stiffly.

''That's a little vague,'' Kane said, his temper fraying. ''If you're going to cover my back, I need to know why you feel so differently, what you've gone through.'' He added wryly, ''You seem to know what's been happening to me.''

Domi acknowledged the comment with a playful smile. ''Heard about it from Quavell and others.''

Domi sighed and stood. She began pacing the room, her black outfit causing her to blend in with the shadows. Linking her hands behind her neck, she stretched, trying work out the kinks. ''For the first couple of days after they found me, they kept me restrained to a bed. Had to feed me with an IV.''

''Were you hurt that badly?''

''No, I just tried to chill anybody who came near me. Then after a while…'' Her words trailed off and Kane waited. At length she shook her head and said, ''I guess I got used to 'em. They didn't hurt me. Quavell and Maddock came every day to talk to me.''

''Talk about what?'' Kane inquired, trying to blunt the sharp edge of suspicion in his voice.

Her answer surprised him. ''Negative conditioning, for one thing. On both sides.''

Kane knew what she was talking about, since Lakesh and Brigid had discussed the matter several times. The similarity between Archons and hybrids and the traditional images of demons had been a matter of academic debate. Brigid opined the physical appearance of Balam's folk accounted for the instant enmity that sprang up between humans and the so-called Archon. Lakesh suggested that ancient depictions of imps, elves and djinns were based on early encounters between Balam's people and primitive man. Therefore, after thousands of years of negative conditioning, humans weren't capable of reaching an accord with creatures who resembled figures of evil.

Even by cross-breeding with humanity, the hybrids were still markedly different from humankind. But of course, different was not the same as alien.

"Quavell told me she had been conditioned to believe all humans were basically vicious apes," Domi went on. "Nothing but savages, not able to learn new things or transcend their roots as killers. Quavell said if she could change her mind, then so could I."

The terminology the girl employed at first amused then disturbed Kane. Almost since the day he had met her more than a year ago, one character trait had never changed; her tendency to never use two syllables when she thought one would do. Slowly he began to realize Domi was far more intelligent than he had ever given her credit for.

"What made Quavell change her mind?" asked Kane.

Domi turned her face toward him. In the dim light she looked like a disembodied wraith. "You did."

"Me?" Kane echoed, nonplussed. "Not just because I—"

"No, not that," she broke in impatiently. "It was

when you spared her life in New Mexico, after we destroyed the mesa facility. She hadn't expected a show of mercy from any human, let alone you. That made her start questioning the whole setup of the baronies, the villes, everything."

Although Kane had come to accept that the barons were not semidivine god-kings, he always wondered if the hybrids, with their purported superior intelligence, would ever reach the same conclusion. Apparently, a few of them had.

"So," Domi continued, "if she could change her mind about us, I guess I could change my mind about them…especially after I saw the babies—"

She clamped her lips tight and to Kane's dismay, he was sure he heard a sob catch at the back of her throat.

"What are you saying?" he demanded. "That the sight of dying hybrid babies turned you around? How many dying human babies have you seen in the Outlands, in the Pits of Cobaltville?"

Domi whirled on him, her eyes blazing with crimson fury, her teeth bared. "Too fucking many!" she shrilled. "Seen 'em, nursed 'em, held 'em when they breathed their last and buried 'em!"

In her agitation, Domi reverted to her clipped outlander mode of speech. "War isn't against babies, not even against hybrids. It's against the barons and—" she stabbed an accusatory finger at him "—against men like you and Grant! Men like you used to be."

Kane felt a flush of astonishment, then one of resentment. But before he could react, Domi said angrily, "I wasn't afraid of hybrids in the Outlands. Didn't even know such as them existed. But I was sure as shit scared of the baron's sec men—the Mags. That's who was my enemy."

She inhaled a deep breath, trying to compose herself. "Mebbe I've thought of a better reason to stay alive than chilling babies, Kane. Mebbe you should, too. If making war is the only reason you can think of to live, then you and Grant might as well die."

Kane was shocked by the passion and reproach in Domi's stance and voice. Death was part of the life she had lived in the raw border territories of the Outlands. He had always assumed she accepted violence and bloodshed as natural parts of existence. Because he had seen her kill frequently, with no outward twinge of conscience, he had presumed she didn't have one. With a pang of guilt, he suddenly realized how little he understood about Domi, and how he had misjudged her.

"You can't live your life hating all the time," she continued. "Always looking for enemies to hate, to fight, to chill."

Kane blew out a frustrated breath and ran his hands through his hair. "This sure doesn't sound like you."

She glared at him defiantly, challengingly. "You and Grant didn't stay what you were. I don't have to stay what I am. If it means working with the hybrids against the barons, against the Mags, then I will. I'll forgive 'em for being born."

Falteringly, Kane said, "I'm not a forgiving man."

In a hollow, ghostly murmur, Domi intoned, "Had

a saying in my settlement, Kane—wind and fire. One wastes its strength in trying to blow down a mountain, the other devours without thought."

"Which are you?" he asked.

She smiled without mirth, without warmth. "Ask me this time tomorrow. Mebbe we'll both know what we are."

Kane studied her, and with a faraway sense of shock, he felt as if he were seeing her for the first time. Her face held a white strength in it, her eyes a crimson blaze of pride and iron will. He couldn't really argue with her about who was the true enemy. Outlanders, sneered at by the elite of the villes, were possibly the last real human beings on the planet, and as a Magistrate, he had chilled scores of them in the performance of his duty.

Kane reached for her, drawing her toward him by her shoulders. She resisted for a moment, then of her own volition pressed herself against his polycarbonate-encased chest. Kane hesitantly enfolded her small frame in his arms and clumsily patted her tousled head.

"Wind and fire," she whispered. "One feeds the other. We'll find who is what."

Chapter 15

The wag shuddered brutally, slamming both Brigid and Grant back against their seats. The nose of the MCP rose as if breasting a wave, but the machine kept advancing. A sheet of sand slid down the exterior surface of the windshield, leaving a dusty film in its wake.

Tensely, Brigid listened for the clattering of a severed tread, but she heard only the steady thud of the drivetrain. She said, "Not a bar mine, I guess."

"No," Grant replied flatly. "Not a Claymore, either. Probably an M-14. Not enough of a charge to damage us, but it would've disabled a Cat...and blown a man's legs off."

"Is the comm link open to the Cats?" she asked anxiously.

Grant tapped the headset and replied, "It's okay. We're still on-line to Ramirez."

Turning in his chair, Grant shouted down the passageway, "Sky Dog! Are you and your men all right?"

After a few moments, Sky Dog called an affirmative. Grant tightened his hands on the wheel. "We don't have any choice but to keep rolling."

He kept the MCP on course for the distant hangar.

The sun rose higher over the mountain peaks, flooding the dry basin with lambent light. Within a minute, another explosion thumped beneath the C2VI. This time the jolt of detonation was accompanied by a clattering, drumming vibration against the undercarriage.

"That was a Claymore," Grant declared. He almost sounded happy about it. "Hear the ball bearings?"

Brigid only nodded, swallowing hard. She repressed the urge to comment on how fraught with danger Grant's agreement was to use the war wag as a mine sweeper. One of the tracks could be sheared away, or the engine disabled, or even the undercoating of armor breached, which could touch off the flammable fuel in storage. But she kept silent, not voicing the litany of things that could go wrong. There were too many of them, for one thing.

Grant glanced out the side window and saw a gap in the convoy. It was split into two sections. The C2VI had pulled well ahead, and two of the Cats followed it in a straight line. The other two vehicles had strayed well off course, flanking the MCP's port side.

"Drop back!" Grant snapped into the mike. "Drop back and close it up!"

One of the Sandcats slowed, slewed around on one track—and vanished in a billowing fireball. The tremendous cracking roar was nearly deafening, even inside the control cabin of the war wag. The shock wave of the explosion jarred the MCP from stem to stern. Pieces of the Sandcat rained down, clanging loudly on the hull of the C2VI.

Grant slowed the wag. "That," he announced grimly, "was a bar mine."

The Cat lay at an angle in the middle of a steaming crater. Black smoke poured from the splits in the hull. Brigid gazed at it, looking for movement behind the ob slits. Only streamers of dark, spark-shot vapor curled out of them.

"Shit." Grant's voice was soft and disgusted. "That mine must have had a tilt-rod delay fuse. When the Cat bent it, the fuse wasn't ignited until it straddled the damn thing."

Peering through the planes of drifting smoke and pulverized dust, Brigid glimpsed dark shapes approaching their position. When the cloud of grit and vapor thinned, she saw ten Hummers rolling in a reversed-horseshoe formation across the lakebed.

The Hummers had huge knobby tires and extremely broad wheel bases. The driver and passenger compartments were enclosed by a superstructure of metal shielding. The front and sides bore slabs of reactive armor, interconnected plates of alloy that distributed and dissipated both kinetic force and explosive penetration. M-60 machine guns were mounted on the roofs, giving the wags a top-heavy appearance. They were about a hundred yards away from the convoy, but closing the gap quickly.

"I guess we're all out of mines," Brigid remarked.

Grant frowned her way. "Why do you say that?"

She pointed out the side window, toward the advancing vehicles. "They wouldn't show up otherwise."

"Shit," Grant said again. Then, into the microphone, he snapped, "Yeah, I see them, Ramirez. Keep your Cats together, don't get separated."

The Hummers traveled at such a high rate of speed, rooster tails of sand and dust spurned from beneath their tires, forming a dense cloud behind them. Grant pressed the gas pedal to the floorboards, saying loudly over the rumble of the engine, "If any of those bastards get in our way, it'll be them all over."

Brigid didn't laugh.

One of the Sandcats that had drifted off course turned and rumbled back to join the convoy. It hadn't crossed more than twenty yards of lakebed when a flower of flame bloomed beneath it. Even before her stunned eardrums recovered from the concussion, Brigid heard the jackhammer clanging of treads shearing away from the rollers. The entire left track thrashed in a long flapping strip, crashing against the hull. Sparks showered and metal screamed as the tread slashed deep scars into the armor. The vehicle rocked to a shuddering, clanking halt.

"I guess there was one more mine," Brigid observed.

The gull-wing doors popped open. Amid a cloud of smoke, six Mags poured out of the Sandcat. They were dazed, unsure of themselves, but not seriously injured. They saw the approaching Hummers and opened up with their handblasters and subguns.

One of the Hummers returned the fire, the perforated snout of the big M-60 machine roaring with flame and thunder. For a moment, the ripping snarls of Sin Eaters and Copperheads on full-auto drowned out the jackhammer roar of the roof-mounted machine gun.

Two of the Magistrates spun in sprays of blood, flinders of black polycarbonate armor flying away from their bodies. The remaining four dashed to cover behind their disabled vehicle. The M-60 continued to rattle and a hail of bullets peppered the Cat's hull. Sparks flared on the metal hide, leaving deep dents to commemorate the multiple impacts of armor-piercing rounds.

Then the ten Hummers were circling the convoy, machine guns chattering. They were far more maneuverable and faster than the Sandcats, and the C2VI. The billowing waves of dust rising in their wakes made for an effective smoke screen. The Hummers weaved in and out between the two Sandcats still mobile. The turrets of the Cats rotated, following their passage, the USMG-73s spitting a staccato hail of bullets at them. Sparks jumped from the chassis of the armored fighting vehicles but the slugs didn't achieve penetration in vital areas.

Three of the Hummers chose to circle the disabled Cat, barreling around it like a pack of wolves cutting a hapless sheep out of the herd. The gunners on the other Cats couldn't open up on the vehicles without hitting their own men.

A Hummer drew close to the C2VI, its M-60 spitting spear points of flame. Brass arced in a glittering rain from the ejector port. Sparks danced on the hull of the war wag, and the left corner of the windshield acquired a starred pattern of cracks. Grant twisted the wheel and the MCP heeled around, making a lunging port-side rush. The MG continued to hammer as it sped away from the war wag's prow. It fired a final burst as it retreated.

Brigid and Grant ducked as part of the Plexiglas shield smashed inward. Cursing, Grant jammed on the brakes and jerked the wheel hard. The MCP slewed around in a sharp ninety-degree turn and came to a halt. Snatching his helmet from its hook and stripping off the headset, Grant bellowed down the companion-way, "Sky Dog! Grab a LAW and meet me at the starboard hatch!"

Brigid started to rise from her chair, but Grant said tersely, "Stand by the fire-control board. I'll give you orders through the helmet comm link."

She gave him a cold look, then nodded and put on the headset. By the time Grant had secured his helmet on his head and reached the starboard side hatch, Sky Dog emerged from a cubicle hefting the long hollow cylinder of a LAW 80 rocket launcher in his arms.

"It's already loaded." He handed the tube to Grant, who pulled apart the two sections to their full extended length and unfolded the reflex collinator sight on its upper surface.

Sky Dog undid the complicated series of levers and latches on the door, then kicked it open. He narrowed his eyes as an astringent blend of smoke and dust drifted inward.

"Stay aboard," Grant told him.

Sky Dog recoiled as a wild round spanged off the

MCP's hide over his head. Dryly he said, "Whatever you say."

Grant leaped to the ground and moved away from the C2VI. Looking toward the disabled Sandcat, he saw one of the pinned-down Mags pitch over onto his face, his armored torso stitched through with a zipper of slugs fired from a Hummer's M-60. The two survivors were completely occupied with avoiding the 7.62 mm rounds crashing and ricocheting from the smoldering Cat's hull.

Placing the launch tube on his right shoulder, Grant inserted his finger into the molded bulge of the trigger on the cylinder's underside. Holding his breath, he placed one of the Hummers in target acquisition, sighting on a small area in the rear not covered by the reactive armor plate. He tracked the wag, led it a few yards, then squeezed into the trigger pull.

Smoke and flame gouted from the hollow bore of the missile launcher as the 94 mm HEAT rocket ignited in the tube. Propelled by a wavering ribbon of vapor and sparks, the projectile seared the air in a direct line toward its target.

The High Explosive Anti-Tank warhead exploded in a flaring fireball on the Hummer's port side aft. The shaped hollow charge smashed a deep cavity into the chassis, and the kinetic force tipped the wag up then over on its side. Fragments clattered against Grant and he flinched, but his polycarbonate sheathing turned them away.

He dropped the launch tube and turned just as a Hummer wheeled around and arrowed for him, its course taking it between him and the safety of the MCP's hatch. Grant stood his ground, his Sin Eater springing into his palm. He fired twice through the ob port at the man behind the Hummer's steering wheel. The bullets punched starred holes through the Plexiglas, coring into the driver's chest. The vehicle immediately slowed, but still maintained its course. The M-60 swung around, trying to align Grant in front of the barrel.

Grant planted a foot against the front bumper of the Hummer and propelled himself onto the wag's hood, then inserted the barrel of the Sin Eater into the gunner's port. He squeezed off a single shot, the round driving through the blasterman's head.

He jumped off the Hummer as it continued to roll. It collided with the disabled Sandcat and bounced to a halt. As Grant edged back toward the MCP, he glanced around the zone. The roar of many engines was loud even through the polystyrene lining of his helmet. The reek of smoke and exhaust fumes filled his nostrils.

Twenty or so yards away, half of the Hummers braked to disgorge men wearing bulletproof vests over gray jumpsuits. Grens hung from canvas bandoliers crisscrossing their chests. They cradled Armalite assault rifles in their arms. The other four Hummers maintained hit-and-run maneuvers around the Sandcats.

There were at least six men, and they ran toward the Cats, using the sandy backwash created by the Hummers as cover. Grant instantly grasped their strategy. Their clothes were neutral colored, and the gunners aboard the Cats were occupied with the Hummers. Creeping under the blanket of dust and smoke, the men intended to chuck grens into ob ports of the Cats.

Grant dropped the Sin Eater's sights over one of the men and squeezed the trigger. The bullet slammed through the sec man's head, jerking him off his feet and throwing him against the man beside him.

Two of the sec men whirled toward Grant, their Armalites blazing. Grant flung himself backward, behind the shield of the open hatch of the MCP. Rounds crashed into it, tearing metal splinters loose and driving sparks high into the air.

Behind him, from the interior, Sky Dog inquired, "Still want me to stay inside?"

"Yes." Ducking beneath the door, Grant fired at one of the men, missing him by inches as he shifted position, sliding into the smoke and dust.

Growling an oath, Grant targeted the man's exposed shoulder. He squeezed the trigger. The 9 mm, 248-grain bullet hit the man in the right thigh and spun him into the open. Aiming for his chest, Grant fired again, but the man staggered and the round struck a gren on the man's bandolier. It instantly exploded and enveloped him in a ballooning ball of flame. The other grens detonated, and the concussion slammed Grant violently against the side of the war wag, the shock wave nearly crowding him back into the open hatch.

He caught only glimpses of sec men's bodies hurtling in fragments in all directions. Arms and legs, and chunks of bloody, ragged flesh thudded down all around. Scarlet sprinkled the ground.

As his stunned ears recovered from multiple explosions, he heard Sky Dog exclaiming in his own language. Grant cautiously moved away from the shield of the hatch door, stepping toward the smoldering crater in the lakebed, searching for other casualties engulfed by the detonations. All he saw was a thick, corkscrewing column of smoke.

A Hummer erupted out of the swirl of gray-black vapor and lunged toward him. Grant leaped backward, but its bumper grazed his hip, nearly knocking the big man from his feet. It roared on by, the M-60 drumming.

Teeth bared, Grant raced after it. When the vehicle slowed to avoid running over a straggling sec man, he bounded onto the back of it. Standing on the bumper, Grant struggled to keep his balance as the Hummer bounced and rocked across the terrain. Bullets from Ramirez's Sandcat scored the Hummer's hull and skimmed across Grant's polycarbonate-sheathed backside. He winced and swore at the pain as the wag crossed twenty yards of lakebed.

Grant crawled to the MG mount and emptied the Sin Eater's clip through the gun port. The M-60 ceased its deadly chatter. Apparently, a couple of rounds found the driver, because the Hummer listed out of control, losing speed and making a slow, leisurely turn to the left.

Dropping from the roof, Grant shoulder-rolled and

came quickly to his knees. He thumbed the Sin Eater's magazine release, ejecting the empty, and slammed a fresh clip home. He chambered the first round and got to his feet, surveying the battle zone. The rushing circle of Hummers had slowed, their movements more deliberate now that their crews realized they'd incurred casualties.

The two Sandcats and seven Hummers raced and whirled around the lakebed, circling and feinting at one another, then veering away. Great clouds of dust hung heavily in the air like curtains of dingy chiffon. Grit and dirt particles coated the visor of Grant's helmet, and he had to constantly palm it clean in order to see.

The Hummers continued to harass the Cats, their big M-60s hammering incessantly, pocking the hulls of the tracked vehicles with fist-sized craters. The heavier Sandcats tried to broadside the Hummers, but the smaller wags were too fast.

Brigid's voice suddenly blared through the comm link, tight with anxiety. "Grant! Two o'clock!"

Grant spun around as two of the Hummers vectored in on him, their engines roaring like rampaging beasts. The barrels of the M-60s trained on him. Instinctively, he opened up with the Sin Eater on full-auto, shifting the flaming barrel from one wag to another. The bullets struck the reactive plate armor and bounced away with keening whines. He fired the blaster dry within a few seconds, but the two vehicles came on.

He knew holding his ground would only get him

shot or flattened, so he turned and ran as fast as he could, his long legs pumping. Although his speed was impressive, Grant could only maintain it for short distances. Flame strobed from the bores of the M-60s, and the bullets thumped the air over his head.

He concentrated on running, praying he wouldn't stumble and hoping the nagging pull of an old injury wouldn't slow him up. Grant's thigh muscles felt as if they were seizing, his lungs were squeezed between the jaws of an ever tightening vise and his vision was shot through with gray spots.

The ground suddenly shuddered beneath his pounding feet, and he felt a blast of withering heat right through his armor. A split second later he heard the report of the MCP's 20 mm cannon, sounding like the handclap of a giant. The incendiary agent of the round impacted squarely on the hood of one of the Hummers. Fire bloomed from the engine block.

The wag swerved into a crazed fishtail, strewing the ground with engine parts. Its front end broadsided the Hummer beside it, and with a shriek of metal grinding into metal and a flurry of sparks, the two wags careened madly in a wild figure eight.

The MCP's cannon belched flame and smoke again, and the second round impacted on the right rear tire of the Hummer with its engine aflame. Both wags went tumbling in a cartwheel. A fuel tank ignited on the third bounce, and the bodywork of both vehicles was swallowed by a mushroom of roiling yellow flame. The crashing Hummers finally came to rest amid a shower of hardware, fire and loose tires.

Breathing hard, his hands resting on his knees, Grant said into the helmet transceiver, "Good thing you didn't wait for me to give you an order."

Brigid's voice responded crisply, "Do I ever? Maybe you'd better get back here—when I fired the cannon, I stalled out the engine. If I fire off any more rounds without the engine running, I'll drain the battery."

Grant straightened, drinking in great gasps of air. He started walking toward the war wag, a couple of hundred feet away. "Just sit tight. I'll be back in a minute."

He had just uttered the words when a man materialized out of the drifting planes of vapor. His eyes were narrowed against the dust and smoke, and he didn't immediately see Grant. Quickly, Grant reached for the combat knife sheathed in his boot, and his hand closed around the Nylex handle. He whipped it free just as the man spotted him, swinging the barrel of the longblaster in a flat arc toward him.

Lunging forward, Grant rammed the fourteen-inch knife into the sec man's lower belly and wrenched upward. The blued, razor-keen blade slit the man's torso from just above his pelvic bone to his clavicle. He yanked the knife free, and the guard fell to his knees, frantically grabbing at his blue-sheened entrails as they spilled into the dust at his feet.

Stepping back, Grant ejected the spent clip from his Sin Eater and slid in a fresh one. He returned the knife to its scabbard just as a bullet punched into his left shoulder and knocked him off balance. Another shot skated along the right side of his helmet. He pivoted on his heel and fired a triple burst into a sec man's chest. The hydrostatic shock of the center-punching rounds dropped him dead.

A Sandcat lumbered past Grant in pursuit of a Hummer. One of the gray-clad men managed to get close enough to it to jam a gren through the ob port, but a stuttering barrage from the MG in the turret tore through his head and dropped him dead less than three seconds after he deposited his gift. The rear hatch swung open and four Magistrates tumbled head-long out of it. A second later, the vehicle jumped, tongues of flame spouting from every seam and opening. The fuel tank ignited and when it exploded, the entire vehicle was engulfed in an orange-yellow fire-ball.

The Hummer skidded around in a fast turn and charged toward the Sandcat's crew. The Mags fired at it, but the wag came on and they scattered in all directions. They were swallowed up by smoke. Grant ground his teeth in angry frustration. The Hummers were too fast for stray shots to blow out tires or strike vulnerable areas, and their AP rounds gave them the distinct edge in a shootout.

Over the roar of engines and the clanking of treads came another sound. It was a faint rustle for a handful of seconds, then a violent downdraft scoured him with an abrasive bath of sand. His visor was occluded by the wind-borne grit, and he cleared it with a swipe of his left hand.

The Deathbird made a low, high-speed pass, diving

down with automatic fire spitting from the chain gun. Streams of .50-caliber slugs slashed long trenches in the lakebed floor, dirt gouting up in high fountains. The streams intersected with a Hummer, banging loudly on the hull as they ripped through both the reactive armor and the shielded bodywork.

The Hummer tipped to the right under the barrage. A rocket burst from the chopper's port stub wing and soared, flaming, directly toward the Hummer. It exploded six feet before impact, causing the wag to list, tilt, then crash over on its right side, wheels spinning. The helicopter hovered over the Hummer like a bird of prey, strafing the undercarriage in steady bursts from the chain gun. One burst punctured the gas tank, and its contents went up in a brilliant fireball.

The Deathbird wheeled away from the licking flames and flew over Grant's head. He ducked as the rotor wash drove a strong puff of grit-laden air down into his face. Spitting, he watched as another puff of smoke and a streak of flame flared from the Deathbird's port-side wing.

The Shrike missile exploded to the right of a racing Hummer in a brilliant red-yellow spout of fire. Shrapnel rattled loudly against the hull. The M-60 on the roof hammered rhythmically, spent shell casings spewing from the ejector port. The Deathbird wagged back and forth, avoiding the machine gun's armor-piercing rounds.

The Deathbird curved around in a wind-screaming arc, points of orange flame dancing from the chain gun. Dirt burst up in columns all around the Hummer, and then came a series of ear-knocking clangs as .50-caliber rounds struck the armor. The black chopper described a swift, strafing circle around the vehicle.

Grant admired the Bird jockey's skill. As a former Deathbird pilot himself, he knew the machines were exceptionally difficult to maneuver, especially when under fire. He also knew that reactive armor or not, the Hummer could not withstand a prolonged hammering of .50-caliber blockbusters. But a Shrike missile with a high-ex warhead had the capacity of piercing even the thickest armor plate to a depth of twelve inches.

As if the pilot had picked up on his thoughts, a missile sprang from the chopper's starboard wing, inscribing a smoking, fiery arc through the air. It struck the Hummer broadside and exploded with such concussive force Grant was sent stumbling backward a few feet. Chunks of the wag rained down for yards around.

Another Hummer plunged out of the dust-laden smoke from behind the helicopter, fire darting from the long barrel like the tongue of a questing serpent. Grant started to call out a warning before he realized the pilot couldn't hear him. Still, when the first shots struck the chopper, twisting a landing skid out of shape, the Deathbird rose in a fast, frantic ascent.

Grant glimpsed metal pieces of the tail-boom assembly fly away in flinders. As the chopper gained altitude, flame flared when an exhaust cowling was shot away. The chopper's engine whined, missed, cut out altogether and caught again.

The Deathbird's rise halted and it hovered for a instant, listing noticeably. Trailing a plume of smoke, it flew away from the lakebed and sank from view behind the ridgeline.

Grant made a wordless utterance of disgust, but still the Deathbird's contribution had evened the odds a bit. A Sandcat lunged out of the dusty pall, the treads missing the toes of Grant's boots by a handbreadth. It roared toward a surviving pair of Hummers. The MG emplacements in the turret fired a solid stream of rounds at the wags.

For a long, stretched-out tick of time, Grant wondered who would blink first, the drivers of the Hummers or the pilot of the Cat. At the last possible microsecond, one of the Hummers veered away, but the blunt prow of the Cat clipped its wheel-well fender. The vehicle spun in a complete circle, the big tires churning up bushels of sand. The Cat rumbled onward toward the hangar.

Grant couldn't be sure, but he felt fairly confident Ramirez was behind the wheel, and that meant Baron Sharpe was aboard. He wondered how the baron was reacting to the little lakebed war. If he was indeed convinced he couldn't die, he more than likely was enjoying himself immensely.

Brigid's voice shouted in his ear through the comm link, and he sprinted back to the MCP. He leaped through the open hatch, running past Sky Dog in the passageway to the control compartment. The shaman pulled the door closed and sealed it.

Taking his seat, he keyed on the ignition and felt

great relief when the engine bellowed to life. He shifted gears, and the huge C2VI lurched forward. He kept the accelerator floored. A fusillade of machine-gun fire chopped into the mammoth war wag as it ran a gauntlet formed by the two remaining Hummers. Despite the AP rounds, the bullets only scored the dense steel planking, but didn't penetrate it.

The racket was deafening, and nerve-racking all the same. The rattling bursts of autofire, the sledgehammer pounding of rounds crashing against the exterior and the high-pitched whines of ricochets all combined to make a hellish cacophony.

From Grant's left, a Hummer arrowed in on an intercept course, its roof-mounted MG spitting flame and lead. There was a gargling cry from behind them. He and Brigid swung their chairs around and saw Red Quill fall from the turret, his hands clasped to his upper chest. Blood bubbled up between his fingers. It had been one hell of a lucky shot for the Hummer's blasterman, but Grant doubted Red Quill would see it that way.

Sky Dog caught the warrior, then handed him off to a comrade. Then the shaman swarmed up the steel rungs of the ladder into the MG blister and squeezed himself into the chair. It wasn't so much as a chair as a sling, cobbled together out of flat pieces of board, canvas strappings and cargo netting. He swung around the barrel of the RPK, pressing on the trigger, weaving short-burst cross-stitch patterns across the path of the racing Hummer, which kept rolling beside the C2VI, returning the fire.

"I'm through playing tag with these bastards," Grant growled.

Savagely, he jerked the wheel and sent the MCP barreling into the Hummer. Although the war wag struck it only a glancing blow, the smaller vehicle was smashed sideways, spinning it, then flipping it completely over.

Grant tried to pace the rolling Sandcat, but the vehicle quickly outdistanced the heavier and more cumbersome MCP. The last Hummer drifted away, at an oblique angle across the flatlands, followed by machine-gun fire from the roof bubble.

Grant turned the wheel slightly to avoid eating the dust churned up by the Sandcat. "Patch us through to Ramirez," he instructed Brigid.

She flicked switches on the comm board and adjusted the frequency knob. Into the microphone she intoned, "Ramirez, are you receiving? This is Titano. Are you receiving me?"

She waited a few seconds, repeated the question, then shook her head. "The frequency is open, but he's not answering. The comm link is clear."

Grant grunted noncommittally.

"You don't seem too surprised by the silent treatment."

"I'm not," he declared. "I knew he wasn't eager to team up with us. I'm sure he was a hoping a mine would damage us enough so he wouldn't have to worry about us."

His lips quirked beneath his mustache in a sardonic smile. "Now he's outmatched in firepower and personnel. He really has something to sweat over now—particularly since he's charged with protecting the baron.''

Brigid considered Grant's words for a thoughtful moment. "They have somebody on the inside, feeding them information," she said. "That still gives them an advantage over us. Ramirez'll know what's coming up next, long before we will.''

"Mebbe. We'll see.''

Uneasily, Brigid said, "We may want to consider he has an ace on the line. If so, we should probably come up with one of our own.''

Under other circumstances, Grant might have grinned at her use of the slang she had picked up over the past year. Because of her precise manner of speaking, it sounded incongruous.

As the MCP clanked across the basin, the hangar swelled quickly in the ob port, growing to truly staggering proportions. Within its shadowed interior, Grant barely discerned flashes of movement, as of sunlight winking briefly on metal.

The plume of dust kicked up in the wake of the Sandcat suddenly lessened in density and height. It curved off to the right, away from the cavernous mouth of the hangar.

Grant leaned over the wheel, muttering, "Where the hell is he going?''

"I'm more interested in why," Brigid commented, her voice humming with tension. Her hand reflexively reached for the fire controls. "Maybe he's acting on some of that inside information.''

The MCP crossed the broad, flat expanse of runway. The surface was rutted with scraggly weeds sprouting from cracks, but it still seemed in fairly good shape. The hangar loomed over them, seeming like a mountain itself. Suddenly, little red fireflies seemed to twinkle from the throat of the dark interior.

The bullets clanged and rattled off the prow of the war wag. Grant flinched as the rounds banged against the thick bulletproof polymer of the windscreen. Most of the bullets bounced away, leaving little white stars to commemorate their impacts, while others splatted into shapeless blobs.

"At least they're not AP rounds," Grant grated from between clenched teeth. He kept the gas pedal pressed to the floor.

A blocky shape hove out of the gloom of the hangar. A boxy, rivet-studded chassis rested atop two treaded tracks, which bore it forward in a clanking, lumbering charge. Grant recognized it immediately as a M-113 APC, the predark template on which the Sandcats were based.

More of a battle taxi than a fast-attack vehicle, the M-113's main armament were a single .50-caliber heavy-barrel machine gun and a .30-caliber machine gun. If he recalled correctly, the M-113 was built of aluminum to give a weight and maneuverability advantage, since the vehicle was capable of crossing large bodies of water. All of the information crossed his mind in a split second, even as the APC's .50-caliber machine gun began gouting flame from the muzzle in a foot-long, wavering tongue.

Brigid slapped at a button on the fire-control console, and cannon fire hammered out a staccato rhythm. The desert hardpan exploded in several mushroom clouds all around the M-113, but she didn't score a direct hit. The APC veered sharply to starboard, the .30-caliber machine gun chattering now.

Grant snarled a profanity and wrestled with the wheel of the C2VI, steering it on a collision course with the smaller vehicle. "I'm *so* sick of this shit!"

Brigid said nothing as Grant literally stood on the accelerator, running the engine temperature to redline vicinity. Bullets from the APC hosed the front of the MCP, ricochets screaming through the air, skimming over the wag's nose and leaving faint scars in the armor.

The armored leviathan rear-ended the M-113, its snout impacting with the aft section of the M-113, pushing it forward a dozen feet.

Brigid lurched from her seat, and Grant slammed chest first into the steering wheel. He kept his foot on the gas pedal as the .30-caliber machine gun continued to spit fire and smoke.

Engine roaring, the drive axles squealing with torque, Grant shifted the transmission into reverse. As the war wag began rumbling backward, he glanced toward Brigid and shouted, "Fire in the hole!"

Without hesitation, she thumbed the red button on the fire-control board and kept it depressed. The flurry of 20 mm HE rounds exploded at extreme close range, shattering the aluminum hide of the M-113.

The flying strips of debris struck the C2VI's hull only glancing blows, since it was rolling backward, equalizing the recoil of the cannon fire and the blowback of the detonating shells.

Grant braked to a halt, gave the burst-apart APC a single, dispassionate glance and shifted gears, rolling once more toward the hangar. "That," he said calmly, "ought to send somebody a message."

Static hissed into his ear, and he sat bolt upright. Brigid noticed his sudden startled movement. "What is it?"

He shushed her into silence, concentrating on focusing through the blur of static to understand the faint murmur of words.

"—receiving—"

His throat was suddenly constricted, but he forced out the words, "Say again."

Grant heard nothing for a moment but fuzzy hisses, pops and crackles. He was on the verge of repeating the request when Kane's voice said, "Slow but sure. What'd you do—walk?"

Chapter 16

The LED on Kane's wrist chron glowed with the numerals 5:29. He watched as the last digit changed to a zero, then said quietly, "Time to make the call."

Domi nodded and rested her hand on the butt of her holstered automatic as if she were preparing herself to shoot the trans-comm in Kane's hand if anything went wrong.

Standing on the monorail platform, looking down the round tunnel stretching to his left and right, Kane keyed in two numbers on the unit and said, "This is Phillipson at station 20."

"Code," came the bored response.

Kane inhaled a calming breath, trying to steady both his nerves and voice. "Jimmy six January."

"Roger," said the voice from the comm. "Powering up."

When the monorail engine emitted a soft electric purr, it required great effort for Kane not to sigh with relief. He and Domi climbed aboard. Kane said into the comm, "Green. Go."

The train hissed along the rail, quickly building up velocity. The train sped down the shaft, passing several stations. Each platform was a potential threat if guards were posted. Fortunately, they saw no one as the car whizzed past the numbered stations.

"Twenty-seven," Kane said as they shot past a pair of faded numbers. "We're getting close."

They whizzed past three more stations without seeing anyone. Domi's tense posture didn't relax. "If power gets cut, we be like rats in trap in here," she muttered.

Kane didn't respond. When they zipped past station 32, he began pulling back on the emergency-brake lever. The metal shoes caught the track with prolonged scraping screeches. He continued to increase the pressure until the car slid to a halt in front of the platform marked 32. As they disembarked and moved into the narrow passageway, Kane said, "Watch our backtrail."

Domi drew her Combat Master and cycled a round into the chamber. The two people cautiously walked through the passage until it opened up on a main corridor. At the far end, two hundred feet away, they saw the double doors of an elevator. Several of the overhead light fixtures were burned out, so Kane relied on his helmet's passive night sight, which turned everything to various shades of gray.

Domi and Kane had crossed about a hundred feet when they heard the scream. It was protracted, exceptionally loud and undeniably an alarm Klaxon.

"Son of a bitch!" Kane snarled out the words. He and Domi broke into sprints.

The elevator doors suddenly slid apart, and a man in a coverall stepped out, holding a trans-comm unit to his mouth. He took one look at the jet-black and snow-white figures racing toward him, and fumbled to draw a long-barreled handblaster from his belt. He yelled, "Intruders!" into the comm unit.

He used a high-velocity slug to emphasize the shout. The round splashed cool air on Kane's cheek as it whipped by. It hit the wall and ricocheted, shattering a ceiling light. He increased his speed, trying to put himself between the guard's pistol and Domi.

The man fired again and the heavy round smashed into the left side of his chest, knocking him backward and nearly driving all the air from his lungs. The molded polycarbonate breastplate had rounded pectorals designed to turn even high-velocity bullets, but the impact still rocked him back on his heels, and the blunt trauma momentarily stunned him.

Domi sidestepped his staggering body and squeezed the trigger of her Combat Master. The booming report sounding like a condensed thunderclap in the confines of the corridor. The steel-jacketed wad of lead punched through the man's chest and erupted from the center of his back amid a geyser of blood and lung tissue. He fell over backward into the elevator car, and the doors closed on his ankles. They popped open again just as she and Kane reached it.

Kane kicked the man's legs out of the way, and the doors slid shut. He breathed heavily, wincing at each inhalation. He never could understand why the duty badge was colored red. He knew it symbolized the Magistrate's oath, the importance of keeping the wheels of justice turning, but to his mind it was nothing more than a target. To blastermen, the red-on-black emblem was an invitation, saying "Shoot here."

Domi eyed him keenly. "You okay?"

Kane forced a rueful grin. "About as okay as I usually am when some bastard shoots me."

He punched the button labeled 10, and as the elevator ascended, he took the trans-comm unit from the dead man's hand, flipped open the cover to see the frequency number and extended it to Domi. His visored eyes met hers. "Once we stop, we need to split up like we talked about. The sec teams are onto us now, and we can't count on Maddock or Quavell being able to run interference for us."

She opened her mouth to protest, but Kane held up a peremptory hand. "No arguments on this, Domi. One of us needs to get out of here. If we travel together we'll end up as either prisoners or corpses. Working independently, we stand a better chance. Understood?"

Domi's ruby eyes were unblinking. She took the trans-comm. Her lips stirred and she whispered, "Understood."

The car bumped to a stop with a pneumatic hiss. The doors slid open to reveal a short stretch of polished flooring leading to a pair of stairwells branching off in a Y. The wall bore a sign reading Z-9. Before Domi took the right-hand stairs, she threw Kane an impudent grin, lifted her index finger to her nose and snapped it away in a smart salute. It was a gesture she had seen Kane and Grant exchange many times,

an acknowledgment of high odds with the chances of
success being one percent.

"Fire," she said.

He smiled fleetingly in appreciation and returned
the salute. "Wind."

Then he entered the stairwell. As he loped up the
steps, he heard the brief chatter of a subgun, then the
unmistakable boom of Domi's Combat Master. He
paused, wrestling with the urge to retrace his steps
and make sure she was all right. The staccato rattling
of the machine gun ended abruptly, cut off by two
explosive reports from Domi's handblaster. He told
himself she had dealt with the blasterman and continued up the stairs to the next level.

Kane came out on another stretch of corridor, identical to the one below. He moved swiftly, walking
heel-to-toe, leading with his Sin Eater. When he
reached a large observation window inset into the
right-hand wall, he carefully edged his head around
the frame for a look at what lay on the other side.

He looked down on a large room lined with two
aisles of computer stations. Only one man was present, sitting at a terminal with his back to the window.
A huge flat-screen vid monitor covered the wall he
faced. The screen was divided into small square sections, each one showing different black-and-white
views of the interior. Kane assumed the exterior was
shown, as well, though it was hard to tell.

One square showed an upright rectangle made of
heavy, cross-braced steel. Kane couldn't understand
what it was, but then massive blast doors opened on

its surface like the interlocking jaws of a trap. A dozen men clad in gray coveralls and wielding Armalite longblasters emerged from the steel box. Bandoliers crisscrossed their chests, and all of them looked tense and more than a little confused.

Shifting his gaze to another section of the screen, he saw Domi, pistol in hand, flit across it, turn a corner and vanish. He smiled in satisfaction. Another square showed a flat, sandy expanse of unbroken desolation. Judging by the quality of the light, he guessed the sun had just risen. He could barely discern a number of dark specks rolling across the lakebed. Puffs of dust floated in their wake.

The section of the screen beside it flickered and displayed the same scene but from a slightly different perspective and much closer. He stared at the dark image dominating the square for so long without blinking his eyes began to sting.

For a chaotic moment, his conscious mind refused to register the recognition signals his optic nerves transmitted to his brain. The huge tracked vehicle looked enough like Titano to be its twin. Finally, with a wild rush of elation, he realized it was Titano—and Grant had to be behind the wheel with Brigid more than likely sitting beside him.

Kane backed up and leaned against the wall, almost light-headed with relief. He had deliberately refused to entertain the concept of a rescue attempt from Cerberus, relegating the possibility to the status of a pipe dream. Now that it was a reality, he was nearly too giddy to move.

He activated his helmet's comm link and wasn't too disappointed when he heard nothing but squawks and crackles. Even if Grant was armored up, the range of the helmet comms was limited to little more than a hundred yards, depending on the terrain and the weather. For that matter, the strongest radio signals would probably have difficulty penetrating the shielded rock surrounding the base.

Kane eased back around and took another swift look at the screen. He saw four ville-issue Sandcats trailing behind the big MCP like shy lion cubs following their mother. The deployment perplexed him for a few seconds, then flame, smoke and sand bloomed from beneath the C2VI. Titano kept rolling, apparently undamaged or even slowed by the land mine. Grant had obviously decided to let the war wag sweep the minefield, depending on its heavy armor to carry it through unscathed. The presence of the Sandcats disquieted him even though he had been told about Barons Sharpe and Snakefish combining forces. Four wags didn't seem to be much in the way of an investment on their part.

Kane strode past the observation window, continuing on down the corridor, following the route outlined on the blueprint. He knew the defenses of Area 51 had to be more extensive than mines, and he suspected his human and hybrid allies had more knowledge of them than they were willing to reveal. Despite Domi's willingness to buy into their antibaron political platform, Kane didn't trust them any farther than he could piss in a chem storm.

Turning a corner, he saw a door hanging ajar. It was stout and thick, sheathed with sheet metal. He crept toward it, barely able to hear the murmur of voices from within over the Klaxon. Instinctively lowering himself to one knee, Kane peered around the door's edge.

The room beyond was crowded with tiers of automatic weapons racked in orderly rows. He also saw an open crate of grens resting on a trestle table. Eight gray-clad men moved about the armory, taking autorifles from the racks and attaching grens to canvas bandoliers. Their motions were quick and expert, their expressions grim.

Standing up, Kane detached the V-60 high-ex mini gren from his web belt. He unpinned it and stepped to the door. One of the men glanced up, looked away, then performed a wild double take. His jaw fell open as if he couldn't believe his eyes. In a move of sheer panic, he fumbled to raise his autorifle. "Kane!" he shouted.

Kane responded by saluting the man, then tossing the gren underhanded into the room. He threw his shoulder against the door and slammed it shut. The electronically controlled solenoids caught with triple clicks.

He sprinted down the corridor, but he had only gone a half dozen yards when heard the detonation of the V-60. It sounded faraway and mushy as if it were only a paper bag bursting. It was followed a few seconds later by a cannonading series of blasts that caused the overhead lights to flicker and dust to fall from the ceiling. At a corner, Kane looked back just as the door flew off its hinges, propelled by a column of hellfire.

The explosion shook the floor beneath his feet, and pieces of ceiling tile showered down. The lights flickered again and went out entirely. A few moments later, emergency lighting kicked in, but it was feeble. The image enhancer mounted on his helmet gathered all available light and made the most of it to provide him with one-color night vision, at least for twenty feet or so.

A new siren began to wail, a high-pitched hooting that sounded like a flock of mutie lake loons in great distress. He wondered if the noise signified something in particular. He didn't wonder long. As he turned the corridor, he saw two men in the corridor ahead of him. They were clad in the gray coveralls of Area 51 security, and the way they held their automatics showed plainly they were combat veterans.

Despite the dim light, the men saw him at the same time and went to opposite sides of the corridor to present more difficult targets and to confuse him. But habit and training took over now, Kane's Magistrate consciousness driving away fears and anxieties.

One of the men shouted something into a transcomm. The other snarled wordlessly and raised his blaster. He didn't fire it, so Kane presumed he had snarled at him to freeze.

Kane didn't know who had given the orders to apprehend rather than kill him, but the sec man should have known chances were slim he would surrender.

Stupe, Kane thought as he squeezed the trigger stud of his Sin Eater. The sound of the 9 mm round exploding from the bore of the Sin Eater was smothered by the siren. The man took the shot in his lower belly. As though he had been slapped off his feet by a giant invisible hand, he catapulted backward down the corridor.

Diving headfirst, Kane went into a somersault and the bullet fired at him from the second man seared the air well above him. Coming out of the roll, Kane triggered the Sin Eater again. The round pounded into the man's chest, picking him up and knocking him down like a disjointed puppet.

Kane regained his feet and ran, leaping over the bleeding bodies of the two guards. A door opened some twenty paces down the hallway, at the outer edge of his night sight. A man ran toward him, and Kane saw he wore one of the infrared vision headsets. Still he seemed oblivious to Kane's presence until he was only a few feet away. He caught a glimpse of a big-bored pistol in the man's hand.

Kane shot him once between the goggles. The man flailed backward, his blood and brains splashing the walls. As Kane stepped to the corpse, he noted the build of a hybrid. Bending, he stripped off the headset and though the light and blood smeared over the man's face made positive identification difficult, Kane thought he was the hybrid named Quaice. What he had mistaken for a blaster was a flare gun.

Kane set his teeth on a groan and squelched a sudden rise of guilt. If the hybrid had been sent to meet him, Maddock should have radioed him and let him know. He walked down the corridor and opened the door Quaice had come through. To his consternation he saw another stairwell extending upward. His trans-comm warbled, and he shut the door behind him to muffle the wail of the siren.

Opening the frequency, he heard Maddock's tense voice ask, "Kane?"

"Right here."

"You won't be able to reach the elevator from level ten. You'll have to take the stairs to level nine. We sent one of our people to lead you."

Kane hesitated a moment before saying, "Yeah, I met up with him."

"Good. Me and Tavares are waiting for you. Be careful. The level is crawling with guards. The orders are to take you alive if possible, but I wouldn't count on that."

"Don't worry—that's the last damn thing I'd count on." Kane cut the connection and put one foot on the first riser.

The door behind him slammed open, shoved by a sec man with an autoblaster in his hand and night-sight goggles over his eyes. He swung the barrel of his pistol in short left-to-right arcs. When he caught sight of the man in black armor, he tried to adjust his aim, but Kane was a shade faster. The Sin Eater spit a stream of 9 mm tumblers that tore through the guard's head, shattering the goggles and pounding his face into red jelly. By the time the dead man fell through the open door, Kane was running up the stairway.

When he reached the landing, he continued to sprint up to the next level, not slowing his pace, the sound of gunfire nearly smothered by the warble of alarm. His breath tore raggedly through his throat, and his lungs ached. Gray spots swam across his eyes, and his legs felt rubbery from the run up stairways and through the hallways. Two weeks of relative inactivity was beginning to take its toll.

When he reached level nine, he eased open the door to the corridor and stopped to catch his breath. Wheezing, he thumbed the magazine release on the Sin Eater, checking the load. The machine pistol's oversize clip still held ten rounds, and he had three spare clips in his belt.

Pushing himself around the corner, he saw a guard standing in the T junction of a hallway. His gray jumpsuit was dark with either sweat or blood. Catching sight of Kane, the guard whipped his assault rifle to his shoulder, but Kane fired his blaster first. Kane's triburst hammered three neat holes in his chest and slapped him to the floor.

Kane moved out, running hard, ignoring the burning muscles in his legs. He raced into another stairwell, literally clawing himself upward by the handrails. Steps went by in a blur. Footfalls slapped against the risers behind him. An over-the-shoulder glance showed him Maddock and Tavares running up behind him.

"On the right track?" he called out hoarsely.

Sounding infuriatingly unwinded, Maddock shouted back, "On track!"

He reached another landing and nearly collided with a dark-haired hybrid. The small man instantly fired an assault rifle at Kane, but the recoil sent him skittering backward across the slick floor. The rounds chewed up ceiling tiles but came nowhere near Kane. Whipping up the Sin Eater, Kane fired a single shot and punched a hole through the hybrid's mouth from less than three feet.

He shouldered open the door to level seven, and almost immediately a fusillade of bullets sizzled through the air where Kane stood. He pulled back to cover. One of the rounds clipped his helmet, jerking his head violently enough to blur his vision and send a wave of nausea through him. No one seemed inclined to take him alive anymore.

He unhooked the flash-bang stun grenade from his belt, pulling the pin and slipping the spoon all in one smooth motion. He threw it toward the knot of guards advancing down the hallway toward his position. He watched it bounce among their feet just before he ducked back into the doorway. A stunning, painfully loud thunderclap battered at his ears. A blazing nova of dazzling white light accompanied the teeth-jarring concussion of compressed air.

Tavares and Maddock reached him, but Kane said nothing to them. He poked his head out and saw three of the hybrids writhing on the floor, hands over their eyes. With their light-sensitive optic nerves, they were completely blinded by the flash.

The two others were human males, and they stumbled and staggered half blind and half deaf. Kane did not hesitate. He extended his Sin Eater, pressing the trigger stud, and six rounds took the men in their torsos, punching dark dots from groin to throat.

The sec men lurched into each other, not knowing what hit them, dazed from the shock of the multiple impacts, tendrils of blood squirting from their chests. As they collapsed, Maddock snapped, "Goddamn you, Kane! They were blind! We could've got through them without chilling them!"

Kane whirled on him, his lips peeled back from his teeth in a silent snarl. The ferocity of his expression drove the man back half a pace. "Then you should've led the fucking way like you claimed you would. When a hand is dealt to me, I play the cards so I can win, not to break even!"

Tavares said flatly, "There's about a quarter mile of hallways between us and the lift. Let's get going, not argue about it."

Kane moved out into the corridor, unconsciously assuming the point position. It was an ingrained habit from his years in the Mag Division. When he acted as point man, he felt electrically alive, sharply attuned to every nuance of his surroundings.

"All hell is breaking loose upstairs," Maddock said lowly. "The assault force has some kind of war wag that nobody here expected. I don't know which ville supplied it."

Kane chose not to correct his misapprehension. He broke into a jog down the corridor, trying to ignore the little flares of pain igniting in his legs. He unhooked the trans-comm unit from his belt and keyed in Domi's frequency. He heard nothing, not even the buzzing of the circuit.

"Who are you trying to call?" Tavares asked.

"Domi."

"Won't work," he replied between pants. "I set a timer to disrupt and jam all local transmitters. It kicked in about three minutes ago."

Kane grunted approvingly. The installation was so gargantuan that by inhibiting communications among the scattered personnel, it minimized their chances of organizing a concerted defense.

"Anyhow," interjected Maddock, "Domi's faster than you. She probably reached the lift and is on the surface by now."

Kane nodded. The three men ran steadily through the dimly lit corridors, not encountering any sec men. Their absence didn't calm Kane's anxieties. "Where the hell is everybody?"

"Most of them went topside," Tavares answered breathlessly. "To either fight or to surrender, depending on how the battle is going."

"That sounds like the Mag way," Kane commented with icy sarcasm. "Either at your feet or at your throat."

The passageway doglegged to the right and opened up into a broad foyerlike area. Kane and his two companions halted. About fifty feet away, feebly illuminated by the emergency lighting fixtures, Kane saw a wide, rectangular opening in the wall. He estimated it to be approximately fifteen feet tall by twelve wide. Because of the shadows and the limited range of his vision enhancer, he couldn't tell its depth.

"There it is," Maddock whispered, hoarse from the exertion of running. "Your ticket out of here. Once you get in, hit the first button on the wall."

Kane didn't move.

"Well?" Tavares demanded impatiently. "We've got your back. Go."

Kane swiveled his head to face the men. "I still don't know about Domi."

Maddock frowned. "If she's still down here, we'll find her and send her up to you. But I'll bet she's already topside and wondering where you are."

Kane's lips compressed in a tight line. "She'd better be, Maddock. If she's not, I'll be coming back. And I won't be alone."

The young man's eyes flickered with uncertainty. "What do you mean?"

Kane shook his head, signifying the conversation was over. Setting himself, he took deep breaths and plunged into the foyer, his legs pumping. He crossed the open area in a sprint, half-expecting Maddock and Tavares to open up on him with their blasters.

When he reached the big elevator car, he fell into it, grabbing a handrail for support. He turned and slapped at the button. A pair of heavy doors rumbled shut, and an overhead light came on. The lift had its own power source, and Kane saw the car was almost the size of a Sandcat's interior.

The elevator shot upward at breathtaking speed,

making Kane's stomach feel as if it were sinking into the soles of his boots. He leaned against one wall, ejecting the nearly empty clip from his Sin Eater and trading it for a fully loaded one on his belt. When the car stopped automatically on level six, he wanted to be prepared for whatever might lie on the other side of the doors.

The cargo elevator jolted to a stop sooner than he'd expected. He staggered and dropped the magazine he'd been inserting into the Sin Eater. As he bent to retrieve it, the doors rolled open and four men stood there, poised to enter. They stared at him and he stared back. All of them were blood streaked and burned, hair crisped and faces blistered.

Kane recognized them as all that was left of the eight-man squad he'd trapped in the armory. He was surprised that even one of them had survived and was ambulatory, much less four. Only one was armed with a blaster, a .38-caliber Walther. Another man gripped a Shockstick. All four of them were unsteady on their feet, and as far as Kane was concerned, they presented no substantial threat even if he couldn't reload.

They gazed at him silently and he returned the stare. Since they were former Magistrates themselves, they weren't intimidated by his grim appearance. In a soft, flat voice, he said, "You were lucky before. Let me pass and I'll let you live."

The man holding the Walther uttered a snarl of derision. "Fuck you, Kane. You stinking traitor. You're not leaving here alive, you shit-faced slagger!'' He hawked up from deep in his lungs and spit a glob of saliva onto Kane's molded left pectoral.

Two weeks of accumulated humiliation, of pent-up rage, of suppressed frustration came boiling up out of Kane in a wild torrent. Sheer homicidal fury took possession of him, the hot blood beating up in him, thundering in his ears. With a slow, deliberately provocative motion, Kane leathered his Sin Eater and said in a gravelly whisper, ''Come on and get the job done.''

The four men rushed forward, milling around him, trying to crowd him into a corner. The Shockstick swung toward his face. Kane sidestepped, locking the man's right wrist in the crook of his left arm at the same time that he secured a grip on the baton. He wrenched it back and up violently, breaking the man's wrist with a wet crunching sound. The man uttered an animal groan and his eyes rolled up in his head. Unconscious, he sagged in Kane's grasp.

The Shockstick clattered to the floor, and Kane kicked it out into the hallway. At the same time he used his left arm to block a fist driving toward his jaw. He dropped the sec man with a backhanded ram's-head jab between the eyes.

He stopped the third man from tackling him from the rear with a sideways snap-kick to the jaw. The fourth man managed to bore in from the other side, knocking Kane off balance just long enough to outmuscle him and apply a full nelson.

''Kill the son of a bitch!'' he gasped, his voice hoarse with fury.

The man he had snap-kicked staggered to his feet, spitting out blood and teeth splinters. He lunged forward, trying to draw a bead on Kane's visor with his Walther. Using the man holding him as support, Kane bunched the muscles in his legs and sprang upward, the thick soles of his boots catching the blasterman squarely between the legs. There was a sound as if a butcher's cleaver had chopped into a side of beef.

The sec man doubled up, croaking in agony, clawing at his crotch. His spasming finger squeezed the trigger and the Walther cracked, the short barrel lipping flame. The bullet sheared through his testicle sac and severed his femoral artery. He fell over on his side, jets of liquid vermilion spraying from between his fingers.

The sec man holding Kane in the full nelson jerked in response to the shot, bleating wordlessly in fear and confusion. Planting his heels firmly on the floor, Kane kicked himself backward. The sec man stumbled the width of the car and his grip loosened. In the split second it required for him to bear down with the full nelson again, Kane flung his arms straight up over his head, relaxed, bent his knees and slipped down between the man's arms.

He pivoted as he did so, knocking the man's legs out from under him with a scything arm sweep. The man fell heavily on his back, and Kane sprang atop him, delivering a *yeko-hija-ate* smash with his polycarbonate-shod elbow into his chest, powering it with his entire weight. Rib bones caved in with grisly snaps, and the kinetic shock stopped the man's heart.

Rising to his feet, Kane glanced dispassionately at the corpses he had just made. In the past, when forced to injure or kill members of his former fraternity, he'd experienced pangs of guilt and remorse. This time he felt nothing at all except a savage satisfaction.

He stooped over to retrieve the fallen ammo clip that had been kicked to the far side of the car. A bass humming sound suddenly filled his head. The magazine suddenly jumped, acquired a deep dent that bent it almost double and, accompanied by a whang of sound, went skittering across the floor into a corner.

Kane whirled and saw a figure standing just outside the doors. "I disobeyed an order," Gifford said genially. "I left my post just in hopes you'd show up around here."

He wore one of the night-sight headsets. Even in the poor light, Kane saw white twists of tissue paper plugged into his swollen, bruised nostrils. In his right hand he carried a slender silver rod. Kane instantly recognized the rod as an infrasound wand. The energy it delivered was far deadlier than the voltage of a Shockstick.

Gifford gestured with it. "Come on out here, Kane. I was told to take you alive."

"That's nice," Kane said. "I'm glad you're here."

"Why?" Gifford asked as Kane shuffle-footed around a corpse.

He turned a motion to step over a pool of blood into a headlong leap. Gifford bent aside, pivoting around on a heel, moving far faster than Kane would have guessed. As Kane's momentum carried him into

the corridor and past the man, the infrasound wand
inscribed a short, humming arc through the air and
touched the back plate of his armor.

Kane heard the polycarbonate crack on impact and
he reeled forward as if he had been drop-kicked by
two men Grant's size. A numbing pain ran up and
down his spine.

Shambling around, Kane performed a clumsy crescent kick with his right leg. Gifford leaned away from
it, and the point tapped Kane twice on the left side.
A rib cracked audibly and Kane staggered sideways,
trying to stay on his feet and not curl into a ball
around the flaring pain.

Gifford pressed the attack, Kane reached down,
plucking the Shockstick from the floor and swinging
it at the sec man's face. Gifford's wand hummed as
he countered the thrust. The pain in Kane's back and
ribs was distracting to his concentration, but he knew
if the wand touched his helmet, his brains would be
blown out his ears. He'd seen it happen.

Gifford slashed with the wand as if it were a saber.
Kane parried the blow and the Shockstick vibrated
furiously, spit sparks and flew from his hand, spinning
end over end.

The man's face was creased by a cold grin as he
advanced on Kane, driving him to the wall. Kane
feinted with a kick, and Gifford backed away hastily.
Kane's hand darted down to his boot, his finger touching the quick-release button of his knife sheath. He
came up with the weapon as Gifford brought up the

wand. Kane flipped the knife, caught it by the point and hurled it at him.

His aim was off. The knife didn't sink into Gifford's thigh. Instead, it split his right kneecap and stayed there, quivering. Gifford screamed in agony and dropped the infrasound wand. He convulsively plucked at the Nylex handle to wrench the blade free.

Kane bounded forward and rammed the heel of his right palm in a *teisho* blow to Gifford's nose, driving splinters of broken cartilage up into his brain. Gifford died still trying to pull the knife from his leg.

"I'm glad I got the chance to say goodbye," Kane husked out. "Give my regards to Baron Cobalt, asshole."

He yanked the knife from the man's kneecap and shambled back into the cargo elevator, his teeth clenched against the throbbing pain in his back and side. He used the carmine-coated point of the blade to depress the button.

The doors slid shut. As the car began to ascend again, a faint crackle of static filtered into his ear. He adjusted the gain with the small knurled knob on the underside of his helmet and said loudly, "Grant! Are you receiving me?" He waited a moment, then half shouted, "Are you receiving me?"

Very faintly, almost on the edges of inaudibility he heard Grant's voice. "Say again."

Kane hung his head, leaning against the handrail. Tension drained out of him, leaving him weak and weary. "Slow but sure," he said. "What'd you do—walk?"

Chapter 17

The elevator doors slid open, and for a second Kane saw only a flat expanse of gray metal. Then a seam appeared in its surface and the massive blast doors rumbled apart with a squeak and groaning of gears. Beyond them lay a scene like an impressionistic painting of Hell.

Smoke drifted in streamers, and he caught only glimpses of shapes moving about. Autofire rattled, interwoven with single-shot cracks and pain-filled screams. Bodies rushed back and forth, shooting and yelling.

A bullet whipped past Kane's head, and he felt rather than heard the little slap of displaced air. It flattened on the metal wall of the elevator car. He had reloaded his Sin Eater during the short ascent, but he duck-walked out of the massive cupola housing the cargo elevator. The ground looked to be acres upon acres of cracked concrete.

He looked above him, but the roof of the hangar was obscured by rising vapors. Sweeping his gaze back and forth, he saw the interior of the hangar was at least dozens of square miles long and broad. He heard a metallic clicking behind him and turned as the elevator's blast doors sealed with a hollow boom.

Squinting in the direction of hangar's open front, he tried to pinpoint Titano in the milling confusion. "Grant!" he said loudly. "Where the hell are you?"

"About twenty yards from the hangar," came the clear response. Now that Kane was out in the open, comm reception was unimpaired. "Where the hell are you and Domi?"

Before Kane could answer, a rush of bodies knocked him sprawling and heavy weights trampled him. Sec men, half-blinded by smoke, were running like panicked deer. Kicking and elbowing, he rolled to one side and got to a knee. A man who had stumbled over him turned, leading with a handblaster. Kane put two bullets through his lungs before he could squeeze the trigger.

A slug plucked at his shoulder and he spun, sighting a gray-clad man leveling an Armalite at him. Kane pressed the trigger stud and sent a wad of lead into the man's chest.

The area was screaming, bloody chaos, bullets splitting the air, men screaming and shouting contradictory orders. Through a part in the roiling vapors, Kane saw at least a dozen gray-clad, bandoliered men hunkering down behind fuel drums and big wooden crates. They frantically reloaded their Armalites.

Grant's voice bellowed in his ear, "What's going on?"

"You tell me." Kane rose to a crouch, choking back a cough. Dust floated in the air, mixing with the drifting planes of cordite smoke to make an impenetrable and eye-irritating fog. "Where are the Cats?"

"All disabled except for one. I don't know where it—"

The air suddenly filled the white phosphorescent threads of tracer bullets. He heard the steady, familiar hammering of two USMG-73s. The rounds smashed into the sec men from the rear, punching holes through them and the metal drums, tearing long splinters from the wooden crates.

Kane instinctively tensed, waiting for the tracers to ignite the fuel, but it didn't happen. The punctured cans were empty. The bullets slapped into the men, ripping away body parts amid mistings of blood. The double fusillade sent them scrambling to take cover on the other side of the crates and drums.

Over the racket, Kane heard the steady drone of an engine and the clanking of machinery. A Sandcat materialized out of the smoke and dust, the turret guns flaming and snapping. Return fire against the vehicle was sporadic and futile. The bullets clanged against the metal sides of the Cat without effect.

It lurched to a halt and the rear hatch opened. Eight black-armored Magistrates tumbled out, armed with Copperheads and Sin Eaters. They opened fire, shooting indiscriminately. Kane flattened himself on the ground. The MGs continued to spray twin streams of steel-jacketed death. More fuel drums were punctured, and one exploded in a ball of flame. A sec man, wreathed in fire, ran a shrieking death race toward the front of the hangar. He crossed less than twenty feet before he was shot dead by a Magistrate. The others broke from cover and ran. Kane watched, a cold knot tightening in his stomach as the Mags calmly back-shot them.

The deep roar of an engine floated through the haze, and mingled with it was the crackle of blaster-fire and frightened outcries. The C2VI exploded out of the fog, driving men ahead of it. They screamed in terror as they sprinted to get out of its path. The MCP kept coming on a straight course. A few sec men triggered their blasters. Ricochets sparked from the hull and the windscreen acquired a few cracks but didn't break.

One of the guards flung a gren in Titano's path, trying to place it beneath a tread. A red-yellow spray of flame erupted under the vehicle's prow and the thunder of its detonation rumbled loudly, but the wag did not deviate from its course.

The MCP suddenly turned sharply to the right and braked at the same time. The resulting skid wasn't controlled, and the rear end arced around in a 180-degree turn. It slapped against a couple of men, swatting them head-over-heels a score or more feet away. The aft and starboard hatches opened and blaster-toting, feather-bedecked, face-painted men streamed out of the wag. They shouted the Lakota war cry: *"Hoka-hey! Hoka-hey!"*

The Indians wore padded body armor that covered their chests, stomachs and groins. The Mags herded the sec men right into the stuttering bores of their M-16 assault rifles.

The men in front crumpled, and the ones behind them threw down their blasters and threw up their arms. A couple of them were killed before the warriors realized their enemies were surrendering. When the Indians understood the battle was over, they voiced an ululating, primeval shout of victory, ending it with their tribe's kill cry, *"Huhn!"* There was a current of disappointment underscoring their cries. The warriors hadn't really joined a battle; they had come in on the tail end of a massacre.

As the Mags and Indians sandwiched the few surviving sec men between them, forcing them to kneel with theirs hands atop their heads, the starboard hatch of the MCP opened. Grant, in full body armor, leaped down, followed by Sky Dog and a heartbeat later by Brigid Baptiste.

She was disheveled, her mane of hair in disarray, and she had obviously neglected both grooming and personal hygiene over the past several days. Still, in Kane's eyes, she was the most beautiful, desirable woman he had ever seen.

Brigid and Grant looked around, trying to find him amid the pall of smoke, dust and other black-armored figures. Kane approached them, taking off his helmet as he did so. Brigid caught sight of him first and made a reflexive move to run to him. She checked the motion but she smiled, transforming her face.

Kane easily recalled when he had first seen that smile, well over a year ago in her little flat in Cobaltville. It was an open smile of relief and honesty, of happiness at finding someone with whom she could discard her emotionless archivist's persona and at last be herself. That same smile now turned her pretty face into something heartachingly beautiful, despite the smears of dirt begriming it.

Kane's eyes suddenly stung, and he wished he hadn't removed his helmet. He told himself it was due to the irritating smoke and dust in the air. He kept walking until he joined his friends. When he stood next to them, all of the humiliation and fears of the past two weeks evaporated like snowflakes on a hot sidewalk. Facing the big black man and the green-eyed woman, he felt a sense of the world righting itself after being out of kilter for a long time.

Grant was the first to speak, saying gruffly, "Slow, my ass. Next time you decide to get captured, would you mind doing it a little closer to home?"

Kane nodded contritely. "I'll arrange it in advance." He glanced at the fresh bullet scars scoring the MCP's hull, then back to Grant. Softly, he said, "You are one hardheaded son of a bitch."

To Brigid, he said simply, "Thanks, Baptiste."

She arched an eyebrow. "For what?"

"For not reaching the logical and understandable conclusion that me and Domi were dead."

She nodded. "If our positions were reversed, would you reach that conclusion?"

He pretended to seriously ponder the question for a few seconds. "Probably."

"But you'd come anyway."

"Probably."

Brigid put her hands behind her back and nodded in complete understanding. Turning to Sky Dog, Kane clasped the shaman's extended hand. "Thanks for loaning out Titano."

Sky Dog smiled. "My pleasure, Unktomi Shunkaha." The nickname translated as Trickster Wolf, and was a reflection of Sky Dog's respect for Kane's courage and cunning. He eyed Kane keenly. "You've been suffering, I can see it. But it's not pain of the body, is it?"

Kane became newly aware of the ache in his back and ribs. "As a point of fact—"

"Where's Domi?" Grant broke in brusquely.

Kane disengaged his grasp from Sky Dog's. "I don't know. I thought she might be up here already. But I haven't seen her."

Grant opened his mouth to respond, then stiffened, gazing at a sight behind Kane. "Best we talk about her later," he commented, quietly.

The back of his neck prickling, Kane turned to see the line of the Magistrates parting to allow three figures through. As he recognized the two in the lead immediately, the tension coiled in his belly like a length of slimy rope. Baron Sharpe, with Crawler wriggling along beside him, beamed at Kane with a wide, friendly grin. "Why, hello, you murderous bastard! Surely you remember me!" he said boisterously.

Kane gave him a cold, imperious nod. "Vividly. And your pet doomie." He nodded down to Crawler, who smirked up in response.

The third figure was a Magistrate of medium height, his lips and chin fixed firmly in grim lines. Sharpe gestured to him indifferently. "This is Ramirez, the commander of this little escapade. Brother Snakefish sent him to nursemaid me.''

Kane wasn't overly surprised by Sharpe's presence on the mission. He had personally led the expedition to Redoubt Papa in Washington Hole. The baron believed he couldn't die, so he wasn't concerned with taking risks, like all the other members of the oligarchy. With a touch of sour regret, Kane realized he had solidified Sharpe's crazy belief in his own immortality by not chilling him when he'd had the chance.

Addressing Crawler, Kane commented, ''Looks like you two have ironed out your differences. I'm glad. There's too much discord in the world today as it is.''

Nobody laughed. Ramirez snorted with contempt and said, ''Kane, we need you for a quick debrief before we occupy the installation.''

Kane looked at the eight Magistrates holding blasters on the surviving sec men. ''You'll be stretching your personnel pretty damn thin to occupy this place. Besides, the doors to the elevator are shut, and I don't know how to get them open.''

''More of us will be coming along,'' Ramirez said harshly, pointing to the front of the hangar. The man exuded hostility like a field of static electricity. Kane sensed it was directed primarily at him.

Turning to follow Ramirez's finger, Kane saw at least a dozen obsidian figures trudging across the lakebed toward them. ''Our wags may've been disabled,'' Ramirez continued, ''but not all of our resources. We've got five kilos of C-4 and remote detonators—that should be enough to blast our way in.''

"One of their resources is a Deathbird," Grant commented casually, so casually Kane knew he was warning him.

"But it's damaged," Brigid put in helpfully.

"That's a shame," Kane said inanely. "There's a member of our party missing, so I'll lead you down so—"

Ramirez cut him off with a sharp hand wave. "You won't be leading us anywhere, Kane. You're under arrest. All of you are under arrest."

The Magistrates snapped up their blasters and covered Sky Dog's warriors. To the kneeling sec men, Ramirez called, "You stupes can either change sides or get bullets in your heads. What's it to be?"

The guards didn't bother even to pretend to think over the offer. They clamored over one another agreeing, thanking and swearing loyalty to Baron Sharpe.

"Let 'em up," Ramirez directed. "Give them back their blasters."

He turned back to Grant, Kane, Brigid and Sky Dog, who gazed at him stone-faced, apparently unmoved or unsurprised by the change of events. Ramirez grinned. "Don't tell me you expected this."

Brigid returned the grin. "One constant is that you can always expect Mags and barons to do the unexpected. Your problem is you never expect anybody to catch on."

Slowly, she brought her hands out from behind her back. Nestled between them was a metal-walled canister. A tiny red light atop it blinked purposefully. Ramirez inhaled sharply between his teeth.

"This," Brigid said matter-of-factly, "is a DM 54 implode grenade. In case you don't know, its effect radius is about thirty feet. And, by coincidence, all of you are within it." She glanced at Grant. "What did you call this kind of gren?"

"The proverbial handful of Hell," Grant supplied helpfully.

"That's right," she replied, bobbing her head in agreement. "But I prefer to call it an ace on the line."

Baron Sharpe tittered wildly. "Well played, Miss Baptiste."

Ramirez cast him a look that bordered on complete contempt. "They're bluffing, my lord."

Sharpe glanced down at Crawler. "Your opinion?"

Crawler peered curiously and intently at Brigid, who affected not to notice him at all. After a few seconds, the crippled doom seer sighed in frustration. "I don't know. Her mind is remarkably structured. I'd hate to gamble my life on whether she's running a bluff or not."

"I'm willing to gamble that she's bluffing," Ramirez snapped.

Baron Sharpe pursed his lips contemplatively. "I can't deny having you three in custody would be an excellent fulcrum by which to tip brother Cobalt from his position. He's been quite obsessed with you, Kane in particular."

In a low voice, Ramirez intoned, "My lord, you forget that Baron Snakefish has questions for these three regarding the Port Morninglight incident and the Tigers of Heaven.''

Sharpe brushed off the Magistrate's objection with an impatient gesture. "He can't very well ask them questions if they've blown themselves up, can he?" His big, back-slanting blue eyes flitted from Kane to Grant and to Brigid. "What do you propose?"

"Simple," answered Grant. "You get Area 51 and we get to go on our way. It's only fair. After all, you wouldn't have been able to take this place without our help."

"It's not taken yet," Ramirez growled. "Besides, you don't dictate terms to us, renegade."

Even concealed by the visor, everyone saw how Grant's eyes flashed with anger. In a quiet, deadly tone he said, "These renegades do, Ramirez. You can watch us leave or watch yourselves die."

"You'd die, too."

Kane joined the conversation with a snort of disdain. "You'd kill us anyway, so what do we have to lose? And I'd get to finish the job I started with Baron Sharpe months ago."

For a long moment, the tableau held. Everybody stared at everybody else—Mags and sec men stared at the Amerindians, who stared back, while Baron Sharpe and Ramirez stared at Grant, Brigid and Kane. Nobody spoke, moved or even appeared to breathe.

The frozen scene was broken by the sudden groaning creak of the elevator's heavy metal doors opening. A slender white wraith stepped cautiously out into the hangar, a streak of blood showing stark and bright against the porcelain hue of her face. Domi caught sight of the standoff, stopped in her tracks and blurted, "Grant!"

A Magistrate whirled toward her, the bore of his Copperhead rising. Domi shot him broadside, the .45-caliber round bowling him off his feet. The bullet didn't breach the armor but when the man fell, his companions voiced a garbled babble of angry profanity. Without hesitation they opened fire on Domi. She leaped back into the elevator, returning the shots.

The Amerindian warriors triggered their assault rifles. The Magistrates stumbled and staggered from the multiple impacts, and they swung their blasters toward them. At the same time Ramirez yelled a wordless warning and threw himself in front of Baron Sharpe.

Grant depressed the trigger stud of his Sin Eater and a triburst stitched across Ramirez's midriff, beating him coughing and cursing to the ground. Sharpe uttered a sobbing laugh, and with a surprising degree of speed and agility dived into the smoke-shrouded shadows. Crawler wriggled along at his heels.

Sky Dog yelled a few words in Lakota, and his warriors began a retreat toward the MCP. The USMG-73 emplacements atop the Sandcat roared in stuttering rhythms, tracer rounds cutting lines of phosphorescence through the massed warriors. Men spun, clutching at themselves as the bullets clawed through the body armor. Fragments of flesh and bone flew off in all directions, accompanied by crimson sprays.

Kane flung himself between Brigid and the Cat,

wresting the gren from her hands. A line of bullets hammered into his back, painful punches even through the armor, doubling the ache in his spine. He let the impacts shove him forward, and he pushed Brigid ahead of him. "Get aboard!" he managed to shout.

He heeled around, flame sputtering from the bore of his handblaster. He and Grant bounded forward, their blazing weapons clearing a path in the massed Magistrates. The Sin Eaters in their hands spit fire and thunder, unleashing round after round of 9 mm slugs.

Return fire ripped the air around Grant, and he dived to his left. Kane held down the trigger of his autoblaster, swinging the flame-belching barrel from left to right. Hot brass spewed from the ejector. When the firing pin clicked dry, he retracted the Sin Eater into its holster with a flexing twist of his wrist.

Even as the cables snapped the weapon back into its holster, Kane transferred the gren from his left to right hand. He thumbed the arming button and whipped his arm back, intending to hurl the gren over the heads of the Mags and plant it right beneath the blunt nose of the Sandcat.

A sledge pounded against his right arm and sent him staggering. The gren fell from his suddenly nerveless fingers and rolled across the concrete away from the Sandcat and toward the elevator housing.

Domi darted out from the cupola, scooped up the gren in one hand and cocked her arm back to throw it at the vehicle. Grant rushed toward her, bellowing at the top of his lungs, "Domi, no! Get back in the—"

A brilliant white incandescent glare suddenly swallowed her form. A tremendous roar, half explosion, half gale-force wind slammed against Grant's and Kane's eardrums. The shock wave of the concussion was more like a riptide, gripping their bodies and yanking them forward in headlong tumbles, dragging them into clumsy somersaults.

A cascade of air, dust, rock particles and powdery sand swirled around them, irresistibly sucked toward the wedge of vacuum created by the detonation of the implode gren.

Then the maelstrom effect created by the implosive device collapsed in on itself and they felt fragments of stone pattering down all around onto them.

Kane found himself on his back, blinking up at the hangar's roof high above. For a few seconds he had no idea of why he was lying there, then Brigid appeared over him. She reached down and hauled at his arm. Her lips worked but he could barely hear her. He struggled to stand, shaking the fog out of his mind. At the periphery of his vision he saw Sky Dog pulling a stunned Grant to his feet.

Kane shambled drunkenly toward the detonation point of the gren. He saw no crater, only a charred star-shaped pattern on the concrete. From the center of it wisps of smoke curled. Several black-armored bodies were asprawl near it, their arms and legs elongated to unnatural lengths. Flat crimson ribbons stretched from their heads toward the epicenter of the implosion.

He knew that beneath the polycarbonate the Mag's bodies were mangled lumps of flesh, their eardrums shattered by the brutal decompression, their eyeballs pulled from their sockets, internal organs burst, blood from ruptured vessels flowing from every orifice, their lungs collapsed to wafers of tissue. Several more men at the edge of the effect radius were unconscious due to the sudden and absolute lack of oxygen.

"Domi!" Grant shouted. His voice had a nasal, snuffling quality as he tried to staunch the blood rivering from ruptured capillaries in his nose.

"She's gone!" Brigid cried, pushing Kane toward the MCP.

Both Grant and Kane resisted Sky Dog's efforts to pull them into the MCP. They saw nothing that might have been the girl's body. Kane had never heard of an implode gren vaporizing organic matter, but that didn't mean it couldn't happen. Soul-freezing horror numbed Kane's mind and body.

The Sandcat's machine guns began to stutter again. Raking autofire smashed up concrete around them, showering their legs with stinging rock chips. Putting her face next to Kane's, Brigid screamed, "We've got to go! We have wounded men to help! We're about to be outnumbered!"

He started to shake her off, but she fought him, crying out, "Damn you, we've got no choice!"

A cold sickness crept over him, a realization that

she spoke the complete truth. Brigid's eyes glittered as she fought back tears. "Do you understand?"

Kane stopped trying to pull away and bent to help one of Sky Dog's bloodied warriors to his feet. Grant and the shaman did likewise. Only four of them still lived. As they retreated toward the MCP, Grant saw Ramirez pushing himself up to his elbows. As he went past him, Grant paused long enough to kick him in the face.

They piled aboard the C2VI, and a warrior bleeding from a superficial wound in his left arm slammed the hatch shut. Grant and Kane turned the wounded men over to the warriors who had made it aboard. In the control compartment, Grant threw himself into the pilot's chair and Kane sat down beside him. Brigid and Sky Dog sat in the pull-down jump seats along the back wall.

Kane's hearing came back, but he still felt as if his ears were plugged with cotton wadding. "Why are we running, goddammit? We can't leave without Domi."

Brigid responded shrilly, "The other Mags will be here in a couple minutes. And remember the five kilos of C-4? Any one of them can jam some in our tracks and immobilize us."

"But Domi—"

"She's gone," Grant bit out. He worked the gearshift lever and popped the clutch. Bullets beat on the MCP's armored sides like outraged fists. "We've got to get out of here or more friends will die."

The C2VI rocked and jounced out of the hangar.

Peering through the ob port, Kane saw two Magistrates run into the path of the vehicle, unpinning grens. Grant slammed his foot against the accelerator, and the war wag surged forward. The Mags lobbed the grens and turned to run, but the MCP rolled right over them. The explosions were muffled and mushy.

"What did you mean?" Kane asked. "What friends will die?"

Grant's hands flexed around the steering wheel. "Other than Sky Dog's wounded men, Baron Snakefish knows about the Tigers of Heaven. He won't let a little thing like a disagreement with Baron Cobalt stop him from finding out where they are...and slaughtering everybody in New Edo. We've got to get there first."

Kane started to say something else, then he leaned back against the chair, hanging his head wearily. He suddenly felt completely worn-out, exhausted to the point of being comatose.

Brigid leaned forward and stroked Kane's sweat-damp hair. She said softly, "Domi gave her life to save ours. To stay and fight against these odds would make her sacrifice completely pointless."

As the war wag clattered across the lakebed, Kane focused his gaze on the burning Sandcats in the distance. "Yeah," he whispered bitterly. "Completely pointless."

Chapter 18

The early-morning sun rose above the flat blue horizon like a fiery jewel, as if it had been disgorged from the depths of the Cific. The open sea at dawn was beautiful with reflected iridescent colors shimmering on the waves.

"Watch your head, missy!" Dubois brayed.

Without looking behind her, Brigid ducked as the boom swung over her head. Grant and Kane, sitting on the other side of the mast, didn't even blink as they lowered their heads.

The single-sailed boat was barely large enough for a fisherman and a moderate-sized catch. With Brigid, Kane, Grant and Dubois all aboard, not to mention piles of equipment, the quarters were worse than cramped, they were barely tolerable, worse than being cooped up in Titano. The only advantage the boat had over the MCP was fresh air, untainted by the smell of blood and wounds turning septic.

The overland journey from Nevada to Port Morninglight on the coast of California had been almost unendurable. If Brigid had thought Grant was reticent, Kane almost matched him in general surliness. Neither man had spoken more than fifty words to anyone, much less to each other since getting out of the

Groom Lake basin. Kane hadn't questioned Brigid's terse explanation about Ramirez's knowledge of New Edo and how the Mag could either follow them or arrange for a Mag force from Snakefish to intercept them.

Kane knew New Edo could prove to be a valuable ally provided they weren't discovered and overrun by Magistrates. He and Grant took turns driving the MCP nonstop. While one slept, the other piloted. Brigid helped Sky Dog attend to his wounded warriors. Out of the seven men who had volunteered to join their shaman in the rescue mission, only two survivors of the firefight were uninjured. Even before they crossed the border into California, one of the wounded died.

The supply of fresh water ran low, and they were forced to strictly ration it, which didn't help buoy anyone's mood. Kane spoke little of his two weeks of captivity, and when Brigid began to tell him what they had learned of the imperator and the alleged return of Balam, he cut her off with a short "I know."

Brigid knew it was hopeless to pepper Kane with questions. He would only talk about his ordeal when and if he thought it had an immediate bearing on their circumstances. The only time they were alone with each other was when he asked her to put a splint-brace on his left wrist, citing a possible cracked bone. She did what he requested, but he refused to elaborate on how and why he had come to be injured. She noticed him favoring his back and gave him analgesics without him asking.

Fortunately for everyone's nerves, the journey to

the coast wasn't as long as the old predark maps indicated. In the months preceding the nukecaust, So-
viet submarines had sown "earthshaker" bombs
along fault lines in what was then called the Pacific.
These detonated when the first mushroom clouds bil-
lowed over Washington, D.C. Thousands of square
miles of California between the ocean and the Sierra
Nevada split open, allowing the sea to come roaring
through in mile-high tsunamis.

Now the Pacific coast was only twenty or so miles
from the foothills of the Sierras. Once they crossed
through Kings Canyon, the sea came into view. Port
Morninglight wasn't difficult to find, since it was in
the general vicinity of a predark ville named, appropriately enough, Porterville. The barony of Snakefish
was located about seventy-five miles up the coast,
where Fresno had once existed.

Brigid hadn't been sanguine about finding anyone
in Port Morninglight inasmuch as the entire popula-
tion had either been slaughtered or enslaved. The survivors had been marched away toward a redoubt in
the Sierras. From there, they could be sent by gateway
to Area 51, where their bodies would be processed
for the raw genetic material the hybrids required.

Brigid presumed the Tigers of Heaven had escorted
the people back to the settlement and returned with
them to New Edo. Still, Ramirez had managed to locate at least one former citizen.

When the MCP chugged into the fishing port near
sundown on the third day, they rolled over the shattered wreckage of a wooden palisade fence and then

past the burned-out husks of huts. Upon disembarking, they found fairly recent gravesites. Magistrates dispatched from Snakefish hadn't been so considerate of the dead, so somebody still resided in the little village. One of the thatch-roofed reed huts showed signs of habitation—primarily a huge collection of bones belonging to freshly filleted fish.

They saw no boats on the beach, but before they had time to curse their misfortune, Sky Dog's keen eyes spotted a speck moving across the heaving blue waves. Grant and Kane weren't wearing their armor, but they drew their blasters just in case the approaching speck turned out to be hostile.

They waited on the shore with frothing waves lapping at their feet until the speck acquired definite shape and form. It was a small, single-masted sailboat piloted by an old man. He had a mop of white hair and a drooping leonine mustache.

Behind the boat bobbed a tightly woven net containing a writhing mass of trapped fish. The old man didn't seem perturbed or even surprised to see the quartet of people standing on the beach waiting for him, even though Brigid knew they must have presented a strange sight. He only squinted at them.

Since he didn't seem to be armed, Brigid waded through the shallows toward the boat's bow. The old fisherman could well have a knife or blaster hidden at the bottom of the boat, but he didn't look like much of a threat.

"Good afternoon," she said politely. "Do you live here?"

By way of a reply, the man tossed her a coil of rope and grunted, "Give me a pull, missy."

Brigid obliged, hauling on the rope as the old man climbed overboard and shoved from astern. When the prow grounded with a crunch of sand, he unhooked the net and struggled to drag it to shore. Glancing toward the three men he brayed, "Well, are you lame or what?"

Grant and Sky Dog waded out to help him land the net. Kane stayed where he was, his arms folded over his chest, his finger hovering over the trigger stud of his Sin Eater.

After the net and its catch were on the beach, the fisherman stated, "I'm the only one who lives here now. My name is Dubois. I was out at sea when the Mags attacked. I came back after they were gone and buried the bodies. Kiyomasa took the folks he rescued over to New Edo. I decided to stay here 'cause I don't care much for that damn spooky island of theirs. Last few days I seen patrol boats from Snakefish cruisin' up and down the coast, so I figured the baron must've heard a word or two about it from somewhere. Not from me, though."

He paused, looked challengingly into the faces of the people around him and demanded, "Satisfied?"

"You saved us a lot of interrogation time," Kane replied wryly.

"Good," snapped Dubois. "I hate answerin' questions. Anything I overlooked?"

"One thing," Grant said. "You don't seem too interested in who we are or why we're here."

Dubois snorted and began trudging across the beach, dragging the net behind him. "That's 'cause I know who you are...three of you, anyhow. Heard all about how you helped the Tigers whip the Mags." He cast a quizzical look toward Sky Dog. "Can't say as I recall them mentionin' the participation of an Injun."

Sky Dog chose to ignore the observation. Brigid said, "We need to get to New Edo. The whole island may be in danger."

Huffing and puffing, Dubois struggled to haul the net of fish toward the settlement. "Don't let me stop you, missy."

Grant said sternly, "We need your boat."

"You need more than that," Dubois said between little grunts of exertion. "You need to know where it is."

"We do know," Brigid replied, and crisply rattled off the longitudinal and latitudinal coordinates she had committed to memory.

Dubois didn't appear to be impressed. "You'd make me feel a whole lot more charitable if one of you strapping youngsters gave an old man a hand."

Grant and Kane took the net from him and carried it to the hut holding the pile of fishbones. As they did so, Brigid explained to Dubois why they feared for the safety of New Edo. Dubois listened with an impassive expression and declared, "Wouldn't surprise me none if ol' Baron Snakefish launched a patrol boat or two to intercept you here."

"We may have been followed overland as it is," Kane said grimly.

Dubois eyed the parked MCP. "A blind cripple wouldn't have no trouble followin' the trail that monster would leave."

Impatiently, Grant said, "Goddammit, you old fart—will you lend us the use of your boat or not?"

"What if I say no?"

With a note of weary exasperation underscoring his voice, Kane asked, "What do you think?"

The old man stroked his mustache. "I 'spect you'd just take it. That be just like Mags...which I heard you two were at one time."

"If we were just like Mags," Grant shot back hotly, "we'd shoot your scrawny ass and just take your boat."

Dubois grinned, exposing brown, cavity-speckled teeth. "I 'spect you would. But none of you look like quarterdeck breed to me. I don't want to lose my boat, so I'll take you to New Edo myself. It's about an eight-hour voyage, so we'll leave about midnight."

"Midnight?" Kane echoed uneasily. He glanced at the seemingly limitless blue expanse of the Cific Ocean. The idea of setting sail in the dark didn't comfort him.

"Full moon tonight," Dubois replied sagely. "Calm waters. An' if any patrol boats are out from Snakefish, we'll have a better chance of sneakin' right past 'em."

Brigid, Kane and Grant exchanged swift, questioning looks, then they agreed. They returned to the

MCP and unloaded equipment from it. Grant told Sky Dog to take the vehicle back to his village. The shaman, though given some training in driving the mammoth machine, didn't look particularly confident in his ability.

"How will you three get back?" he asked.

Brigid replied, "There's a redoubt about twenty miles away with a gateway unit. We'll use that to jump back to Cerberus."

Although they had explained the mat-trans network and the scientific principles upon which it was based, Sky Dog hadn't completely accepted such a manner of travel. He didn't argue with them. His concern for his wounded men was overwhelming, and he knew they stood a better chance of recovering from their injuries among their own people.

Fortunately, Port Morninglight had an ample supply of fresh water, and they replenished the MCP's dwindling reserves. Now that there were three less people to keep alive, the water should last them on the trip back.

They spent the rest of the evening eating, checking out their ordnance and resting. Shortly before midnight, Kane, Brigid and Grant exchanged grave goodbyes with Sky Dog and his warriors. They loaded the fishing boat with their possessions and set sail.

The little ship moved swiftly across the sea, her sail filled by the thrust of the wind. The surface of the Cific parted before her prow in silent ripples. Dubois knew what he was doing, whereas his passengers did not, so he attended to the rigging, tacking and furling. After the first hour of swinging the boom arm back and forth, and nearly braining all three of them at least once, he managed to achieve the navigational course he wanted. After that, he drowsed over the sweep.

Despite being on the open waters, the humidity was oppressive. Sweat gathered on everyone's faces, and their shirts stuck to their backs. There was something oppressively ominous about the sea itself. Brigid remembered how the ocean's name, the Pacific, was something of a deliberate misnomer. According to nautical lore, the Pacific Ocean was anything but placid, but then nothing in her life had been for the past year or so.

She cast a glance toward Kane, lying half-prone in the bow, his hand propping up his chin. She couldn't tell if his eyes were open, and even if he were napping, the slightest change in speed or direction would probably awaken him. Brigid considered trying to engage him in conversation, but all of her attempts during the journey from Area 51 had met with either monosyllables or a request to be left alone.

She hadn't been offended, though she knew she should have been. Something had happened to him that went deeper than either grief or guilt over Domi's death. Although she had often thought Kane was one of the most emotional men she had ever met, that didn't mean he always expressed what he was feeling.

Brigid knew he turned his grief over Domi's death inward, presenting only a detached mask to her and everyone else. She could relate to his reaction. During her years as an archivist in Cobaltville's Historical Division, Brigid had perfected a poker face. Because historians were always watched, it didn't do for them to show emotional reaction to a scrap of knowledge that might have escaped the censor's notice. Grant obviously didn't want to talk about it, either, so she gave the two men the privacy they wanted and needed. Both were obviously grappling with their emotions, trying to come to terms with Domi's death.

In many ways, Brigid reflected, she, Kane and Grant had spent most of their exile trying to accept and come to terms with new knowledge and perspectives. Even after all this time, Brigid still had difficulty accepting what she had learned about the nukecaust and the so-called Archon Directorate's involvement in it. Until a year or so ago, neither she, Grant or Kane had even the vaguest inkling of the existence of the Archons, much less the fact that they had coexisted with humanity and directed human affairs for thousands of years.

Brigid rested her chin on her knees, desperately wishing she had something to think about other than what they had all lost over the past year. She watched the sun climb a handbreadth above the flat horizon, trying to concentrate on its beauty. A cluster of clouds wreathed the bottom edge of the sun. Beneath them, a dark shape rose from the sea.

"We're coming to the strait," Dubois suddenly announced. "Almost there. I hope you three will be welcome after what we'll go through getting into the damn place."

Chapter 19

"See there?" Dubois pointed, and Grant made out the shadowy cliffs looming up from the horizon. "There's a channel we have to navigate. It's some wild water, but once we're through it we'll be in New Edo."

He altered course to port, saying happily, "It's a sweet ride, if you like that sort of thing."

His passengers offered no comment. When Grant saw the island, he could barely restrain a sigh of relief. He desperately wanted to get out of the company of Kane and Brigid, at least for a few hours. His mind kept replaying his last sight of Domi, her small figure vanishing in a blinding flare of light. Every time he closed his eyes, he saw her standing there, her arm poised to hurl the gren, like a poorly edited vid tape on continuous loop. The image lingered in his heart and head, like a wound that refused to heal.

Grant had gone through his life feeling he always knew what should be done and when, and the death of Domi proved he had deluded himself. He realized he hadn't known her, not really. Until a month or so ago, he had deliberately dismissed her as something of a caricature of an outlander, having only a set of characteristics not a true identity. It hadn't occurred to him they had forged a relationship deeper than he knew or cared to admit.

In the past he had tried to cite the age difference as the reason he didn't want to get involved with her, sexually or otherwise. Domi had been patient and understanding for a year but grew tired of waiting. In truth, Grant had deliberately maintained a distance between himself and Domi so if either she or he died—or simply went away—the vacuum wouldn't be so difficult to endure. He recalled with crystal clarity what she had said to him a month or so ago when she confronted him: "If you can't do it, if you're impotent, then let me know right now so I can make plans."

When he angrily denied a physical disability was the reason, she snarled, "Then it *is* me, you lying sack of shit." With contempt dripping from every syllable, she said, "Big man, big chest, big shoulders, legs like trees. Guess they don't tell the story, huh?"

That was the last private conversation they had. Her angry outburst cut him like a knife, and now he burned from the brand of his own regret. When he remembered the recrimination in her voice, he knew he couldn't make up for anything he had done to use her.

Grant glanced at Kane. He was only a few feet away, but he exuded such an aura of isolation he might as well have been in another dimension. There was an emotional distance between them for similar reasons. If one were lost, the other could go on. He suspected that what kept Kane silent and distant was not the fresh trauma he might have suffered in Area 51 but guilt. Because the gren had been in his hand, he felt Domi's life had been in it, too.

By Grant's way of thinking, Kane was purposefully punishing himself, but the man had always exhibited some peculiar whims when it came to setting standards of success and failure. He had partnered with Kane for many years and still didn't fully understand him. But the years they had spent together, fighting on the same side and guarding each other's back, hadn't made them much closer than the first day they had met.

He suddenly decided the distance he had observed with Domi, like the distance Kane maintained with Brigid and both of them demonstrated with each other, wasn't about remaining self-reliant—it was about a fear of commitment, a terror of not being able to accept the potential for personal loss or control the fates of others.

He remembered his helplessness and rage when Olivia had been torn from him by the caste standards of the villes. He could only watch as she fell away from him and his life. Her absence was never filled, but the pain it left strengthened him—he had silently vowed never to let anyone take control from him again. Now, because of that vow, guilt filled him like a cup. The taste of self-loathing was a bitter coating on his tongue and soul.

Grant focused his vision and concentration on the island, which grew closer with every passing minute. The rising sun reflected blindingly from the water as if the Cific were a huge mirror, forcing everyone to put on sunglasses. From his pocket, he took the compact set of microbinoculars and scanned the irregular hump rising out of the horizon.

The seas grew rougher as the sailboat pushed through the waters, skipping on the chop like a flat stone on a pond. Grant tried to keep the binoculars trained on the island, though with the way the boat bounced, it wasn't easy. The bridge of his nose was sore by the time he was able to pick out more details. He saw that the island was the largest of a smaller string consisting of four islets. The main landmass reared out of the sea like a massive cube of black volcanic rock, but he saw green vegetation on the summit of a small peak. Atop it he discerned the outline of a watch or bell tower. Castellated cliffs loomed at least a hundred feet above the surface of the Cific. Thundering waves crashed and broke on the bare rock, foaming spray flying in all directions.

Dubois worked the steering sweep, and the little ship began to pick up speed. He directed it into the grip of a current that swept toward the cliffs, like a thin river racing more swiftly than the sea itself. The dark walls seemed to plunge toward them. Kane turned toward the old man, demanding, "Are we supposed climb those damn cliffs?"

Shaking his head, Dubois said, "There's a passage. You just have to know where to look for it."

Grant squinted through the eyepieces toward the rock walls. At first, he could see no passage whatsoever. Then, suddenly, a narrow streak of light appeared. The sea heaved under the boat as Dubois steered it closer. The gap widened and became a gushing channel swirling around broken rocks, spray rising like smoke.

Dubois swiftly furled the sail as the current caught the boat. The ship quivered, sprang ahead, then tore like a wild animal into the heart of the churning, foaming strait. In spite of himself, Grant's hands tightened on the gunwales of the fishing boat as it rushed along the wild sweep of the current. Mist and spray swirled past the prow. The old man threw back his head and made a yelping outcry of pure exultation.

The fishing boat plunged into the strait between the slick, seaweed-draped walls of the narrow channel. It pitched and jumped as it followed the twisting passage. The boat picked up speed, shooting forward, threading its way between upthrusts of pitted rock. Everyone and everything was drenched by the cresting waves and flying foam.

The strait widened, and with startling abruptness the boat plunged into a lagoon. Even within the inlet, the sea was turbulent and swells threatened to pile the vessel up on the rocks. Dubois tilted his head back and shouted, *"Hin'yuu! Hin'yuu!"*

An upward glance showed Grant that the walls of the strait were defended on both sides. Squat, boxlike structures were built over deep clefts in the cliff face. Behind them, sunlight winked from metal helmets. He also saw windlasses and ballista arms for the dropping and drawing of nets across the narrow passage. According to Kiyomasa, New Edo had reason for such

defenses. Not only had the settlers fled from political
strife on Japan, but also the inhabitants of other Western Islands depended on piracy and plunder.

The boiling sea calmed the farther the ship moved
from the throat of the strait. It seemed to Grant the
boat barely moved. His impatience and the subtle
sense of danger deepened. Dubois unfurled the sail
and when a breeze filled it, he steered the ship toward
a stone jetty on the far side of the lagoon. Several
quays and docks were built around a spit of volcanic
rock that jutted into the blue waters. A cluster of vessels was tied up there, mainly barges and skiffs, but
he saw three large vessels that had all the characteristics of warships.

They were all of a type, riding high above the wa-
terline, consisting of sharp angles, arches and but-
tresses. The sails didn't look like broadcloth. They
reminded him of window blinds made of a waxed and
oiled paper. He, Kane and Brigid had seen similar
craft before, on the island of Autarkic. As he recollected, the ships were called junks. Beyond the ships
and the docks, he saw a crescent of a white sandy
beach, bracketed by stunted palm trees and tropical
ferns.

The port wasn't a beehive of activity. Only a few
people, most of them wearing a simple ensemble of
cotton T-shirts and shorts, seemed to be at the water-
front area. Green nets hung from pilings and were
spread out over the docks. It struck Grant as decidedly
odd that no fishermen were out at sea, particularly so
early in the day.

Dubois docked the sailboat at the jetty. Kane tossed the mooring line to a boy who called Dubois by name. He tied it expertly around a cleat bolted into a support post. All of them disembarked, but no one spoke to them. The people moved away, giving them surreptitious up-from-under looks. "Something's wrong here," Brigid commented uneasily.

No sooner had she spoken than the tramp of many running feet reached them. Along a cobbled path that twisted between the foliage jogged a troop of armored figures.

"Setting loose the tigers on guests doesn't seem very hospitable," Kane commented.

Grant and Brigid silently agreed with his observation. The Tigers of Heaven were attired in suits of segmented armor made from wafers of metal held together by small, delicate chain. Overlaid with a dark brown lacquer, the interlocked and overlapping plates were trimmed in scarlet and gold. Between flaring shoulder epaulets, war helmets fanned out with sweeping curves of metal. Some resembled wings, others horns. The face guards, wrought of a semitransparent material, presented the inhuman visage of a snarling tiger.

Quivers of arrows dangled from their shoulders, and longbows made of lacquered wood were strapped to their backs. Each samurai carried two longswords in black scabbards swinging back from each hip. None of them carried firearms, but their skill with the *katanas* and the bows was such they didn't really need them. Besides, Grant knew the few blasters they had at their disposal were hardly state-of-the-art. He had been told that ammunition was hard to come by, nor did New Edo have the natural resources to manufacture it themselves.

The troop, consisting of fourteen Tigers, collected in a knot at the far end of the dock. One samurai marched toward them, his gait aggressive, the wooden planks thumping hollowly under his boots. In one hand he carried a weapon that resembled a sheaving scythe topping a five-foot-long wooden staff wrapped by many turnings of rawhide. The polished, curving blade glinted in the sunlight. Its edge looked exceptionally sharp, and Grant briefly wondered if the process that made the *katanas* so razor keen had been applied to it.

Brigid said, under her breath, "He's carrying a *naginata*...a weapon better suited for foot soldiers than samurai. It's a butcher's weapon."

Grant and Kane eyed his approach dispassionately, but both of them unconsciously began tensing their wrist tendons just in case their Sin Eaters were needed.

The samurai halted abruptly and regarded the four people coldly. His helmet's visor was up, and they saw he was much younger than they expected, perhaps only in his early twenties. His body was square and strong, his legs long and straight. Still, he was slightly under medium height.

To Dubois, the samurai snapped, "Instead of trade goods, you bring us more gaijin?"

His English was excellent, which wasn't surprising.

According to Shizuka, English had developed into a second language, the tongue of business and politics.

The samurai's rudeness was uncharacteristic of the other Tigers they had met. Rather than react to it in kind, Grant said, "We're friends. My name is—"

"I know who you are," the man broke in with an autocratic lift of his chin. "I've heard about you—all of you—for weeks now. The black samurai."

In a mild, inoffensive tone, Kane asked, "And may I inquire as to your name?"

"It is Shoki."

Kane nodded to him politely. "Well, Shoki, if you've heard about us, then you should have also heard we deserve a bit more respect than what you're showing. I'll attribute it to your youth and poor upbringing—this time."

Shoki's eyes flashed and spots of red appeared on his cheeks. His hand tightened around the handle of the *naginata*. He opened his mouth to speak, but the clatter of hooves on cobblestones commanded his attention.

A roan horse cantered through the line of armored men, who quickly gave ground. A small, lithe figure sat on its back, easily controlling the horse with an air of authority. It was another Tiger of Heaven, but not wearing a helmet. When Grant saw who it was, he felt a surge of relief, comingled with intense happiness.

Shizuka reined her mount to a halt and vaulted lightly from the saddle. She spoke a stream of rapid-fire Japanese to the samurai, who instantly began drifting away as if all of them had suddenly remembered something else they needed to do. She strode swiftly up the dock, and Shoki addressed her in angry tones, gesturing to Grant with his weapon. Her response was curt and sharp, and the young man backed away, casting his eyes downward.

Shizuka smiled at them all in turn. Her glossy black hair tumbled down over the shoulder epaulets of her armor, framing a smoothly sculpted face of extraordinary beauty. Her complexion was a very pale gold with roses and milk for an accent. The almond-shaped eyes held the fierce, proud gleam of a young eagle.

In flawless English she said, ''I'm gratified to see all of you again.'' Her eyes never left Grant's face. ''Truthfully, I did not expect it so soon.''

''Neither did we,'' Brigid said.

Shizuka threw her a fleeting, almost apologetic smile. Her eyes narrowed. ''Where is the ghost girl who accompanied you before?''

No one answered for a long moment. Finally, Kane intoned flatly, ''She's no longer with us.''

Shizuka bowed her head respectfully. ''*Ah so desu ka.* I understand. I offer my condolences. She was a brave warrior.''

In a strained voice, Brigid said, ''We're here because the barons—one of them anyway—has learned of New Edo.''

Shizuka's lips compressed. ''*Hai.* We have observed mysterious craft in our waters over the past few days engaged in a search pattern. We knew our discovery was inevitable, but such an event could not have come at a worse time. We are torn by strife and discord.''

Grant recollected Shizuka mentioning the disagreement between Captain Kiyomasa and the daimyo, Lord Takaun, about the path the future of New Edo should follow. Takaun wished to remain isolated and self-sufficient, while Kiyomasa wanted to expand New Edo's influence into the mainland and establish a colony on the Cific coast—a colony that would be within Baron Snakefish's territory.

''You'd better figure out a way to put your differences aside and make common cause,'' Grant said grimly. ''I'm pretty sure we were followed to Port Morninglight by Magistrates.'' He hooked a thumb toward Dubois. ''He told us he'd seen ville patrol boats, too.''

Dubois nodded. ''I have. That's one of the reasons I brought 'em here. Figured they might have some information Lord Takaun could use.''

Shizuka sighed and ran a hand through her raven's-wing hair. ''We must bring this to him immediately.''

She wheeled and began walking swiftly toward the end of the dock. ''Follow me.''

''What about our possessions?'' Brigid called after her.

Shizuka spoke a few words to Shoki, who glowered in response but bowed deferentially as she passed by. ''Shoki will be happy to bring them to the castle,'' she announced breezily.

Brigid, Kane and Grant fell into step behind her. Dubois elected to remain with his boat. Shizuka didn't mount her horse but led it by the reins along the cobblestoned path.

Grant caught up to her. "What's Shoki's problem?"

She tried to shrug but it wasn't easy beneath her shoulder epaulets. "Besides being young and headstrong, he is commited to Lord Takaun's isolationist viewpoint. When we brought the survivors from the Port Morninglight massacre, he objected strenuously. He, like many others, feels that offering sanctuary to gaijin will only bring disaster down on us."

Grant pitched his voice low so Kane and Brigid couldn't hear over the clopping of the horse's hooves. "Seems like he has a personal problem with me."

Shizuka nodded, a faint smile playing over her beautifully shaped lips. "Shoki claims to be in love with me, the differences in our ages and rank notwithstanding. I fear he took the news very hard when I told him my heart was pledged to another."

Grant felt his stomach muscles jerk in reaction to her words. Disappointment felt like a knife turning in his guts, but he didn't allow it to show on his face. In a studiedly noncommittal tone, he asked, "Who is that? Another Tiger?"

"In a way." Shizuka raised her gaze, staring into his face directly and boldly. "A black tiger."

Chapter 20

The cobblestoned road wound up and around a series of gently rolling hills, all with green rich grass. Cattle grazed inside split-rail fences. Cultivated fields made a patchwork pattern over the terrain.

Gravel-covered footpaths branched off from the main thoroughfare, leading to modest single-level homes made primarily of carpentered driftwood.

Kane was struck by the overall cleanliness of the village. He saw no litter anywhere, and all the shrubbery and undergrowth was trimmed back neatly. Some of the hedgerows had been clipped into interesting shapes resembling cranes and snakes. The few people they encountered stared at them and bowed whenever eye contact was made.

They didn't whisper among themselves about the strangers, which Kane found a little strange. Other than the refugees from Port Morninglight, he doubted the New Edoans had seen so many gaijin that the novelty had worn off. The tense silence that hung over the houses and paths was more nerve-racking than people talking and pointing at them.

At the top of a hill, Shizuka gestured and said, "There is the castle of our daimyo and the seat of New Edo government."

The fortress of Lord Takaun stretched like a slumbering animal among gardened terraces. It was not particularly tall, but it sprawled out with many windows, balconies and carved frames. The columns supporting the many porches and loggias were made of lengths of thick bamboo, bent into unusual shapes. The upcurving roof arches and interlocking shingles all seemed to be made of lacquered wood. To Kane's eye, it was well laid out with deep moats on three sides and cliffs on the other. At the top of the walls were parapets and protected positions for archers and blastermen.

Kane was deeply impressed not just with the size of the fortress and its architecture, but the knowledge Takaun's people had accomplished so much in only eight years. Most of the Outland settlements he had seen, even those that had existed for decades, generally resembled the temporary camps of nomads. An image of Domi's squalid settlement on the Snake River drifted through his mind, and he deliberately quashed the memory.

He recalled what Kiyomasa had said about their first few years on the island. He described the many problems that had to be overcome, referring to demons and monsters that haunted the craggy coves and inland forests. Kiyomasa claimed they possessed a malevolent intelligence and cruel sense of humor and would creep into the camp at night to urinate in the well water or defecate in the gardens. The House of Mashashige not only persevered, but it also thrived, hacking out first a settlement then an entire city from the wilderness.

When they reached an outer gate of the castle, Shizuka handed the reins of her horse to a man wearing a black kimono and proceeded under the archway. A short bridge spanned one of the moats, leading to a cobblestoned footpath. The cobbled walk began to narrow as it became flanked by twenty-foot-high walls of highly polished bamboo without handholds. On either side of the fortress rose two corner towers, which Shizuka called *yagura,* that overlooked the road and the lagoon. Armed men stood atop the towers and patrolled the walls. Kane suspected there were others out of sight in the gardened terraces and lowlands around the castle.

There was definitely something going on. The castle was on a battle alert, and the tension in the air was thick and palpable. Shizuka was greeted at the portal leading to the inner gate by a woman richly dressed in many layers of smoothly woven silk. Her face was whitened by powder and her cheeks rouged. She looked with a certain distaste at Kane and Grant but bowed to them anyway. She smiled at Brigid as she bowed.

Shizuka led her three guests down a passageway made of highly polished panels of wood. She said, "That was Yoshika, my sister. She decided to become a geisha rather than a samurai."

"It's nice to learn women in your society are given the choice," Brigid said dryly.

"Our society was changing even before skydark," Shizuka retorted a bit peevishly.

She stopped in front of a door made of opaque oiled paper and laths, guarded by a samurai. The man bowed to Shizuka and spoke softly to her. She turned to Kane and Grant. "I'm afraid you must give up your weapons if you wish an audience with the daimyo. It's palace etiquette and a security measure."

Kane and Grant exchanged long looks, then with shrugs, they undid the buckles and Velcro tabs on their forearm holsters and handed the Sin Eaters over to the guard. The man examined them curiously.

"Tell him not to fool around with them," Grant advised. "They're damn dangerous for a novice."

Shizuka repeated Grant's instructions in Japanese, but the samurai only smiled in response. He opened the door a crack and whispered to someone on the other side. A moment passed before a voice whispered back. The doors began to slide open, pulled by an attendant wearing a bright blue kimono. In the room beyond, seated cross-legged on the center of a long low dais and flanked by Captain Kiyomasa on his left, was Lord Takaun, daimyo of the House of Mashashige and ruler of New Edo.

Kane, Grant and Brigid kept their eyes on Shizuka and tried to emulate every movement. Shizuka entered first, bowing her head toward the tatami on the floor. Slightly behind her, the three guests did the same.

Takaun wasn't quite the impressive physical specimen they had expected, certainly not looking at all like a man who commanded such respect and had forced the wild environment of the island to his will. He was slender and of medium height. He wore an unadorned black kimono, and the sword hilt protruding from his blue sash bore no ornamentation at all. His clean-shaved face was narrow, with heavy eyebrows above hooded eyes. His long black hair, shot through with silvery threads, was knotted at his nape by a coil of silver.

Except for eye and hair color, Kiyomasa was almost his exact opposite. His features were full fleshed with a sharp hooked nose set between and below heavy eyebrows. His eyes were very thin slits with no emotion in them. A thin mustache drooped at the corners of the grim, unsmiling slash of a mouth. There were faint hairline scars on his face and neck. He, too, carried a *katana,* and Kane took this to mean that despite their differences Takaun trusted him and was showing him respect by permitting him to have his weapon in his presence.

Lord Takaun motioned for them to come closer, but he did not invite them to sit on the floor mats. He studied all of their faces for a silent, tense tick of time. Kane became very aware of how unwashed and unshaved he and Grant were. Even Brigid was unusually untidy.

Quietly, Takaun said, ''Captain Kiyomasa has told me of your service to him, and through him, to me. He told me that you have slain the killers of our friends on the mainland.''

Kane waited for Brigid or Grant to say something

in response. When they didn't, he murmured, "There is nothing like spilling the blood of a mutual enemy to make new friends."

The phrase was one Kiyomasa had employed upon their initial meeting, and he saw the samurai captain's eyes flicker briefly in appreciation. Lord Takaun acted as if he hadn't heard.

"Unfortunately," he continued in that same soft, apologetic tone, "it is with great regret and a certain degree of shame that I cannot offer you the welcome warriors such as yourselves deserve. I will permit you to remain here for the day, but you must leave by dawn tommorrow."

"That may not be wise," Grant rumbled.

Takaun raised a challenging eyebrow. "And why is that?"

"We didn't come here to freeload off you—we came to warn you. Patrol boats sent out from Baron Snakefish are scouring these waters. His Magistrates caught one of the survivors from Port Morninglight and he talked about you. They may not know the exact location of this island, but they have a good idea of New Edo's general vicinity. They'll recce— reconnoiter—every island in this part of the Cific if they have to. It's only a matter of time before they find you."

Takaun clenched his jaws tightly. Scowling, he turned to Kiyomasa. "This is exactly what I feared would happen if we engaged in trade on the mainland. Now we must contend with threats from within, as well as without."

Kiyomasa grunted before he replied. "We don't know if we face an actual threat from either quarter as of yet."

"What kind of threat are you talking about?" Brigid asked.

Lord Takaun scrutinized her. "Are you the scholar my captain and his lieutenant spoke of?"

With a wan smile, Brigid answered, "I've been called that, yes."

"Then perhaps you may be of some further service to us other than acting as a portent of doom."

Brigid wasn't sure if the daimyo was being sarcastic or melodramatic, so she opted to remain silent. Takaun and Kiyomasa arose together, uncrossing their ankles, rocking forward on their knees and then on their heels. They came to their feet in one smooth, flowing motion. The two men strode across the room, Takaun gesturing for them to follow. Grant and Kane hesitated, but Shizuka whispered, "It's all right."

They joined the two men in an adjoining room with a balcony overlooking craggy rocks and a small bay. The rocks thrust up out of the foaming surf like the blunt fangs and led in an irregular path to a small islet. At the balcony's railing stood a tripod-mounted telescope. On a bookcase built into one wall was a curious collection of artifacts, all of which were out of place in the castle. Resting on one shelf, dented and dull, was a metal casque from the days of the conquistadores. On another was a crude knife made from a flake of flint, the handle wrapped with leather thongs. The blade was shaped somewhat like a laurel leaf with deep lengthwise grooves on either side. A rusty flintlock pistol lay beside it. There were other items less recognizable.

Takaun directed his attention to a long, low table. Upon it lay an object covered in canvas. He said, "That thing was killed last night in our rice fields. The farmer who killed it brought it here this morning. Captain Kiyomasa and I were discussing the implications of its discovery when you arrived."

Brigid stepped close as the daimyo whipped the stiff cloth aside in a theaterical gesture. She bit back a cry of surprise mixed in with incredulity. A long-necked and long-legged creature lay dead on the tabletop. From the tip of its whiplike tail to its blunt, scaled snout, she estimated it was about eight feet long. Clawed forelegs were drawn up to its chest, and its thickly muscled hind legs were equipped with three hooked talons. The legs were bent at the knee, so it looked smaller than it actually was.

Grant and Kane moved to either side of her, eyeing the mottled, red-striped scaly hide. Its open eyes were piercing black, holding a glassy sheen in death. The long underjaw gaped open slightly, revealing rows of needlelike fangs thrusting up from purple gums. A small bleeding hole showed in its chest, obviously made by an arrow that had penetrated its heart.

"What the hell is it?" Grant demanded. "Some kind of mutie?"

Brigid shook her head. In an enthralled half whisper she declared, "Not a mutie unless radiation can reverse the process of evolution. Paleontology isn't my favorite field, but I know this is a dinosaur—a Dryosaurus...from the Jurassic period, I believe.''

She poked its pebbled hide with a forefinger. ''It's real.''

Takaun snapped gruffly, ''Of course it is.''

Kane said skeptically, ''That thing didn't come from the Jurassic period.''

''No,'' Kiyomasa stated stolidly. He waved an arm toward the balcony. ''It came from that little island.''

Brigid swiveled her head toward him, lines of confused consternation creasing her forehead. ''What?''

Lord Takaun nodded grimly. ''When we first arrived here, we became aware of a cyclical phenomenon occurring on that isle.''

''What kind of phenomenon?'' she asked, her eyes glinting with interest.

''Lightning that seemed to strike up,'' the daimyo answered. ''Or that's what it looked like. Sounds like thunder always came with it, that's why we named it Ikazuchi Kojima—Thunder Isle. We never knew if it really was thunder or what caused it. What we do know is that shortly thereafter, demons would make incursions here—or so some of my people claimed.'' He nodded toward Kiyomasa.

''There was evidence,'' the samurai commander bit out.

''Yes, there was evidence,'' Takaun agreed. ''Footprints in our fields, signs that our food stores had been raided. Even animal spoor that could not be identified.'' He gestured toward the odd collection of artifacts on the shelves. ''I sent an expedition to the isle, and they brought those items back. I'm not a scholar like you, but I know that helmet comes from an era six hundred or more years in the past. And that knife from an even earlier time.''

Brigid glanced at the knife and said, ''It resembles a Folsom point, so named for Folsom, New Mexico, the archaeological site where the first one was found. It was evidence of a prehistoric culture, many thousands of years old.''

''What the hell has a knife got to do with a dinosaur?'' Grant demanded.

Takaun said, ''I ask that same question and receive no answers. For the past five years, the phenomena have been very sporadic, occurring only a few times. Now a new cycle has begun, and it's happening far more regularly.'' He walked to the balcony and adjusted the telescope. ''Take a look.''

Brigid leaned down and squinted through the eyepiece. All she saw was an islet that resembled a saucer crafted from volcanic rock. It was almost bare of vegetation. ''What am I looking for?'' she asked.

''Keep watching,'' Takaun said.

Then light flickered and flashed somewhere on the surface of the black saucer. It wasn't an optical illusion. Squinting through the eyepiece, she tightened the focus. Light flickered again, white and bright, far too bright to be a reflection. Or if it was, the reflecting surface had to be gigantic. The flare had to have been blinding on the island. In the distance she heard a rumble. At first she thought it was thunder, but it was far too brief. It sounded more like a handclap.

She straightened, rubbing the flash-induced spots

from her eye. "Something's going on over there, but I'm afraid I can't offer even a provisional hypothesis without making a hands-on recce."

Kiyomasa declared, "We've sent our people over. Some found nothing, some never came back." He drew an index finger across his throat. "And some were found decapitated."

Grant remarked, "I recollect you mentioning that. I thought you were just being colorful."

Kiyomasa's lips twitched in an effort to repress either a smile or a frown. "Hardly, Grant-san."

"It seems to me," ventured Kane, "that the threat of Mags storming New Edo is a bit more immediate than a light show on that island and an overgrown lizard in your rice paddies."

Takaun cast him a glare. "Who is to say, gaijin? I know one thing for certain—your presence here will only serve to inflame the passions of my people who share my attitude toward contact with foreigners. I will treat you as guests for this day only. If you remain I'll treat you as prisoners. If you return, I'll have no choice but to treat you like invaders."

Brigid said icily, "You have some very peculiar notions of gratitude. We came here to warn you and offer our help."

"And you may have drawn to our shores the very forces for which we would need your help." Takaun's thick eyebrows drew down over the bridge of his nose. "Did Shizuka or the captain happen to mention the Black Dragon Society to you?"

When the daimyo received headshakes from the three outlanders, he planted his hands on his hips and stated, "Not everything we brought from our home-land is good. Three centuries or so ago, when the old feudal system of Nippon ended, a group of *ronin*, masterless and unemployed samurai, formed an organization to fight the spread of Western influence. They were terrorists of the most extreme kind, rabidly xenophobic. It has been revived here."

"In New Edo?" Brigid inquired suspiciously. "After all this time?"

"Sects of that nature never die out completely. There are always messianic fanatics to breathe new life into them."

"This just gets better and better." Kane didn't even try to disguise the sarcasm in his voice. "New Edo isn't so big they can stay hidden from the Tigers of Heaven."

Takaun nodded in sour agreement. "They can hide in plain sight, since most of the Black Dragons are drawn from the ranks of the samurai trainees. They are young and are utterly devoted to *otoko ni michi*, the manly and honorable samurai tradition. That's why I cannot afford to imprison, execute or exile any of them I suspect of being a member. Unlike my captain here, I am not willing to alienate the samurai. Therefore, though I wish it were otherwise, I won't countenace any further trade with the mainland peoples. If I do so, I risk a rebellion, perhaps even a coup."

He passed a weary hand over his forehead and added sadly, "I hope you understand my position."

Without waiting for a response, the daimyo pushed past them and returned to the audience chamber.

Kane, Brigid, Grant and Kiyomasa followed him. As they entered, they saw the attendant pull open the door, allowing Shoki to come in. He carried their packs of armor and equipment. Takaun spoke to him impatiently, and Shoki immediately backed out with the packs.

Kane made a motion to go after him, but Kiyomasa caught his eye and shook his head. Turning to Takaun, Kane said, "With all respect, we'd prefer to have our weapons, especially after what you just told us about these Black Dragons of yours."

Lord Takaun reseated himself at the dais. "If the Black Dragons learn I allow you to stay here in the palace bearing weapons, then your safety most certainly will be in question."

"In that case," Kane said, a steel edge in his voice, "we won't stay in the palace. Give us back our possessions and we'll leave right now."

Takaun shook his head. "Not during daylight hours. You could be spotted by patrol boats. No, you will remain here at least until after dark. I will provide you with food, quarters and even baths if you so desire."

He spoke so tersely and flatly, everyone knew he was signifying that the audience and the conversation were over. Both Kane and Grant stared at him with narrowed eyes, but Shizuka stepped up between them. "Come with me." In a whisper, she said, "There's no point in arguing. So please, come with me."

Chapter 21

The room Kane was given was small, with a futon and wooden pillow for sleeping and a few scraps of furniture. Before he was allowed to enter it, Shizuka bade him to take off his shoes and socks. He did so, noting that she didn't so much as wrinkle her nose at the ripe odor. Once the door was closed, he removed the nickel-plated Mustang .380 from beneath his shirt where he had stuck it in his waistband before disembarking from Dubois's fishing boat. He hid it beneath the futon mattress.

A few minutes later, a small girl barely into her teens brought him a covered dish of warm bean curd and rice with a little ceramic pot of tea. She seemed afraid of him and wasn't inclined to linger. He ate and drank without tasting the food and then lay on the futon, staring up at the accordion-like paper lantern hanging from a roof beam. He was so tired even the square block of wood serving as a pillow felt as soft as a mass of cotton wadding.

He hungered for a cigar, but Grant had neglected to bring any along from Cerberus. Dreamland had apparently been a nosmoking facility, since he hadn't seen or smelled any tobacco there.

Kane tried very hard to think of anything but Domi,

but the treacherous human mind always zeroed in on the most painful subject. He had no trouble admitting to himself that not only had he yet to come to terms with her death, but also he couldn't even grasp the concept except in the most abstract way. The very notion slipped through the fingers of his mind like a wisp of smoke.

It wasn't as if he didn't recognize the inevitability of death. He was accustomed to a lot of inevitables—loneliness, pain, fear, the emptiness of dreams. He had accepted all of them with equanimity, yet he couldn't accept the fact Domi was truly dead. Something inside of him, almost instinctual, refused to acknowledge it. He knew his denial was due in part to his ingrained opposition to blindly embracing the superficial. Although he wasn't an expert on explosives, he was fairly certain implode grens couldn't vaporize targets without leaving some trace—a spattering of blood, a scrap of bone, a hank of hair.

A suspicion lurked at the very back of his mind that what he had seen, what all of them had seen, wasn't Domi dying. A subliminal afterimage of an object or movement at the very instant of detonation bobbed at the fringes of his memory, but his conscious mind couldn't analyze it.

On a more visceral level, Domi's death simply *felt* wrong, as if it weren't supposed to have happened. It was an error, a miscalculation like the alternate event horizon Lakesh postulated that had set into motion the events leading to the nukecaust.

There was more to it than that, of course. He hadn't

known Domi, not really. The compassion she'd displayed for the dying hybrid babies had profoundly shaken him. He closed his eyes and tried to work up a bitter laugh at his ridiculous theorizing. He recognized the symptoms of shock and tension. His aching muscles screamed at him to be allowed to relax, and his mind begged him to go to sleep. But every time he closed his eyes, the vision of Domi being swallowed by a blaze of light crowded into his mind, pushing aside all other thoughts. He had been trained to catch sleep whenever he could, so as to build up a reserve, in case he had to go for long periods without it. He began a relaxation exercise, regulating his breathing. By degrees he allowed the waves of sleep to wash over him. Just as he drifted off, he heard his own voice whisper, "She's not dead."

His sleep was fitful, disturbed by the choppy fragments of dreams and none of the pieces made any sense. He heard someone from far, far away calling his name, asking him if he was all right. He realized the voice was not wafting from a dream but from somewhere above him.

With great effort, Kane forced his eyes to open. The room was dim and all he could see for a moment was a blurred halo of gold falling in waves around a pale, indistinct face. He blinked repeatedly, and Brigid Baptiste's face came into focus and sharpened into clarity.

She knelt on the floor beside the futon, her emerald eyes intense and worried. "Kane—answer me. Are you all right?"

Knuckling his eyes, he pushed himself up to his

elbows and looked around. Diffuse late-afternoon sunlight slanted in through the opaque paper and wood door, casting golden highlights in Brigid's mane of hair. He saw she was wearing a sky-blue kimono with a heron embroidered on the left breast in red thread. She looked very clean, and he caught a delightful whiff of sandalwood and soap.

"Yeah," he grunted, clearing a dry-as-dust throat. "Why wouldn't I be all right?"

"I heard you out in the hallway. You were moaning, talking in your sleep."

Kane hiked up to a sitting position, dry-scrubbing his itchy scalp with his fingers. Embarrassed but refusing to show it, he asked, "Did you hear anything you can use against me?"

Brigid didn't answer immediately. When she did, her voice was pitched low to disguise the tremor in her voice. "It sounded like you were saying 'she's not dead.'"

Kane reached for the ceramic pot on the little table. It still held a couple of mouthfuls of tea, and though it was cold and bitter, he gulped it down.

"But she is, Kane." Brigid spoke barely above a whisper. "None of us have had the time to deal with what happened to Domi, but all of us have to accept it. She's gone."

"We didn't see a body." He spoke more harshly than he intended.

A line of worry creased Brigid's high forehead. "Is that what it'll take to convince you—a maimed corpse?"

"It would be more convincing than *not* seeing any corpse at all, maimed or otherwise."

Testily, she said, "Kane, her body was probably drawn into the vacuum and completely compressed. After the effect passed, it was scattered all over the hangar."

Kane angled an eyebrow at her. "When did you become an expert on implode grens?"

"I'm not. But I've become something of an expert on you over the past year or so. Something happened to you in Area 51, something you don't want to talk about or even want to remember. I sense it—I can see it in your eyes."

Trying but failing to squash a rise of annoyance, he demanded, "What makes you so sure?"

Calmly, Brigid replied, "Simple logic, for one thing. If Baron Cobalt occupied the place, he wouldn't have been content to simply toss you in a cell and keep you a prisoner. He would've devised some kind of torture but one that served his interests, too. I don't see any marks on your body, so whatever he did to you wasn't primarily physical. Whatever he did to you, maybe even to Domi, is something you're loath to tell me or even Grant about."

Kane glared at her, opening his mouth, closing it, then shaking his head in resignation. A profanity-salted sigh issued from between his lips. "Baptiste, if I told you about it, you'd be very sorry that I did. It's over now. What we should concern ourselves with is a war between the barons and this so-called imperator. We've got to get back to Cerberus as soon as possible. Lakesh can—''

"You're obfuscating," she snapped.

"Fluently. And I'm hungry as hell, too. And I've got to pee. So what's your point?"

She only stared at him steadily.

Kane inhaled a deep breath. "Baptiste, do you remember when you learned you were barren?"

She jerked slightly in reaction to his question, but she nodded.

"I learned about it, too, but I didn't ask you about it. I waited until you were ready to tell me. I respected your privacy. I'm asking you to show me that same kind of consideration."

Brigid nodded again. "Understood. So when you're ready, you'll talk about it?"

He forced a smile. "You'll be the first to know."

She tried to match his smile, but it didn't reach her eyes. "That might offend Grant."

"He offends too easy nowadays as it is. Where is he, anyway?"

She gestured toward the wall. "He woke up a while ago and went to the bathhouse." Her smile widened. "You could probably benefit from a visit yourself."

Kane ran a hand over his jawline, producing a sound like sandpaper being drawn over a rasp. He sniffed the collar of his shirt and murmured in horror, "Almighty God."

Brigid laughed, and the chain of tension stretched between them relaxed. She rose to her feet and offered him a hand. He took it and she helped him to his feet. He stumbled slightly, and she reached out to steady him. For an instant they stood very close together.

Gazing into the jade depths of her eyes, he said falteringly, "I want to thank you again for—"

The black-robed-and-hooded man chose that instant to slash through the rear wall with a *katana*.

THE BATHHOUSE WAS at the rear of the palace and was surrounded by tidily trimmed thickets and little rock gardens. From the exterior, it looked like a storage building made of stone and wood. Grant entered, ducking his head beneath the low doorway, and saw polished wood floors, benches and a large aboveground tub. The far wall was made of the oiled paper and laths he had seen in the other parts of the fortress.

The circular tub was about ten feet in diameter with a bench running around the inside, all of it made of planks of seasoned hardwood and sealed with pitch. It rose three feet above the floor. As Grant entered, he saw that it was already three-quarters full. Two girls poured buckets of steaming water into it. They were small and petite, wearing loosely woven shifts that left their arms and most of their legs bare.

They bowed to him as he entered and, by hand gestures, indicated he should disrobe. He unlaced his boots and stepped out of them. After he shrugged out of his shirt, he stood and waited as one of the girls topped off the tub with a final bucket of water. The other one tugged at his pants. Grant glowered down

at her and held her small hand where it was. She
looked up at him and said a few words in an exasperated tone, gesturing to the tub with her other hand.

Grant told himself he wasn't the first naked man
they'd ever seen and probably wouldn't be the last.
Reluctantly, he unbuckled his belt, undid the snaps on
his trousers and dropped them, as well as his under-
wear. Both girls gazed at him for a long silent moment, their dark eyes widening as far as the epicanthic
folds allowed.

They quickly averted their faces, giggling into their
hands. Grant felt a hot flush of irritation and embarrassment spread up his neck. Then the truth dawned
on him. The girls had never seen a gaijin male un-
clothed before, and he guessed that the average penile
size of their men was more than likely in direct pro-
portion to their bodies. Grant wasn't a small man regardless of how he was measured, either in height,
breadth, length or thickness. To them he must have
seemed like a giant out of one of their legends—in
more ways than one.

He climbed into the tub and sat on the bench, making shooing motions with his hands. Rather reluctantly, the two girls left the room. He splashed water
over his face and chest. His joints were stiff, his muscles aching. A dull headache throbbed at the back of
his skull. Leaning over the edge of the tub, he removed his straight razor from the kit bag.

After a few minutes of insistent arguing earlier in
the day, Shizuka had arranged for the return of his
bag. It was waiting for him when he awoke from his

day-long slumber. When he passed Brigid on the way back from the bathhouse they spoke for a couple of minutes, both of them hoping that when and if dinner was served, it would be a bit more substantial than bean curd and rice.

Covering his face in soap suds, he shaved away more than a week's worth of whiskers from his face. He rarely used the razor as a personal grooming tool. He usually carried it out in the field as a hideout weapon, a way to cut and slash high odds down to his favor.

He rinsed his face and filled a bucketful of water and let it trickle across the back of his neck, the muscles of which felt like clenched fists. Even sleeping for nearly eight hours hadn't relaxed him. He poured more water over his head, hoping it would wash away the residue of his dreams.

He couldn't really remember them, but he knew Domi figured in them prominently. Although Grant had witnessed the deaths of many people, he still would not have been surprised if she popped her white-haired head up above the rim of the tub and chirped, "Had you big-time fooled, didn't I?"

He told himself she never would. The dead never returned to life like that. Leaning back, arms propped on the edge of the tub, he was content to soak and doze for what seemed like an hour. When fingers touched the back of his neck, his body snapped taut like a bowstring and he spun on the bench, sloshing water out of the tub.

"Do you wish me to massage you?"

Grant expected to see one of the serving girls. His mouth gaped open when he saw Shizuka standing there, backlit by the lantern. She was dressed in the same short white linen shift as the female attendants, and with her raven hair hanging loose and free she was heart-wrenchingly lovely. His blood seemed to race through his arteries like stampeding horses.

Grant tried to sound casual, but knew he failed at it when he replied, "If you have nothing better to do…"

Shizuka chuckled. "I don't. I can make it as prolonged or as delightful as you wish."

"Let's just see how it goes."

Grant put his back against the wall of the tub, and she leaned into him, working at the thick muscles of his neck and shoulders with surprisingly strong, practiced fingers. As she kneaded the tendons, he felt the soft brush of her hair against his bare shoulder. Within minutes, the pressure of her fingertips pushed out the stiffness and undid the knots in his muscles. He noticed his headache was receding, as well.

He felt the gentle touch of her soft, budlike lips as Shizuka kissed the side of his neck. Her hands went around him to his chest, and he felt the teasing pressure of her breasts pressing against his back. Her hands trailed across his chest, one sharp nail tracing a thin line over his belly.

Grant caught his breath sharply, and her hand paused. "What is it?"

Although he felt his muscles tightening under her touch, he husked out, "It's been a long time for me,

Shizuka. A very long time. And I don't know if this is the right time—''

Her dark eyes looked liquid. "You feel you would be unfaithful to your little ghost girl?"

"No—yes. No. There was nothing like this between us."

Shizuka kissed the side of his face. "What was between you, then?"

Grant shifted uncomfortably on the bench as his penis engorged and thickened. He tried to ignore it as he began to talk. He rarely spoke of his past, of personal matters, but now he told her of his life.

He spoke of his youth in Cobaltville, of his heritage as a Magistrate and how he abided by the family tradition to become one himself. He told her of his many long years as a spiritually and legally sanctioned killer, using only violence to impose order on the baron's definition of chaos.

His voice low, he described some of his bloody deeds as a Mag and the wounds he incurred, not only of body but of soul. When he spoke of Olivia, he cursed the slight quaver in his voice, and he noticed how Shizuka's lips pursed momentarily.

He told her of his many uncertainties in life but revealed to her the one thing he was certain of—sooner or later, pain or death or both came to all who got too close to him.

Shizuka shook her head and pressed her cheek against the side of his face. "A sad tale, Grant-san."

He forced a lopsided grin. "Compared to some of the suffering I've seen, it's not sad at all."

Shizuka kissed him, her lips moving from his cheek to his lips. "But still your warrior's heart suffers. Let me ease it a bit."

Shizuka's fingers trailed down his belly again to his groin. They found his erection, and she let out a brief, startled murmur. Her hand encircled his shaft, hefting him, measuring him with curious but gentle fingers. Shizuka undid the drawstrings on her shift and gracefully slid out of it at the same time she slid over the rim of the tub.

"Is this part of the samurai code?" Grant muttered.

She laughed melodiously and caught his hand. "I'm amending it just this once."

Shizuka guided his hand to the firm swell of her small but perfectly shaped breast. He felt the gem-hard nipple pressing against his callused palm. Leaning forward, he kissed her yielding mouth as he ran his free hand over the smooth, taut skin of her shoulders.

Then the same mad passion that had consumed him on the night they had first met after the battle with the Cobaltville Magistrates engulfed him again. He showered her face, throat and breasts with kisses.

Panting, Shizuka straddled his thighs, putting her knees on the bench. Clasping her hands at the back of his neck, her forearms resting on the broad yoke of his shoulders, she began lowering herself on him. When he felt her velvety warmth on the swollen tip of his shaft, he couldn't repress a groan.

Shizuka groaned, too, as she worked his rock-hard

length into her. Her hips moved back and forth. She bit her lower lip, her face a mask of concentration.

When he was fully embedded within the heat of her, Grant cradled her buttocks with his big hands and set a steady rhythm, lifting her up to him while he lunged upward with his hips. Voicing a keening cry, Shizuka thrust up and down, gasping, whimpering and moaning. She clutched at his biceps, her fingernails digging into the flesh.

Steam and lust and sweat blinded him. He tongued the desire-hard nipples of her breasts, and her body suddenly stiffened. Back arching, she convulsed and shuddered in a spasming orgasm so fierce and unrestrained that Grant began trembling in a contraction. Gripping her tightly by the waist, he burst deep inside her, an eruption of liquid fire that seemed to last forever.

Grant embraced her while both of them trembled through the aftermath of their mutual release. His senses slowly returned to him and Shizuka breathed a long, final sigh of satisfaction. Her liquid brown eyes gazed steadily into his and she whispered, "Grant-san, I am so glad the winds of fate blew you here."

He smiled. "Me, too, even if I didn't have anything in mind except to get a bath."

Shizuka stared at him, puzzled, then she threw her head back and laughed in genuine amusement. She pulled away from him and leaned against the side of the tub, her head tilted back, eyes closed. "I think I'll rest for a minute or ten."

Grant waited until his respiration had returned to normal, then climbed out of the tub. He took a towel from a bench and rubbed his chest and shoulders dry. As he turned to hand the towel to her, Shoki came through the door in a lunge.

Chapter 22

Kane straight-armed Brigid out of the path of the black-garbed man. He dived for the futon and the blaster hidden beneath it.

The swordsman launched himself forward, the long, slightly curved blade cutting a whipping path through the air toward his head.

Kane managed to drop to a half-crouch and duck as the *katana* slashed over his head. Snatching at the futon, he yanked it from the floor and flung it at the hooded assassin. The sword edge hacked through it, sending up a spray of chicken feathers. He stabbed his hand out for the Mustang .380, but the *katana* chopped into the floor a quarter of an inch from his middle finger.

As Kane threw himself backward, the man kicked out with a slippered foot and sent the blaster skittering across the room. Kane managed to grab the wooden-block pillow, and he held it before him between both hands. A snarling, contemptuous laugh issued from beneath the black hood. The *katana* rose and fell in a lightning-quick motion, and the pillow fell from Kane's hands, sliced neatly in two. The assassin spun gracefully on the ball of one foot and thrust the sword at Kane's midsection.

Kane sidestepped, feeling the blade cut through his shirt right over his left ribs. As the blade cut a flat arc toward his throat, Kane flung himself across the room in a backward somersault, rolling into a ball to make himself a smaller target. Then muzzle-flashes strobed in the gathering shadows of the room and three shots cracked, one following the other so closely they sounded like a single report. The thunder of the gunfire was deafening. The flimsy walls of the room beat it back and magnified it.

The swordsman jerked and doubled over, bleeding from three wounds in his belly. He fell facedown barely two feet from Kane's position on the floor, rendered unconscious by the shock of the triple shots fired at such close quarters.

Brigid, holding the Mustang in a double-handed grip, her legs spread wide in a combat stance, intoned, "So you smuggled in a blaster."

Kane rose to his feet and fanned away a wisp of cordite smoke. "Good thing, too. Looks like the Black Dragons weren't so much offended by the idea of gaijin carrying weapons in the palace as encouraged by the fact we weren't."

Brigid eyed the pistol curiously. "Where'd you get this?"

Kane picked up the dead man's sword and hefted it, testing its balance. "A small memento of Area 51. Did you say Grant was in the bathhouse?"

She nodded tensely. "If the Black Dragons are planning to sweep all foreigners from New Edo, they'll be after him, too."

Kane didn't waste time putting on his boots. He opened the door a crack and peered out into the dimly lit corridor. It appeared empty and sepulchrally quiet. It was still early evening, and all the lamps had yet to be lit. In a whisper, he said, "We don't know if Takaun himself is behind this. Regardless, we've got to find where they're keeping our weapons."

Brigid took up position on the other side of the door. "We'd better find Grant first."

Kane nodded, slid the door open and stepped out into the hallway. He took the point, padding along barefoot with Brigid bringing up the rear, blaster held with its barrel pointed toward the ceiling. They had progressed less than a dozen yards when a side door opened and a black-kimonoed figure stepped out into the hallway. Light glinted along the length of his sword.

Kane and Brigid halted as the figure moved gracefully toward him. "Want me to plug him?" she asked.

He didn't show his surprise at Brigid's sudden willingness to employ violence. "No," he side mouthed to her. "At least, not now. We may need all the rounds later." Raising his voice, he said, "Do you speak English?"

"*Hai,*" came the response, sounding as if a teenager had spoken. "I know your vile tongue, gaijin. We Black Dragons can barely speak a word of it without vomiting."

"Then you don't have to say anything. Just listen.

I don't want any trouble with your society. Let me pass and we'll leave New Edo right now.''

The Black Dragon eased closer, and Kane saw he looked to be about seventeen years old. His face was smooth and unlined, but his dark eyes glinted with a fanatic's fervor. "It's too late for that. We must send a message, not just to other gaijin-lovers on our island but to the daimyo himself.''

He said nothing more. Kane set himself, and his youthful opponent moved immediately to the attack. His blade work was fast, but his technique was not as good or clever as other samurai he had seen. Still it required all of Kane's speed and reflexes to keep the Black Dragon's glittering blade from breaking through his guard.

"This isn't necessary," Kane grated between his clenched teeth.

The Black Dragon paid no attention to him. He made a sideways slice that Kane blocked, then he stepped in close, his *katana* locking against the other man's blade, freezing it in position. His opponent's face was a mask of complete strain as he strove to break contact, but Kane didn't relent with the pressure. The young man was faster than him but he was by far the stronger.

Kane shoved him backward down the hallway and then stepped back. The unexpected release of resistance caused the young man to stumble, and as he regained his balance and made a clumsy thrust with his blade, Kane dropped to one knee and plunged his *katana* into the Black Dragon's lower belly.

He set himself to take the man's weight as he impaled himself on the sword. The Black Dragon screamed, his face a mask of rage and agony. Then he simply shuddered and died. Kane stood, and the young man's body slid wetly down his blade.

Without looking at Brigid, he started down the hallway again. As he reached the door leading to the outside, he saw three dark shapes creeping across the lawn. One turned toward him and he heard a semimusical twang. He dropped into a crouch just in time to avoid an arrow that whistled over his head. Brigid fired the Mustang through one of the paper panels, and Kane saw one of the shadow-shapes clutch himself and fall heavily.

Kane made a move to step outside again, but a man standing just outside the door reacted to the rustle of his clothes and slashed out with a *katana*. Kane kicked himself backward as Brigid leveled the blaster.

The round took the man in the right shoulder. The sound of the steel-jacketed slug smacking into flesh was ugly, but the awful animal howl he uttered was worse. The wounded man lurched across the lawn, wild with pain, dazed from the shock of impact. He screamed a long string of indecipherable words.

A dozen helmeted men in body armor and armed with *katanas* came running through the open gate. Black-robed figures, long blades glittering in the last rays of daylight, rushed to intercept them. Then figures were shouting and swearing and running all across the lawn.

The Black Dragons attacked the Tigers of Heaven,

fighting stubbornly and skillfully, for they had nothing to lose, and therefore everything to fight for.

SHOKI'S SLIPPERED FEET WERE silent against the polished cedar floor. Grant caught only a whisper of sound, a glimpse of a flitting shadow. He rolled away, flinging himself clear as Shoki hurtled through the air, driving down with his *naginata*. The curved blade buried itself in the edge of the tub, inches from Grant's right arm.

In that peculiar slowing of time perception in combat, Grant saw everything at once. Shoki's face was twisted with savage anger. Shizuka pressed against the wall of the tub, her eyes wide in shock. The flame of the lantern flickered in the breeze wafting in through the open door.

Grant saw it all in a single shaved sliver of a second. While his mind registered it, his body reacted to the attack. As Shoki tried to free his blade from the tub, Grant punched him with his right fist on the point of the samurai's chin.

The idea was to break his damn neck with one blow, but Shoki released the long handle of the *naginata* and rolled with the blow. He staggered half the length of the room but managed to retain his balance. Grant coiled the muscles in his legs and bounded forward, his broad bare chest colliding violently with that of the Japanese man.

Arms windmilling, Shoki was catapulted backward through the rear wall, taking laths and oiled-paper squares with him in a loud, clattering crash. The air was nearly driven from his lungs, but he got to his feet again, kicking and tearing his way through the wreckage to renew the attack. Shizuka shouted shrill words at him, but the man paid her no attention.

He launched a straight leg kick at Grant's exposed genitals, but Grant turned sideways and the foot landed on his upper thigh not his groin. Still the impact hurt and in response, he hooked a punishing right fist into the samurai's ribs. He heard the crunch of bone, and the Japanese staggered back with a grunt of pained surprise.

Grant moved after him, not wanting to let the man regain his balance or find a new weapon. Shoki kicked out at his groin again and then at his kneecaps. Grant sidestepped the first kick but the second one landed on his shin, peeling the flesh up over the bone.

"You little prick!" Grant growled between clenched teeth. Angrily, he kicked out himself, but Shoki dived aside. His dive brought him back to the tub, where he closed his hands around the handle of his *naginata.*

He wrenched the blade loose from the wood, but Grant leaped on him like a black panther. His right hand encircled Shoki's wrist, and he put his left arm around the man's neck, as he drove his knee into the base of the samurai's spine. Shoki screamed in pain but managed to slam the blunt butt end of his weapon hard into Grant's lower belly.

Air left Grant's lungs in an agonzied grunt and his grip loosened. Shoki wriggled free and spun, raising the *naginata* for an overhead blow in order to split Grant's skull like a melon.

Shizuka chose that instant to vault over the edge of the tub, water trailing from her naked limbs. Both of her feet struck Shoki between his shoulder blades, and he stumbled forward, his back arched. The blade hissed down and chopped into the floor barely a finger's width from the tip of Grant's big toe.

Shoki pulled it free and began circling Grant slowly. To Shizuka, he growled, "Stay back."

Grant couldn't afford to have his attention divided. One wrong move, one misstep and he was dead—or at the very least, grievously wounded by a castrating scythelike sweep of the *naginata*.

When Shoki feinted, pretending to slash at Grant's groin, the big man took the feint and cursed himself an instant later when the samurai shifted in midmotion and hacked at this throat. Grant ducked but he felt the passage of the blade over his head, so close he wouldn't have been surprised if it shaved off a few twists of his hair.

From between clenched teeth, Shoki hissed, *"Hiretsukan!"*

Grant didn't know what it meant, but he assumed it wasn't an endearment. Shoki crab-stepped forward, trying a different tactic, whipping the blunt end of the *naginata* toward Grant's throat. Lifting his hands, he crossed his wrists and caught the end of the wooden shaft between them. Grasping it tightly, he pivoted and yanked the weapon from Shoki's grasp. He howled as the pole slid through his hands, inflicting painful friction burns on both palms.

He tossed it aside and advanced on the samurai, half expecting him to flee. Instead he leaped forward, bending diagonally at the waist. He extended his leg straight out, and the sole of his foot thudded solidly into Grant's midsection. Air left his lungs in a loud whoosh, and he stumbled, off balance. Shoki followed through with his leap, chopping with the edge of his hand at the base of Grant's neck.

Although his hand rebounded from the thick ropes of neck muscle, the impact caused little pinwheels to ignite behind Grant's eyes. Before they stopped whirling, Shoki secured a stranglehold.

Fingers like flexible iron bands locked around Grant's throat, the thumbs pressing against his larynx. A grin of triumph and exertion creased his face, and Grant growled from deep in his chest. The samurai had a great deal of experience in hand-to-hand fighting, but he hadn't ever pitted himself against someone like Grant.

He brought up his forearms and knocked the samurai's hands away. At the same time he drove a knee into Shoki's groin and, as he doubled over, folding in the direction of the pain, Grant brought his right fist down like a piledriver on the back of the man's neck. His face hit the floor first, followed a second later by his knees, then the rest of his body.

Grant stood over him, panting and massaging his hand. He had broken a few knuckles before and he was pretty sure he had done it again. Shizuka came to his side, her dark eyes wide with worry and a flickering gleam of anger. "Are you all right?"

He shook his aching right hand and said, "You'd think after all this time I'd have learned to hit the soft parts."

Shizuka didn't laugh. She bent and wrestled Shoki onto his back. He wasn't a pretty sight. One eye was swollen shut and his mouth and nostrils leaked blood. A couple of teeth lay on the floor in a little puddle of crimson. She jerked open his robe, lifted his left arm and pointed to a tiny black figure tattooed in his armpit.

"A Black Dragon!" she spit out. "I knew he was hotheaded, but I never dreamed he would—"

From somewhere in the vicinity of the palace, three gunshots cracked, sounding like firecrackers going off under a tin can. Wordlessly, Grant and Shizuka threw on their clothes.

She took less time than he did, and he simply stuffed his feet into his boots without putting on socks or lacing his boots. Carrying the *naginata*, Grant followed Shizuka out of the bathhouse. They did not leave its shadow, because Shizuka suddenly went on one knee and gestured for Grant to do the same. They sidled up to a sculpted corner hedge and hazarded a quick look around it.

In the gathering gloom, they saw many dark figures flitting across the lawn, moving in on the rear wall of the castle. "What the hell is going on?" he whispered into her ear.

"The Black Dragons are staging a coup," she responded angrily. "I don't know if they intend to overthrow Lord Takaun or merely bend him to their will, but the Tigers of Heaven can't allow either one to happen."

Grimly, Grant said, "If you can take me to where you stored our weapons, I think we may able to tip the scales in your favor."

She shook her head in frustration. "The room is all the way on the other side of the fortress. It would be the miracle of miracles if we could reach it undetected."

Another cracking gunshot split the sunset. Grant craned to see around the corner of the bathhouse. "Somebody's got a working blaster in there," he murmured. "One guess who."

Shizuka regarded him with a searching stare. "Kane-san?"

He smiled bleakly. "He'd be my first choice."

Sounding scandalized, Shizuka demanded in a fierce whisper, "You mean he smuggled a firearm into the palace?"

"Yeah. I wish I'd thought of that."

Shizuka's rejoinder clogged in her throat as one more snapping report sounded. This one was followed by howls of pain. They eased closer and saw a man reeling across the lawn, clutching at his shoulder. Through an open gate came a surge of Tigers of Heaven, their armor glinting in the sunset.

From almost every shadowed point on the lawn between the bathhouse and the castle rushed a horde of black-garbed Dragons wielding swords and lances.

They struck the Tigers from both flanks, pushing them toward the rear of the fortress. A resounding roar arose from the ranks of the Black Dragons: *"Banzai, banzai!"*

There was almost no room to manuever, and the *katanas* of the Black Dragons penetrated chinks in the Tigers' armor and sank deep into eyes through the slits in the visors. Screams blended in with the clash of steel on steel. The gloom lit up with little flares as blue sparks flew from impact points.

Then, over the clash and clamor of battle, a new sound floated in on the warm sea breeze. It was the brazen tolling of a bell. It rang in a three-one pattern and then repeated. Shizuka stiffened and stood, wheeling around to face the direction of the tolling.

Grant tugged at her hand. "Get down, goddammit! They'll see you."

Shizuka struggled, wresting away from his grip. "No," she said in a strained, hoarse whisper. "The watchman—he's ringing the signal for *raikou!*"

"Who's that?" Grant demanded.

Voice trembling, eyes suddenly wide and wild with terror, Shizuka cried, "Not who—a what. *Invasion!*"

Chapter 23

Lakesh gazed in awed fascination at the transparent sphere. Six feet in diameter, it occupied the center of the room from floor to ceiling—at least, Lakesh assumed the room had a floor and ceiling even if he couldn't see them. He had jumped from the Cerberus redoubt with Erica and Sam without knowing their destination. The walls, ceiling and floor of the room were such a total black they seemed to absorb all light like a vast ebony sponge. It was a blackness usually associated with the gulfs of deep space and gave no clue of their location.

Within the suspended globe glittered thousands of pinpoints of light, scattered seemingly at random, but all connected by glowing lines similar to the redoubt's Mercator relief map that delineated all the functioning gateway units of the Cerberus network. But the map had never gripped his imagination like the sphere.

He couldn't tear his eyes away from the flashing splendor, recalling how Plato had looked up at the stars and dreamed that each one made its own glorious, heavenly music. It was as though he stood before the whole blazing, wheeling galaxy in miniature. He felt as if he were a disembodied spirit flying through interstellar space rather than standing in a room looking at a three-dimensional representation of the electromagnetic power grid of the planet.

Erica van Sloan sidled up from the blackness, her satiny blouse rustling softly. In a voice no less soft and rustling, she said, "Impressive, isn't it? I thought at first it was a work of art."

Lakesh nodded distractedly. "In a way it is. It's not just a geomantic map of Earth, but it's my entire field of study condensed and captured."

He gestured to the flickering points of light. "The power points of the planet, places that naturally generate specific types of energy. Some have positive and projective frequencies, others are negative and receptive. There are funnel-type vortices, cylindrical and even beacon types."

Pointing to one glowing speck, brighter than the rest, he said, "Chomolungma in the Himalayas—Mount Everest. According to ancient lore, that vortex is the single most powerful point on the planet. The energy it radiates sustains life and spreads prana all over the globe."

She cocked her raven-tressed head quizzically. "Prana?"

"An old Sanskrit term, meaning in a general way the world soul."

"Was that what you were you trying to spread with your quantum interphase mat-trans inducers?"

Lakesh chuckled self-consciously. "I was just trying to make quota. At the time I didn't know I was going over ground already broken millennia before."

Lakesh had achieved his breakthrough in the Pro-

ject Cerberus researches only by coming to the conclusion that matter transmission was absolutely impossible through the employment of Einsteinian
physics. Only quantum physics, coupled with quantum mechanics, had made it work.

But he was by no means the first to make this discovery. The forebears of Balam's people possessed
the knowledge of hyperdimensional physics. The so-
called Archons shared this knowledge in piecemeal
fashion with the scientists of the Totality Concept.
But they had kept to themselves the knowledge that
the gateways could accomplish far more than linear
travel from point to point along a quantum channel.

Project Cerberus and Operation Chronos were all
aspects of the same mechanism, only the applications
of the principle differed. It had occurred to Lakesh
that perhaps the entire undertaking had been codenamed the Totality Concept because it encompassed
the totality of everything, the entire workings of the
universe.

Of course, the human scientists and military offi-
cials involved in the endeavor were too fixated on
reaching short-term goals, making quota and earning
bonuses to devote much thought to the workings of
the universe or even where the basic components to
build the first mat-trans unit had come from. Lakesh
included himself in this number, although he hadn't
been so much fixated as blinded to the disastrous consequences that could result from the Totality Concept's myriad divisions.

"I was attached to Operation Chronos, remem-

ber?'' Erica reminded him. "It was your first suc-
cesses with the mat-trans inducers that allowed us to
pierce the chronon stream."

"I know," replied Lakesh. "But every bit of Totality Concept technology was only a synthetic imitation of the power Balam's folk tapped into and
wielded." He smiled bitterly. "We were all frauds,
you know."

Lakesh still remembered his dismay and outright
shock when, in his position of Project Cerberus overseer he had learned that quantum scientific principles
by which the gateways operated were not a form of
new physics at all, but a rediscovery of ancient
knowledge.

Before and after the nukecaust, he had studied the
body of scientific theory that claimed megalithic
structures such as the dolmans of Newgrange in Ireland and Stonehenge in England were expressions of
an old, long-forgotten system of physics. The theory,
based on hyperdimensional mathematics, provided a
fundamental connection between the four forces of
nature, an up-and-down link with invisible higher dimensions. Evidence indicated there were many natural vortex points, centers of intense energy on Earth
and even other celestial bodies in the solar system.

Lakesh became convinced that some ancient peo-
ples were aware of this, and could manipulate these
symmetrical earth energies to open portals not just for
linear travel like the gateways but perhaps into other
realms of existence. He suspected the knowledge was
suppressed over the centuries, an act of repression he

believed was the responsibility of the Archons or the secret societies in their service.

To test the theory, Lakesh saw to the construction of a miniaturized version of a mat-trans unit, utilizing much of the same hardware and operating principles. He called it an interphaser and like the gateways, the interphaser functioned by tapping into the quantum stream. Although the interphaser opened dimensional rifts as did the gateways, he envisioned using the gaps as a transit tunnel through the gaps in normal space-time.

The instrument was designed to interact with a natural vortex's quantum energy and create an intersection point, a discontinuous quantum jump. The device worked, but in ways he hadn't dreamed. Lakesh had always wanted to discuss the phenomenon with Balam, but the entity had refused to reveal any of his people's secrets outright. When Balam left his custody, he had despaired of ever learning anything more. Now it appeared he had a second chance.

Erica took his hand. "They're ready for you."

"Who?" he asked, resisting a moment, surprised by how strong she was. "Sam or Balam?"

She smiled seductively. "Come with me and find out."

Reluctantly, Lakesh allowed himself to be led away from the map of the global energy grid. He figured he had studied it for long enough. More than half an hour before he, Sam and Erica materialized in a gateway unit with rich, golden walls, as if ingots had been melted down and applied to the armaglass like molten paint.

Outside the chamber was a stone-block-walled, low-ceilinged corridor. Lakesh had no idea where they were. When he asked if they were in Agartha, where Kane and Brigid had left Balam, neither of his companions gave him a definite answer. Regardless, he sensed they were deep underground, beneath inestimable tons of rock.

The location was of secondary importance as far as Lakesh was concerned. If Erica and Sam had wanted to kill him, they could've done so during the many hours he spent alone with them in the Cerberus redoubt. They certainly would not have had to cajole, argue and finally plead with him to accompany them on a mat-trans jaunt.

Most of his questions about Balam, Sam's origins and particularly Erica's restored youth had been neatly deflected. Both Sam and Erica were adept at teasing him with hints and inferences about an undertaking that would forever change the nuke-scarred face of the planet. They wanted his involvement, but they refused to reveal anything but tantalizing scraps of information.

Lakesh couldn't help but be intrigued. He was suspicious of both of them, especially Erica, but she answered all of his questions about the inner workings of the Totality Concept and the personnel involved without hesitation. At length he accepted she was who she claimed to be and he agreed to accompany them to their unnamed destination, where not only Balam awaited him but also where he would find answers to his questions.

Over the strenuous and profane objections put forth by DeFore, Bry and even Banks, Lakesh entered a set of coordinates provided by Erica in the gateway's keypad and away they went. He felt a little guilty about leaving Cerberus while the fates of Domi and Kane were still unknown, but both Erica and Sam vowed to return him in twelve hours. He believed them, and he didn't know why.

Although he experienced a strong physical attraction for the woman, he found it required a great deal of mental effort to refuse Sam anything or question anything he said. The boy possessed exceptionally strong powers of persuasion and whether it was just charisma or something else, Lakesh was completely charmed by him. Actually, he was more than charmed—he trusted him and felt protective of him in a paternal way.

To his everlasting regret, Lakesh had never married or fathered children. The closest he came to producing offspring was when he rifled the ville's genetic records to find desirable qualifications in order to build a covert resistance movement against the baronies. He used the baron's own fixation with purity control against them. By his own confession, he was a physicist cast in the role of an archivist, pretending to be a geneticist, manipulating a political system that was still in a state of flux. Kane was one such example of that political and genetic manipulation.

Erica van Sloan strode purposefully down the pas-

sageway, taking long-legged strides, her boot heels
clacking in a steady rhythm against the stone floor.
Lakesh could not reconcile his memories of the withered, crippled old hag with the tall, vibrant and beautiful woman he followed. He shook his head a little
remorsefully as he watched the sensuous twitch of her
buttocks beneath the tight jodhpurs. She had a body
built for sex and if she was attempting to entice him
with her restored youth and vitality, it was a cruel
game.

Erica stepped through an open doorway. Lakesh
followed her and came to a halt, blinking owlishly at
the furnishings of the room. It wasn't so much the
lavish appointments that startled him as the sensation
of stepping back in time several thousand years into
a central clearinghouse of several ancient cultures.

A tall, round sandstone pillar bearing ornate carv-
ings of birds and animal heads was bracketed by two
large sculptures, one a feathered jaguar and the other
a serpent with wings. Silken tapestries depicting
Asian ideographs hung from the walls. There were
other tapestries, all bearing flowing geometric designs.

Suspended from the ceiling by thin steel wires was
a huge gold disk in the form of the Re-Horakhte fal-
con. The upcurving wings were inlaid with colored
glass. The sun disk atop the beaked head was a cab-
ochon-cut carnelian.

Ceramic effigy jars and elegantly crafted vessels
depicting animal-headed gods and goddesses from the
Egyptian pantheon were stacked in neat pyramids. Ar-

rayed on a long shelf on the opposite wall were a dozen ushabtis figures, small statuettes representing laborers in the Land of the Dead. Against the right wall was a granite twelve-foot-tall replica of the seated figure of Ramses III. It towered over a cluster of dark basalt blocks inscribed with deep rune markings.

A huge, gilt-framed mirror, at least ten feet tall and five wide, stood amid stacks of weaponry—swords, shields and lances. A spearhead with a single drop of blood on its nicked point rested on a table.

The center and corners of the floor were crammed with artifacts from every possible time, every culture—Inca, Maya, China, Egypt and others Lakesh could not quickly identify. He wasn't even sure if he wanted to, since he had believed some the relics were pure myth, such as the mirror of Prester John and the Spear of Destiny.

Each and every item appeared to be in perfect condition. The huge room was an archaeologist's paradise. Lakesh struggled to comprehend the enormity of the collection and why it was here. Finally, he realized it was a representative sampling from every human culture ever influenced by the race he knew as Archons.

He looked around, trying to find Balam in the collection. For an instant he thought he spotted him, then realized it was only a statue that closely resembled him. Standing in an erect position, less than five feet tall, the sculpture represented a humanoid creature with a slender, gracile build draped in robes. The features were sharp, the domed head disproportionately large and hairless. The eyes were huge, slanted and fathomless. Cradled in its six-fingered hands was what appeared to be a human infant.

Lakesh repressed a shudder and nearly jumped straight up when he felt a light touch on his arm. He spun clumsily to see Sam beaming up at him. Forcing an aggrieved note into his voice, he said, "You took ten years off my life, and at my age I can ill afford to squander even an hour of it."

Sam's cherubic smile broadened. "Perhaps we'll do something about that, Mohandas."

Lakesh felt a distant unease at the comfortable way the boy called him by his first name, but he didn't comment on it. "Where is Balam?"

"You'll see him once you're convinced."

"Convinced of what, young man?" Lakesh demanded in his best authoritarian tone.

"Of who I am," Sam answered blandly. "Of the energies flowing through me."

Erica stepped up to Lakesh and caressed his deeply seamed cheek with cool, soft fingers. Teasingly, she said, "You've been consumed with curiosity about how Sam restored me, haven't you?"

"Among other things," Lakesh retorted gruffly. "Least of all why you refer to him as your son."

Erica chuckled. "First things first, Mohandas. Secrets must be revealed in the order of their importance."

"Secrets?"

"The first secret is energy," Sam stated. "It always

has been, always will be. The science of moving it in precise harmony and in perfect balance, harmonizing it with other forms of energy.''

Lakesh bobbed his head in irritated impatience. ''You're not telling me anything I haven't spent my entire adult life studying.''

''Perhaps,'' Sam replied calmly. ''But studying and understanding all the principles and applications are often very different things.''

Lakesh bristled at the boy's patronizing tone. He drew on an untapped reservoir of strength and managed to work himself up to a high state of annoyance, despite Sam's powers of persuasion. ''Demonstrate what you mean or I'm leaving.''

The corners of Sam's mouth turned down in a frown. ''You've come too far to dictate terms, Mohandas. I want you to understand what I am. I am an avatar.''

Chill fingers of dread stroked the buttons of Lakesh's spine. ''An avatar of what?''

''There must be an order to things. If war is necessary for that order to be established, then I am willing to wage it. But you must teach me certain things, make me more than I am.''

''I know nothing of war.''

''But you know deception, do you not? Is not all war based on deception, on misdirection and misinformation?''

Lakesh dredged his memory and came up with a quote from Sun Tzu. '''Use deception when you have not the power to win in open battle,' " he said quietly.

Sam nodded. "Exactly. You have followed that philosophy in your war against the baronies. I can learn much from you."

"And if you win your war, what kind of order do you intend to build?"

"One where the old humans and the new humans rally around me, the bridge between both, and coexist peacefully."

Lakesh gazed into the boy's eyes of many colors and felt a little ill and frightened. He sensed the king's robes around the child even if he could not see them. But he also sensed Sam was either cursed or blessed with something outside the pale of normal humanity—or inhumanity. Hoarsely, he inquired, "Coexist under your single authority?"

Sam's frown deepened as if he were irritated by Lakesh stating the obvious. "Of course. I thought you understood that."

Lakesh exhaled a weary breath. "I understand, Sam. You're just another damn megalomaniac, another mutie with an attitude." He turned toward the door. "I don't know what powers you have, but it's obvious you lured me here under the pretense of a meeting with Balam. He's not and probably never has been here. You disappoint me."

Lakesh caught only a glimpse of Sam making a flicking hand gesture, then Erica van Sloan was on him, securing a hammerlock on his right arm and wrenching it up between his shoulder blades. She kicked the backs of his knees and his legs buckled. Crying out in pain and outrage, Lakesh collapsed. Only Erica's surprising strength prevented him from falling on his face. Into his ear she murmured, "I'm sorry about this, Mohandas, but you'll thank me when it's over."

He struggled, but she cinched down even tighter on his captured arm. "When what is over?" he brayed.

Sam stepped toward him, pulling back the belled right sleeve of his robe. In a very soft, sympathetic tone he said, "When I'm finished moving energy in precise harmony and perfect balance."

Sam spread his right hand wide and laid it against Lakesh's midriff. From it seeped a tingling warmth. Ice seemed to melt his body and he felt painfully searing heat, like liquid fire, rippling through his veins and arteries. His heartbeat picked up in tempo, seeming to spread the heart through the rest of his body, a pulsing web of energy suffusing every separate cell and organ. He squeezed his eyes shut.

Lakesh's lungs gave a jerking, labored spasm as they sucked in air involuntarily, expanding so much in his chest he feared his ribs would break. His mouth opened and a scream came forth, but his voice was not reedy or strained. The cry was a full-bodied utterance of pain. He was aflame with it, the same kind of agony a man feels when circulation is suddenly restored to a numb limb. His back arched, and for the first time in more than fifty years, he felt a stirring in his loins. His entire metabolism seemed to awaken to furious life from a long slumber, as if it had been jump-started by a powerful battery.

The heat faded from his body, and he sagged within Erica's grip, panting and sweating. She released him and he caught himself on his hands. Slowly, Lakesh opened his eyes. They burned slightly, feeling somewhat sticky, but his vision was not blurred or fogged. He tried to push himself up, but his body felt like a foreign thing, and it moved sluggishly.

Erica said softly, "Careful now, Mohandas. Take it easy at first."

Carefully, she helped him to his feet. His legs wobbled like those of a newborn foal. When he raised a hand to wipe away the film of perspiration on his face, he realized two things more or less simultaneously— he wasn't wearing his glasses but he could see his hand perfectly. By that perfect vision, he saw the flesh of his hand was smooth, the prominent veins having sunk back into firm flesh. The liver spots faded away even as he watched.

Wildly, Lakesh stumbled toward the huge mirror. He nearly fell twice, but Erica helped him along. He stood before it, stupefied into silence. The face reflected in its glossy surface bore little resemblance to the one that looked as if he had borrowed it from a cadaver. His hair, though still thin, was not ash gray, but an iron color. It seemed to darken with every passing second. Uttering a wordless cry of wonder, Lakesh brought his hands up to his cheeks, his fingertips exploring the smooth, unseamed cheeks.

A voice spoke from behind him, hoarse, faint and

scratchy. "Now we will speak of the future, Mohandas Lakesh Singh."

The familiar voice sent cold prickles up and down his backbone. Slowly, he turned, keeping his expression as neutral and composed as possible.

A figure stood beside Sam, dressed in a similar robe. Lakesh gazed without blinking at the high, domed cranium that narrowed to an elongated chin. The faint grayish-pink skin was stretched drum tight over a structure of facial bones that seemed all cheek and brow, with little in between but two great upslanting eyes like black pools. The slit of a mouth held the faintest suggestion of a smile.

"Yes, Balam," said Lakesh gravely. "We must speak of the future and my place in it."

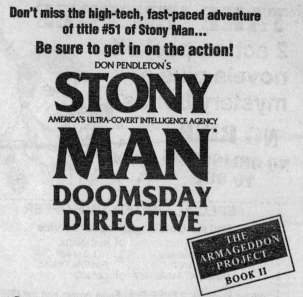

She Felt A Comforting Warmth Spreading Through Her . . .

Brandy knew it was dangerous, this peaceful sleepy feeling. But it was so much better than the earlier pain of the cold. No, she wouldn't move now; it was so nice here. The snow went on about its gentle business of covering her.

Someone was pulling at her, shaking her, picking her up. Her blood poured like fire, searing its way back into her frozen limbs. She screamed in protest.

Grey's face was close to hers. "I've got to get you back."

She remembered the child lost in the storm, and the shivering started again, adding agony. "Missy's out here. I couldn't find her. Oh, Grey, I couldn't find her."

She slipped from the jarring pain of being carried into darkness. She did not feel Grey's strong hands holding her fiercely against his own warmth; she did not hear him repeating her name over and over.

The
Night Child

Celeste De Blasis

BANTAM BOOKS
TORONTO · NEW YORK · LONDON · SYDNEY · AUCKLAND

All the characters in this book are fictitious, and any resemblance to actual persons living or dead is purely coincidental.

This low-priced Bantam Book has been completely reset in a type face designed for easy reading, and was printed from new plates. It contains the complete text of the original hard-cover edition.

THE NIGHT CHILD

A Bantam Book / published by arrangement with the author

PRINTING HISTORY

Bantam edition / March 1986

ISBN 0–553–25458–8

Published simultaneously in the United States and Canada

Bantam Books are published by Bantam Books, Inc. Its trademark, consisting of the words "Bantam Books" and the portrayal of a rooster, is Registered in U.S. Patent and Trademark Office and in other countries. Marca Registrada. Bantam Books, Inc., 666 Fifth Avenue, New York, New York 10103.

With love and thanks
   To my parents
      for giving me space,
   To my grandmother
      for teaching me to see,
   And to my brother
      for believing.
Ciao, Captain Nirvana. Sail on.

Acknowledgments

I trust that the background research for this book does not intrude on the reader's pleasure. The story was written to amuse, not to present a lecture in history or in childhood behavior. However, when one writes outside one's own century, locale, and knowledge, debts of gratitude are incurred, and so it is with *The Night Child*.

To my friends in San Francisco, particularly to Jeffrey B. Leith, I owe much for their eternal pride in their city, their joy in its past and present, and their ability to make each day of its existence live in the instant.

To Kathy Poncy I owe my gratitude for her deep dedication to autistic children and for her generous sharing of her hard-earned knowledge.

But my deepest thanks goes to my aunt, Donna Pollard Campbell, and her brother, C. Owen Pollard, who began my love affair with Maine with the strange, beautiful cadence of their words and the luminous memories of their Down East childhood.

CHAPTER I

Brandy trembled from her effort to control the waves of laughter washing up toward sound. The voice of Mr. Ponsby droned on, speaking for the directors of the school, enumerating her sins against decency: She had taught unexpurgated Shakespeare, pouring ancient obscenities into young minds; she had stated that there were valid beliefs in religions other than Christianity; she had introduced Mr. Darwin's theory of the Origin of Species to the children; she had destroyed the discipline of Greenfield Academy, turning well-behaved students into disobedient fiends. And worst of all, she had been observed wearing trousers and engaging in horse racing on a Sunday.

The trousers and the racing were sins aplenty; the day of the week damned her for sure. She put her handkerchief to her mouth, trying to turn a giggle into a cough. It was absurd—all that destructive power attributed to her. They would never see that their collective narrow-mindedness and bigotry made them vulnerable. That was pathetic because it would be passed on to the children. But Mr. Ponsby's being the one to dismiss her, Lord, that was amusing! There he was, speaking ponderously in his good citizen's voice, the same paunchy little man who eyed every young woman hungrily, who terrified his wife and daughter,

1

who tithed at church and charged double for the dry goods he sold.

Brandy tried to think of something sad, something which would lend her dignity of a serious expression. Her mind went back a year to her father's death, but it was no use. His legacy was what was tripping her up now, that constant appreciation of the foolishness of human behavior.

The voice had now moved to her general moral tone and was receiving a hum of agreement that it wasn't good.

Her eyes wandered over the faces in the small room. Most of the expressions were tight-lipped, forbidding, but here and there she saw friendly ones, translated into sadness because, though they did not believe her guilty, they would not risk anything to prove her worthy and keep her on.

She stopped her inventory. At the back of the room was a stranger, glaringly obvious because everyone in the smallness of Greenfield was familiar. He was leaning negligently against the wall; when he stood, he would be very tall. He was well dressed. His shock of black hair and his straight black brows did nothing to soften the arrogant sculpture of his face—the prominent cheekbones underscored with hollows, the high-bridge nose, the heavily carved mouth, and the decisive angle of chin. Harsh lines had etched away youth. He looked like the devil come to a church social. The distance between them was short enough for Brandy to see that he too was amused. Her own impulse to laugh died abruptly.

Ponsby's voice was impatient; he must have asked the question several times. "Well, Miss Claybourne, what have you to say for yourself?"

Nothing would do any good. They had no intention of allowing her to remain. They simply wanted to hear an apology which would confirm their charges. Brandy wasn't sorry. Her voice was quiet and even, words dropping like stones into the silent room.

"Mr. Ponsby, ladies and gentlemen. Ignorance is excusable when there has been no opportunity to remedy it; pride in one's ignorance is never excusable. This is eighteen hundred and sixty-nine, the Dark Ages ended years ago in most places; apparently they are to continue at Greenfield. New ideas, new theories, and knowledge of foreign cultures and alien ways of thought are not harmful, but suppression of them is. The bloodiest wars in history have been fought because of intolerance. And unfortunately, there will always be people such as you who are willing to continue the wars.

"There is no hope for you—your minds are rigid with the hate and fear of anything new. The tragedy is that you will inflict your narrow visions on your children, and they will perpetuate your ignorance. Even had I the opportunity, I would not continue to teach in such an atmosphere. You have done me a great service by dismissing me."

Voices rose in outrage as Brandy made her way out of the room. Her height served her well. She held herself proudly erect, walked slowly, and stared coolly down at the contorted faces. She heard the comments and did not flinch. "What, that slut, how dare she?" "To think she has been allowed near our children." "Should never have been hired. She's from the West; just goes to show you how uncivilized they are out there."

At the door she stopped and turned, making her voice loud enough for all to hear. "By the way, I am sure you must be wondering about the race. I won."

She heard a shout of laughter amid the angry buzz, but she did not pause or look his way. Once in the corridor, she felt her knees giving way, but she made it outside to lean against one of the massive pillars of the portico, thinking irrelevantly that the Greeks would have hated their architecture to be used in a place of so little enlightenment.

Well, now you've really done it, she thought. *There will be references all right, all bad. Just try to find another teaching post. How delighted Aunt Beatrice*

*will be that I finally got my comeuppance—that's what
I can't bear to think about—leaving the Adamses' house
to go back to live with Aunt Beatrice.*

She was startled by the voice beside her. "Miss
Claybourne, I am Grey King." His voice was deep with
a strange drawl which sounded almost British. His
handshake was firm, and even though she was eight
inches over five feet, he towered above her. His eyes
were so dark, pupil and iris merged. The devil indeed
and still looking amused, at her expense.

"I hope you enjoyed my performance!" she snapped,
and glared at him.

"I did. I wouldn't have missed it for the world. But I
did not follow you out here to congratulate you. I would
like to offer you a job."

Brandy stared up at him suspiciously. "Doing what?"

"Teaching, of course," he said impatiently, and Brandy
was about to ask him if he was mad or just cruel, but
the change in him stopped her. All humor was gone,
the lines cutting deeper, his face a graven mask with
glittering eyes. Brandy felt a tremor of fear and resisted
the impulse to step back.

The sound was harsh. "I'm not offering you another
Greenfield. I'm offering you what I think is an impossible
job with one pupil. I have a daughter. Melissa is five
years old, but she has not spoke since my wife died two
years ago. She does not play; she does nothing but rock
and stare. I have taken her to doctors, and they all
agree it is hopeless. They think it would be for the best
if she were put in an asylum. I have had a succession of
governesses, but none of them has been able to reach
her, and they have all left with great relief. My home is
in an isolated spot in the state of Maine. I will pay you
double what you've been paid here, but if you come,
you must agree to stay for at least six months. Do you
want the position?"

Brandy tried to sort it out—a strange offer to work
with a deranged child in the middle of nowhere or
going back to live with Aunt Beatrice in her cheerless

house in noisy Boston. And how had this man known she was to be fired?

He saw the question before she asked it; maybe he was more than a little like the devil. "George Adams is an old friend. He's seen Missy, and he knows the problems I've had keeping anyone to work with her. I saw him in Boston yesterday and told him I was trying to find another woman. With reluctance he told me about your situation. He too thinks Missy's condition is incurable, and he made it clear that he would prefer you did not get involved. But in fairness, he thought you should have the chance to decide."

Brandy was getting her wind back. Unconsciously she assumed what her father had called her "let's find some trouble stance"—head up, chin out, eyes wide and deceptively innocent, feet apart and planted firmly in unladylike strength to meet all comers. "Mr. King, you sound as if you hope I will not take the job, but you're out of luck. I accept, and I agree to the six months' clause. But you must understand that I have never taught a child such as yours, and there is every possibility that not only may I not be able to help her, but I might make her worse. If that is the case, I'll not hold you to the time limit if you wish me to leave."

Satisfaction gleamed in the obsidian eyes, and he said, more to himself than to her, "Perhaps I've finally found what Missy needs, someone who is willing to fight for her." Then in a brisker tone: "Can you be ready to leave by tomorrow?"

"Yes," she said without hesitation, not asking how they were to travel or whether she would be properly chaperoned. The quirk of his eyebrows told her he had noticed the omission. She reflected glumly that she would never look or behave like a governess. She liked the feeling of moving freely like a colt sure of quick-springing muscles; sedate steps were beyond her. On her neck she could feel the tendrils of hair which had escaped from the briefly decorous chignon. Her hair was the color of her name, a rich red brown, a strange combination with her tawny eyes, wide-spaced and almond-long under arching brows. Her nose was straight, her mouth full and red. She always felt too earthy, too brightly colored around the small, round women of fashion.

Mr. King's eyes moved over every detail of her appearance and gleamed suddenly as though in appreciation of a private joke.

She broke his silence. "Well, have you finished your survey? Do you think I'll do? You look as if you're buying a horse."

His smile softened the grim lines, but Brandy was aware again of her uneasiness. Under the disciplined exterior there was a volcano, and though she wasn't afraid of many things, she guessed his anger, if it were ever unleashed, would be terrible. "I apologize, Miss Claybourne, my mind was wandering."

He escorted her back to the Adamses' house, making arrangements for the next day as they walked. He would return with a carriage to pick her up, and they would leave Boston on his schooner for the trip to Maine. *Private schooner*, thought Brandy, *what am I getting myself into?* But outwardly she accepted the instructions calmly.

The Adamses' house was a rambling affair which had been built on a farm and had then seen Greenfield grow into a stately little village with easy access to Boston. The oaks and maples around it were bright with autumn, and Brandy felt a pang about leaving. The Adamses had become family, and Hugh would have liked the relationship to be closer than that. But she could not take advantage of them, remaining there without a job. Dorothea was all the help her husband, George, and son, Hugh, needed in dealing with their patients. And no school for miles around would hire Brandy now.

Dorothea saw them coming up the walk and came out to greet them. The number of carriages and horses indicated that the doctors were having a busy day, as usual, but Mrs. Adams invited Grey to stay for the evening meal, telling him he could relax in the library until then.

"Thank you, Dorothea, I would like to accept, but I brought a guest with me. She's been shopping in Boston and will expect me to dine with her tonight."

"Ruth?" asked Mrs Adams.

"Who else?"

"Grey King, why don't you marry that girl and make a decent woman of her? You've had long enough to get to know each other." Trust Dorothea to say what she was thinking. She spoke to him as though he were a young boy; obviously they had known each other for years, and he did not frighten her.

"What a novel idea. I'll think about it," he said sarcastically.

"You're impossible, and I'm busy." She gave him a hu_ and went back into the house.

He had left his horse hitched to the rail, and when Brandy saw the beautiful bay, she gave a low whistle of appreciation and saw Grey's renewed amusement— a governess who whistled. It was a wonder Greenfield had not listed that among her sins.

"Yours?" she asked, running her hands gently over the horse's face and rubbing behind his ears as she spoke softly to him.

Grey's amazement showed plainly. Calaban was not a friendly animal and usually rolled his eyes and nipped at strangers, but now he was hanging his head with an idiotic look of contentment.

"He's out of my stock, but he belongs to a friend in Boston who is kind enough to let me use him when I'm up this way. Sorry, but I can't lend him to you for any races," he added as he mounted in one easy movement from ground to saddle.

Brandy stepped back, and Grey looked down at her. "I'd better get him back before he falls asleep and I have to carry him. See you in the morning."

She watched him leave, watched the road for a long thoughtful moment before she went in.

Her packing did not take long. She was not in the habit of collecting things casually. Her books and music went in first, followed by her small wardrobe. Defiantly she put her Levi's on top of the dresses. Her special treasures from the West went on top—the gown from Pearl, the jade pendant from Chen Lee, and the watch and gold nugget from her father.

She saw Dorothea first in the hour before supper, but her questions were forestalled. "My dear, you've decided to take the post Grey offered. I can't say I'm pleased about it; I would like you to stay with us, with Hugh especially, forever, but you are as stubborn as ever either of your parents were, and I know it would be useless to try to dissuade you. And I know there are things you would like to know about Grey, but I'm not the one to tell you. Let George do it."

Mrs. Adams was not the crying sort, but she gave a surreptitious wipe at her eyes as she bustled off, and Brandy realized how much of a mother this busy little woman had been to her.

She saw Hugh next as he came down the hall which linked the office with the rest of the house. Hugh, blond, laughing Hugh, dependable and kind, favorite with all of his patients from the youngest to the oldest. He look so safe after Mr. King. Why couldn't she love Hugh, settle down with him, have his children?

He caught her by the shoulders and held her, looking at her with the same penetrating gaze he used when he was diagnosing a case.

"I haven't got the measles or any other contagion," she protested, feeling uncomfortable under his eyes.

"I know. You haven't caught me either, and I've done my best to make sure you did. I can tell, you're really leaving us, leaving me. I am going to try to be civilized about the whole thing, but it isn't easy. I love you, Brandy, you know that. I want you to marry me, and that's nothing new either. I don't want you going off to the wilds of Maine to live under King's roof with his incurable child. I haven't seen her, but Father has, and he doesn't think there is a chance she will ever be normal.

"Please stay. I'm sure we can find another job for you, and I promise not to push about us. I am responsible for your losing your position. If I hadn't let you race Blue, this would never have happened."

"Don't be silly, Hugh. It was my idea, and besides, the race was just the last in a long series of my sins. I'm quite certain they were already thinking of letting me go at the end of last year. They're just so slow that it took them until now to add everything up and decide. Anyway, I'm determined to take this new job, and I won't be told that the child is hopeless until I've seen for myself. But from the way you talk, there's something I ought to know about Mr. King which no one has told me yet."

Hugh shook his head ruefully. "No, it's just plain old jealousy. Oh, I've heard he's been a bit of a rakehell but never with anyone who wasn't willing. I don't know him that well. He's nine or ten years older than I, and Father knows him much better than I do."

He kissed her gently on the forehead and drew her against him. "Darling, I am going to let you go because I haven't any choice in the matter. But I'm going to hope that you won't like it there, that you'll come back. I want you to promise that you won't hesitate to get in touch with me if you need me or if you want to come home."

He tipped her head back, and Brandy saw the concern in his eyes. She smiled at him. "I promise I'll give a yell that you'll hear down here if I need you."

He kissed her on the mouth, not gently, and let her go. "That's to remind you of how I feel," he said, his voice suddenly rough. He left her standing there wondering why such a marvelous man stirred no more than feelings of friendship in her. *Be honest, Brandy, he's too safe, and life with him would be much too even and easy, and you must be mad not to want that.*

Nine or ten years older than Hugh—that meant Mr. King was thirty-five or thirty-six. Her mind supplied the figures automatically, quickly dismissing Hugh, intent on Grey King.

The evening meal lacked its usual casual conversation and gaiety. Brandy's imminent departure hung so heavily in the atmosphere that she thought if something didn't happen soon, she was going to burst into tears like a child and flee the table. But what happened did not make things any easier.

In the middle of the meal, Mrs. Ponsby and her daughter, Judith, came to tell Brandy good-bye, bringing with them a bouquet of late flowers and a letter signed by her pupils saying how much they would miss her, how much they had liked her as a teacher. The letter was written in Judith's careful hand, and Brandy recognized the individual signing of each child's name. She was speechless, not only from the sweetness of the children's gesture, but because Mrs. Ponsby had had the courage to come. Her husband would make life hellish for her if he found out.

The nervous little woman saw her concern and rushed into speech, giving Brandy time. "Miss Claybourne, I just had to come. Judith and the other children thought of the letter all by themselves. They are so distraught that you are leaving. And I'm ashamed that it was my husband who did it."

Brandy answered huskily, "You have no idea how much this means to me. As long as the children were happy and learned something, none of the rest matters. And your husband was only the spokesman; the decision was made by several people. You aren't to blame. I have a new job already. I'm leaving tomorrow, but I won't forget you."

She saw the tears welling in Judith's eyes, and she knelt down and drew her close. "Judith, you have a wonderful mind. Go on learning everything you can, and try to like your next teacher. As long as you can read about new places and new ideas, you'll be free and nothing can really hurt you." Including your father, she added silently. She stroked the little girl's hair, and the tears stopped. Judith gave her a quick, shy kiss, took her mother's hand, and they were gone.

Brandy had no stomach to finish the meal, and Dr. Adams didn't either. He rose from the table and took Brandy with him to his study, leaving Hugh and Dorothea looking preoccupied and sad.

Brandy loved old Dr. George. He was nothing like her flamboyant father except that they both carried about them the same air of authority and concern for the well-being of their patients.

He settled himself in his chair, rumpled his white hair in his characteristic way, and lit his pipe before he began. "My dear child, I am not going to try to talk you into staying; I'm sure Hugh and Dorothea have already covered that ground thoroughly. But I am going to claim a sentimental old man's privilege to be maudlin for a minute.

"Your father was ever a direct man. When he persuaded you to come East, he knew he was dying. I had not heard from him more than a few times since he and your mother headed for California, but I loved them both, and it was a personal loss when I learned that your mother had died so soon after their arrival, so soon after your birth.

"Of you I knew very little. When his last letter arrived, I didn't know what to think. He said that because of family ties, he was sending you to your mother's sister, Beatrice, but that he was quite sure it would not work. Kathryn was never like Beatrice; she was always wild and willful, enchanting, and ready for any adventure. Beatrice has been purse-lipped and frightened of God's wrath since birth. Your father knew you resembled your mother too much to get along with your aunt, but he felt honor-bound to give her the first chance of providing you with a home. You see, he considered it a privilege, he loved you so much. But he was honest. The letter to me explained that he had reared a girl who was as wild as the country she was born in. Dorothea and I didn't know what to think, and frankly, we dreaded the day when we might become responsible for you. When you got in touch with us because you were unhappy with your aunt and had gotten the job at the academy, our hearts sank. But the rest you know. Within twenty-four hours we had both fallen in love with you. We always wanted a daughter, and we could not love you more or be more pleased with you even if you were our own. We will always feel that way, and this will always be your home."

Brandy sat quietly with her hands in her lap, making no effort to wipe away the tears.

Dr. George continued: "Of all that they gave you, Brandy, the finest gift from your parents is your honesty. You laugh and cry and love with no pretense. What happened at the academy should leave no stigma on you, only on the power that caused your dismissal. Some people find honesty and an open mind intolerable affronts, but that is their loss, not yours. And you have my deepest gratitude for the way you have treated Hugh. Perhaps in the future you will come to love him, but you do not now, and you have not led him to believe that you do. To choose the truth over a comfortable offer of marriage is something few women do. Kathryn did." His voice had a sudden tightness, and Brandy glanced at him quickly, trying to see him clearly through the blur of tears. He swallowed and went on more evenly. "She was wise to do so. She liked me very much, but she adored your father. And I learned to love Dorothea deeply, to know that she was the woman to share my peaceful existence, to be happy with one place and never want to cross the mountains. Your mother and father were both born wanting to know what was on the other side."

The silence stretched on, but it was not uneasy. Brandy's tears had stopped with her startling new knowledge of Dr. Adams. She could see his face clearly now, and she knew he was seeing her parents as he remembered them, with love. His voice was pensive when he began to speak again.

"King and his daughter seem to be your next mountain, a very difficult climb. I knew Grey's father, and I've known Grey since he was small. He is a man of great wealth and power, but little joy. Too many things have happened to make him bitter. But I knew him when he was young and full of laughter and high spirits, in spite of the fact that his parents died of cholera when he was only eighteen, and he had to step into his father's shoes. His mother was always frail, but the death of his father was a real shock. Now all his energy goes into his empire. He owns shipyards, textile and lumber mills, granite quarries, breeding farms for fine horses, and just about anything else you could name. He drives himself relentlessly, probably because he doesn't want to think too much about his daughter or her mother." His face assumed the brooding expression of the times when he had patients who were beyond his help.

"Greg's wife was a girl named Jasmine Lavelle. She was from New Orleans." He saw Brandy's expression of surprise. "Oh, yes, strangely enough, because of the cotton trade, the ties between Maine shipowners and the South were very strong before the war, closer in many cases than between Maine and the rest of New England.

"Grey met Jasmine in New Orleans, fell in love with her, and married her against her family's wishes—they had no use for Yankees, and she was only seventeen. He brought her north to live and as far as I know, she never visited the South again. Of course, the war came and broke communications, but from what little I know, Jasmine had no desire to see her people again anyway. I met her only once when Grey brought her to Boston. She was very beautiful, but not likable. She was one of those women who radiate discontent. She had nothing but contempt for the provincialism of Maine, and she talked incessantly about how much she missed a civilized social life. Grey bore it in good humor because he loved her and because he believed that love would be enough to make her happy.

"Then when the war came, Grey was nearly killed at Gettysburg. He was sent home to die, but he was just too stubborn. And about a year later the little girl was born. I don't know too much about those three years with Missy, but from what I gather, the marriage went along with the child as the center. At least in that Jasmine was normal. Mutual friends said that both parents adored the child, whatever their personal problems were. But those problems certainly existed. Grey has a brother, Raleigh, and he seemed to have been involved. He's younger, gay, charming, and financially dependent on Grey. He didn't go to war, and perhaps he kept the home fires burning too brightly. There were rumors that he and Jasmine were much too close in Grey's absence. I've met Raleigh a few times, and he is a hard man to hate, so I have no idea whether or not there was any truth in the gossip. Jasmine was the type who would have liked to create a scandalous reputation whether or not it had any basis in fact.

"What is important is that what little remained of Grey's youth after the war was shattered in one night. I don't think anyone will ever know what actually happened. Grey had been home, but apparently he was not when the fire started."

"Fire," echoed Brandy stupidly. She was having a difficult time connecting everything Dr. George was saying with the man she had met so briefly and accepted a job from so quickly.

His words were steady. "The fire that killed Jasmine. God knows why she was in the stables late at night when they burned to the ground. No one knows how the fire started. What is known is that Jasmine died that night, and the little girl has not spoken since. Whether that is simply because her mother died so suddenly or because she saw her die in the fire is not known either. But I've seen the child, and my diagnosis is that she will never be healed. Maybe in the future we will discover how to persuade such children to come back into the world, but we don't know how yet, and all I can foresee for you is frustration and sorrow."

All Brandy could see at the moment was pity for Mr. King, and the last part of the gruesome tale brought him into even sharper focus.

"I would rather not tell you, but I think you ought to be warned. The stableman swore that Grey did not arrive until the fire was roaring and that he made valiant attempts to save the horses and thus found his wife's body. But the story persists that he murdered her. I do not believe it; from what I know of Grey, it is impossible. But even I must allow that strong emotion can make the sanest man unstable."

His voice died away. Brandy got up and put her arms around him. "I love you as I loved my father," was all she could manage, but by his look it was enough. She went up to her room without seeking out Dorothea or Hugh; there was no sense in making the parting harder by more anxious time together.

She was exhausted by the events of the day, but she did not sleep peacefully. She had learned too much too soon about Grey King, and it was impossible to reconcile the separate images of that arrogant devil of a man with one who had suffered so much and might have committed murder out of desperate love.

CHAPTER II

By the time Mr. King arrived the next morning Brandy was anxious to be on her way. It was one of the things her father had emphasized from the time she was small—to make decisions courageously and, once having made them, not to fret. She was going to Maine, and nothing would be gained by prolonging her departure or wondering if she was doing the proper thing. She kissed the Adamses good-bye, ignored their looks of concern, promised to keep in touch, and gave Dr. George a note to be delivered to her aunt when next he went to Boston. She had no intention of hearing her aunt's opinion of what she had decided to do.

Beyond a brief "good morning," Mr. King said very little, though Brandy had felt him watching as she made her farewells. Now driving out of Greenfield, he confirmed this. "Are you sure you want this job, Miss Claybourne? Obviously Hugh Adams feels more than brotherly affection for you. Or perhaps that is why you are putting such a distance between the two of you?"

Brandy's compassion for the man evaporated. "Mr. King, I have taken the job with no regrets. I am looking forward to teaching your daughter. But my private life is entirely my own, and I'll thank you to keep out of it."

His reaction was not what she expected; she suspected

his responses would never be predictable. He laughed, turning his attention from the horses he was driving to her. "Point taken. And I knew you wouldn't wear a bustle."

The *non sequitur* amused her, and she joined his laughter. She knew very well that the russet of her traveling costume set off her coloring and that there had been approval, not offense, in his comment. "Silly things, I hate them," she said. "They make women so impractical; even sitting down is a chore. You talk more like the Western men I knew than an Easterner. Most of the men here are afraid God will strike them dead if they so much as think about an undergarment, let alone mention it."

"What kind of men did you know in the West?" he asked, and she started to bristle again but then realized he was really curious, not just prying, and that he had a right to know something about her background.

"I knew miners, gamblers, sea captains, farmers, horse thieves, doctors, and lawyers, just about any kind you could name, good and bad. But most of them shared one thing—they were kind and gentle to me while I was growing up, and a lot of them helped to raise me. You see, my mother came with my father to California in forty-nine, and she was already carrying me when they boarded the ship, but she didn't tell my father for fear he would cancel the trip. He was a good doctor, but she was over thirty, and up till then there had been no sign of a child, so perhaps that made it easier to keep it from him. It was a long, hard voyage, and it ruined her health. In spite of all he could do, she died in childbirth a few months after they arrived. Women and children were as rare in San Francisco as the mother lode in those days, and the few there were treated as exotic creatures who needed protecting. Father used to tell stories of miners who offered gold dust just to kiss a woman or hold a child because they missed their own families left in the East.

"I think you have the right to know something else. The first women who arrived in any numbers were what you would expect, prostitutes and dance hall girls, and many of them helped bring me up, too. One in particular who called herself Pearl Orient was the closest thing I had to a mother." Brandy caught his look of sympathy. "Oh, don't think that! Pearl was wonderful, and so was my childhood. As far as I know no one knew Pearl's real name or where exactly in the East she had come from, and nobody cared. She ran a saloon in front of her building and had rooms with girls in the back. Her house was clean and honest, and even the girls who worked for her liked her. We stayed there when we were in San Francisco. Father never set up a practice; he was sort of a traveling medicine man going from one isolated camp to the next, and how glad they all were to see him. Pearl gave us a home when we were in the city; we wouldn't have had one otherwise. When I left two years ago, she had long since retired and was living in a beautiful house overlooking the bay, and Father still stayed with her when he was in San Francisco. She was the one who wrote to tell me that he was dead, that he had died peacefully in her arms."

Two years ago, that was when Grey's wife had died, not peacefully but in an inferno. Brandy went on quickly.

"Pearl must have come from a special background. Her English was very proper; she could speak French perfectly, too, and even learned passable Cantonese in San Francisco. She had a well-stocked library, and most ships coming in brought the additional volumes she coveted. She played the piano, and her customers loved to hear her play and sing. She taught me how. She taught me a great deal more than I learned when I finally started my formal education. Even when so-called modish society became a reality in the city, my father and I preferred Pearl and the others like her, the people who had faced the first hard years and survived.

"I thought it only fair to tell you while you still have time to change your mind about me. You might not want someone with my background around your daughter."

He hesitated so long that she thought he was indeed disturbed by the prospect. His voice was leaden. "What I want is for the day to come when Missy can understand well enough for you to tell her about Pearl and the West."

Brandy was touched, and she didn't know what to say. She was relieved when he continued on a lighter note. "Two more questions, both of them personal, but permissible, I hope. First, how did you happen to be named Brandy?"

"That's simple. My father drank the stuff for a week after my mother died and then decided that his child had better be as strong as the liquor if she were to survive. I guess it was like giving me an Indian medicine name, and Brandy's better than Eagle's Wing or Bear's Claw."

That drew a smile from him. Amazing what a difference it made in the hooded face.

"Next question?"

"Did Pearl ever want you to follow in her footsteps?" he asked.

Brandy gave a peal of laughter. "Good heavens, no! She was perfectly happy herself, but she had no intention of letting me become a prostitute. She said some were cut out for it, but I wasn't. She was stricter than the most straitlaced matron about some things. When her girls were entertaining the customers in the back rooms, I was either asleep or doing lessons in her study. But she was always open and answered any questions I asked. She just made it clear to the men that I was not part of her business, that I was to be treated as a daughter of any respectable woman would be. I only remember a couple of men misbehaving, and they both ended up on the street, forbidden to visit Pearl's place again. She was the one who started my father on the

notion that I should come East. She said both coasts
should be tasted."

They finished the ride in companionable silence. Mr.
King seemed to use words only for extracting or giving
information; small talk was not one of his habits, and
Brandy agreed with him.

It took them scarcely more than an hour to reach
Boston and the harbor from Greenfield. The sounds of
the city closed in, and the peculiar smell of the wharves
grew stronger—tar and hemp and the thousand strange
things being handled there. Brandy was becoming ever
more aware of how important Mr. King was. An agent
was on hand to take the carriage and pair back to their
Boston stable. And when Brandy discovered which ship
they were to board, she stopped dead and breathed,
"Now that's a yacht!" More than fifty feet long, the
Isabella rode proudly with every surface gleaming from
constant care.

Grey was amused. "No, actually she's not. *Isabella*
isn't used solely for pleasure; she's a working vessel,
does coastal trading when she's not transporting me or
Raleigh. On her normal route, her arrival is quite an
event in the small ports. She doesn't match up in size;
there are many ships which are twice as big as she is,
but she's appreciated nonetheless. Why, right now her
hold is full of goods bound for Wiscasset. Most of it is
special orders such as a rare blend of pipe tobacco for
Joe Samuels, a bolt of fine cloth for Jane Alman's
wedding dress, and if I remember correctly, a new
whalebone corset for Mrs. Pettigrew." Brandy giggled at
the picture of Mrs. Pettigrew waiting anxiously for her
new corset to sail in.

Captain Hackett, a broadly built man with white hair
and sea-faded eyes surrounded by permanent squint
creases, greeted them as they came on board. Besides
the busy crewmen, there was a woman on deck. She
was pacing impatiently when Brandy first caught sight
of her, but she stopped when she saw them. The old
come-to-me trick, thought Brandy cynically as they

walked toward the figure. Grey introduced her to Ruth Collins.

There was no denying that she was beautiful. She was a good head shorter than Brandy, slender-boned and elegant but round in the right places. Her blond hair was carefully coiffed under a charming blue hat trimmed with tiny roses. Her matching blue dress was finely tailored with a bustled skirt and fitted jacket. Stupid wide skirt to wear on a ship, decided Brandy irreverently. Ruth's eyes were long-lashed under delicate brows. Her nose was small and straight, her mouth a perfect rosebud. She looked younger than the thirty years Dorothea Adams had put to her credit.

And there was no denying that she disliked Brandy on sight. Her eyes widened in surprise quickly hidden. She forced a smile as the introduction was made, but her voice was tense in spite of her efforts to make it casual. "Why, Grey darling, Miss Claybourne hardly looks like a governess. She's terribly young. What will she find to do in our backward state?"

Brandy's temper flared. She hated being talked about as if she weren't there. She spoke before Grey had a chance. "I wasn't aware that governesses are all cut in the same pattern. I am nineteen and have already taught school for over a year. And I'm going to Maine to work, not to be entertained."

She was instantly sorry for her outburst. She saw anger flash on Ruth's face, but it was followed by a faint shadow of fear. Poor Ruth, from what Brandy gathered, she had been in love with Grey for years and hopeful of marrying him, so why shouldn't she be suspicious and resentful of a younger woman who was joining Grey's household? She put out her hand impulsively. "Please, let's be friends. I'm sure there is so much you can tell me about Missy that would take me a long time to discover on my own."

Ruth took her hand, and this time she really smiled. Grey seemed satisfied that they were not going to start pulling out each other's hair, and he walked off to talk to the captain and so missed the change in Ruth's expression and her words.

"There's nothing I can tell you about Melissa that you won't know the minute you see her. I can tell you that she was a normal, laughing little girl before. Even her mother, the most hateful woman I have ever known, loved her. But all that is gone. The child is an empty shell, and she's ruining Grey's life. That's awful to say, isn't it? But it's true. He is so guilt-ridden that sometimes I wonder if he's sane. He can shut himself so far away that he resembles his daughter. Miss Claybourne, the best thing you can do for him and for me is to agree that the child belongs in an asylum so that we can get on with our lives."

Brandy still felt sorry for her, and for a moment she had thought they might be friends, but nothing could excuse such a callous attitude toward a child; surely if there was love between Grey and Ruth, they could make a life which included Missy. Brandy felt her facial muscles tighten with dislike, and Ruth saw it.

Her voice was harsh. "You are too young to understand how desperate love can make one. And you will not cooperate. You will struggle and fail like all the others, but it will take you months to admit it. If you took my advice, you could save yourself and me a lot of wasted time."

"Thank you for your concern, Miss Collins," said Brandy stiffly, and was relieved to see Grey coming back their way. He asked if she would like to see her quarters, and she agreed with alacrity. Ruth watched them go, her polite smile frozen into a grimace.

The crew's sleeping quarters were forward; the passenger cabins aft. Though the *Isabella* was fairly broad-beamed, the living space below deck was cramped, and Brandy could see why everything was so carefully stowed in its proper place. Her quarters were small but neat and comfortable. She saw Grey's cabin and Ruth's and noticed the connecting door. How convenient.

But in spite of her feelings about Ruth, the trip

proved a pure delight for Brandy. She had little experience of ships beyond her passage East by steamer, and she found to her relief that she was a good sailor. She loved the gentle undulating motion, the singing of the lines, the snap and rustle of canvas, the faint bell sounds. The weather held clear and fairly calm, so there was no rough water to contend with.

She persuaded one of the crew to tell her why Grey had referred to going up to Boston while going to Maine was going down, clearly a reversal of the actual directions. He told her that it was on account of the wind—you sailed up the prevailing winds to Boston, down back to Maine. From him she began to get a better idea of how closely Maine was tied to the sea—his own family had been bound to it one way or another as far back as anyone could remember, being either builders of boats, members of a crew, or fishermen. And in his voice she heard the strange broad vowels, soft tones, and hesitant, careful use of words peculiar to his state and much more intense than in Grey's speech.

Beyond mealtimes, she spoke little with Grey and never without Ruth present. Captain Hackett took his meals with them, and Brandy enjoyed his company, though she suspected that Grey had asked him to eat with them to reduce the tension between the two women. The captain told wonderful tales about his days on the clippers, and Brandy envied his wife who, like many of the clipper captains' wives, had voyaged with him, staying at home only when the arrival of a child was imminent. When she told him so, the captain shook his head sadly. "Ayuh, those were th' days, but they're fast passin', an' I'm thinkin' my Samantha misses 'em more'n I do. She hates steam for doin' in th' sails."

He and Grey went on to talk about the new Suez Canal, another sure blow to sailing ships, for now the steamers would be able to cut down the distance between coaling stops, and the less fuel they had to carry, the more profitable cargo space they had. And the newly completed transcontinental railway would also bring a change. Brandy listened in fascination, thinking of how vast a seaman's boundaries were—a change half the world away affected him as if it had happened next door. Ruth did not bother to hide her yawn of boredom.

Grey spent most of his time with the captain or members of the crew. He was well liked and respected for his seaman's knowledge, something the captain said most owners sorely lacked. And the sea was good for Grey; he looked younger, less careworn, almost at peace.

Brandy was perfectly happy exploring the ship and watching the seabirds, other vessels, and the changing shoreline. They were within sight of land most of the time, and she watched sandy shores of New Hampshire change to the rough granite of the Maine coast jutting out from tall stands of pine and spruce. Here and there isolated houses, compact and practical, looked out on the sea, each with a boat tied close by, and there were a multitude of tiny harbors. The ruggedness reminded her of the West, and already she felt a kinship with the state.

Ruth made no attempt to speak about Missy again, and that suited Brandy. She caused a stir on the first morning out by appearing in her fitted denim trousers. Grey's mouth twitched, and some of the crew were startled enough to forget what they were doing for a moment of frozen wonder. But only Ruth felt impelled to reprimand her. "Do you think those are quite proper, Miss Claybourne?" she asked, her judgment clear in her tone.

Brandy returned her cool stare. "Yes, I do, quite proper for climbing around on a ship; much more sensible than trailing skirts or those idiotic Turkish trousers which are bound to trip me. Besides, my figure is hardly enough to be called indecent, whatever I wear." Ruth was flushed with anger and shock, Brandy noticed with satisfaction.

"That's a matter of opinion," Grey said, his eyes taking in every detail of her appearance, the long, slender lines softly rounded. Brandy had always dismissed her figure as too boyish for fashions; apparently Mr. King did not share her view.

Ruth's face was rigid as she took Grey's arm possessively and asked him to escort her back to her cabin. She was not as easy with the boat's motion as Brandy was. Brandy felt the little tremor of fear again—Grey was not a man to tamper with or try to bind too closely. Poor Ruth, she should have learned that by now.

On the third day, they sailed up the wide Sheepscot River to Wiscasset, where Grey had his major shipyard. Brandy was delighted with the lovely white sea captains' houses, many of them complete with widow's walks around the roofs. The port still looked very busy to her, but Grey said that the war had changed things radically, and now that steam was so popular, many shipyards were closing down because they could not compete with the British builders of steamships. Brandy saw his hardness again; he had no pity for men who could not anticipate new trends and prepare for them.

Not far from where they docked, a man was waiting with a wagon. Grey accepted it as a matter of course that he would be there, but Brandy thought rebelliously that far too many people seemed to spend their lives waiting to do Mr. King's bidding. Either that or he had an uncannily accurate sense of timing which he passed on to his employees.

Grey went to speak to the man and returned with him. Ruth gave a small, cold nod of recognition; obviously she did not like him. As Brandy was introduced to Raphael Joly, she wondered if Ruth's dislike might stem from fear, for his appearance was not reassuring. Such a soft name for a hard-looking man. He could be anywhere from forty to fifty years old. He was not as tall as Grey, but he was much broader, and his skin was as brown and grained as bark, his hands as gnarled as the wind-warped trees she had known on the coast of the Pacific. But none of that was difficult to accept. Brandy had seen men shaped by the elements before. It was his face which gave him a baleful aspect. He had heavy brows, a hooked nose which had encountered fists often enough to be bumped and off center, and a heavy-lipped mouth. And his face was set in a perpetual, twisted leer because a puckered scar pulled skin and muscles tight from the outer tip of his left eyebrow to the corner of his mouth. Raphael Joly did not get along well with his fellowman, that was certain.

Brandy found it difficult to look away from the scar as they were introduced. She forced her eyes to meet his and experienced a shock. His eyes were a clear brown, and they were as gentle and innocent as a child's, completely out of place in the contorted face. She smiled at him and, hearing his thick accent, acknowledged the introduction in French.

His eyes gleamed with pleasure, and he said, "Please, it is better for me in English. I have still much to learn."

Brandy wondered where Grey had found him and how he had got the scar. It was not that old, probably no more than a few years. No matter; Brandy already liked him because of his eyes and because of his manner with Grey. There was no subservience in it, and obviously Grey expected none. They treated each other as equals. Brandy wondered what bond they shared.

The wagon they were to travel in had been built for durability, not style, as had the matched pair of ponderous grays hitched to it. Brandy had a good idea of what the road was going to be like by looking at the equipage. She envied Mr. King, for there was a sleek black horse tied to the wagon, saddled and ready for him to ride. She wished she had worn her breeches instead of her civilized clothes, then she might have had a fighting chance of riding horseback part of the way.

She was amused by Ruth's reaction. With all of Ruth's luggage, her own trunk, and sacks of supplies, they did look like tinkers on the move, and Ruth's face showed clearly that she would have preferred a carriage and pair even for so short a trip. She lived in a trim white town house, and they stopped to let her out. Grey wanted to be at his own house by nightfall, so there was no question of tarrying. But Ruth made her position known.

She reached up and kissed Grey deliberately, and her voice carried to the wagon. "When will you be back, darling?" And Grey's answer must have pleased her, for she smiled and said, "I'll have your favorite supper ready."

Grey rode along beside the wagon. People hailed him now and then, and he paused courteously but made it clear that he had little time to spare. Brandy returned the curious stares she was getting with her own.

She was amazed by how swiftly the road changed. For some distance it was suitable for carriage travel, but soon it degenerated into a track of connecting ruts. Grey still rode beside them, but there was no conversation, and Brandy didn't find the silence offensive. She was concentrating on seeing everything while maintaining her seat on the hard planking of the wagon. After the civilization of the port, she was astonished by the wildness of the country. There were trees everywhere—maple, oak, spruce, and pine—making a quilt of autumnal color: the reds, golds, and yellows made more brilliant by the dark-green emphasis of the evergreens. There was an abundance of water; rivers, lakes, and the small threads of wetness on their path flashed silver in the sun. The land rolled from one hill to another, and here and there were solitary farmhouses, small patches of cultivated land stolen by endless toil from the woods.

The farther inland they went, the more puzzled Brandy became. For a seafaring family, the Kings certainly lived far from the sea. She asked Grey the question, turning to look at him as she did. Her voice trailed away, but he did not seem to notice. As the countryside had changed, so had his face. He looked ten years older, all traces of humor gone. His mouth was a rigid line, his words as mechanical as the steady beat of the dray horses' hooves.

"My great-grandmother lost her youngest son to the sea, and after his death, she wanted to be out of sound and sight of the tide. My great-grandfather built King's Inland for her the following year, in seventeen hundred and ninety. But he kept a house in Wiscasset, and my brother, Raleigh, lives there. The country is much too quiet for him. And now if you will excuse me, I will trust Rafe to deliver you safely."

He touched his hat politely. The great black horse sprang forward, and they were soon lost in the trees.

Brandy stared after him blankly. The change to cold formality had been so abrupt, the shutting down of all warmth so sudden. She turned to Raphael. "What in the world was that all about? I can understand how anxious he must be to see his child, but lordy, that wasn't a happy man who just rode off."

Raphael said nothing for a moment. The sunlight of his eyes regarded her intently. She felt him probing her mind, sorting through the impulses of her heart. She had never felt so open to judgment or cared so much about the verdict. Finally he spoke.

"You are to live in his house, you should know. That one, he has many demons with him, but always the most difficult is his child. She fears him above all things. She is a child of the silence, but when he is near, she cries out. He does not go often to her. I do not know what the infant thought she saw that night, but she has the fear of her father since then."

Brandy's heart beat loudly against her silence. Children saw things so clearly, judged so ruthlessly until they were taught that civilization required a certain blindness for survival. What if it had been Grey, what if the child had seen it—the deliberate murder of her mother by fire? That was the worst possibility of all, that fire had been used as a weapon. There was more savagery in that than in a gun or knife or even bare hands. Brandy knew. She had seen San Francisco in flames often enough to realize fully the horror of dying that way. But Dr. George had said that Mr. Joly had testified to Grey's innocence, so surely it was true.

Her courage flooded out of her, and she wanted to ask him to take her back to the port; she would get passage back to Boston somehow. But something stayed her. "Why, damn you for a coward, Brandy Claybourne, if it is true, then the child needs you more than ever."

Raphael reached over and patted her hand clumsily. She had not realized she had spoken aloud. "It is good. And this one, Rafe, he would like to be your friend," he said, and urged the grays to a faster pace.

The sun was going down by the time they reached King's Inland, and Brandy had been seeing everything through a haze of weariness for the past hour. She never wanted to sit on a wagon seat again; it was going to be difficult to sit on anything comfortably for several days. Not even the occasional herds of deer leaping the track held any appeal for her now. But her first view of the house enlivened her senses in an instant.

She didn't know what she'd expected, certainly not a hovel, but not this magnificence either. Three stories of elegant simplicity rose from the clearing at the end of the treelined lane. Golden light flowed from the many paned windows of the first floor. Even in the semidarkness, Brandy could see the richness of the exterior, the weathered wood lovely in itself without the coats of white paint which seemed the rule in Maine. To the right and some distance from the house was the barn with its two low-lying side wings which Brandy guessed to be extra stalls for the horses Grey raised. The barn and stables were glaringly new. Of course, the fire. Brandy looked away.

Rafe broke the silence. "It is like a magic place, no? And there is the enchanted princess. Perhaps you will break the spell." A strange man this, Brandy thought. He looked like the product of years of saloon brawls, and yet his ways were gentle, his speech was courtly.

He pulled the wagon up to the front door, and Brandy climbed down stiffly, thankful to stretch her limbs. The door opened, flooding the entrance with light, silhouetting the woman who emerged. She was of medium height. Her gray hair was dressed neatly in a bun; her blue eyes sparkled with benign curiosity behind gold-trimmed spectacles; her tendency to plumpness eased the lines of sixty years or so. She took Brandy's hand in her own capable ones and greeted her.

"I am Mrs. Bailey, Grey's cook and housekeeper. Welcome to King's Inland." She regarded Brandy intently. "Well, my dear, you are younger than I expected, but perhaps that will be good for Missy." Her accent was of New England but did not have the peculiar Maine sound.

Rafe broke in. "Eh, that one, calling herself housekeeper, cook. She is *la châtelaine*. One must stay always on her good side, or it is great trouble. She has been here a hundred years, I think."

"Away with you," said Mrs. Bailey, flapping her apron at him. "Where is Grey? I thought he was coming in with you."

Rafe's face pulled, and he shook his head. "He came before us. I thought he would be already here. He must have need to be alone."

Mrs. Bailey sighed. "Well, poor man, he has problems enough to fret him. Come, Miss Claybourne, I'll show you your room so that you can freshen up, and then we'll have supper."

"Please, call me Brandy."

Brandy's laugh was cut off by a gasp as she got her first look at the interior of the house. She had never seen such opulence. The floors were of shining, inlaid wood with intricately patterned carpets spread here and there. There were beautiful pieces of furniture, and the woodwork of the house itself carried fantastic carved designs. Porcelain, jade, and sculpture in metals and stone rested on tables and behind the glass doors of cabinets. And yet the large rooms bore it all without being cluttered. It would take days to explore the whole house.

Mrs. Bailey smiled at her obvious wonder. "Sea captains are compulsive collectors, and this house holds almost eighty years of booty." She ran her hands lovingly over the wood of one of the cabinets.

Brandy was so busy catching glimpses of the rooms that she did not see the girl standing shyly at the bottom of the staircase until Mrs. Bailey introduced her. "Brandy, this is Persia Cowperwaithe. She lives with her family on a farm a few miles from here, but she comes in five days of the week to help me keep this place in order. Two people can scarcely do it all, but I prefer that to an army of servants who just clutter the place and break things."

Persia was not as tall as Brandy, but she was large-boned and well fleshed. Brandy guessed they were probably of an age. Persia looked as if she had been conjured out of the autumn woods. Her hair was a fiery tousle of red, her eyes were leafy green brown, and golden freckles ran over her fair skin. Her smile was wide and infectious, revealing white, slightly crooked teeth. She was intensely alive and sturdy-looking, conveying the impression that hard work and joy went together with no conflict.

"Persia, please show Brandy her room. I'll have supper ready in a trifle. Rafe can bring her trunk up when he has Grey to help him," said Mrs. Bailey, and Persia turned obediently to lead Brandy up the stairs.

She hesitated. "Shouldn't I meet Missy first?"

Both the faces took on that expression of sadness which Brandy already associated with any mention of the child. Mrs. Bailey shook her head. "No, tomorrow will be soon enough for that. She's asleep now, which is a blessing. Sometimes she lies for hours with her eyes open. It wouldn't do to wake her."

"No, of course not," agreed Brandy, following Persia up the stairs, but inwardly she was feeling more doubt-

ful than before. What had she got herself into? The
child didn't even sleep as other children did.

The staircase wound up and to the right from the
middle of the hall, and when they reached the second
floor, Persia explained which rooms were which. Brandy grinned to herself; Persia's accent, like that of the
schooner's crew, was so strange-sounding to her ears
that she had to listen very closely to understand.

There were seven rooms, three on each side of the
hall and one at the end, which was Grey's. Missy's room
was the center one on the right-hand side; Brandy's was
across from it. The house had been built to hold a large
family and many guests; on this floor alone there were
four unoccupied rooms. Persia explained that Mrs. Bailey had her own suite of rooms on the first floor, toward
the back of the house.

"And there's a whole floor above this one!"

"Yes, ma'am, but kept mostly shut an' used for storage an' such."

"Oh, Persia, please don't call me ma'am. It makes me
sound a hundred years old."

"Yes, ma'am," said Persia, and they both started to
laugh, trying not to make noise that would wake the
child.

Persia opened the door to Brandy's room, and Brandy gave a low whistle of pleasure. The room was large,
and in spite of the glow of several lamps and the fire
burning in the open hearth, there were shadows. But
she could see enough detail to be stunned that this was
to be hers. The walls were covered with Chinese
wallpaper patterned with pairs of brilliantly plummaged
birds. It was old, hand-painted, and had nothing in
common with the modern monotony seen in most
houses these days. Persia pointed out the owl—the only
bird without a mate—and explained that the paper fit
the saying "Love and beauty walk hand in hand, but
wisdom stands alone." Brandy felt an immediate affection for the lonesome little fellow staring saucer-eyed
from the wall.

The bed too was old-fashioned, huge and canopied in heavy yellow silk which matched the window draperies and one of the predominant colors in the wallpaper. The chair by the fireplace had side wings to screen the heat and was covered in lavishly embroidered figures of flowers, trees, and fantastic beasts.

The ample desk had ornately carved, curving legs and a chair to match, but what intrigued Brandy most of all was the traveling desk on top of it. Intricately inlaid with mother-of-pearl and the initials "M.K.," it had obviously been designed for a woman, yet it was larger than any she had ever seen. It must have belonged to someone whose correspondence had been widespread, whose household paperwork had been demanding even when she was away. Brandy lifted the lid and peeked inside. The drawers and pigeonholes were empty, though under the writing surface the bottom held an ample supply of creamy writing paper of the finest quality. A long rectangular space with a separate lid formed the back of the box and held steel pens, an inkwell, fine sand, and some old quills. As Persia put it, the house was "full o' other folks' things." She made it sound as if the previous generations of King's Inland had just stepped out for a stroll and would come collect their belongings later.

Everything gleamed with the evidence of good care, and the air smelled pleasantly of cedar, lavender, and burning wood. "It's heavenly!" exclaimed Brandy. "I can't believe I'm to stay here."

Persia smiled proudly, and Brandy knew she must have had much to do with getting the room in order. "Thank you, I can see your hand in this," she said, and the girl blushed with pleasure.

Then she said briskly, "There's water in th' pitcher if you're wantin' to have a wash. I'd better be along to help with supper."

"I'll hurry," Brandy promised.

She took off her bonnet, bathed her face and hands, and was brushing her hair back into some semblance of order when she heard a door shut softly in the corridor. She wouldn't have heard it at all except that her own door had been left ajar. She froze for a second, then gave herself a mental shake. What in the world was she so jumpy about? It was probably just Mr. King coming in. No, he would have made more noise than that; he wasn't the type to creep about in his own house. The child then. Brandy went into the hallway. There was no sign of anyone, and Missy's door was shut. She went and opened it carefully.

She was stunned. There was a lamp burning beside the bed, and she could see the child clearly. In all the things she had been told about her, no one had mentioned how beautiful Missy was. Her hair was sun gold, thick and curly. She was tiny for her age; everything about her was petite and exquisitely formed except her eyes. They were large and dark in her small face. Brandy's heart missed a beat. In color and shape, the eyes were Grey King's, but there the similarity ended. The child's eyes were absolutely blank, wide and seeming to be fixed on some object through and far beyond Brandy. Brandy was surely in her field of vision, but not by the slightest sign did the child betray that she saw her. It was far worse than looking into physically blind eyes. Brandy steeled herself against a nervous shudder. It must have been the child at the door; therefore, she could not be totally withdrawn if she had heard the voices and responded with curiosity.

Brandy went and sat on the bed, making no attempt to touch her. The eyes remained fixed. Brandy spoke slowly. "Hello, Missy, I'm Brandy. I've come to stay with you. I hope we'll be friends and that someday when you feel like it, you will talk to me."

She got no further. Missy's body did not stir, but something moved for an instant in her eyes, and she started to scream. Brandy whirled around, and there stood Grey. His voice was as expressionless as the eyes of his child had been. "I see you've met my daughter," he said, and walked out.

The piercing wail of terror tore at Brandy's heart. She knew she might make it worse, but she gathered Missy into her arms anyway, crooning to her and rocking the frail body gently. It was another thing outside her experience—the child's body remained rigid, her muscles not relaxing at all in response to being held. But some contact must have been made, for the screaming gradually died to whimpers, then ceased altogether. Either that, or simply having the object of fear gone was enough.

The weariness of the day washed over Brandy; she felt totally incapable, and when Persia appeared, saying that she would sit with the child until she slept, Brandy could have wept with relief. Persia insisted she go downstairs and get something to eat. " 'Tis a bit much to take in all at once. Missy an' me, we get on all right. Don't fret. She'll be fine."

Grey met her at the bottom of the stairs, and she wanted desperately to reassure him, but she could think of nothing to say; Missy's behavior left no doubt about how she felt toward her father.

Grey spoke first, his voice oddly gentle. "I know better than to appear in Missy's room, but somehow I always think this time will be different, for once she won't be afraid. I have as many delusions as my child. Rafe and I had just brought your trunk up, and I wondered if you were with Missy."

They were in the dining room now, at the back of the house. It was connected to the kitchen by a pantryway, and Brandy could hear Mrs. Bailey moving around in the kitchen. Impulsively she put her hand on Grey's arm. "Don't worry. There must be a way to change her. And perhaps it is a good sign, though terribly difficult for you—at least she reacts to you; she doesn't seem to see me at all."

"Thank you," was all he said as Mrs. Bailey bustled in carrying a tray heavily laden with covered dishes.

Brandy moved to help her, but she refused. "No, this is my bailiwick. You looked starved to death and tuckered out anyway, wouldn't want you falling over and breaking the best china. Now sit."

Brandy laughed and did as she was told. The table would have seated twelve people easily; it looked bare with only three places set, but the candlelight from a pair of silver candelabra softened the scene. The walls were hung with tapestries, and the padded cushions of the chairs were covered in burgundy-red velvet. Brandy didn't think she would ever become accustomed to the richness of King's Inland. She felt very countrified in contrast with the grandeur.

"What about Persia and Rafe, won't they be eating with us?" she asked, thinking she would be very glad of their earthy presence.

Grey was much too quick; he read between the lines easily, and she knew he was aware of her reaction to her surroundings. "No," he said. "Rafe only comes under the pressure of formal occasions. He has his own cabin in the woods, and he guards his solitude fiercely. Persia was raised in this country, and she thinks nothing of walking home after dark. I've offered her the use of a horse, but she insists her legs are much more trustworthy than any beast's, and she is probably right. She likes to be with her family in the evenings. She'll probably be down soon and on her way." The shadows crossed his face.

Brandy knew she owed some explanation for being in Missy's room. "I really am sorry for all the fuss; I'm to blame. But the oddest thing happened—I heard a door shut in the hall, and I thought it was the child, so I went into her room. She was wide awake, so I told her who I am. It seemed hopeful. I mean, she was curious about the new arrival, so she can't be totally oblivious to what goes on, can she?"

She could not judge whether or not the small space of silence held any hope; if it had, it was overcome by doubt. "Brandy, we all want to believe, as you do, that there is a normal child hidden somewhere in Missy and that she peeks out now and then, but it is impossible that the noise you heard was caused by her. She does not go out of her room by herself," said Mrs. Bailey. "You must not get your hopes too high; the disappointment could be dreadful."

Grey nodded wearily in assent but said nothing. Brandy felt her temper rising and hoped it didn't show. How could the child ever improve if everyone around her accepted her as ill forever? Come on, Missy, come on, she pleaded silently, I'm sure it was you, and you know I'm here. Let's show them, let's show them soon!

But outwardly she shrugged and let it go, making a polite comment about the food which she could hardly taste because she was so weary. Persia stuck her head in briefly and bid them good-night. The only conversation at the table was between Grey and Mrs. Bailey concerning various problems at King's Inland. Late apples and early colts swam together in Brandy's mind, and her muscles protested the day's wagon ride. She was just considering going to sleep right there when Grey said, "Miss Claybourne, if there is anything I cannot bear, it is a pretty woman with blueberry pie on her forehead, and that is exactly what you are going to be if you fall asleep. You are excused."

She felt like a child, but she answered his smile with a rueful one of her own. Any humor he showed in this house was a good sign. He walked with her to the foot of the stairs.

"Unless you are an extremely early riser, I'll be gone when you awaken. If you need anything, ask Margaret or Persia. I've already given orders to Rafe that you are to be given a horse if you wish to ride. And there is a piano in the music room if you wish to use it. Good night and good luck."

He turned and left her. She was amazed by his memory for details, that out of the rush of his daily life, he had remembered she liked to ride and to play the piano. She was glad she had not followed a perverse impulse to ask him to give her best to Ruth.

She had a thousand things to ask, to think about, but

she considered none of them. She barely got her clothes off and her hair down before she collapsed in bed and fell asleep. She did not hear her door open or see the small figure of the child watching from the shadows.

CHAPTER III

Brandy roused briefly in the predawn when she heard Grey come up to his room. She was vaguely satisfied that at least he was going to get a few hours of sleep, but he left again almost immediately. Poor man, she thought as she drifted back into sleep, he can't even rest peacefully in his own house.

When next she opened her eyes, it was to full sun and Persia peeking in the door, trying not to let the dishes of the breakfast tray rattle. "Oh, I'm sorry, I wasn't to waken you, but I reckoned you might be up an' hungry by now," she explained.

"Heavens, I am embarrassed! I've nearly slept the clock around, and now I'm being waited on. You shouldn't have let me be so lazy."

Persia shook her head. "You'd no choice, Mr. King's orders. He said you were to sleep as long as you might after yesterday's journeyin'."

"Is he still here then?"

"No. He left word with Mrs. Bailey last night. I expect he pried up the sun this morn."

"Oh," said Brandy, trying to sound surprised, unwilling to admit she had been so attuned to his movements. She patted the bed. "Can't you stay a minute? I've so many things to ask you."

Persia put the tray within Brandy's reach and sat carefully on the bed. As she did so, Brandy heard a soft mew, and then two cats, one after the other, landed on the bed. "Why, you rascals, followed me right up, didn't you? Shall I put them out?"

"No, don't. They're lovely. Introduce me, please. I've never seen cats quite like these," said Brandy, staring at them. One was mottled white, orange and black, and the other had a lovely coat of soft gray faintly ringed.

Persia laughed. "Cats in the state o' Maine are more spoilt than th' children. Th' captains collected them an' brought them back like all th' other oddments from th' world. Th' spotted one, Tiger, she's a money-cat, an' they're always female. T'other, she's Iris, an' she's a coon-cat. Some say they come from wild coons an' house cats gettin' together, but I don't believe it. We've a tom here too, his name's Horace, but he don't like people much, 'ceptin' Rafe, so he's usually there." The way she said Rafe's name made Brandy glance at her quickly, and she saw the telltale flushing of the fair skin. Well, well, so that's the way the wind blows, she thought, but she didn't want to embarrass the girl by commenting on it.

"What about dogs?" she asked instead. She liked cats well enough, but she preferred dogs. "I didn't hear any bark when we arrived."

Persia's face fell, and Brandy knew before she spoke that it had something to do with the child. "Mr. King won't allow any on th' place, even though he fancies 'em himself. Missy's scairt to death of 'em." Her face brightened. "But we've quite a passel at our farm, an' one o' th' best bitches is fixin' to whelp any day now, so you can come there if you get lonesome for a good dog. I'd be pleased to have you meet my people anyway, if you've a mind to."

"I'd love to," Brandy said, but she wanted the talk to turn back to Missy. She was beginning to suspect that though the people of this region probably kept track of everything, they were disinclined to gossip with strangers. She approved, but she needed information. "Persia, what else is Missy afraid of and do you know why?"

Persia hesitated; then she shrugged hopelessly. "She's scairt o' so many things, you can't hardly keep track o' 'em. She's scairt o' goin' out o' her room, o' th' dark, o' th' outdoors, o' dogs. She hates things to be moved about, an' she's scairt o' fire, even in th' hearth, but most o' all, she's scairt o' her father. Now some o' that, like th' fire, that makes sense, but th' rest's beyond me."

Brandy wondered if she also thought Missy's fear of Grey was reasonable, but she knew she would not say. "How do you know about her being afraid, does she scream like she did last night?"

"No. She only screams when Mr. King's about," Persia said sadly. "For th' other things, she rocks an' stares. Sometimes it gives me th' collywobbles to watch her. You'd think she'd be tuckered out, but she just goes on an' on. An' th' oddest thing, there're things she should be scairt by, but she's not. She don't hear loud noises—you could drop th' roof in an' she wouldn't jump, an' she can stay in a cold room an' not seem to feel it at all."

Brandy stared pensively at a pair of birds on the wallpaper, her half-eaten breakfast forgotten. Persia saw her abstraction and was not offended by it. "I'd better be about my chores," she said, picking up the tray. "Missy's awake, so just go on in when you want, but try not to be too down-hearted by what you see."

Brandy brought her attention back for a moment. "Thank you. I'm awfully glad you're here." Persia's ready smile flashed, and she bobbed her head as she left the room.

Brandy dressed quickly, her mind whirling with what she'd been told. If so many of Missy's fears were unreasonable, could it not also be true that her fear of her father was equally unfounded? She sighed; she wished it was so, but she doubted it. The child's terror was so specific toward Grey.

When she went to the room, she found Missy sitting motionless on the floor. There were dolls and toys spread temptingly about, but not by the child. She did not play. Her hands were in a strange position—elbows out, wrists dropping, fingers curled uselessly.

Brandy settled down on the floor beside her. She began to talk, telling the child again who she was and why she was there. She changed the pitch and volume of her voice constantly so that Missy could not slip away easily from a monotonous sound. She kept at it for more than an hour, watching the little girl for any sign that she heard. There was none, and Brandy was exhausted. She made a rule for herself then. She must allow herself time away from her charge; otherwise she knew the lack of response would make her angry and frustrated, and that would be a victory for the child. She would be groping her way blindly toward helping Missy; she knew no sure methods, but some things she was already beginning to sense—the child had rigid control over what she saw, heard, and touched, and somehow that must be broken.

Brandy got up stiffly. "Missy, I'm going now, but I'll be back. I'll be back again and again because I want to help you."

There was no danger in leaving the child alone; she never did anything. As Brandy headed down the stairs, she met Persia coming up with a tray of food. The food was cut into small pieces and arranged precisely.

"Does she always eat in her room?" asked Brandy.

"Yes, an' always at th' same times."

"Does she feed herself?"

"I don't reckon so. I've left th' tray sometimes, an' once I thought she might've taken a mite on her own, but I couldn't tell for sure. You see, she don't seem to get hungry, but she'll open her mouth an' eat a little when I feed her."

Brandy continued down the stairs mulling this over. To her it was one more example of the child's control, and this too had to be changed. She wondered if they had ever let the child go hungry enough so that her body would compel her to eat.

On her way outside she saw Mrs. Bailey, who was busy polishing a cabinet in the hall. She offered to help, but the housekeeper shooed her out. "I'll call on you if I need help, but I'm terribly fussy about the treasures in my charge. If anything's to happen to them, I'd better be to blame. Not that I'd judge you clumsy," she added. "But with the burden you've taken on, you're going to need all the free time and fresh air you can manage. Go explore the grounds and get Rafe to show you the horses. Grey said you are a good rider." She said it with no hint of mockery, so Mr. King must not have told her about the disgraceful race—that was thoughtful of him.

The day was perfectly golden, and she skipped a little as she walked. She saw the flower beds in front of the house. They were bare of blossoms now but would be beautiful in the spring, she guessed, for gardens seemed to be important in Maine. All the houses they had passed the day before, even the most isolated ones, had had pots solely for flowers. Nice to know that Maine women considered beauty as essential as food.

She found the spring- and smokehouses and the vegetable garden in the back, finished save for the bright pumpkins and plump ears of corn yet to be harvested. Beyond it lay the brown stubble of a hay-field, a small orchard, and then the woods. She marveled again at the pervasiveness of the forest, guarding its darkness, surrounding every patch of cleared land which had been wrested from it. She could see a path leading from the field into the trees, and she looked forward to following it. She liked the wildness of the growth and wanted to see the creatures whose voices drifted to her from the shadows. But first she wanted to see the horses.

She found Rafe cleaning out stalls. His eyes brightened in welcome, and he was happy to take her on tour, obviously proud of his domain. He had a right to be; the horses were beautifully groomed, their tack meticulously kept. The center part was the true barn, high-ceilinged with a long loft piled with hay over several box stalls. Chickens scratched and chuckled in the hay. There were five additional stalls in each of the two wings connected to the barn. And behind the building was a paddock where the horses could be exercised. Brandy inhaled the sweet hay and warm horseflesh smell with delight.

There was one cow which supplied King's Inland dairy needs, and there were five horses in addition to Pete and Polly, who had pulled the wagon. Two of the five were yearling colts in training. That left three— Prince Lucky, Tally, and Lady—to choose from for riding. The only horse which was off limits was Orpheus, Grey's stallion, but in any case, he was usually gone as now with Grey.

Brandy looked the three over carefully. They were all magnificent, long-legged, satin-coated, high-strung aristocrats of their species. She chose Lady without hesitation. Lady was a chestnut, a little larger than the other two, but just as finely built. Brandy appreciated all the points of her confirmation, but she chose the horse for a certain look in her eyes. They were large, wide-set, and gentle, but there was just enough mischief gleaming in them to make Brandy want to try her. She told Rafe she'd go riding the next morning and asked him what she ought to expect.

"She is good, but she has only three years, so sometimes she plays as a child. But already you have seen that, no?" Brandy smiled and nodded, and Rafe continued, "Now, for the jumping, she is agreeable to it but in that still an infant. She needs more working to make the grand ones. Go carefully, yes?"

Brandy agreed, and they went on talking as Rafe led her out and around to the back where the two colts were playing in the paddock. Brandy settled herself contentedly on the warm, stubbled grass, and Rafe sat beside her.

"I thought Mr. King raised a lot of horses. Are these all he has?"

Rafe gave a deep chuckle. "All here? Oh, no, there are many more in other places, more south and warmer with more persons for training. And at the finish of the summer, we have sold many that were here, fat on the fine grasses. Not that the winter here is too bad," he amended hastily. "It is not as in the north." Brandy saw the sudden tightening of his muscles as he said it—a winter in the north and the north country itself, something that had happened there? She did not know him well enough to ask. Instead she questioned him about Missy.

"Rafe, was the little child normal when you first came? Did she like the outdoors?"

Whatever his other thought had been, it vanished in his concern for the child. "Like the butterfly she was beautiful, laughing, dancing, running every place, as from flower to flower, fearing nothing. Like that I knew her for a short time before the fire. Often I would take her with me on the horse, and she had not fear, only joy."

Brandy swallowed the lump in her throat. The way Rafe spoke English made everything sound strangely beautiful and profound. How deeply he had loved the child, and this too Missy had relinquished.

Brandy thanked him and walked back to the house, going straight up to Missy's room. The child was in the same spot, and she wondered if she had moved at all. She went patiently to work again. She quit when her voice began to get hoarse. Nothing stirred in the blank eyes.

That night after supper Mrs. Bailey invited Brandy in for tea in her rooms across the hall from the dining room, and Brandy liked what she saw. Mrs. Bailey had a sitting room and a bedroom, both of ample proportions. The quarters provided her with some privacy as there was a back room leading outside. She smiled softly in remembrance as she pointed out the special conveniences of her apartment.

"Mr. King, the boys' father, hired me and brought me

to this house to be housekeeper and companion for his wife more than forty years ago. The grandparents were still living then, too, and all four of them, the old and young people, were people of strong character. Mr. King knew that, and he wanted me to have some life of my own, so he gave me these rooms and declared them off limits to the family. No one was allowed to trouble me here, and I was most grateful. I was only twenty when Mr. King hired me, but I was already a widow; I had lost both my husband and my baby son. They died of typhoid fever."

"Oh, I'm so sorry!" exclaimed Brandy, knowing the words were inadequate but at a loss for others.

"It was a long time ago, and the Kings gave me a new life, a new family. When Grey and later Raleigh came along, it was as if they were my own boys, though I must admit Grey wanted no confusion about it. He used to tell visitors, 'This is not my mother, but she takes good care of me.' I think he felt some sort of misguided pity for his mother when in fact, Mrs. King was glad to have help raising them; she was frail, and they both had more than a touch of high spirits and mischief in them."

As Brandy sipped her tea, Mrs. Bailey showed her some of her special treasures—pieces of ivory, jade, porcelain, and silver given her by the generous Kings of several generations. But it was a much humbler article which caught Brandy's interest. It was difficult to imagine Grey as a child, even when she held the tiny ship carved from a single piece of wood and initialed "G. K." There was something vulnerable about the patient care which had been lavished on the figure. She shifted her mind away from the inexplicable sadness it gave her.

"Does Raleigh ever come here?" she asked.

Mrs. Bailey's face lighted with joy. "My, yes, he does. I give him a good scolding when he stays away too long. But Grey and he don't get along at all. It's just one of those things. So he only comes when Grey is gone." She explained it with complete acceptance that sometimes brothers did not feel the blood bond, but Brandy wondered how much the estrangement had to do with Grey's wife.

She rose to go. "I've taken up enough of your time, but I do thank you for showing me everything. And now, if it won't disturb you, I would like to try the piano."

"Disturb me? Mercy, no! The music room is clear in the front. Besides, it will be nice to have music in the house again. Come along, I'll show you the room, and tomorrow I'll take you on a full tour."

As they walked down the hall, Brandy asked who used to play.

"Why, of course, you wouldn't know. Jasmine was the last one." Mrs. Bailey's voice held no rancor when she said the name. "I swear I don't think that girl could have baked a loaf of bread if her life had depended on it. She didn't do that sort of thing, but she could play the piano, dance, and ride, things like that. And she was good to Missy."

"It's awfully difficult to get any clear idea of what she was like," mused Brandy.

Mrs. Bailey opened the door to the room. "Maybe that will give you a better view." She pointed to a painting hanging on one of the walls.

The room was lovely, its gilt chairs exquisite, the piano magnificent, all of the decorative touches perfect. But nothing was as beautiful as the portrait of Jasmine King.

Brandy stared speechlessly at the image of Missy's mother. With the crinolined skirts of her time billowing around her, she looked like an exotic flower come to life. The fitted bodice of her dress accentuated her slim, yet sensuous figure, leaving her creamy shoulders bare. Her neck was long and slender, her face a perfect oval framed by the sunlit wealth of her hair, Missy's hair. Her eyes were enormous, their unbelievable violet-blue depths fringed by surprisingly dark, long lashes. The mouth was full, the lips slightly pouting. But despite its great beauty, there was nothing vapid about the face. There was a recklessness, a lurking mockery, and above all, a determination to have her own way in her expression.

Brandy had a sudden vision of the burning—the exquisite face distorted by pain, destroyed by flames—and she spoke quickly to erase it. "Was she really that beautiful? It seems impossible."

"No painting could do her justice, not even that one."

"No wonder Mr. King loved her!"

"Yes, any man would." There was no sarcasm in Mrs. Bailey's voice, only admiration.

"Did you get along with her?" she asked hesitantly.

"Well enough. Even though I have been in this house for a long time, I have no illusions about my position. The wife of the house is the first lady. Jasmine was. She was quite content to let me run the day-to-day business since she had no interest in housekeeping. When the child came, Jasmine didn't want me to have much to do with her, but that was all right, too. I was already getting too old to keep up with a youngster." Brandy made a gesture of protest, but Mrs. Bailey forestalled her. "No, that's the truth. Missy was so full of energy, I could not have kept track of her properly. How I wish she was still like that." She hurried on. "I expect Ruth Collins will be first lady soon, and that will be fine with me and good for Grey. The house needs a mistress."

Brandy had a better knowledge now of how much the house and the King dynasty meant to Mrs. Bailey, who had spent most of her life helping to keep both going. "Well, now," she said briskly. "I'll leave you to your music."

It gave Brandy an eerie sense to be in the room with Jasmine's portrait, as though she were not alone, as though the painting were a living presence. She shivered a little, imagining an echo of mocking laughter. Then she chided herself. In a way, the picture was a good sign; Grey had not destroyed all traces of his wife. She did not want to consider the idea that he might be punishing himself.

She pushed such thoughts away as she touched the piano. It was a wing-shaped grand some ten feet long. She recognized the famous name of Jonas Chickering of Boston. There was no finer piano to be had, and she was awed to be allowed to play it. Its tone was full and perfect; it had been kept in good tune.

She did not know how long she had played when her muscles finally protested enough to make her stop. She was tired and content as she rose, taking the lamp with her. She did not look at the portrait as she left.

She was halfway up the stairs when she heard them, light footsteps running down the hall, a door closing with a careful click.

It had to be Missy. Missy alone in the dark of the hall? Brandy moved as swiftly as she could carrying the lamp until she put it down impatiently and ran the rest of the way. A light was burning in Missy's room as always, and the child lay on the bed, eyes closed.

Brandy stood looking down at her, seeing the racing pulse beating under the thin skin at the base of the tiny throat, and was shocked by the swift impulse to anger which flowed through her. She wanted to shake Missy until the child had to cry out to her to stop.

She was instantly ashamed, and her voice was gentle as she sat down on the bed and gathered the tense body into her arms. "I know it was you; I heard you. Did you come out to hear the music? That was very brave. But I'll play for you anytime you wish. All you have to do is ask me." *Ask me, that's a good one! Missy, if you asked me out loud, in a real voice, to jump up and grab the moon for you, I'd try, and I'd be so happy, I just might be able to reach it.*

She continued holding her, talking to her, stroking the fair hair. The pulse slowed, and the slight relaxation of muscles, of which Brandy was already so aware, came, telling her the child was truly asleep.

She went wearily to her room, the peace of her music lost. She lay awake for a long while, wondering what had caused Missy to creep closer to the sound—was it because it reminded her of her mother or simply because the music pleased her?

She awakened once to find she had slept so restlessly that she had pulled the pillow over her face and tangled the bedclothes. She fell back to sleep still fretting over Missy.

By the next morning she had decided several things. First she met Persia bringing up Missy's breakfast. She held out her hands for the tray. "Please, I'd like to take over feeding her, if you don't mind."

Persia's eyes filled, but she handed the tray over obediently. Brandy hastened to reassure her. "Please, don't look like that. It isn't because of anything you've done. I know how patient and good you are with her. It's just that I want to get as close to her as I can. If I'm to do her any good at all, she's got to recognize me as an important part of her world. And eating is pretty basic for all of us, even Missy, I suspect."

Persia's face cleared. "Well, just look at me, won't you? Here I am going green an' tetchy over such a thin'. I surely can use th' extra time to redd up this house. But you call on me sometimes, if you're too busy, won't you?"

"I certainly will," Brandy assured her, loving her for her concern for the child.

Missy, already neatly dressed by Persia, was sitting in her usual spot on the floor. Brandy looked at the snowy fabric of her dress, the gleaming gold of her hair, everything so still and doll-like. She nearly laughed aloud at herself; here she was hoping for the day when Missy would be dirty and mussed from playing, a state most governesses abhorred in their charges.

She settled down beside Missy. She couldn't tell exactly what it was, but something warned her that Missy was aware of the change in her schedule and resented it. "Persia and I are going to take turns, darling," she explained, holding out the first morsel of food.

Missy's action surprised Brandy so that she nearly dropped the fork. Her hand came up, and Brandy thought for a moment she was going to strike her, but instead she held her hand in front of her face and started flicking her fingers. Brandy stared at her, at the relentlessly mechanical motion of the fingers, at the dark eyes fixed on them, and she realized that the child must feel the need for an added barrier against her.

"No, Missy, don't do that," she commanded, reaching out and taking hold of the hand. The flexing continued in her grasp, and she knew that she had done the wrong thing—Missy was winning the point, for as soon as Brandy let go, the hand would screen the little face again. She let it happen, and then she brought her own hand up in front of her face, copying Missy's actions exactly. She could hardly breathe, so desperately did she want to win the battle of the wills.

It worked. Missy's hand dropped to her side. So Missy was normal in this. Brandy had learned in her teaching experience that children hated the ridicule of being imitated; she had seen her younger students do it to each other, often to the point where she had to intervene before someone got a bloodied nose.

For the first time, the strange eyes were looking directly at her, with anger or hate, she didn't care which. She offered the bit of food again. Missy's mouth opened, and she took it. Brandy was amazed at the wild rush of blood she felt from such a minor victory.

She was still beaming when she handed the tray to Persia downstairs. Persia grinned back at her. "I'm so glad it went well, on th' first try, too! Mr. King will be pleased."

"Oh, is he coming back so soon?" Brandy tried to keep the anxiety out of her voice; she wanted to have much more than this morning's work to show him when he returned.

Persia understood. "No, I don't know when he'll be

back, but don't you worry, you're doin' fine with Missy. Little things mean so much with a child like that one."

When Brandy arrived at the stables, Rafe took one look at her face and said, "So it is a good morning?" He eyed her trousers with approval. "Better than a dress. Now you will not need the foolish lady's saddle."

He readied Lady for her and gave her a leg up. She asked about riding in the woods, and he said it was fine as long as she kept to the trail and did not lose her bearings.

Lady snorted and shied playfully. Brandy reined her firmly, speaking to her quietly, letting the mare know her rider could be trusted. Rafe nodded. "I will not fear. It is well between you."

She waved her thanks as she rode off. They crossed the meadow and entered the woods, and Brandy drew breath at the beauty. Sunlight fell in delicate patterns through the gold and red leaves; the singing of the birds surrounded her, and she inhaled the sharp pine scent until she knew the farthest boundaries of her lungs. Lady was willing and obedient, and Brandy let her canter on the smooth parts of the trail. She took a slight detour on a well-trod path and discovered the tidy little cabin which had to be Rafe's. He took great care of his place; everything was in repair, and neatly cultivated land surrounded the building.

She went back to the main trail and found a lovely little pond deep in the woods. It would be a good place to bring Missy someday. A herd of deer, startled by her approach, escaped in graceful leaps as she watched with pleasure. She found a couple of low log falls and tested Lady's jumping ability and judged Rafe's opinion to be correct—with patience and practice the mare could be trained to be a fine jumper. She felt utterly content by the time she turned the horse for home, keeping her at a slow pace to match her own dreaming state.

Lady's start and her snicker of welcome jolted Brandy out of her daze. Another rider was coming down the trail. Grey King on a big bay. Where was Orpheus? She raised her hand in greeting, then dropped in confusion as he came closer. His grin was wide and mischievous; all the same features were there, but much more lightly drawn on the youthful face. Brandy blinked and stared.

"Sorry to disappoint you," he said, tipping his hat to her, "but my big brother is still in town, so I thought I'd sneak out to meet the new addition to the household. I'm Raleigh."

His dancing black eyes took in everything about her at a glance. "My, my, I thought you must be special; the fair Ruth turns green at the mere mention of you. But special is hardly adequate. My brother is becoming a connoisseur in his old age. I must congratulate him."

She knew she ought to be insulted, but Raleigh's gaiety was infectious. She shook her head in mock disapproval. "Are you always so full of flattery? That has to be some of the worst nonsense I've ever heard!"

"My dear Brandy—Miss Claybourne is too formal—you wound me. I am a sincere fellow driven to flowery speech by your surpassing beauty."

They laughed and chatted all the way back like lighthearted children. Raleigh was so easy to be with that Brandy could not get over the contrast in personalities between him and his brother, made so much more noticeable by the physical similarities. It gave her a strange sense of double vision, as though she were looking into Grey's face of ten years ago.

When they got back to the stables, Brandy was startled by Rafe's reaction to Raleigh. He was polite and willing to take care of Casco, Raleigh's horse, but his manner was distant, all light in his eyes extinguished. *Why*, thought Brandy, *he's so protective of Grey that he resents Raleigh's even being here, or maybe for being with me*. She felt a faint flicker of fear in a sudden new thought—as gentle as Rafe might be in most things, she had no doubt that he would be savage in defense of Grey. She suppressed a shiver; fanaticism in any form was dangerous.

If Raleigh's reception at the stables was cool, it was

not so at the house. Mrs. Bailey heard them come in, and her face was joyous as she came down the hall. Raleigh lifted her right off her feet and kissed her, leaving her blushing like a young girl as she tried to make her voice angry. "You incorrigible boy, I'll have you remember that I am a dignified old woman!"

"Not my Margaret, not if I can help it."

"It's no use," said Mrs. Bailey, "he's been like this since he was born, even with all my efforts to bring him up right."

She prepared a light meal for them, and Brandy ate hers quickly and left to take Missy's tray up despite Raleigh's protest. She knew they wouldn't miss her. They were talking rapidly and laughing when she left, obviously old favorites with each other.

Her morning's victory held; Missy ate without any problem. Brandy set the tray aside and talked to her about her ride and what she'd seen.

She was interrupted by Raleigh saying from the doorway, "Mind if I come in and say hello to my niece?" There was nothing to say since he was already coming toward them. Brandy could see no change in Missy, but her own body was tense, and she realized she wanted Missy to react to Raleigh as she did to Grey. Why? To show there might have been some mistake? She didn't understand her motives for wanting it.

But Missy did not oblige. She didn't scream or move when Raleigh picked her up and kissed her. "How's my little one, now that the nice lady has come to stay with you?" Brandy knew he expected no answer, but she was touched by the kindness in his voice. She put away the wish that it was Grey instead of Raleigh holding the child.

When she came down for dinner, she was pleased to learn that Raleigh was staying for a few days. She was too honest to deny that his company gave her pleasure.

After the meal, Mrs. Bailey and Raleigh took her on the promised tour of the house. There were endless cabinets of silver, gold, porcelain, jade, and ivory. There was a collection of tiny, fully rigged ship models representing every vessel built by the Kings. Brandy recognized the *Isabella* with delight and could almost see a tiny figure on deck, Grey looking out to sea. And even the pieces of furniture were by famous makers, proudly listed by Mrs. Bailey. Brandy recognized some of the names—Chippendale, Sheraton, and Hepplewhite—but she felt very ignorant as Mrs. Bailey elaborated on the different joints, finishes, and woods used to make the articles, touching each piece as gently as if it were a beloved child.

Treasure after treasure passed before Brandy's eyes until she was dizzy with the richness of it all. Without stopping to think, she asked impulsively, "Do you ever mind being the second son, not having King's Inland for your own?" She gasped as the rudeness of what she'd said assailed her. "Oh, I am so sorry! What a dreadful thing to say!"

Raleigh smiled easily. "Don't be embarrassed. It's a fair question, and I like your directness. No, I don't mind at all. What would I do with this lot except gawk at it as we are now? And being second relieves me of a lot of responsibility. I don't want to be old and grim before my time, like Grey. Besides, Margaret has always spoiled me terribly, probably to make up for it. It has its compensations."

"You are a wicked young man," chided Mrs. Bailey.

"Can't help it, all second sons are, you know, way they're raised," he teased, but Brandy suspected that her question had hurt more than he admitted, especially since the formidable Mrs. Bailey's eyes rested on him with such troubled intensity. It made her feel guilty, and she was especially nice to him for the rest of the evening.

CHAPTER IV

Brandy had to curb her tendency to do everything too fast in her dealings with Missy, but her knowledge that the child did leave her room at night gave her courage for the next part of her plan. Missy's lack of response except for terror had gradually defeated everyone so that they allowed the child to keep to the safe prison of her room. Brandy thought it was one of the unhealthiest things of all, and she wanted it changed immediately. It was Saturday, one of Persia's days off, and Raleigh was taking Mrs. Bailey out for a ride in the wagon to visit some of the farms, so only Rafe would be around. That suited Brandy perfectly. In case of a disaster, she did not want extra spectators.

Despite the frosty mornings, the Indian summer still held and softened the edges of the days, and Brandy couldn't wait to be outdoors. And so when Missy had finished eating, Brandy picked her up. She was so slight that her weight was easy to carry; only the rigidity of her body made it difficult. "I know you go out of your room sometimes, so now you're going to go out with me. It's time you saw the sun again."

The trembling didn't begin until Brandy had carried her down the stairs. She steeled herself against giving in to it; it was pathetic—the little body quivered in her arms as if touched by deadly cold. When she finally got outdoors with her burden, she felt as if her own teeth must be chattering from mere contact, but she didn't put Missy down until they were out by the paddock where the two colts were already busy teasing each other. She settled herself and the child on the ground, keeping her arm around her. The cats ran up, mewing for attention, and Tiger rubbed against Missy. The child did not reach out to touch the animal, but it did not seem to add to her fright.

The shivering slowed, then stopped altogether. Missy's eyes had been tightly shut since Brandy had picked her up; now they opened and Missy's head turned slightly. Brandy nearly crowed aloud with delight. The colts were in the child's line of vision, and Brandy knew she was seeing them, really seeing them, not looking through to some invisible point beyond. Brandy sat very still, watching every small movement which told of new things being looked at, one by one.

She heard a step and looked up to find Rafe staring at them, mouth open in amazement. Missy gave no sign that she was aware of him, and he recovered quickly. He sat down beside Brandy. "It is a beautiful day to be under the sky. I am glad to see you, my little friend." Just that, nicely said. Brandy could have kissed him for it—no mention of the long time past, no demands on the child. They sat for a good while, Brandy and Rafe talking about the animals, not letting Missy's silence become their own.

Finally, Rafe excused himself to go back to work, and Brandy said to Missy, "We'd better go in now, too. I am too tired to carry you. Will you walk, please?" Gently she stood the child upright and then put out her hand. Nothing was offered in return, but when she took hold of the small hand, it was not withdrawn, and when she started off, Missy walked stiff-legged and clumsy but obediently at her side.

So much had been accomplished that Brandy nearly lost her nerve for the next step, but it was important to try it while Persia was gone—Persia was so tender-hearted that she would suffer more than the child.

Brandy brought Missy's midday meal up and set it before her, explaining firmly, "Missy, I fed you breakfast. People have been feeding you like a baby for a very long time, but I want it to stop. You are five years old, and I know you can feed yourself. I'm going to leave this; eat what you want." She left quickly because she felt if she looked one second longer at the frail body, she would go right back to hand-feeding the child.

She found she didn't want anything to eat at all. *You are as bad as Missy,* she accused herself, and tried not to feel so anxious. When she went back to get the tray, it had not been touched. "All right," she said, picking it up, "you are probably not hungry now, but perhaps you will be by supper time."

Apart from another talking session with Missy, she spent the afternoon writing letters to the Adamses and to Pearl, and she was very happy to hear Mrs. Bailey and Raleigh coming in. She went down to meet them. Raleigh eyed her and said, "We had a very nice day, but it doesn't look as if you did. You look like a fox caught in a hen house. What have you found to do around here that's as bad as that?"

Brandy laughed louder than she meant to, but her protest was sincere. "No, I've had a marvelous day!" She told them about Missy's excursion, and after their first stunned disbelief and Mrs. Bailey's protest of "It can't be!" they were properly joyous. She didn't mention her experiment with Missy's eating, and she had to fight the wild impulse to say, "Oh, yes, and I'm seeing if I can get her to eat by herself. I'm starving her."

When she took Missy her supper, she repeated her earlier words. The eyes did not flicker; the body rocked slowly, steadily. She knew what she would find when she went back for the tray. She looked at the untouched food, then at Missy. "I know you can do it, I know you can, if not for your hunger, then for mine because I am not going to eat until you do. So if you care about me at all, you will do as I ask. We'll try again tomorrow."

Out in the hall she fed bits of the meal to Tiger and Iris. She had let them follow her up; she could see how cats could come in handy sometimes. She did not want Mrs. Bailey to see the full tray.

It wasn't difficult to refuse food at supper; she wasn't hungry. She felt as if she could go for days, but Missy couldn't, not tiny Missy.

When Mrs. Bailey asked if she was feeling all right, she laughed and said she certainly was, so much so that she'd been an awful pig when she made her midday meal. Raleigh was skeptical and teased her about being lovesick. In truth, she did feel a little feverish with anxiety about whether or not she was doing the right thing. She was relieved when they asked her to play the piano. Her music had always brought instant escape, but now as she played, it was difficult not to think of a hungry little girl huddled at the head of the stairs, listening.

And when she finally slept, it was to wake again tangled in the bedclothes and feeling suffocated—a strange thing since she usually slept so quietly. Work with Missy was taking its toll of her, she admitted as she tried to sleep again. But another thought struck her, and she sat bolt upright. Now that she was more fully conscious, she thought she remembered hearing her door click shut just as she had awakened. She crossed her room swiftly, yanked the door open, and looked up and down the hall. There was no one there. She shrugged and went back to bed. Waking from bad dreams often leaves one unsure of what is fantasy, what is truth.

Breakfast brought no change. Iris and Tiger ate well. Brandy looked at Missy and sighed, amazed she could still be rocking. "I am sure you're hungry by now; I know I am. We'll try again midday."

She skipped the morning session with the child,

hoping the solitude would make her hungrier. She went for a ride with Raleigh, feeling light-headed and reckless, drawing repeated warnings from him about going too fast and trying impossible jumps. She settled down only because she might endanger Lady.

Raleigh was puzzled by her behavior, but his only comment was: "I thought you had some bee in your bonnet, but it seems to be a granddaddy hornet instead."

By the time she took the next meal to Missy her hands were shaking so that she could hardly carry the tray. It had to work; she had to win, but she couldn't go on this way much longer—Missy's control might be enough to bring death by starvation.

She put the tray down before the child without hope and turned to go. The clink of silver on china turned her unbelieving eyes. Not with her fingers but with the calm precision of a longtime use of tableware, Missy was feeding herself.

Brandy swallowed her tears and made her voice steady. "That's very, very good. I knew you could do it. Thank you. Now I can eat, too. I'm awfully hungry."

Of course, Missy paid no attention to her, but Brandy was completely satisfied, watching the competent movement of the small hands. When Missy had finished, Brandy kissed her. "I am so proud of you. How I love you!" The rocking was not resumed.

Her relief that the battle was over and won left her bemused, and she was not aware of the voices until she reached the bottom of the stairs; then the words broke over her in an angry wave. Grey was home.

He was facing Raleigh in the hall. His whole stance was one of violence barely restrained. "Can't you ever do a man's job? You were supposed to be there when the *Lisbeth* docked. You knew that. Instead I find you in my house, amusing yourself with my servants. Now get out!"

Neither heard Brandy's outraged gasp.

Raleigh grinned mockingly at his brother, and his voice was lazy. "There are plenty of other men there to check in the cargo; another useless job to keep me occupied, wasn't it, big brother? Bit possessive of your belongings, aren't you? Guess I would be too if I had such good taste in governesses."

The tray crashed to the floor, startling both men, and before she knew what she was doing, Brandy was between them screaming, "Stop it, stop it! You're behaving like horrid, hateful children. And I belong to no one!" She had a glimpse of their stunned faces before the world tipped crazily and the light whirled away.

She was aware of the rough weave of Grey's coat; that was nice, he must have caught her as she fell. He was carrying her. She looked up into his white face. "Well, I'll be damned," he said.

"I'm sure you will. Now put me down!" snapped Brandy, remembering the scene that had caused all this.

Grey placed her carefully on the sofa in the drawing room. His anxious, guilty expression made him look momentarily younger, more like Raleigh. Raleigh was hovering in the background. They reminded Brandy so much of ten-year-old boys caught in a prank that she had to smile.

Grey's face eased. "That's better. You are not the sort of woman I would have thought suffers from the vapors, even though I've heard it's fashionable. Do you faint often? May I get you some whiskey?"

"No to both. I never faint, well, never until now, and the last thing I want is whiskey. It was hunger, not fashion, which caused that bit of idiocy."

His eyebrows rose in bewilderment. "You certainly don't wish to be any thinner than you are?"

Brandy laughed ruefully; he had none of Raleigh's talent for a compliment. But then her joy in Missy's progress welled up again, and the words tumbled out in explanation.

When she had finished, she saw incredibly that his face was not nearly as pleased as she had expected. It was more than a little angry. "That," he said, "was a very foolish thing to do."

"Oh, I know it was a risk, but I had to try it. I wouldn't have let any harm come to her, you know that, don't you?"

"I'm not talking about Missy. I would agree to anything which would help her. But for you to go hungry on her account is beyond my understanding."

"Don't you see, I promised!"

He eyed her curiously. "Did it never occur to you that she would not have known?"

"That would have been dishonest. Promises I make, I keep. But you're missing the whole point. I think she really cares about other people. I think she finally fed herself for my sake, not for her own. That means she is still capable of feeling something besides terror, of loving."

Grey's face was old again. He shook his head wearily. "I think it means the child finally got hungry enough to do something about it. But I am, of course, pleased with her progress, whatever the motives. And I apologize for my behavior with my brother." He looked around for Raleigh, but there was no sign of him, and Grey shrugged. "We don't see eye to eye. My words about servants were unforgivably rude, but I ask your pardon anyway."

Brandy smiled at him as she stood. "Apology accepted because if this goes on any longer, I never will get anything to eat."

Grey smiled back at her, but it never reached his eyes. She had a sudden lonesome wish for Raleigh's blithe presence.

Brandy would not have mentioned it, but Grey told Mrs. Bailey what had happened, adding that she'd better keep an eye on Miss Claybourne, who seemed unable to take care of herself. Before Brandy could make a nasty retort, Mrs. Bailey said, "I think she's quite capable. Just think, she managed to do what I've been trying to accomplish for years—she ended one of your dreadful rows. It would be so much simpler if you boys got along." Grey's mouth tightened, but he said nothing.

Mrs. Bailey asked Brandy to play the piano again that night, saying that she was getting quite spoiled by having music so readily available once more. She led the way to the music room, and Brandy hesitated, putting her hand out to stop Grey. "If you'd rather I didn't play, I can say I'm still feeling too wobbly." She didn't know how else to approach the subject, but her meaning was clear to him.

"You take me for more of a sentimentalist than I am, Miss Claybourne. My wife played the piano, rode horses, danced, and did many other things. I still enjoy all of them." His voice was calm, but his expression was grim, and Brandy wondered how he could bear to have the picture of Jasmine in his sight.

There was no easy slipping away with Grey present. Brandy was acutely conscious of him sitting where he could watch her hands. He could also see the portrait. She could not resist stealing occasional glances at him as she played, nor could she deny the feeling of triumph when she saw his absorption in the sound, the easing of his guard. She played well, her fingers finding the keys not only without fault but with passionate conviction, offering the best she could without knowing why it was so important.

She didn't know what warned her—it was like picking up the small changes in Missy—and she played the English suite to the end without faltering. But she saw it all—the sudden shifting of Grey's eyes to the painting, the mocking lift of his eyebrows, the twist of his mouth, his whole sardonic salute, as though he had said aloud, "All right, Jasmine, you have reminded me; I cannot forget."

Brandy felt sick, as if she had been spying on an intimate scene between lovers. She rose after the last note. "Thank you for your patient listening. I must go to bed now; it has been a long day. Good night." She was thankful for the steadiness of her voice. She left swiftly, hearing Mrs. Bailey's words trailing behind her. "She does look worn out. It was thoughtless of me to ask her to play tonight." Brandy did not hear Grey's reply. Instead, as she made her way without a lamp, she heard the sounds of Missy in the darkness, deserting her post, scurrying down the hall, shutting the door.

She was very desperate to sleep, but every time she shut her eyes she saw Grey and Jasmine, mocking, hating, loving each other. She concentrated on the night sounds. A loon's hysteria rose to meet the chuckling bark of a fox. She did not hear Grey come up to his room, and in the morning he was gone. He had only come to King's Inland because he knew Raleigh was there. But even so, his precise attention to details had not faltered. Mrs. Bailey told her he had taken her letters to start them on their separate journeys.

Persia was late, but when she arrived, she was in even better spirits than usual. The new puppies had arrived that morning, and she had tarried to make sure the bitch was all right. "Five little ones she had, all perfect. Now, you'll have to come visitin' right soon, so you can see 'em while they're wee." She thought a minute. "How 'bout tomorrow afternoon? I could finish early, an' we could get Rafe to take us in th' wagon. Then you could both stay to supper."

Brandy hid her amusement; she guessed how much Persia wanted Rafe to be included in the plan. It was fine with her, but she hesitated, not wanting to leave Mrs. Bailey out. The housekeeper saw her doubt. "Don't go mothering me! I've been in this house more than double the years you've been alive. And I'm perfectly capable of giving Missy her evening meal, especially now."

Persia's puzzlement turned to incredulous pleasure when she heard about Missy's accomplishments. Her laughter and tears were in what she termed "a regular tangle."

Later, when Brandy carried the child down the stairs

again, Persia had control enough to say, "Good morning, Missy," as though it were normal for her to be out of her room.

As soon as they were outside, Brandy put the child down and took her hand. She seemed less awkward than she had the day before, but Brandy realized she was setting her steps toward the stables. Even this Missy was trying to form into a pattern. There was a moment of resistance when Brandy resolutely started in the direction of the orchard behind the house, but then Missy started to walk again. When they had settled down beneath an apple tree, Brandy took Missy into her lap, cuddling her, talking, and singing nonsense rhymes. By the time she was ready to take her back to the house she thought she could feel a slight bending of the body to fit her own.

The next day she made her walk from her room and was amazed that there was no problem. The stairs were awkward for her; she went down them with infinite care, making sure that both feet were firmly planted on one step before she tried the next, but as far as Brandy was concerned, she could take all day if she wished, as long as she kept going. Beyond a slight hesitation as they passed the door to the music room, Missy did not even protest walking through the house. And she made no attempt to determine the direction of their walk, apparently accepting the fact that it would be different and Brandy would decide. Brandy's heart was singing as she led Missy into the beauty of the woods, and she enjoyed every minute of their time there.

Persia finished her chores at three, and Brandy went to see Missy before they left. She checked at the doorway, wondering what was different, and then it hit her. Many of the dolls, books, and various toys so long untouched had been moved. She was so attuned to this room that she could see clearly that things had been picked up, and though there had been some attempt to put them back in their usual places, either the time had been too short, or in the excitement of touching them, Missy had forgotten how they had been arranged. And as added proof, a brightly painted rocking horse still swayed back and forth slowly, as if a hand had given it a sly push.

Brandy had a moment of vicarious pleasure, of knowing what it must be like to touch all sorts of different objects, to feel the various shapes and textures after so long a time of nontouching, of dead hands. Her eyes flew to Missy's hands. The fingers were no longer curled; the wrists no longer dropped; the strange bend of the elbows was gone. The hands rested naturally in her lap.

Brandy swooped her up in her arms, laughing her joy and telling her how marvelous she was. She hated to leave her after such a discovery, but Persia's family was expecting them, so she explained carefully, telling Missy that Mrs. Bailey would bring her supper but that she, Brandy, was going away only for a short while. She hoped Missy understood, but her reaction wasn't encouraging; her body was rigid again as though ice had suddenly frozen where blood had flowed.

Brandy was quiet for most of the wagon ride, disinclined to mention the latest developments until she understood them better herself. She knew what was happening was good, but also one-sided. Missy was reestablishing contact with objects but only indirectly with people. At least she made no violent protest to being touched. Brandy sighed and brought her mind back into focus. Rafe and Persia had not minded her lack of attention; they were engaged in a silence of their own. Rafe had been very polite and willing to be their driver, but Brandy could see the wariness in his eyes, the tenseness in his body, holding away as if afraid to touch Persia, who sat beside him. Through Missy, Brandy was learning a great deal about the ways a body could whisper and shout without uttering a sound. Persia's face was more open, anxious at Rafe's coldness but nonetheless blissful because she was with him.

They reached the Cowperwaithe farm in less than an

hour, but on foot it would have taken quite a bit longer. Brandy asked Persia in wonder, "Do you really hate horses so much that you'd rather walk all this way twice a day than ride?"

Persia grinned. "Well, that's part of it, though I always know Rafe'll give me a lift if I need it. But you see, things are lively in our house, an' my walkin' time is peaceful like."

As soon as she met Persia's family, Brandy could see her point. The house overflowed with cats, dogs, and children. Mrs. Cowperwaithe was short, round, red-headed, and energetic, a good thing seeing all she had to manage. Lean and lantern-jawed, her husband gave a first impression of dourness, but it was soon belied by the wry good humor in the far-seeing blue eyes. When Brandy complimented him on the beauty of the farm, he said, "It'll do till somethin' better comes along."

Persia's older brother, Ben, was a youthful copy of his father. Hank and Amos, the other two boys, were still in the toddler stage; what the family called "the gaggle of girls" came in between. Persia had two sisters, India and Ivory, both younger than she. Ivory, in spite of her name, was dark-haired and brown-skinned; India was another of the fiery-haired Cowperwaithes. The richness of the girls' names was another reminder of the legacy of a seafaring state.

The family greeted Brandy with diffidence but no servility. They were proud and warm, tempered into strength by their unceasing battle to wrest a good life from the unyielding ground.

Brandy duly admired the new puppies and stroked the head of the mother who seemed to think it her just due for a job well done. But it wasn't until she saw the outcast that the idea came to her. He was not a member of the new litter. He was past weaning but every once in a while he would wander hopefully over and try to creep in among the puppies until the bitch would send him away with a low growl and teeth bared. He was small and liver-colored with floppy ears and a potbelly.

He looked as if he were made of random parts of several breeds.

Brandy picked him up, and he snuggled gratefully against her. "Where did he come from?" she asked.

"Well, we aren't rightly sure," drawled Mr. Cowperwaithe, face straight, eyes dancing, "that's why we call him Mebbe, 'cos mebbe he's a dog, mebbe not. Th' others that came with him, they are dogs all right, an' we've given 'em all t'other farms. But him, well, we aren't extra-proud o' him, so runty he's a shame to th' family."

Brandy regarded him with admiration; she bet he could spin tall tales by the hours. She put the dog down and tried to put him out of her mind.

Time passed much too quickly. Brandy had a merry time, and even Rafe relaxed, helpless against the atmosphere of goodwill.

Brandy resisted almost until it was time to go, but then she picked Mebbe up again. "Please, may I buy him from you?"

"Nope, but you can sure have him so long as you don't let on where he came from," said Mr. Cowperwaithe.

"Thank you, thank you," she cried, hugging Mebbe. But she saw the doubt in their eyes; they knew about the no dog rule at King's Inland. "Don't worry. It will be fine. I'm sure it will. Missy needs something alive to have as her own. I don't think she'll be able to resist him."

"If it don't work out, just send him along home with Persia," said Mrs. Cowperwaithe practically.

The family saw Brandy and Rafe off, telling them to come by anytime. The lanterns hanging on the wagon cast shards of light, and Rafe kept the pace slow so that Pete and Polly wouldn't stumble. The creak and rumble of the wagon, the warm weight of the puppy asleep on her lap, and the quiet man beside her filled Brandy with peace. She sighed contentedly. "They're a very special family, aren't they?"

"Yes, good people they are, all of them." Brandy

heard the wistful note in Rafe's voice and tried to think of a way to shift the subject casually to Persia. She turned her head to see Rafe more clearly, and out of the corner of her eye, she caught sight of wide-set green eyes pooling the lantern light. She started, grabbed Rafe's arm, and woke the puppy in the process. "Good grief, what's that?" She tried to point out where the eyes had been, but nothing glinted.

Rafe laughed softly. "You will see him again. He is following us. It is the lynx cat. They are full of a great curiousness about people and light, but they will not harm."

The opportunity for talking about Persia was lost, but Brandy decided it was just as well; she probably would have made a bad job of it. As Rafe predicted, the cat stalked them most of the way, jade eyes gleaming and then disappearing, but Brandy didn't mind; now that she knew it was just a bobcat, it seemed rather comforting, like having a woods' guardian.

Mrs. Bailey met her in the hall when she got home. Her welcoming smile died at the sight of the puppy. "My dear Miss Claybourne, I am sorry you didn't understand. Dogs are not allowed in this house. Missy is afraid of them, and Grey forbids them. He got rid of his kennel on account of the child."

Brandy didn't want to be defiant, but small points were so important. She was also reluctant to suggest that perhaps Missy had feared Grey's dogs simply because they were his. Instead she said, "I am sure I'll make many mistakes, but one thing is clear to me— Missy's world must be changed, her fears overcome each in turn. I think the dog will be another small beginning, but if not, I will send him back."

Mrs. Bailey shook her head ruefully, her smile returning. "Miss Claybourne, under that meekness, I detect an iron will. But it's not me you have to answer to, it's Grey. I admit you are making remarkable progress, though, and that should please him. The child ate her supper like a perfect lamb."

Brandy thanked her, and carrying Mebbe, she went to see if Missy was asleep and found her sitting up in bed, eyes wide and staring, body rocking. She rushed to her, putting the puppy down and taking the child in her arms. "Poor darling, did you think I'd left you forever? I went to meet Persia's family, and they sent you a present. Isn't he beautiful? His old name was Mebbe, but that isn't nearly good enough for him." *A maybe dog for a maybe child; no, not nearly good enough.* "I think we ought to call him something special like Panza. There was a man named Panza, and he was a fine friend." *To another human being who lived in a fantasy world*, she added mentally. She hardly dared breathe as she waited for a reaction, any reaction.

The golden head turned, the black eyes focused and widened, a shiver ran from the child's body to Brandy's. *Please, please*, Brandy prayed silently, *let the fear pass.* Panza looked up at Missy, whined and wiggled closer, rolling on his back and begging to be petted. A small hand was extended tentatively, and Panza licked it shyly. The hand drew back a little, and the puppy lowered his head as though sure he had done something wrong. For one awful moment, Bandy thought the child might strike him.

Missy put her hand out toward him again, holding it uncertainly over him, and then gently, gently she touched his face. He licked her hand again, squeaking joyfully, and this time there was no withdrawal. With infinite care and complete absorption, Missy touched his ears and the soft skin of the little round belly and ran her hand down his back. It was too much for Panza; he snuggled closer, then climbed clumsily into Missy's lap, ecstatic with acceptance, reaching up to lick her chin. Her head bent to him, her arms held him close. Brandy's vision blurred as she hugged them both to her. The first miraculous contact had been made; of her own accord, Missy had reached out to touch something warm and alive, to touch it gently with awareness of its vulnerability.

Brandy wished the moment could go on forever, but she was well content when she left the pair. Missy was asleep, her body not rigid but slightly curled to provide the hollow where Panza dozed contentedly close to her warmth.

CHAPTER V

When they went walking the next day, Panza followed at Missy's heels, and Missy turned her head every once in a while to make sure he was there. The child walked independently, no longer needing a hand to keep her going. Brandy saw her own idiotic grin of delight reflected on the other faces at King's Inland, Rafe's especially noticeable because his scar distorted his countenance so much when he smiled.

Brandy brought food this time, having decided they would picnic in the woods if Missy did not seem too tired to keep wandering. They ambled along under the trees, Missy walking gracefully now, and it was Panza who showed the first signs of weariness, his short, fat legs having to trot to keep up. Brandy picked him up to give him a rest, and Missy reached out to touch him every now and then, though she was careful not to touch Brandy. Brandy put Panza down at intervals, and at one point he saw a squirrel and gave chase, barking in his ridiculously small voice, tumbling over a log in the way. He looked so funny that Brandy laughed and glanced at Missy in time to see a small lift of her mouth. In other children it would have been nothing; in Missy it was the tiniest beginning of a smile. Brandy could not imagine how beautiful she would be if she truly smiled.

A short distance from the pond, a muffled growl and

the rising hackles on Panza gave her a first warning.
The puppy shivered in her arms. Brandy stopped and
looked around carefully. At first she could see nothing,
but then a faint snorting grunt gave her direction. She
stared hard at the shade- and sun-dappled thicket and
saw, as if he had appeared in an instant, a great brown
bear, sitting up on its haunches, its beady eyes watching
them, its nose twitching as it tested their scent. The
rush of fear made her giddy, and she looked around
wildly for refuge—looked around to see Missy walking
toward the beast. Brandy was beside her in an instant,
holding her firmly but trying not to communicate her
terror.

The instant of panic seemed endless to Brandy, as
though time had stopped while her mind worked crazily at high speed. Run? No, how far would she get
carrying a child, and what would be more likely to start
the bear after them? If the bear came after her, could
she keep it busy until Missy could get away, would
Missy run on command, would she know the way? *Oh,
Grey, I never thought!*

The bear gave a low, snuffling growl, followed by a
human-sounding snort of disgust; then it dropped to all
fours and shambled into the brush, leaving only a faint
trail of sound to tell Brandy it was moving away from
them. She stared at it in disbelief, and her knees gave
way so that she sat down abruptly, pulling Missy into
her lap, bringing a squeal of outrage from Panza, who
had barely avoided being sat on. Brandy heard her own
laughter rising hysterically. *Must get a grip on yourself,
mustn't frighten Missy*. She stopped with a choke and
offered a shaky explanation. "Well, he was something to
see, wasn't he? I'm glad you weren't afraid of him, but
you must be awfully careful around bears. You never
want to get too close to them; they're big and strong,
and they might squash you flat just trying to give you a
friendly hug." *Friendly hug, my soul and body*, thought
Brandy as she held Missy, *more like a predinner preparation*. She knew the truth now of another facet of

Missy's strangeness; though afraid of something as harmless as a dog, she would have walked right up to the bear.

Brandy drew a deep breath and got to her feet, helping Missy up. Resolutely she headed for the pond rather than home, making herself let go of Missy's hand in deference to the child's new independence. Having faced what seemed the ultimate calamity and having escaped unharmed, Brandy decided it was foolish to change plans, and she felt rewarded for her conviction by their time at the pond.

It was so peaceful there with the water reflecting the embers of the trees' autumnal fire. Bare branches etched the sky, and heavy drifts and fallen leaves rustled with the busy scurryings of mice hard at work to make winter a time of plenty. Two otters played ceaselessly on the mud slide on the far bank, and Panza rolled and bounced and yipped through his explorations while Missy watched him. Brandy got the food out, and Missy ate with good appetite, and with no prompting, she gave Panza a piece of meat when he begged. Brandy didn't care how spoiled he became as long as he provided a living link with Missy.

When they passed the thicket on the way back, Brandy was relieved to see no sign of the bear, but sometime later she was not so sure they had been lucky. Missy stopped and stiffened, and at her heels, Panza sat down and cocked his ears, whining a question. Then Brandy too heard the hoofbeats, and as soon as Raleigh was in view, Missy relaxed. She knew the difference between her father and her uncle, even to the horses they rode.

"At last I've found the pilgrims," Raleigh said as he reined Casco to a stop, and Brandy was very happy to see him, even though it might mean more trouble with Grey.

He dismounted, saw the puppy beside the child, and comprehension dawned in his face. "Well, I'll be, introduce me to the new member of the family, won't you?"

He caught on to the name too. "Very apt, trust a schoolmarm to find the right word."

He squatted down so that his eyes were level with Missy's and put his hands on her shoulders. "Hello, little flower, you look all rosy from your walk, very pretty, in fact. Would you like to ride a ways with me on Casco?"

Brandy watched her carefully—her eyes were looking directly at Raleigh, and she did not rock or flick her fingers to provide a shield. Brandy decided it was worth a try.

"Why don't you get on, and then I'll give her a boost up?"

Though Missy did nothing to help the plan, she did not hinder it, but once she was in the saddle in front of Raleigh, she put out her hands. Brandy thought for a moment she was actually reaching out to another human, wanting to get off the horse, but then Panza's jumping and whining told her what was going on. She handed the puppy to Missy, and the child's thin arms held the fat little weight firmly. Raleigh steadied her with one arm. He kept the pace slow, and Brandy walked, which, according to Raleigh, was the way things should be. Brandy stuck her tongue out at him, but she agreed with the situation; Casco might not be so gentle with an unfamiliar rider.

When they arrived home, Rafe was so pleased with the procession that he even greeted Raleigh warmly, and he treated it as the greatest privilege to be allowed to lift Missy down. The little girl's lack of protest at being touched by several different people and at being on a horse was wonderful, and Brandy gave full credit to Panza. It was as though the sensation of the soft body under her hand had given Missy back the knowledge that physical contact with living things was a pleasant and necessary part of existence. If only her part of it, the reaching out, could be extended beyond Panza's warm fur to a human hand.

The child was fast asleep by early evening, proving to

Brandy that much of her tenseness and her hours of wide-open eyes had come from what lack of exercise had added to the illness of her mind. Brandy resolved that under her regime that was one problem which would cease.

Raleigh's presence made it easier. For the next few days he walked and rode with them. When they rode, they took turns holding the child and the puppy, and Brandy was amazed by the sedate behavior of Lady and Casco, who acted as if they knew how precious the added burden was. The busy days had the desired effect on Missy, and some afternoons she even napped, Panza snoring beside her. She made it clear she did not want the puppy out of her sight, looking around anxiously when he was gone.

As much as she loved the child, the afternoons when Missy slept were a delight to Brandy because of Raleigh. She would check in with Persia or Mrs. Bailey, and then she and Raleigh would go for long rides, letting the horses behave with more freedom than on the careful mornings. Brandy tried to suppress an eerie feeling about the whole situation, but it kept returning. It was not helped by the fact that Persia, Mrs. Bailey, and even Rafe appeared to be reconciled to it. She, Raleigh, and Missy felt like a family. They fit comfortably together, and Grey's dark image was an intrusion. Brandy dreaded his return; he brought with him mockery, anger, bitterness—a barely controlled universe of violence.

Her feeling was stronger than ever one afternoon as she and Raleigh sat on the grass in a clearing beside the road which led to King's Inland. They had ridden out on it because it provided better places for jumping than the more overgrown woods trail. They had ridden hard, and Brandy was pleased with the way Lady was coming along, not refusing jumps, sailing over them easily.

The days were cooler now, but the afternoons still held the sun, and Brandy was relaxed and content resting on the warm earth. She turned her head slightly and saw Raleigh watching her, his smile lighting his face as her eyes met his. He reached out, and she was in his arms. He kissed her slowly, thoroughly, and she responded; there was no urgency or clash of wills in the act, only a gentle sharing of a perfect moment.

Silently she cursed Grey for it as she drew away. She countered Raleigh's puzzled frown by putting her hand against his cheek in a gesture which reassured, yet told that the magic was, for now, finished. She shut her eyes, trying to destroy his presence, but he was there still—Grey, enraged by the kiss, jealous of his child, of her, willing and capable of doing harm to anyone who displeased him. She tried not to shiver, not to show Raleigh how cold she was in spite of the warmth of the glade. She rose swiftly, mounted Lady, and called to him to hurry before the good light for jumping was gone.

She knew his male pride was enough. Though he was still confused by her reaction, his expression showed that he was rapidly deciding her withdrawal had come from an excess of emotion and maidenly confusion. *Maidenly confusion, hell*, thought Brandy, but she was grateful he did not suspect that his brother, though miles away, was with them.

She wanted to outride his image, and her urgency communicated itself to Lady. They were off before Raleigh was in the saddle. She heard his shout of surprise and asked Lady for more speed, heading for another clearing ahead, wanting the difficulty of the obstacle there.

She heard Casco thundering behind her, but she knew she could clear the jump well before him. The log fall loomed ahead. She collected herself and the mare. Lady left the ground just as the shout rang out. Brandy felt the midair jerk of the horse's body, the front legs fumbling on the logs, the girth giving way, her own body flying through the air.

Rough hands were poking and prodding, a voice telling her to wake up. She said very clearly, "Keep

your filthy hands off me!" and looked up into Grey's
strained face. He was standing now, his body taut with
rage. She sat up abruptly and cried out at the excruciat-
ing pain shooting through her shoulder. Her left arm
hung uselessly. She clamped her good hand over it and
looked around desperately. "Lady, is Lady all right?"

She caught sight of the saddleless mare placidly
nuzzling Orpheus just as Grey snapped, "She's fine."

Brandy decided to attack first. "You fool, don't you
know better than to startle a horse in mid-jump? Where
did you come from anyway?"

For a minute she thought he might accomplish what
her fall had failed to do. His hands flexed involuntarily,
and she was sure they itched to encircle her neck.

"You stupid little bitch, if you want to commit sui-
cide, do it on your own time and your own horse
somewhere away from here. You should know Lady isn't
good enough to take a jump like that," he snarled. "And
I come and go from my home as I please."

"Lady's good enough if her rider knows how to ask
her. We would have made it anyway if the saddle hadn't
come off," she said, but her voice lacked conviction.
Things were fuzzy at best, but it was becoming clear
that Grey didn't give a damn about the horse, that he
was masking his concern for her with anger. Suddenly
she could see the reason—she was the only one who
had got anywhere with Missy; what would happen if
she died as abruptly as the child's mother had?

"Where's Raleigh?" she asked, still trying to sort
things out.

"I sent him to get Rafe and the wagon," he said,
dismissing his brother with a few words. Then he was
kneeling beside her again. He took her hand away from
the injured shoulder, and she closed her eyes as his
hands explored the damage.

"Don't think it's broken, just dislocated," she gasped
through clenched teeth, opening her eyes in time to
see him nod.

His own face was as rigid as hers as he laid her back

on the ground. She shut her eyes tightly again as he braced her shoulder with his boot and took hold of her arm; she had seen her father do it often enough. The jerk came, snapping the bone back into the socket, and Brandy was disgusted by the sound she made. She rolled over onto her good side, swallowing convulsively. Being sick in front of Grey would be too humiliating.

She was so accustomed to dueling with him that she found his gentleness difficult to accept. His arms held her firmly until she was breathing regularly again. Her shoulder still ached as if badly bruised, but the sharp pain of the displaced bone was gone.

"Thank you. I'm fine now. I'd like to get up, and I'm sure I can ride home."

His face eased and his habitual mockery was back as he helped her to her feet. "I am convinced you could ride home, but I won't allow it. Lady isn't really hurt, but she's bruised and probably getting stiffer by the minute. She doesn't need a rider on her back. You'll ride in the wagon."

"Yes, sir," Brandy said, and admitted privately that she would be quite happy to go back via the wagon. She still had a case of Persia's collywobbles, and falling off of Lady a second time would complete her disgrace.

When the wagon came into sight, she froze and rubbed her eyes, but the vision remained. Raleigh wasn't with Rafe, but Missy was; Missy outside for the first time without her. Joy shot through her; she gave Grey's hand a quick squeeze and then ran to the wagon. She expected Missy to sit composedly as she usually did, but when she got there, the little girl put her arms out, and Brandy responded with her own, swinging the child down, holding her, feeling no pain at all from her shoulder.

"My brave Missy, my brave, wonderful girl! You came all the way with Rafe. And I'm fine, nothing is the matter. I just did a silly thing and fell off Lady. Oh, I am so proud of you!"

Missy's hands were around her neck, her head hidden against her. Brandy looked up at Rafe and saw the sun rising in his eyes. His face was warped by a huge smile. For once he spoke in French to explain. When Raleigh had gotten back to the house, Missy had seen him from a window. At the anxious, tugging insistence of the little girl, Persia had taken her downstairs earlier—now it made sense. Missy had wanted to be able to see toward the stables, had wanted to be that much closer to them, and when she had seen Raleigh, she had flown to the front door. Persia had let her out, and she ran to Rafe, grabbing hold of him, insisting without words that she be taken along. Rafe finished by telling Brandy that she had been right all along: Missy did know what was going on; she had known something was wrong with Brandy.

He added in English, for Missy's benefit, "The little one, she is a good one, yes?"

"A very, very good one," agreed Brandy, stroking Missy's hair. She would have liked more than anything else to hand the child to Grey. She looked around for him. He was standing a little ways off, holding the broken saddle and the reins of the horses. He looked utterly forsaken, his face drawn with the acceptance of the fact that even in her triumph, Missy barred him from her world. Brandy sighed; she was sure Missy knew exactly where Grey was, for she was keeping her head turned away from the spot, and Brandy felt her muscles tensing. But at least the screaming did not start.

Brandy met Grey's eyes, trying to keep the tears out of her own, and gave a small shake of her head. Grey turned away and mounted Orpheus without a word. Then he said, "I'll lead Lady home so you won't have to worry about her." His words were so tightly controlled that Brandy could feel his throat muscles closed around them. He looked at Rafe. "Where's Raleigh?"

"Eh, that one, he does not like the trouble. He has left in a hurry." His accent, the long e's and rolling r's added extra contempt to his opinion of Raleigh. Grey

merely nodded, staring thoughtfully down at the saddle
he had dropped on the ground. He asked Rafe to pick it
up and started for home, urging even poor Lady into a
brisk trot. Brandy knew it was because he could not
bear the sight of Missy with her and Rafe, with no place
for him. Rafe understood, too, and waited until Grey
was out of sight before he helped them up onto the
high seat.

For the first time, Missy spoke eloquently with her
body, and Brandy was so happy she hardly noticed the
absence of words. Missy patted her every once in a
while as though to reassure herself that Brandy was still
alive and with her, and she reached out and touched
Rafe occasionally as if to thank him. When Brandy put
her arm around her, the child snuggled against her.

Orpheus was in his stall when they arrived home, but
Casco was gone. Though Rafe attributed Raleigh's disappearance to cowardice, Brandy believed he had left to
avoid another scene with Grey because she had left no
doubt about how she felt when they shouted at each other.

She still felt dizzy from her fall, but something in
Rafe's manner as he picked up her saddle from the back
of the wagon brought her pause. His motions were
normally slow and steady, but he was in a clumsy hurry
to get the saddle into the barn.

"Wait!" she commanded, taking hold of the girth. For
a moment she thought they were going to have a
tug-of-war, but then he stopped, his eyes not meeting
hers.

Turning it, she stared at the place where the strap
had broken. Broken! Her heart thudded uncomfortably.
It was possible that the leather had just given way but
unlikely. Tack was so well cared for at King's Inland.
And the break was odd—ragged and fibrous on the top
side as if torn, but sharp and clean on the back. Her
hands shook as she held it. There was no way to prove
it, but she was quite sure someone had cut it so that
with enough strain it would give way. Her mouth went
dry at the thought of Missy in front of her on the

saddle. They had ridden slowly, so a fall might have left them unhurt, but it would have undoubtedly terrified the child and reversed much of the progress they had made. Or perhaps the damage had been done just for her own hard afternoon rides. Everyone at King's Inland knew about them; everyone except Grey—unless he had been home before she knew, unless he had found out about the time spent with Raleigh. Perhaps the shout had been an attempt to prevent his own plan from working. Then why had he looked so carefully at the saddle? Her mind spun with all the possibilities. Someone wanted her at the very least injured, at the most dead. She shook her head to clear it.

"Please, forgive me. It is my fault that such a thing should happen. But I do not understand; I am very careful with all of the leathers." Rafe's voice was anxious, pleading.

Brandy looked at him, her face empty of expression. Did he really not suspect it had been deliberately done or was he covering his own crime with feigned innocence? He would do nothing unless she threatened Grey, and surely he did not think that of her. No, she could not believe it. She trusted him too much, loved him too much. Her face softened, and she put her hand on his shoulder. "It was my fault as much as yours. I saddled Lady myself this afternoon, and I am a good enough horsewoman to know how to check my own tack."

She turned to look for Missy and found her sitting on the ground with a frantic Panza licking her face. Persia was with them. "That pup went near crazy when she left him." She looked closely at Brandy. "Are you all o' a piece? What a terrible thing!"

Could she have done it? No. Brandy managed a smile. "I'm fine. I've taken quite a few tumbles before, and I'll probably take many more before I'm done." But not because of a cut girth, she added mentally.

She did not believe that something good always came of something bad, but in this case it had. Missy's new responsiveness was not a transient phase arising out of an interval of shock. When Brandy went to her, Missy reached out as though the barrier had never existed, and hand in hand they went into the house.

Grey was probably in his study, and Brandy hoped he stayed there because she did not want this delicate new part of Missy to be cut off by terror. As they went up the stairs, Missy ran her hand over the smooth wood of the banister and touched everything within reach on her way to her room. Once there, she picked up one toy after another, openly savoring the texture of each as Brandy knew she had done secretly.

Brandy left her to wash the dirt of her fall away and met Mrs. Bailey in the hall. Mrs. Bailey? No, not her either; her normally serene face was white and tense with worry. "My dear, I am so glad you were not badly hurt. I don't think any of us could have borne it; you have become so much a part of us. And I have never seen Grey so upset. He wants to see you immediately in his study."

Brandy thanked her for her concern, but some inner defiance moved against Grey, and she said, "Please tell Mr. King I will be down as soon as I have had a chance to freshen up and to give Missy her supper. And will you ask Persia if she would bring the tray up to me?"

Mrs. Bailey was obviously surprised that Brandy would defy Grey, but she complied.

Brandy brushed the dirt out of her hair and surveyed the damage. A fine bruise and an aching shoulder were all the fall had given her. She knew how lucky she had been. She shivered and dressed hurriedly.

Missy was calmly holding Panza when Brandy went back to her. She stayed with her until she had eaten her supper and fallen asleep, and then she went down to see Grey.

He was working at his desk, and he rose politely when she entered. He made no comment on her defiant lateness, but his face was forbidding, and he scrutinized her carefully before he spoke. "I am glad to see you in one piece, Miss Claybourne. You might easily have broken your neck."

"I know that, but I've had enough experience to know how to fall."

She expected him to be amused, but he wasn't. "I have no doubt of that. Anyone who mismatches horse and jump like that must be prepared to fall quite often. But it is difficult for me to understand Raleigh letting you attempt it. He must be even more empty-headed that I thought."

Brandy's temper flashed, but she tried to keep her voice even. "That's unfair, both ways. I told you before, I've been doing a lot of work with Lady; she's taken that jump easily on several occasions. Your shout and the girth breaking were to blame, not the horse. And Raleigh had nothing to do with it. I went ahead of him and chose the jump." She blushed at the sudden memory of Raleigh's kiss, and Grey's mouth curled sardonically as if he were seeing it.

"I can't say I have much respect for your choice of companions, but then, Ruth was probably right, there is so little to amuse a young woman here." Brandy kept her hands clenched in her lap because she wanted to slap him. But when he continued, his voice was weary, the sarcasm gone. "I will take you back with me tomorrow. I will pay you for the full six months plus your passage back to Boston."

Brandy stared at him incredulously. "You'll what? You'll send me packing just because I fell off a horse?" The image of the cut leather rose again in her mind.

"Not because you fell off a horse, but because you might have been killed. And the very last thing I can afford is to have another woman die accidentally at King's Inland."

Brandy heard the emphasis on "accidentally" and met his eyes squarely. "All right, so it might not have been an accident. I saw the strap, too, and it was either a very odd break or someone cut it. I will be more careful about checking my tack in the future. But I'll not leave. We made a bargain, a six-month bargain, and I'm going to hold you to it. The only way you are going to make me leave is to haul me off bodily, and I'll kick and scream all the way. I've thought about it, and I can only find two people who might have a motive for wanting to be rid of me. One is Ruth, but unless she has someone hiding in the woods to do her work, she can hardly have managed it from miles away. The other is you, and if it's true, then it's very strange indeed. Missy now goes outdoors; she is no longer afraid of dogs or horses; she feeds herself; she touches not only objects, but people; and she sees, really sees. In a very short time, we've made tremendous progress, she and I, and I'm proud of both of us. I have no doubt that she will speak one day, and I want to be here to hear her. Now, the only reason I can find for your wanting me gone is that this whole business of your wanting to help her is a sham, that what Miss Collins told me is more of the truth than even she realized—that you and she would be much better off without the burden of the child."

She had never seen such blazing anger. She noticed the details with an odd detachment. His eyes were narrowed to mere slits of darkness; a vein pulsed in his temples; the lines in his face looked deep enough to have been carved with a knife. But when he spoke, his voice was devoid of emotion, flat, dead. "That will be all, Miss Claybourne. Right now I would not mind in the least if you broke your neck or if someone did it for you. I myself am more than tempted. Get out."

Mrs. Bailey was puzzled by Grey's absence at supper, but Brandy did not enlighten her. Brandy's anger lasted through most of the meal until she heard first the study and then the front door opening and slamming shut, and Mrs. Bailey shook her head, saying, "He's off on one of his wild rides on that great black devil. It's a wonder to me he ever comes back whole."

Brandy's anger dissolved, and the dismay that had been creeping around the edges of her mind flooded in.

She felt so guilty she could hardly bear it. If anything happened to Grey on his ride, she would be to blame. She desperately wanted to drown her consciousness in music, and she wanted no audience. Mrs. Bailey accepted her explanation that she wished to do some practicing without anyone there to hear her mistakes.

She played classics, popular tunes, and the haunting melodies of lonely ballads she had learned in the West. She played until her hands ached and her injured shoulder throbbed with a life of its own. And then she played past the pain until she felt disembodied, as if she were listening to someone else making the instrument ring.

She did not hear him come in, did not know how long he had been standing at the doorway before she felt his presence. The music died abruptly as she spun around to face him.

He was dust-grimed, and his face was bleached with fatigue except for the scarlet lines across one cheek where a branch had hit him. She could not meet his eyes, afraid of what she might see there. Her voice was queer and choked to her own ears. "Mr. King, I am so ashamed about what I said. I made accusations for which I have no proof, and I don't even believe them anyway. I spoke out of anger because I care so much about Missy I could not bear the thought of leaving her. I can't bear it now. Don't you see, she is the most important consideration. She will be ready to let me go someday, but not yet. And there is no proof that the strap was cut, no reason in spite of what I said that anyone would want to harm me. I'll just be more careful. But I'll never be more sorry than I am right now, and I have never wanted anything more than I want your pardon."

Silence filled the space which had held so much music minutes before, and finally, Brandy could not forbear looking at him. He was staring at her, a queer light which was not anger in his eyes. She had never heard so kind a voice from him.

"I hired you because I thought you had the spirit to fight for Missy. You have proved you do to a much greater degree than I would have guessed. I would be a fool to dismiss you; God knows what it would do to the child. But if you ever feel frightened enough to want to leave, my offer still holds. Good night, Miss Claybourne."

Threat or concerned promise—she could not decide.

Her sleep was broken once more by the hot choking feeling which was becoming distressingly familiar. She checked the hall and found it empty, and as far as she could tell, Missy was truly asleep.

CHAPTER VI

Brandy had become so accustomed to Grey's quick exits that she was astonished to find he was still at King's Inland the next day. Missy knew it too; she was tense, her eyes were fixed again, her body rocked rhythmically.

Brandy picked her up, speaking gently but firmly. "No, you mustn't do that anymore. You are all right; I won't let anything happen to you."

The dark eyes focused, the rocking stopped, and Brandy felt the childish body relaxing, curving to fit her own. She wondered how much Missy might have heard the night before; her return to old ways might have been from the fear that Brandy was leaving as much as from her father's presence.

She spent the day outdoors with the child. The weather was much colder now, and that was a good excuse for being very active. Brandy wanted Missy to be weary by nightfall. They even ran together down one smooth stretch, and Brandy was pleased to see that the child's new coordination extended even to this; she ran gracefully, though without the smile and playful gestures which were so characteristic of normal children.

Grey was obviously making an effort to stay out of sight, and Brandy thought of how painful that must be and wondered how much he was observing from the shadows. That evening when Missy was blessedly fast asleep, and Brandy was eating dinner with Mrs. Bailey and Grey, he told her.

"I saw you with Missy today. I find it difficult to credit the change in her. She looked much like she used to, running with that puppy at her heels." His mouth quirked, and Brandy got ready to argue. This was his first mention of the dog, but she relaxed at his next words. "Panza I believe you've named him, a romantic name for such an odd little beast. Your taste in horse-flesh is commendable, but I cannot say the same for your choice of a dog. The kennels of King's Inland used to have quite a reputation, forever lost now, I fear."

Brandy laughed. "Mr. Cowperwaithe had the same opinion. Poor Panza, only Missy and I are able to see his finer points." She hesitated; it was presumptuous to give permission to the master of the house, but then she went on because she wanted desperately for Missy's progress to give Grey some direct gift. "I heard you had some fine dogs here, and I think if you wish you could have them again. I don't think Missy will be afraid of them now."

Grey always seemed to know her motives; to him she must be a pane of glass. "Thank you, I appreciate your thoughtfulness, Miss Claybourne, but I think it would be better to wait. Panza belongs to her as the cats belonged to Jasmine. Missy feared the hounds because they were mine. There is no assurance that she will not associate them with me again." No anger or bitterness, just resignation. Brandy swallowed hard.

To Mrs. Bailey at least, Grey's next words were as startling as a gun shot. "I regret that it will mean more work for you, Margaret, but in two weeks' time I plan to give a party here. I know it's short notice, but the Lord only knows when the first snow will come, which would make it difficult for Ruth and several others to come from Wiscasset. The weather should hold until then. Perhaps you can hire some extra help from Persia's family."

Mrs. Bailey's normal composure had fled. She stared

at him for a moment before she stuttered, "But I . . . we . . . there hasn't been a party here since. . ." Her voice trailed away.

Grey said steadily, "Yes, I know, since Jasmine died. But I think King's Inland has had a decent interval of mourning, don't you? I will leave a list of local people whom I would like you to invite. Use Rafe to deliver the invitations. And please make sure enough rooms are prepared to accommodate Ruth, the Coopers, the Robinsons, and several musicians."

Mrs. Bailey was recovering. Her eyes began to sparkle in anticipation. She accepted Brandy's offer of assistance gratefully and was already enumerating the things which Ivory, India, and Ben Cowperwaithe could do if they were willing. She went to her own quarters right after dinner to make a list of tasks to be done, saying that the orderly rows of words gave her a nice, if false, sense of competence.

For once Brandy did not feel at ease in Grey's presence, and she accepted his invitation to sit in the front parlor. She was, however, relieved that they were not in the music room under Jasmine's painted eyes.

Brandy settled on a wide sofa, and Tiger, who had followed them, jumped into her lap and settled herself with no apologies. Grey remained standing, and oddly for him, he seemed to be having difficulty with something he wanted to say. Brandy looked up at him inquiringly.

"I . . . well, that is, you are of course invited to the party."

Brandy giggled. "Thank you, I'm glad you're not one of those employers who locks the governess in the nursery when company comes."

He smiled briefly, but he still hadn't said everything, and he went on quickly. "What I wanted to ask, well, do you have a dress for the occasion? If not, I am sure Ruth would be quite willing to help."

She was touched that he had thought of it, but the last person in the world she would let choose for her was Ruth; she could imagine the miserable, pale-shaded, fussily fashioned creation she would foist on her. Mischief rose in her as she thought of what she would wear. "Thank you for the offer but honestly, I do have a dress which will suffice. Hugh liked it, so I shouldn't disgrace anyone. I promise I won't wear my trousers."

No smile answered her own. "Damn, I nearly forgot!" Grey exclaimed, pulling something from his coat pocket and handing it to her. "This came by my yard in Wiscasset."

It was a letter from Hugh. He had not received hers yet, and he was waiting anxiously to hear from her. The letter was full of love and bits of news about the family, his patients, and her students. He described the teacher who had taken her place as "a whey-faced gentlewoman of ninety years or so." Brandy laughed at that, but she felt sorry for her former pupils. The letter finished with a plea for her return. She felt a moment's lonesomeness for the uncomplicated household at Greenfield, and she sighed as she put the letter down.

Grey's question startled her. "Homesick?"

"Just for a moment," she admitted, "but I wouldn't leave Missy for the world." The finality of her voice left no room for argument. Grey shrugged and went to a cabinet and took out a decanter of brandy and two glasses.

When he handed her a glass, she was tempted to refuse it. It was not a lady's drink, and she suspected he was teasing her about her rowdiness by offering it. Then she was amused by her pique—with her name and her upbringing, she could hardly claim the right to delicate sensibilities. Defiantly she took a sip of the liquid fire and managed not to gasp.

"Thank you, it's very good, but isn't this against the law here?"

"Yes, it is, but surely you've seen enough of the people in the state of Maine to realize a little thing like that isn't going to stop us—it just makes procuring it more challenging."

She could well believe it. He looked like a prime candidate for a rumrunner himself.

Cynically Brandy suspected the liquor, but for whatever reason, she and Grey managed to chat amiably for quite some time. He told her about the high-hope horses he had at other farms, about things such as the first Maine pulp mill, which had been built the year before in Topham, about the state's desperate need for new industries and more people owing to the changes brought by the war. He spoke with disgust about the conditions in most factories throughout the country—the long hours which came with increased demand for a product and then the long days without job or pay when the demand lessened—and in the surrounding areas where people lived in squalor with too little light, air, and food. "It is not only inhumane," he said, his voice intense, his look no longer withdrawn, "it is impractical. If a man is tired, ill fed, ill clothed, and generally wretched, he cannot work efficiently, and he stands a much higher chance of coming to serious harm from one of the machines. And he's a danger to other workers. I have the ledgers to prove it from my own businesses—offer a man steady, reasonable hours and wages, add a decent place to live, and he will give you a better-made article and higher profits. It's such a simple balance, but you would be amazed by the number of factory owners who don't think they're getting their just due unless their employees are miserable."

Brandy asked about his family and saw them come alive with his tales. His ancestors had been gallant and stubborn, surviving the War for Independence, Indian raids, losses at sea, and violent deaths at home to build an empire based on far-flung trade—an empire Grey had inherited and expanded greatly, Brandy knew, though he did not say so. She found that Grey and Melissa were the only King family names which had no connection with the sea; the others—Amanda, Drake, Cabot, Isabella, Miranda, and Raleigh—all carried images of the tide. He and Missy's namesakes had been Grey's great-grandparents. The writing box in Brandy's room had belonged to the first Melissa. As far as Grey knew, he, Raleigh, and Missy were the only surviving members of the family; an uncle had gone West and had never been heard of since, so he was presumed dead.

"I wonder if perhaps he is somewhere in California. Maybe I even met him once," said Brandy.

"Not a chance! I only saw him a few times before he left, but young as I was, I could tell he didn't like people at all. If he's still alive, he's in the wilderness miles from anyone else. All right, I've done my part. Now it's your turn."

She told him stories about Pearl, about her father, about Chen Lee, who took the time to make kites of magic colors for the children in spite of the demands of his many ventures. She told of the marvelous madness which was so much a part of San Francisco; of the fire companies that raced each other to be first at a blaze; of the strange little man who had proclaimed himself Emperor Norton and who was given tickets not only for himself, but for his two dogs, Bummer and Lazarus, to every major event in the city; of the famous performers who came to sing or dance or act and were never again free of the city's enchantment.

They talked on, and though Brandy's head was full of memories of her past and new things learned about the Kings and Maine, she was not too oblivious to notice that Grey was drinking steadily, refilling his glass often while she still had more than half of her first glass left. His words began to stretch and drawl much more than usual. He really is getting drunk, she thought, fascinated because he was such a disciplined man; it seemed completely out of character. *Like killing your wife,* her mind added involuntarily. But she stayed where she was, her eyes narrowed and golden, gleaming like Tiger's. Pearl had taught her long ago not to be afraid.

He poured himself another drink and glanced at hers. His face became exaggeratedly sad. "What's a matter, won't you drink for your namesake's sake?" he asked, grinning at his pun, words sliding into each other.

Brandy laughed aloud; he was being so ridiculous, so boyish. She had never seen him so stripped of his cold arrogance, and the change was remarkable. She could imagine what he had been like when he had been young, wild, and foolish. He looked younger than Raleigh right now. Her laughter died abruptly as she watched the change—his smile vanishing, his face becoming a mask with midnight eyes. Tiger landed on the floor with an outraged yowl as Grey lunged for Brandy, and she stood and stepped aside in the same instant. But Grey's rage made him quick, and his reach was long. He spun and caught her before she could get out of range. His hands were hard and bruising on her arm, his face distorted as he spat out the words: "Little cat, judging me, always judging, killed one, he'll kill one more. Destroyed his child, killed her too, another way. Why not keep on?"

Brandy still wasn't frightened, but she was in trouble, and there was no way to reason with him. She brought her foot down as hard as she could on his foot, and as he lurched forward, she brought her knee up. His hands dropped away as he grunted in agony, but he was a strong man further enraged by pain, and she was only a few steps away before his hand was clamped around her left arm. She had gone far enough; her right hand found the heavy silver box on the side table. He didn't even see it coming as it crashed into the side of his head and he fell.

Brandy suppressed her start of panic; she was quite sure she hadn't killed him; it took a great deal of strength and good placement to do that. She found his pulse; it was rapid but strong. She sat back on her heels, thinking about what to do next. She was thankful Mrs. Bailey had not appeared; explaining why Grey was stretched out unconscious on the floor would be difficult.

She went quietly to the kitchen and brought back two bowls, one full of cold water, and some toweling.

She knelt beside him again and felt the lump which was already rising, blood oozing from a small cut where the corner of the box had struck.

She put a cold compress against it, using the edge to wipe Grey's face. He began to toss his head from side to side, mumbling unintelligibly. His eyes opened, wide and unseeing, narrowing as he brought her into focus.

"My head. I . . ." was as far as he got. She held his head and the empty bowl skillfully. She had done it many times before, helping her father and Pearl with their similar patients; it didn't bother her. When his retching had stopped, she settled his head back in her lap and sponged his face with cool water.

His voice was muffled. "I haven't had many occasions to be ashamed in front of a woman, but this will do for a lifetime." He was completely sober.

Brandy's response was sharp because she found to her surprise that Grey's being humble was something she could not bear. She remembered when she had fallen from Lady how she had dreaded losing her dignity in front of Grey. "Nonsense, you wouldn't have had any problem if I hadn't knocked you out. And you forget, my two best teachers were a doctor and a saloonkeeper; holding heads was part of the course. Now, do you think you can stand?"

His color was improving and he managed a wry grin. "I'm proof that Pearl taught you a deal more than holding heads," he said as she helped him up. He winced as he put weight on his injured foot. Brandy put an arm around him, tugged at his own until he put it around her shoulders; obviously the world was still spinning enough for him to be thankful for the support.

"Come on," she ordered, "no falling down again until you're in your own bed."

He swayed a little partway up the stairs, and she held on tighter, laughing softly. "Oh, no, you don't! If we both go crashing down, Mrs. Bailey will surely hear us, and my good name will be ruined forever." She got him to his own room, and she heard no sound to indicate that Missy had wakened.

He refused to lie down. His voice was firm as he stood looking down at her. "Miss Claybourne, there is no excuse for my behavior. Maybe I am as mad as some think I am. You must reconsider leaving now with full pay."

Brandy stared at him in open amazement. "I must have done more damage to your head than I thought, Grey King. What do you think I am, some missish ninny who goes to pieces because a man has a little too much to drink now and then? Do you think I would leave Missy just because you suffered a lapse in manners? No one can live as you do, strung tightly as a bow, without snapping sometimes. Besides, you came off much worse for it than I. Do as I tell you, lie down!"

"Yes, ma'am," he said with mock meekness, much more the Grey she knew.

He settled back on the bed, and she worked to get his shoes off in spite of his protests. "Too bad for you I'm such a large woman," she said, running her hands over the bruised arch of his foot, "but I don't think I broke anything. You stay put, and I'll get something cold to put on that." She headed for the door.

"Ruth would have had me thrown out," Grey commented sleepily.

"Well, I'm not Ruth!" Brandy snapped with more vehemence than she intended.

"You certainly aren't," she heard him say as she shut the door behind her.

Downstairs she carefully removed all traces of the battle. Then she added more wood to the embers of the fire in the stove and brewed a strong cup of tea. She worked quietly, and Mrs. Bailey did not emerge from her rooms. She carried the tea up to Grey. He was half asleep but roused as she came in. He grimaced at the teacup. "You may not want it, but your stomach needs it, so drink it all," she commanded as she deftly slipped the pillows behind him so that he could sit up.

She held a wet towel against his foot to help bring the bruises out. She felt him watching her and turned her head to look inquiringly at him. "Sorry, am I hurting you?"

"No," he said, the intensity of his expression unaltered. "I was just thinking that California lost a gold mine when you came East."

Mockery she could handle, but the compliment made her blush furiously. As though Grey sensed this, deviltry danced in his eyes, and he asked sweetly, "I have another injury. Aren't you going to take care of that, too?"

Brandy gave a snort of laughter. "No, I'll leave that to Ruth."

"I deserved that," said Grey ruefully, and Brandy saw the bleakness in his eyes.

As she made him lie flat again, pulling the coverlet up over him, she had a sudden revelation. He grumbled, "You make me feel just about Missy's age."

She stood looking down at him, hands on her hips. She nodded in agreement. "That's just about how old you were tonight. Drunk as you may have been, that was all deliberate, wasn't it? Though I think you let it get a bit out of hand. You were providing me with one more reason to leave King's Inland, weren't you? Good Lord, you are determined to have your own way!"

"Didn't work, you're even more stubborn..." His voice trailed off, and he was asleep.

She stared at him for a moment, thinking how changed faces were by sleep. Grey looked weary and sad, all traces of ruthlessness erased. She searched for the word—he looked vulnerable. She shook her head in disgust at herself for the late-night fantasies; no word was more unfitting than that for Grey King.

She checked on Missy and found her sleeping peacefully. Suddenly she was so tired it took an immense effort to get to her own bed, and she slept as soon as her head touched the pillow.

When she awakened in the morning light, she knew

Grey had gone again. Beside her pillow was a small box and a note. She opened the note slowly and read: "You win. I expect you always will. Please accept these with my compliments for a brave battle. They belonged to my great-grandmother, Melissa. G. K."

She stared at the bold handwriting for a long time before she opened the box. She thought of Grey coming in and leaving the offering while she slept; it gave her a strange feeling, fear or pleasure she couldn't tell. In the box lay a pair of earrings, the jade of each delicately carved into flower buds with golden leaves. The green was deep and pure, perfect for her coloring. She knew it was as improper for her to accept them as it was for him to give them, and she knew she was going to keep them anyway.

CHAPTER VII

The next two weeks were the busiest and happiest Brandy had known at King's Inland. Ben, India, and Ivory often came with Persia, and sometimes even Hank and Amos were allowed to accompany them. The little ones were very well behaved and would play together for hours, quiet, eyes full of wonder. Persia said it was because they thought they were in God's house so they'd better be good. Brandy suspected Persia had started that rumor.

The house rang with laughter and bustle as rooms were aired and every surface polished. Mrs. Bailey was in her element—as though returning King's Inland to its old splendor were her own responsibility, her own passion. For the first time Brandy saw the rooms on the third floor and found them equal in magnificence to those on the second. They moved the extra furniture into the storage room at the end and prepared the others for guests. It seemed as if there were space for an army to sleep comfortably. For what she hoped was casual asking, Brandy learned that most of the guests were to sleep on the upper floor while Miss Collins would, of course, have the room next to Mr. King's, the room which had been Jasmine's. Of course, thought Brandy, and wondered why she felt so vicious about it, but at least the room had not been locked up and left as a morbid shrine to Grey's wife.

Rafe helped in the house when he could, and when he did, Persia's face glowed so brightly that Brandy thought he must feel the light, but he gave no sign. Most of the time he was off with the wagon, going to deliver invitations to neighboring farms, bringing back extra foodstuffs for the party.

Brandy watched Missy carefully, fearing at first that all the added confusion would upset her, but quite the contrary, she seemed to be enjoying it, though without laughter or smiling, it was hard to tell. At least she did not grow tense or rock or try to build the wall again. Brandy wondered if perhaps the excitement stirred some joyful memories of when her mother had been alive, her world in order. She was touched by Missy's reaction to Hank and Amos, for after staring at them for a moment, she patted each one gently as she did Panza, as though she recognized all three as fragile young things. If the boys thought it odd that she touched them but did not speak or play, they made no point of it, accepting her on her own terms.

By the time Ruth and Grey arrived the day before the party everything was in order. The house gleamed; the kitchen and springhouse were full to overflowing with crocks of butter, freshly baked bread, slabs of meat, fowl, salted fish, relishes, jellies, and pies. And as soon as she was in the house Ruth behaved as if she were its mistress and responsible for the work which had been done. Though Mrs. Bailey did not seem at all offended and chatted amiably with her, Ruth's attitude annoyed Brandy so that she excused herself, saying that she had to take Lady out since the horse had had so little exercise lately. Beyond a brief greeting, Ruth had managed to ignore her presence but when Grey said pointedly, "Do be careful where you jump, Miss Claybourne," Ruth's dislike and suspicion flashed openly for an instant.

Brandy said demurely, "Thank you for your concern, Mr. King."

She changed into her trousers and left Missy in

Persia's care. She took Lady out, and they worked off their excess energies together. But when she got back, Persia met her, and Brandy knew something was dreadfully wrong. Persia's words tumbled over each other in her anxiety. "Oh, Brandy, I didn't want to, but what could I do? She told me to leave her alone with Missy, an' she's still there with her."

Brandy didn't have to ask who "she" was. She said, "All right, Persia, thank you, I'll attend to it." She was amazed that a calm voice was possible in the midst of so much anger.

The door to Missy's room was ajar, and Ruth did not hear Brandy approach; she was too busy scolding. "The idea, no discipline, that dog should not be in your room." Panza was on the floor, looking miserable and cowed. Missy was rocking, her fingers flickering furiously in front of her face. "Progress indeed! You are as mad, as empty as you ever were, aren't you, you blank-faced little idiot, destroying our lives. You can be sure I'll bear your father no brats; one fool is enough."

"Get out, get out right now, Ruth, before I throw you out!" Brandy muttered. She was afraid of what she would do to the woman if she got close to her.

Ruth spun around, her mouth hanging open in shock before she collected herself enough to speak. "How dare you! I shall tell Grey immediately."

"Please do. Then I can tell him how you treat his child."

"I've heard enough about you to know you aren't fit to be in this household. I am going to be mistress here soon, and you, Miss Claybourne, will be the first to leave."

"That may be, but it isn't so yet, and if you don't leave this room this instant, you are going to go to the party tomorrow with a very bruised face." Brandy's hands curved into claws.

Fear supplanted arrogance on Ruth's face. She gathered her skirts and sidled past Brandy, her voice reduced to a gasp. "You'll be sorry for this."

Brandy ignored her, caring for nothing but comforting Missy. She gathered the child into her arms rocking, soothing her. "My darling, don't mind her, she's a bad woman. She doesn't like you because you are so beautiful and because everyone loves you so. She's jealous of you." She didn't know how much Missy understood, but it was enough, for the child relaxed in her arms, burrowing against her warmth. Brandy lifted Panza up and Missy cradled him tightly.

She stayed with her all afternoon and into the evening until the child had eaten at least some of the supper Persia brought up and had finally fallen asleep. Brandy did not want to go down for dinner, but she felt her absence would be a victory for Ruth, so she changed into a dress and arrived late at the table.

Grey asked instantly, "Is something wrong with Missy?"

Brandy answered quietly, but her eyes never left Ruth's face. "No, she is all right. I think she was just a little upset by all the excitement." She could not say, "By that bitch, your mistress," but she knew Ruth heard the silent words, for she flushed an unbecoming red and chattered aimlessly.

Grey's eyebrows quirked as he looked from one woman to the other, but he made no comment, and Brandy knew he was attributing the tenseness to simple jealousy. For her it was a miserable meal, and she went upstairs as soon as it was over, wanting to be asleep before Grey and Ruth came up to bed.

Her last thought before she slept was of Ruth's claim that she had "heard" things about her. Who would wish or bother to spread lies about her, she wondered, then dismissed the words as the false claim of a jealous woman.

The next day dawned cold and clear. Brandy spent it with Missy, trying to explain to her that there would be many people in the house but that they wouldn't hurt her and she mustn't mind. Brandy didn't want to be downstairs where she would have to watch Ruth greeting people as if she were Grey's wife.

The guests from farthest away arrived first, and Brandy heard the traffic of footsteps on the staircase and overhead as they were shown their rooms. And late in the afternoon she answered the knock on Missy's door with no idea of who it might be. To her surprise, she found Raleigh standing there. She was so delighted to see him that she hugged him and received a kiss of greeting in return. Neither of them saw Grey at the end of the hall as they turned and went into the room.

Brandy had been afraid to ask whether or not Raleigh was invited, and so his coming was a special gift. He laughed about it. "Even Grey has to keep up some show of being civilized, so he had to invite his only brother. My, my, how he must hate it!"

He stayed with them for about an hour, holding Missy and telling outrageous stories about sidehill badgers which had short legs on one side for hill living, about a marvelous city of crystal and gold somewhere in Maine, about lumbermen, Indians, and pirates. Brandy was sure Missy was enjoying it; she looked so contented.

He left with admonitions to Brandy not to be late to the party because he wanted the first dance. But in spite of that, she did not leave until Missy had had her supper and was asleep. As she went to her room to get ready, the first strains of music drifted up the stairwell, but she resisted the impulse to hurry; tonight she wanted to look her best.

She pinned her hair up, letting the heavy curls fall in a cascade from the back. She needed no rouge; her honey skin was already glowing with excitement. And finally she was ready to put on her dress. She took it from the wardrobe, her fingers touching it lovingly, remembering the careful work Pearl had put into its making as a going-away gift. The amber velvet held the same rich light as the brandy of her name, and Pearl had made it to suit her with total disregard for what the fashion plates demanded. The bodice was cut in a low curve, and the material was molded to every line of her long, supple figure until it fell into soft fullness from her hip bones to the floor. The long sleeves with tiny buttons fitted her slender arms perfectly.

When she was dressed, she put on the pendant from Chen Lee. The exquisitely carved birds and flowers had all been done from one delicate piece of jade which hung from an intricately wrought gold chain—California gold; she touched it for luck. The last things she put on were the earrings from Grey.

She surveyed herself in the mirror. She knew Ruth would be scandalized, as she knew Grey would approve, and there was pleasure in the knowledge.

As she descended the stairs, however, her courage deserted her. The air hummed with many voices underlaid with music, and several people who were on their way to find refreshments in the dining room eyed her curiously. She could not quell the hot blood rising in her cheeks; she didn't think she could face so many strangers. As kind as it had been of Grey to include her, she felt the awkwardness of her position and had a sudden longing to be back upstairs where she belonged. But as she turned to go, Raleigh stopped her. He had been watching for her from the door of the music room.

"Oh, no, you don't," he called, coming down the hall in long strides. "Shame on you, Brandy, I wouldn't have taken you for a coward, but I was beginning to think I was going to have to come up and drag you down by your hair, which looks lovely by the way. You're beautiful head to toe, and I am claiming the privilege of showing you off."

Her confidence flooded back as he took her arm. He made everything seem so easy. He escorted her into the music room, introducing her to the people they passed. She received only admiring comments about her dress. She was delighted to see the Cowperwaithes and to meet others from the region's farms. Whatever his faults, Grey was not snobbish in his choice of guests. The farmers and their families were just as welcome as the modish people from town. She stopped to talk to Mr. and Mrs. Cowperwaithe, telling them of the great success Panza was with Missy. She saw Persia looking very pretty in a green dress which complemented her bright curls. One of the local boys asked Persia to dance, and she accepted, but Brandy saw her looking wistfully across the room. Rafe stood alone against one wall, obviously ill at ease and wishing to be gone. She also caught sight of Grey and Ruth dancing. One she could do something about; the other she could ignore.

Raleigh said there had been enough talking and swept her out onto the floor. He was a good dancer, and their steps matched well together. The musicians played a variety of dances from polkas to waltzes to the Scottish set dances—reels, and flings, and the lovely slow strathspeys. Brandy managed to smile politely at Grey and Ruth when the sets brought the couples in contact.

Grey left Ruth every now and then to dance with other ladies, and Brandy chided Raleigh for shirking his duty.

"Ah, but I have no duty. Luckily for me, I am not master here. I can dance with you. Another privilege of the second son." Brandy heard no bitterness in the words.

"Well, there's one duty you're going to perform, if only for a minute," she said, and explained her scheme.

Raleigh shook his head. "I never would have thought you were a matchmaker."

"This is special, and don't you dare tease them about it," she retorted.

Raleigh agreed, and at the next slow tune he was at Persia's side, asking her for the dance while Brandy headed for Rafe. "I know this is unladylike, but it's the only way I am going to get a chance to dance with you," she said, holding out her hand. "Please?"

Rafe stammered in his embarrassment. "I am . . . I do not dance well. Your feet, they will be in great danger."

"I'll take that risk. Come on, before it's finished." She pulled at him, laughing, giving him no choice.

He wasn't at all bad, just a bit stiff with unease, and her plan worked splendidly. Raleigh maneuvered himself and his partner close to them and said apologetically, "I know it's most ungentlemanly of me, especially since I am dancing with such a lovely girl, but I find it impossible to see Brandy in another man's arms without becoming extremely jealous. If you permit . . ." The change was smoothly made, and there was no way out for Rafe except by being rude to Persia, which Brandy was sure he would not be.

As she glided away with Raleigh, she looked back at the couple. There was an instant's pause, and then Rafe took Persia in his arms, and they joined the slow measure. Persia's face was radiant, and Rafe's body was no longer tense. Brandy knew her ruse had been transparent and Raleigh's excuse overdone, but Persia and Rafe were accepting it gladly because it brought them together without either of them having to take the initiative.

Brandy was standing beside Raleigh, who was talking to the Robinsons when the next waltz began. Grey's voice startled her; she had assumed he was with Ruth.

"May I have this dance, Miss Claybourne?" he asked formally. She wanted to make a caustic comment about duty dances not including governesses, but she found the words wouldn't come. She caught a glimpse of Raleigh's angry look as he turned and of Ruth glaring as Grey swept her away, and then she forgot everything save for being in his arms. He was a fine dancer, better even than Raleigh. He executed the steps with perfect grace, but Brandy was aware of the barely harnessed strength of him in every movement they shared. She gave herself up to the joy of it, wishing it would never end. But had it not been for his strong lead, she would have faltered toward the end of the dance when he said calmly, as if commenting on the weather, "Thank you for wearing the earrings. They suit you. You are the most beautiful woman here tonight." She looked up at him. All his attention was fixed on her; he meant exactly what he said.

Her mind was still whirling in confusion when the

dance ended. Grey signaled to the musicians that they could rest for a while. Brandy saw Raleigh coming toward her, his face still mutinous, and then she heard Ruth's voice, deliberately raised. "Yes, it is an odd dress, but then Miss Claybourne is a rather strange person. Her background is interesting, to say the least, but I really can't bring myself to discuss it."

The last thing Brandy wanted was a cat fight at Grey's party, but the sudden silence and the eyes turned curiously on her destroyed her good intentions. She made her voice loud enough to be heard clearly throughout the room but kept it sweet and even. "Why, Miss Collins, you mustn't suffer any shame on my account. I'll be happy to tell them about my dress." She pirouetted gracefully, causing the skirt to swirl and ripple with amber light. "It was given to me by Pearl Orient, the woman who raised me. She was a prostitute, you know, and many of her gentleman friends gave her gifts, they liked her so much. That's where this material came from. Pearl made the dress during the day, when she didn't work." She touched the jade at her throat. "The necklace was given to me by Chen Lee; he too was one of her friends and mine." She did not mention the earrings, not wishing to involve Grey.

She had the satisfaction of seeing several reactions: Ruth's face was alternating between chalk and hot red; Raleigh looked as if he were enjoying it; Mrs. Cowperwaithe was beaming, and Mr. Cowperwaithe's taciturn face was showing a gleam of humor in the eyes, the twitch of a smile in the mouth; Persia was glaring with open dislike at Ruth. There were a few shocked faces, but Brandy felt the overwhelming response of approval. Stupid Ruth to forget that the right to be different was one of the most closely guarded privileges in Maine.

Then she saw Grey, and her glow of triumph vanished. Even here, across the room from him, she could feel his anger. She knew what she would see in his eyes if she were close enough. She turned her back on him just as he signaled for them to resume. She began to chat mindlessly with an elderly woman who was smiling at her, and she could hear the dancers taking to the floor, but all she could think of was what she had done to Grey. *Brandy, you absolute fool, fine to revenge yourself on Ruth, she deserved it, but you embarrassed Grey, too.* It was one thing for him to have accepted her despite her upbringing; it was quite another for her to be bragging about it, casting doubt on Grey's choice of a governess for his child.

Brandy burned with shame, and she escaped as soon as she could. She did not think anyone had noticed as she slipped out into the hall and went up the stairs. She stopped short when she was within sight of the landing and then hurried on. There was Missy, huddled in the cold corridor, listening to the music with Panza beside her.

"Hello, little lamb, I bet you're lonesome all by yourself," she said as she sat on the floor and drew the child and the puppy into her arms. Panza slid halfway off her lap and went back to sleep. Missy had made no attempt to flee on being discovered and now she reached for the softness of Brandy's velvet dress timidly. Brandy experienced the same thrill she had every time the child made some new contact with the world. She gave her an extra hug. "Isn't that nice to touch? I'll make you a dress that feels the same."

Missy made her small nestling movement which signaled her contentment, and Brandy hadn't the heart to move her. In spite of the chill air, she felt very peaceful sitting there, cuddling the child, music drifting up around them. She began to hum and then to sing the soft, nursery rhyme words from her own childhood with Pearl:

> Rest, my sweetling, rest.
> The dove is in her nest.
> The dreaming way is best
> Rest, my sweetling, rest.

Sleep, my darling, sleep.
There is no cause to weep.
You have my love to keep.
Sleep, my darling, sleep.

Missy's eyes were closed, her breathing deep and even when Brandy finished.

The creak of a board gave him away, and Brandy stilled her start of terror as she turned her head and looked up at Grey. He put his finger to his lips, signifying he would keep the silence. Then he walked carefully until he stood above them. Panza woke up and thumped his little tail happily. Grey reached down to take Missy out of Brandy's arms, and her heart lurched. She couldn't deny the man his own child, but she didn't know what Missy would do if she awakened in his arms.

The absorption in Grey's face prevented her from stopping him. She made no protest as the child was lifted away from her. She got up, holding Panza, and followed Grey down the hall to Missy's room. She watched him as he put his daughter down on the bed; his face was completely open, full of love and yearning for the child. As he put her down, her tiny hand touched him for a moment before it dropped to her side, but she did not awake.

Brandy barely choked back her sob before she turned and fled the room, unable to witness any more of his pain.

Her eyes were still blurred, but she was in better control by the time he met her at the head of the stairs. Before she knew his intent, he leaned down and kissed her gently on the mouth. "Thank you for letting me carry her," he said.

His gratitude threatened to start her tears again, and her voice was brusque. "Good grief, she's your child!" She could not interpret the strange look on his face, and she rushed on before he could shut himself in again.

"I'm truly sorry about what I did down there. It was childish, and hurtful to you, besides."

He gazed at her in amazement. "What are you saying—that it was your fault? That you shouldn't have told the truth?"

"But I... the way you looked, I thought you were furious with me and for good reason."

His voice was very quiet. "You must think me a monster indeed. I expect I deserve it, but I don't quite see how. I haven't many virtues, but one of the few I possess is, I hope, a sense of justice. Ruth was deliberately trying to slander you with half-told tales, and I could have wrung her neck for it. She got exactly what she deserved. Most of the people down there have even more admiration for you than they would have, much to Ruth's sorrow."

Brandy's relief that he had not been angry with her was so great that she even felt generous toward Ruth. "Don't judge her too harshly. She loves you so much it's difficult for her to see that I'm no threat."

The dangerous light kindled in his eyes again. "Yes, I suppose it is," he said as he drew her hard against him. His mouth came down on hers, and this time it was not gentle.

It was Grey who ended the kiss. Brandy's mouth was bruised, she could taste blood where her teeth had cut into her lip, her whole body felt shaken and weak, and she had done nothing to stop him. She backed away, more astonished at her lack of resistance than his behavior. The sunlight eyes met the midnight without flinching. Grey's laugh was harsh. "That, my dear Brandy, was punishment for underestimating yourself. Now shall we go down? My guests will be wondering."

Her hand flew involuntarily to her mouth, and Grey said mockingly, "No, no one will notice. I didn't brand you. I only kissed you. Your mouth is just a shade fuller and redder now, very tempting."

He gestured to her impatiently to descend ahead of him, and she obeyed. She seemed to be doing everything he wanted without protest, and she couldn't even find the gumption to be disgusted with herself. "My dear Brandy" he had said, not "Miss Claybourne."

She watched him make his way across the room to Ruth and she jumped when Raleigh touched her arm and asked her to dance. She looked up at the soft copy of Grey's face. Raleigh grinned maliciously at her. "My, my, when the lord and master beckons and even when he doesn't, people do take notice, don't they? You had better be careful of your reputation, little Golden Eyes, my brother has a way of ruining them."

Brandy stamped her foot. "Do you or do you not want this dance?"

"Always forgetting the kitten has claws," he said as he swept her out onto the floor.

She followed her partner and answered when he spoke to her, but all she could see was Grey, all she could feel was his kiss. It meant nothing at all to him, she told herself ruthlessly, and still could not stop the strong singing of her heart.

It was stopped for her at midnight when Grey, with Ruth at his side, announced their engagement. The wedding would be sometime in the spring; the exact date would be announced later.

CHAPTER VIII

Brandy knew she had managed well. She had congratulated Ruth, countering her cat-with-the-cream expression with wishes for her happy marriage. And her voice had not faltered when she had moved on to offer her felicitations to Grey, though she could not meet his eyes. He had said what sounded like "It is for the best," as though it were a sentence of some kind, but Brandy could not be sure in the babble, and she had no thought for anything save maintaining her own control.

She danced the last dance with Raleigh, laughing and talking as they whirled around the room. "Why, you really don't care, do you?" he asked in amazement.

She did not pretend to misunderstand. She widened her eyes deliberately and said, "Care, why should I care? I am only here to work with Missy, and that is going very well. Grey needs a wife, and I hope the child will be ready for a new mother by spring. Then my job will be done." In her highly sensitive state, she had the feeling that this did not please Raleigh, that he would have liked it better had she wanted Grey, but that made no sense at all, and Brandy dismissed the idea.

By the time she retired to her room she had herself in hand. Her first impulse, to throw herself on the bed and weep, was checked. She was ashamed of herself for being such a green girl, for thinking herself in love with

112

Grey because of a kiss—a kiss most likely initiated by
the hard liquor the men had been drinking in the back.
Grey most certainly had had his share, and a taste of
Brandy was just one more, she thought ruefully.

What really mattered was that before too long, Ruth
would have charge of Missy. That was horrifying, and
Brandy was newly resolved to equip Missy with all the
weapons of normality so she could hold her own against
the woman.

She was lying with weariness edging her closer to
sleep when a new thought struck her, and she sat up
suddenly, sure it was true. Missy had known she was in
Grey's arms, and she had touched him on purpose
when he put her down. It had to be, because Missy,
even with her great progress, did not touch involuntarily, not even in sleep. Each time she reached out it was
to make contact deliberately.

Brandy shook her head with the effort to understand.
It was as though Missy were playing an elaborate game
in which she was not responsible for things she did
while others thought her asleep. So what did that
mean? What sort of self-defeating act was it to accept
her father only while feigning sleep? Even with all of
the child's problems, Brandy had refused to think her
mad—a sickness of the mind and true madness were
very different things to Brandy. But now she felt her
first chill doubt, her first realization that there might be
two very separate children in Missy, a day and a night
child living under completely different rules. Before
she had accepted the night prowlings as part of one
problem; now she was unsure.

She settled down to sleep exhaustedly, knowing she
must speak to Grey before he left again. She was dozing
fretfully when the door creaked open. She lay frozen,
heart thundering in her ears, as she watched the small,
barely discernible shape of the child pause at the
doorway and then come partway into the room. Brandy
was lost; she didn't know whether to call out or keep
silent, and to her horror, she found she was afraid,

afraid of a tiny child. She had a sudden vision of Missy in her room not to seek comfort but to glare malevolently from the darkness or to prowl close to suffocate her. She remembered the torment of waking with face covered by pillow or bedclothes, something which had never been self-inflicted before, something which she doubted was self-inflicted now. An ineffectual way to kill someone, but would a child know that? She lay still and made her breathing deep and even. With a little sigh, Missy turned and left the room, carefully closing the door behind her.

Brandy rolled over and clenched the pillow, moaning audibly. "Dear God, it can't be! She can't mean me any harm. She's got to be the same frightened, lost little girl all the way through. She's just checking to make sure I haven't left her in the night as her mother did." The words echoed hollowly in her ears as she lay waiting for the safety of the sun.

She dressed in the first pallid light and made herself sit at the desk writing letters until she heard Grey open his door and go downstairs. She had counted on his usual early rising so much that she felt as if she had been holding her breath since dawn.

She went down and knocked on the door of his study. His voice was brusque as he bid her enter, obviously annoyed at being interrupted at this early hour, but it changed to surprise when he saw her.

"Up with the dawn, Miss Claybourne, and after such a late night! Something on your conscience?" The memory of the kiss gleamed wickedly in his eyes.

His sarcasm made her own voice cool. "No, sir. But there is something about Missy which I think you ought to know." His eyebrows lifted in question, and she forgot her reserve. "Missy knew who picked her up last night. She touched your hand on purpose!"

His response was controlled, but his face was tense and the telltale vein throbbed at his temple. "And how did you come to that conclusion?"

Brandy tried to make her answer coherent, explaining

what had led her to the knowledge, but Missy's mode of expression was so subtle that it was difficult, and in the pause that followed her disjointed words, she thought she had failed.

But then Grey said, "All right, in case you are correct, what do you suggest I do about it?"

Brandy frowned in bewilderment; she hadn't thought that far. She supposed they ought to test it, but not with Ruth around, and Ruth and Grey were due to return to town today. She was still mulling it over when Grey solved the problem.

"I'll remain here for another twenty-four hours. Ruth can go back with the Coopers."

Brandy's words were choked as she thanked him and left. Honestly, it wasn't fair, the way he could see straight into her head. She blushed at the thought of what else he might have seen.

The morning was hectic with the guests' departures, and one in particular Brandy wished she'd never witnessed. She had gone to Missy's room with the child's breakfast, and her first sight of the slight golden girl made all her imaginings of the late hours seem not only impossible, but insane on her part. Missy reached out to her immediately and ate her breakfast docilely. There simply couldn't be room in Missy for an evil twin.

Brandy was crossing the hall to her own room when she heard Ruth's voice coming from Grey's room. She stopped, wondering if Missy could hear it too, deciding she could not through the closed door. She knew she should close her own door on the sound, but she stood where she was, eavesdropping shamelessly, transfixed by the rising venom of the words.

"I'll not go back with the Coopers! What will everyone think? We've just become engaged; they know you and I were to go back together, and now you are sending me back like some ship's cargo. I won't have it! Either you take me back, or I'll stay here until you're ready to go."

Grey's voice was harder to hear in its quiet, precise anger. Brandy shivered involuntarily at its quality. "You will go back with the Coopers. And you will learn to do as I say while you are in my house. I don't give a damn what people think, and if you are going to marry me, you had better learn not to care either. Perhaps you've made a mistake."

Brandy expected Ruth to become placating at that, but her anger had carried her too far. "Oh, no, I haven't made any mistake at all. I want you and I want King's Inland. I think the regret is yours; you know I won't let you keep that woman once I'm mistress here."

Brandy's reaction was simple—she wanted to go scratch out Ruth's eyes. She expected Grey's reaction to be similar, but with a mixture of chagrin and acceptance of her just deserts, she heard him laugh. "My God, Ruth, I know what you are thinking, but you might as well accuse me of having an affair with Margaret Bailey— she's years older than I am, and Miss Claybourne is years younger. Between them there is a wasteland with me in the dead center. Now run along like a good girl with the Coopers. I'll be in town by tomorrow night."

Brandy hurried to get into her room, but she needn't have bothered; it was quite a few minutes before Ruth, accompanied by Grey, passed her door and went downstairs.

She was consoling herself with the thought that Grey's dismissal of her as a woman was just too glib—after all, if he trusted her with Missy, he could hardly consider her a child; unless, of course, he thought of her on the level of an informative playmate for his daughter. "Enough, Brandy," she said angrily to herself, "you can't have him, he belongs to her. Don't want him anyway," she added defiantly, "he's a dangerous piece of work."

She jumped when someone knocked at her door, fearing for a moment that Grey in his omniscience knew of her eavesdropping, but it was only Raleigh coming to say good-bye. His smile lit up the morning, and he gave her a casual kiss of farewell, but he was as preoccupied as she and in a hurry to be off so that he could catch up with the Coopers and Ruth. The disquieting idea she had been trying to ignore rose again; she was beginning to think that Raleigh, for all his charm, operated from one desire—to take the greater part of what Grey possessed, to take Missy's and Mrs. Bailey's affection, her own, and, now that the pact was sealed, Ruth's. All perhaps because he could not have King's Inland. As she had suspected before, it seemed that the bitterness of being second son ran deep, probably deeper than even Raleigh knew. She shook her head wearily to brush away the thought; the Kings' problems were her concern only when they affected Missy.

The next knock on her door was Grey's. He had come to ask what she wished him to do about testing her new theory. He was twisting his hat in his hands, seemingly unaware he carried such an odd thing for indoor use, and Brandy felt his fear of failure as if it were her own. Her voice was gentle and pleading. "I know it may not work, but we've got to keep trying. I think the best plan would be for me to take her for a walk down the woods trail. You wait and then come riding down it. The woods are neutral territory and maybe she will feel easier there than if you walked into her room."

He agreed, but his voice was so hopeless that pity welled in Brandy's throat, making her voice uneven. "I know how hard it is for you, but I swear she's not nearly as afraid of you as she seems. Maybe someday she will be able to tell us why she acts the way she does with you."

Brandy couldn't help thinking of the appalling possibility that Missy's first words might be: "I'm afraid because you killed my mother."

"Even that would be better than silence," said Grey as he turned and left. Brandy was certain she had not said the words aloud.

She dressed Missy warmly for their walk, thinking as she did that this was another area where the child must achieve some independence. But even for a normal child of five, dressing oneself wasn't easy with sashes to be tied and gaiter boots to be pulled on. And as finely made and pretty as Missy's clothes were, Brandy considered them too fussy for a good romp and felt remiss that she had not thought of making some simpler things before this. No one had thought to provide the child with playclothes—why should they when she never played?

They set off at a brisk pace to ward off the cold. Panza ran in glad circles, and Missy seemed very eager. Brandy hoped it was not because she knew her father was still at home and wanted to be well away from him. The trees were quite bare now, spiny against the still-luxuriant evergreens. The thick carpet of leaves crackled beneath their feet and gave off a faint, spicy dust.

When Brandy judged the time to be right, she turned the little party for home. She had to take Missy's hand for a moment because the child seemed bent on continuing onward, and Brandy suspected she wanted to go to the pond. "No, Missy, we must go back. We didn't bring any lunch with us today, and we'd be awfully hungry if we stayed out all day." Her voice sounded calm and reasonable, but she hoped her inner tension wasn't communicating itself to Missy, who had so little need of words to tell her what was happening.

Missy and Panza were walking ahead of her when the hoofbeats became audible. The dog sat down and cocked his head. Missy stopped, but nothing happened; obviously she assumed it was going to be another meeting with her uncle. But when Orpheus was visible, Missy swung around and stared at Brandy for an instant before she sat on the ground abruptly and began to rock, flicking her fingers in front of her eyes.

Brandy's cry was a wail of despair. Missy's brief look had told her she knew she had been tricked. "Missy, oh, Missy, don't, please don't! He loves you, and I know from last night you love him."

A shudder passed through Missy, but the rocking

continued jaggedly, as though the slight body were being pulled two ways. Brandy, cradling the child against her on the ground, wasn't aware of Grey's nearness until he spoke. He towered above them on the black horse. "Don't fret, child. I won't bother you. You're safe with Brandy." The kindness in his voice made Brandy want to weep; she would have preferred it had he yelled at both of them. She didn't watch him as he rode off.

Missy's hand stopped fluttering, her body stopped rocking as soon as the sound had died away. Brandy heard a strange noise, and her heart jumped. She looked around for Panza; he was sitting a little ways off, looking puzzled by the strange behavior of the humans. Brandy was sure he had not made the sound, sure that Missy had made that one small, strangled sob of grief. A sound of grief, not anger or fear, from a child who neither laughed nor cried. Tears were too much to expect, but she saw the suspicious brightness in the dark eyes. The full horror of Missy's world washed over her anew—not to speak, to laugh, to cry, not by any outward means to acknowledge the emotional turmoil inside.

She continued to hold Missy until the cold forced them to start back. She knew she was at the stage where she took comfort from any crumb, but still the fact that Missy had been moved enough by Grey to let that sound escape had to be of major importance. Her mind started on another of its endless spirals of wondering about Missy's motives—was she grieved because her father had committed an unforgivable crime or because she loved him and shared his sorrow but could not overcome some barrier of her own making?

Grey was not home by nightfall, and Brandy wondered if he had ridden on to Wiscasset; she wouldn't have blamed him. But even without knowledge of the day's disaster, Mrs. Bailey thought he was probably off on one of his hard rides. "He'll come in mud-splattered and tired, but at least he'll be at peace for a while," she said sadly. "I can hardly wait until he's married. Ruth is such a nice woman. She'll be able to make him happy."

Brandy had difficulty keeping her savage disbelief to herself—happy with a woman who hated his child and would give him no others? It amazed her that Mrs. Bailey was taken in by Ruth, but she realized that could easily stem from a readier acceptance of things as they were and would be than she herself possessed. After all, Grey loved Ruth.

The house was very quiet after Mrs. Bailey had retired. Missy was long asleep, and Brandy hoped she would stay that way. Persia had left early after seeing to much of the disorder created by the guests. It was strange to Brandy that one party had made her so aware of how empty the house was, as if it still craved the numbers it had been built to contain. She went to the music room, and though the furniture was neatly back in place, it did nothing to dispel the memory of waltzing in Grey's arms.

She knew why she wanted to play the piano. It wasn't just to fill the silence with music; it was to pass the time waiting to see if Grey was coming home, to be sure he was safe.

She started with the clean precision of Bach, but for once it did not satisfy her, so she began to play and sing the songs Pearl had taught her and the many she had learned since. She could not brood much when she was both playing and singing. Her voice rose clearly, rich and well trained. She took the same impersonal pleasure in it as she did in the piano which played the proper notes on command; in her mind its quality was just one more gift from Pearl.

She was singing the last lines of "Shenandoah," seeing the rhythmic hoisting of the countless anchors for which the song had been used, when Grey came in. She heard him and stopped, but he protested, "No, please, if you're not too tired, continue."

Tired! she thought. *I am many things when you are near, but never tired.* Her hands wandered aimlessly over the keys while she caught her breath. Grey was the weary one; her brief glance had taken in his stained clothing and lined face the color of his name. Outriding the devil was work indeed.

When she began to sing again, she did so with fierce energy; if it gave her solace, so might it give him. She sang "Oh, Susanna" which had been so much a part of the early gold seekers in California; she sang silly songs such as "The Girl That Keeps the Peanut Stand" and drew appreciative laughter from Grey; she sang ballads and lullabies and anything that occurred to her, not wanting the gift to end. The lyrics did not seem overly important to her, but apparently they did to him, for when she had sung the lines "Oh, that I was where I would be, Then should I be where I am not; Here I am where I must be, Where I would be, I cannot," from "Katy Cruel," he stopped her. "And where would you be, Brandy?" he asked very softly.

"Exactly where I am," she replied firmly, and she chose as her final piece the Shaker song "Simple Gifts," enunciating every word clearly:

'Tis the gift to be simple, 'tis the gift to be free,
'Tis the gift to come down where we ought to be.
And when we find ourselves in the place just right,
'Twill be in the valley of love and delight.

When true simplicity is gain'd
To bow and to bend we shan't be asham'd,
To turn, turn will be our delight
'Til by turning, turning, we come round right.

"Love and delight at King's Inland? I hardly think that's what you've found." But there was no mockery in his voice, only rueful disbelief.

"Missy is my love and delight," she said, but she avoided his eyes. She was on the verge of telling him that Missy had sobbed for him, but she realized she couldn't explain why that was a good sign; Grey had been too badly bruised by the whole situation to think that crying was any better than a scream of terror. So instead, she mumbled something about Missy's having accepted the meeting much better than her outward actions showed.

Grey looked at her in silence for a long moment before he spoke. "Well, as long as you go on believing in her, I suppose there is hope." There was none in his voice. "Thank you for the music. Good night." He went down the hall and into his study. Not once had Brandy seen him look at Jasmine's portrait; he had not even glanced at it as he left the room.

When Brandy went upstairs, there was no sound of Missy scampering, and when she checked on her both child and puppy were asleep, only their heads showing from the heavy coverings. Brandy sighed; here was another problem. Winter's first snow would come soon, and already the rooms were cold unless a fire was kept burning. But Missy would not allow a fire in her room. The flame for light in the lamp she tolerated because of her fear of the dark, but she seemed indifferent to the cold, and Persia had told Brandy that the minute a fire was lighted in Missy's hearth, the child would retreat across the room and rock blindly until it was extinguished. Brandy wanted to change this, too, but she felt her ground was less firm here than in other areas; since her mother had died by fire, Missy certainly had a right to fear it.

She resisted the impulse to lock her door against Missy's night wandering; it would show a lack of trust and would undoubtedly frighten Missy if she found it bolted against her. And she was sure the child did not have the strength to suffocate her. Even if those episodes had been Missy's doing, she had only covered Brandy's face and departed before Brandy awoke. Certainly her hands did not have the power to hold the wrappings firmly enough to kill while Brandy struggled.

She heard Grey come up as she climbed into bed, hoping the events of the last twenty-four hours and her lack of sleep the night before would give her instant oblivion. And she did doze peacefully until the dreaming began and her sleep became a restless confusion of people and places, her dream eyes seeing first New England, then California, then both together. There was a fire in San Francisco, and she was going with her father to help, but it was Aunt Beatrice's Boston house which was burning. And the smell was getting stronger.

Brandy's terror awakened her. It was no nightmare. The flames were licking at the floor under one of the windows and beginning to run up the heavy draperies. She was at the desk without knowing she had moved. She hitched up her night rail and clambered up on the desk. Reaching as high as she could, she could just manage it; her hand found the protruding end of the heavy rod holding the curtains. She tried to push it up and out of its metal cradle; it moved but did not fall. In desperation she gave a little jump and hit the rod as hard as she could with the palm of her hand. It crashed to the floor, breaking a pane of glass on the way, and landed in a crumpled heap of heavy cloth. She jumped from the desk and began to use the material to smother the flames.

She screamed when rough hands grabbed her and shoved, and Grey's voice yelled, "Stay out of my way!"

She stood tight-lipped, watching him put out the fire. When he was done, he turned to her, his face grim, but she spoke first. "I was doing very well, thank you. You didn't have to push me!"

He stared at her for a stunned second, and then he burst out laughing. "Sweet Christ, Brandy, you are the only woman I know who would demand the right to fight her own fire!"

As suddenly as it had come, the humor drained from his face. "All right, how did it start?"

"How in the hell should I know!" she snapped. "Things have been rather busy since I woke up."

He examined the scene closely and found what he was looking for. The desk lamp lay on its side on the floor, its chimney blackened by the trail of oil fire it had bled. "That was very careless; you could have burned the house down." Implacable anger sounded in each word.

Brandy felt very strange. She sat down with a thump. "But I didn't leave the lamp burning. I never do when I go to bed. Even the one in Missy's room makes me nervous. Spending any time at all in San Francisco teaches one to be careful. And isn't it peculiar that it fell off without me hearing it and that it didn't break? Was the door open when you came bursting in?"

He nodded slowly.

"It was closed, though not locked, when I went to bed. And how did you know to come anyway?"

"I heard the crash, and then the smell . . ." His voice trailed off as he met her eyes. "My God," he said incredulously, "you don't think I did this? What do you think I came in here for, to see you burn?"

The world blurred, and Brandy could not bear the look on Grey's face. She hid her own face in her hands, and her voice was barely audible. "I don't know, I really don't. But someone started the fire, and whoever it was must be quite mad."

"Missy?" he asked, very quietly.

"How dare you suggest such a thing?" hissed Brandy, shooting out of the chair. "Your own child! She's terrified of fire; even if she did wish to harm me, which she doesn't, she would never do it that way." She believed what she said, but she could not quell a sudden doubt. Missy was brave enough to creep out of her room sometimes at night, even to go as far as entering Brandy's room; perhaps brave enough to have attempted smothering. The night child at work? What a choice, the child or the father.

"I will have a lock put on the outside of Missy's door, and I want it to be locked every night, Miss Claybourne."

The return to formality added an extra spur to her fury. "I'll see you with the devil first, Mr. King," she snarled, trying to keep her voice steady. "If anyone locks that door, I will unlock it. Missy is in enough of a prison without adding bolts and keys. If you knew your own child at all, you would know she is not capable of causing what happened tonight."

He watched her, the demonic light which unnerved her so beginning to show in his eyes. "As a matter of fact," he said very deliberately, "I have no idea what Missy is capable of. Perhaps the sins of the fathers are visited on the daughters when no sons are available."

She was blind to his leaving. It was as though he had admitted killing Jasmine. She did not check to see if Missy was awake. She climbed into bed and lay staring at the canopy above her. Even if Grey had started the fire, he had had enough remorse to come to her aid—unless he had thought the noise of the falling rod sufficient to alert Missy and maybe Margaret. He had been dressed in trousers but no shirt, still enough to cover him if he had had to leave the house quickly. It made no difference; she was too weary. She sobbed out her grief for him and did not know when the tears ended and sleep began.

When she awakened and looked at herself in the mirror, she wished she had done neither. She looked awful. She bathed her eyes to ease the swelling and pinched her cheeks to add some color, but the results weren't encouraging. For once she would have liked to possess some of Pearl's beauty potions. Then she chastised herself for being idiotic; what did it matter, everyone would know about it anyway.

As she went down the stairs, her assumption was confirmed. Persia and Mrs. Bailey met her, their faces full of shock and concern. "Oh, Brandy, how terrible for you!" cried Persia, hugging her tightly.

Brandy drew away and said firmly, "It's all right, though I am sorry about the draperies; you can be sure I won't do it again."

She watched them closely, but neither gave any sign that she doubted it was an accident. At least Grey hadn't told them he suspected Missy.

She went to brew a cup of tea and found Grey finishing his breakfast in the kitchen. Neither of them said anything until Mrs. Bailey had assured herself that Brandy had all she wanted to hand and had bustled out. Grey's face was pale in spite of his weathered skin. He regarded her intently, but said nothing, and Brandy spoke quickly out of nervousness.

"Thank you. I know you didn't tell them that you thought Missy started the fire or that she ought to be locked up."

"I still believe both," he said flatly, "but I am leaving the decision up to you. For all I care, this whole place can burn down, but since it is a most unpleasant way to die, much worse than a quick fall from a horse, perhaps you will reconsider. I am leaving, so one of your worries at least will be absent."

She should have been relieved that he was going, but instead, she was desolate and barely restrained herself from running to ask when he would return. She heard the faraway thud of the front door.

When she went to Missy, she paused in shock on the threshold of the room. The child was sitting on her bed, rocking furiously. Brandy had never seen her rock so hard. She felt all the ground they had gained together slipping away. She sat on the bed and gathered Missy into her arms, joining the motion of her own body with the child's, crooning to her as she rocked. "Missy, Missy love, I know you are upset; I know you know something about what happened last night. Don't worry, it was an accident, nobody did it, and nobody was hurt."

A shiver passed through the child as Brandy said that, but the rocking went on. Why? Had Missy started the fire, after all, or did she know who had? Or had she heard what Grey had said about her? All the possibilities were terrible, and the only comfort Brandy could find was that Missy's reaction was one more sign that the child was aware of what went on.

It took much longer than it had before, but it worked.

Brandy continued to rock, and Missy stopped. Brandy laid her back on the bed when her eyes closed and waited until she was sure sleep had come. She was sure Missy had not slept much of the night.

She knew why she didn't want to do it; she was afraid of what she might learn. But she steeled herself and went to find Rafe. He was in the stables, and one look into his eyes was enough to tell her that he knew about the fire.

"Please, Rafe, I need to talk to you."

"It is better for me not," he mumbled, not looking at her.

"You are the only one who can tell me. It was no accident, someone tried to kill me last night and I suspect on several other nights, and it was undoubtedly the same person who cut the girth. I don't want to be part of a pattern which was started long ago."

The silence between them thickened like a dangerous fog until Rafe began to speak, his words coming slowly with great effort. "You think he began the fire with the purpose to kill you. For why would he do that thing when the other has brought only sorrow? You have given life again to the house and a new beginning for his child, for why would he finish it?"

Brandy shook her head in despair. "I don't know, I don't! He says he thinks Missy did it, but I can't believe that. And Jasmine died by fire. You testified for him; you said he wasn't responsible. Is that true?"

His scarred face was wrenched with pain. "God, I should not say it, but you are in danger, you have the right to know. I did not tell the truth of that night as I saw it but as I knew it to be. You know my house; it is in the woods, away from the view of the stables. That night I was outside of it to listen to the dark things singing, to think dreams under the stars. The smell of the burning came to me strongly, and then I saw a light in the sky which was not of the night. I ran, hearing the distress of the horses as I was nearer. I saw Grey's horse tied away from the danger. Yes, he was there before my coming, and I do not know for how long before it.

"The fire was very bad; many of the fine horses died in it. Grey was wanting to go in to help them, most especially the young one, Orpheus, who was chosen for his own. I could not prevent him and so I went with him. It was such terror, I do not remember all that happened, but we reached the black colt, and near we found Jasmine. I led Orpheus away; Grey carried the burned body of his woman."

"Then it is true; he could have killed her himself."

"No!" He sounded furious with his effort to make her understand. "Because I did not see him come does not make it that he did something he would not do. In the war it is sure he killed other men as they tried to kill him. But not this thing, not this killing of a woman he loved. Some men, yes, not Grey." Brandy stared at him, ice beginning in her bones. His eyes were dead, and without their light, his face was truly ugly, menacing. She knew without doubt that he included himself in the phrase "some men." Had he killed Jasmine? No, she believed his harsh admission—Grey had been there before him. Then his own woman, had he killed her? And the fire in her room, had he set it? She knew two things at once: She knew that he would have no hesitation in committing such an act if he thought it was necessary to protect Grey, and she knew that she was no threat to Grey. She could still not see any way in which Rafe could judge her so. The frantic beating of her heart slowed. She sensed there was no use in asking him what his own crime had been, no use in admitting she knew there must have been one. If he wanted to tell her, he would have done so. Instead, she asked him how he had come to work for Grey.

As he spoke, she watched the light rekindle in his eyes. "From my life in the north country, I came south. I drank the whiskey and fought and did not care. I wanted to die, but I had not the courage to do it. Then one day I was by the docks. There was much going on, many ships being unloaded. Close to me was a wagon, very heavy, and hitched to it were a pair of horses, very big, very beautiful ones. While the men were taking things from the ship and putting them on the wagon, one of the horses, he fell. The stones under his feet were wet from the morning and the sea. He fell against his mate, and both went down, tangled with the wagon going over too. They were screaming in fear and hurt, but only one man went to them, all others were as stone. I was there helping him before I knew. Together we made them quiet and got them to their feet. They were cut and had swellings, but not of a serious nature. The horses, they were Pete and Polly, and they were my friends starting then. They are kind, for they judge a man only by what they know of him in the instant.

"For me, it was enough to have given succor. It was the first thing of value I had done in a year's time. But not for the man, not for Grey. He said he had need of a man to work with horses, and to me he gave the work. I told him I had not much knowledge of them except for the ones I had known on a farm as a boy. I remember, he laughed and said the knowledge was easy to teach if the love was there in the first. I told him of all the evil things of myself; it made not a difference. I have worked for him since that day."

He had explained more than he meant to, Brandy guessed. She remembered the bleak look he had had when once before he had mentioned the north. He had committed some unspeakable crime there and fled his home and his first language. And in his solitary way, he was still fleeing most people. Most people except for Grey. She was certain that Grey knew what he had done and that it made no difference; Rafe was too loyal to him not to have made his confession complete in every detail. It explained the strange bond between them. But there was no comfort in knowing that Rafe maintained Grey's innocence so vehemently, not because he had proof of it, but because he worshiped Grey and believed him to be superior to himself. *Oh,*

Rafe, she thought, *don't you see, in spite of whatever you did, you are basically kind and gentle, and you love him enough to damn yourself that he may appear to better advantage. He is more ruthless than you have ever been, much more likely to have committed a savage act and with less reason.*

She voiced none of this to him. His expression stilled her doubts. He stood patiently, as though waiting for her to turn from him in disgust at the picture of a wharfside drunkard and brawler. She touched his marked face lightly and said, "Rafe, whatever is in your past is past, and you've paid for it. You mustn't spend the rest of your life in a prison like Missy's. It isn't fair to you or to the people who love you; it isn't fair to Persia." She believed it as she said it; Grey and Persia were two people he would never harm.

The scar was white against the sudden ruddiness of his face. "How do you know of this?" he demanded harshly.

"I know because of the way the two of you look at each other and the way you try not to. I know because of the things you say to each other and more because of all the things you don't say. And I know because Persia is happy or sad according to whether or not she's seen you. She doesn't hide things very well."

"I have done nothing to give her sorrow, nothing," he said in despair.

"That's exactly what you've done—nothing. It's the hardest thing for her to bear, loving you the way she does."

"She must not love me then. It is not right. She is too young, with too much of life, with too much innocence. I have not anything to give her."

"You are a coward, Raphael Joly, and you're wrong about her. Persia's deep and true and as stubborn as this land. She can handle whatever you have to tell her. Why do you think she looked so bored with all those country boys at the dance? She doesn't want someone young and green. She wants you, seasoned by years, gentle and strong. And she'll go on wanting you even after you tell her about your past. Nothing will change her mind or her heart."

His face was still, but his beautiful eyes had the light of hope beginning. Brandy wished she did not feel compelled to ask her last question.

"Rafe, can you tell me anything about Jasmine?"

He shook his head. "I cannot speak badly of another's dead, of Grey's dead. But I will say because he is my friend that he was deserving of a better woman than he had, and in his brother also he deserves more than such a one who takes much and gives little."

"Well, perhaps Grey will be happy with Ruth."

"No, she and Raleigh, they are both the same nature. Not dangerous, but like little winds having no bodies and no hearts, blowing to make small noises and small mischiefs."

Poor things, not even full of sound and fury, she thought. She felt disloyal to Raleigh, but she could see the truth in Rafe's judgment. His unconscious raising of Raleigh's name with Jasmine's told a great deal.

"Thank you, my friend, for trusting me with so much of yourself," she said, hugging him briefly and pretending not to see the sudden brightness in his eyes.

When she got back to the house, she found Mrs. Bailey busy as usual dusting one of the cabinets in the hall, even doing the inside, handling each object with loving care. "You make me ashamed, Mrs. Bailey, don't you ever rest?"

As the housekeeper turned to smile, she lost her grip on the slippery piece of jade she was holding. There was a moment of midair gasping before she got hold of it again and set it back in the cabinet with trembling hands. Her face was so white that Brandy was alarmed and put a steadying arm around her. "That's quite enough cleaning for today," she admonished her gently. "Let's go make a cup of tea."

Mrs. Bailey closed her eyes for a moment and

gasped, "I've never broken anything in this house, never! That was so dreadfully careless of me."

"I think it was very agile of you to catch it, and you didn't break it, so come along," Brandy soothed her as she led her toward the kitchen, but privately she was a little taken aback by the housekeeper's distress. She was quite sure Grey wouldn't make any fuss over an accidental breakage. She realized anew how deeply Mrs. Bailey was dedicated to preserving every small part of King's Inland.

She made the tea strong and sweet and watched the color come back into the older woman's face. Mrs. Bailey smiled and nodded at her. "My, that does taste good! An old lady should know when to stop for a moment."

"Old lady, she says," snorted Brandy.

They were chatting about inconsequential things when Brandy heard herself ask abruptly, "Do you know what it was Rafe did that caused him to leave the north?" She was appalled to have asked. She hadn't meant to. It was as though the question had grown swiftly of its own accord to ask itself at the earliest opportunity. "I'm so sorry! Forget I ever asked. It's none of my business," she apologized.

Mrs. Bailey's face had grown very still and thoughtful, but then she shrugged. "No, my dear, you have a right to know since we live in such close quarters here. I think Rafe is a changed man, but at one time he must have been a very jealous, very violent one." She drew a deep breath before she continued. "He was married to a woman much younger than himself, and that is often bad business and cause for distrust. I think her name was Marianne. He only told the story once, to Grey and then to me when he first came here. He killed his wife because she had been unfaithful. He got the scar on his face in the struggle. That's all I know, but I don't think he is dangerous. That was, after all, a special case. And I'm happy to see you don't look too shocked."

"No, I'm not. That sort of thing happens in any part

of the country, and out West my father treated many cases where jealousy didn't have a very good aim with a gun or a knife. If you are capable of great love, then you must also be capable of great hate, or so it seems to me."

"Yes, that is very true," Mrs. Bailey said slowly. "I've lived long enough to see it proved time and again." Brandy excused herself and went slowly up the stairs to check on Missy. It was true, she wasn't shocked. She had suspected as much. But she did have a curious double feeling about what she'd learned. She could understand the impulse to kill for infidelity, but the actual picture of Rafe murdering his wife was gruesome and chilling. She did not want it to taint her friendship with him, and so she would just have to believe that her faith in him was justified, that what he had done had been necessary for him, and that one impulsive act in the past did not predict the future.

CHAPTER IX

For the next few days Brandy wondered if her mind would ever function properly again; every time she thought about the fire it went blank, refusing to consider the possibilities.

She could easily have moved to another room, but the one she occupied was the only part of the house that was particularly hers. She did not want to leave the solitary owl, Melissa King's writing box, the figured chair, or any of the other things which had become so familiar. Mrs. Bailey and Persia understood and helped her to put up new draperies borrowed from one of the third-floor rooms. The soft blue complemented the yellows of the room, but it was a constant reminder of what had happened to the original hangings. Rafe replaced the pane of glass from a store kept for repairs; windows did, after all, get broken now and then. But not many were broken under such circumstances, thought Brandy when she saw the clearer piece, which did not match the older, heavier panes.

Seeing Rafe with her new knowledge of him gave her an instant's pause, but she was relieved to find it was no more than that. She simply could not believe that his gentle eyes were the eyes of a habitual murderer. It was no hardship at all to smile at him and thank him for repairing the window.

Her numbness was broken by the arrival of a package

brought by special messenger from Grey. It contained a velvet dress for Missy, made in the same style as Brandy's, though the bodice was higher to fit the childish figure. It was sapphire blue, perfect for Missy's coloring. It said so many things that Brandy could hardly take them all in. It meant that Grey had witnessed the whole scene of Brandy holding Missy and singing to her at the top of the stairwell; that he had watched until the creaking board had given him away. It meant that he knew Missy well enough to describe her size exactly; Brandy was sure the dress would be a good fit. It meant that he had noticed every detail of Brandy's dress and that he cared about what his daughter wanted, cared enough to have done some very fast work in getting the fabric and having the dress made.

Every time she looked at the gift she thought of Grey and of the fire. She was faced again with the choice of the same five people: Rafe, Persia, Mrs. Bailey, Missy, and Grey. Only they had been around both when the girth had given way and when the fire had started. Persia, Rafe, Mrs. Bailey? They all accepted her, or at least they seemed to, and they had nothing to gain and everything to lose by a catastrophe at King's Inland.

Missy or Grey? She loved them both; it was agonizing to suspect either. And if either had done it, the action must have arisen out of madness. If it were Grey, then the gift to Missy was a weak protestation of innocence or a manifestation of a good side, one which loved and built rather than a side which hated and destroyed. She knew her love for him was clouding her judgment, and it was no easier to transfer the guilt to Missy. But in spite of herself, Brandy could see that the child might have a very good motive. Perhaps she did not wish to come back into the regular scheme of things; perhaps the night child was the stronger of the two and resented the intrusions Brandy had made.

She was still not convinced that the covering of her face had been intentional, and she willed herself not to believe it had been, for Missy was the one with the most opportunity to have done it. If true, it would seem the final proof of the night child's work.

In addition, she had to consider Raleigh, for if he was as jealous of Grey's position as she suspected, then his was the best motive of all. The house was easy to enter; there were many windows, and the front door was never bolted as far as she knew—why bother in the middle of nowhere? But Raleigh had gone back to Wiscasset, as had Ruth, long before the fire broke out. And even taking him at his worst, accepting the possibility that he operated out of sly greed, Brandy did not think it was in character for him to attempt murder. She agreed with Rafe's judgment, that Raleigh was a "little wind making small noises and small mischiefs."

Her jealousy and dislike interfered with her judgment of Ruth. She wondered if the woman was cruel enough to bribe someone, for she surmised she was too cowardly to soil her own hands with murder. But who at King's Inland would do such bidding, even for a price? Brandy couldn't believe it anyway; Ruth was too petty surely to be involved in any killing passion. Full, useless circle again.

She wished she could believe all the incidents had been accidental, but that was impossible. She had to face the fact that someone had made at least two outright attempts on her life. And accepting that meant she had two choices—to flee or to stay at King's Inland. She saw Hugh welcoming her home. But it was small temptation; her decision had been made with her first sight of Missy. She would go on with her work, and she would be very careful. But she would not abandon the child, not even if she found her to be guilty.

Though Missy still wandered at night, by no sign did she show hatred of Brandy or a wish to harm her, and Brandy did not awaken again to find anything pressed over her face. And while the nocturnal visits unnerved Brandy when she woke and lay silently watching Missy, she did not lock the door, and she took comfort from the fact that Missy never carried anything—no weapons at all. Her decision made for good or ill, she took up the task of expanding Missy's world again.

From Mrs. Bailey Brandy acquired some lengths of muslin, calico, and wool to make playclothes for Missy. It was possible now to order patterns by mail and even to acquire garments which only needed to be stitched together, but Brandy was a good seamstress, thanks to Pearl, and she had her own ideas about what she wanted to make. Everything was to be very simple so that Missy might be taught to dress herself. The lighter materials would do for indoor wear, and Brandy made dresses which buttoned down the front. From the wool she made Missy a pair of fitted trousers for the expeditions outside. She worked in Missy's room, and the child watched the movement of the needle with apparent fascination. Brandy guessed that wonder about how things were made and where they came from had not been part of Missy's shuttered existence until now, and she was delighted with her first interest.

When the first dress was completed, Brandy tried to explain to Missy how to put it on. She took the small hands in her own and showed them how a button went through a buttonhole, but it seemed to make no impression at all. Missy was quite content to wear the dress hanging open if Brandy didn't button it for her, even though they went through the learning exercise every day. And to her wry amusement, Brandy discovered that Missy didn't mind wearing no clothes at all if no one dressed her.

The child did take particular interest in the trousers, touching the material often and anxiously as Brandy worked on them, and Brandy was sure that was because she understood they were for going outdoors, something Missy was growing very fond of, even on the coldest days.

Brandy did not show Missy the dress from Grey until she judged the child to be, she hoped, happy and relaxed enough to accept it. Missy was sitting on the floor with Panza in her lap. Brandy had brought the

parcel with her that morning. Missy had shown no
curiosity about it then, but Brandy saw the sudden
tenseness as she unwrapped it, explaining where it had
come from.

"Isn't it beautiful? Your father sent it to you. He cares
so much for you he had it specially made."

Brandy held the dress out to her, and she watched
the conflict which was becoming so familiar. She was
willing to swear Missy wanted desperately to touch the
soft luxury of the velvet; her hand reached out tentatively, but then the fingers curved into rigid claws as
though inner strings were pulling them back puppet-
fashion. The dress was from her father; therefore, she
would not touch it. The strength of her control was
awesome. Brandy sighed and hung the dress in Missy's
wardrobe; if the child wanted it, she could reach it. No
one else would put it on for her; the decision had to be
her own.

Brandy went back to her sewing, and out of scraps of
material, yarn, and buttons, she made something else
for Missy—a rag doll with floppy hair and a happy
mouth. Missy had more dolls than any child Brandy
had ever known, and to Brandy they constituted a sad
mockery of Missy's inability to play. The dolls were the
finest from several decades, but they were all of wax,
wood, or china, and even those with cloth or leather
bodies had an unyielding formality to them which made
them seem more like showpieces than toys. Missy now
picked them up once in a while, but she obviously did
not see them as characters in imaginary situations, only
as objects to touch. She seemed to take everything at
its face value, not as a representation of anything else,
so a doll to her was simply a collection of materials put
together in a certain way.

When the rag doll was finished, Brandy presented it
to her and struggled to give it new meaning. "You saw
me make this, so you know it's just bits of things sewn
together. But now we are going to pretend it's a little
girl like you. Let's call her Molly. You can make believe

that Molly goes for walks, or rides, or anything you wish. Missy, do you remember, a long time ago, when you used to pretend things?"

Playing was so natural for normal children that Brandy felt there was no adequate explanation for it; she could explain what to do, could set up mechanical games, but that had nothing to do with the essence of playing or why it was done. She watched Missy anxiously. The hands reached out and took the doll, holding it limply for a moment, but then a strange cast came into her eyes. They shifted beyond Brandy, narrowed as though with the effort to see something very elusive and far away, and then came back to Brandy and finally to the doll. With a convulsive movement, Missy clutched the soft thing to her chest. Her body jerked a little, and Brandy knew what she was doing—she was remembering holding and rocking a doll in her arms.

"I'm very proud of you, darling," Brandy said unevenly. "Remembering how to do things is hard sometimes, but you've done it." Inwardly she hoped she was doing the right thing; too much remembering might be very damaging.

It was close to Thanksgiving before Brandy tested her next line of attack. The velvet dress still had not been touched as far as she could see, but at least Molly had been fully accepted and went everywhere with Missy. Brandy wanted to believe it was because she provided an imaginary playmate, but she was too realistic not to suspect it was much more likely that the doll represented a security link between herself and the child.

Grey had not been home since the day after the fire, and Margaret had received word that he would be spending the holiday in town with Ruth. Though Brandy missed his disturbing presence more than she liked to admit, this fitted in perfectly with her plans. She wondered fleetingly about Grey's reaction to Thanksgiving. Considering that President Lincoln had made it an official holiday after Gettysburg, she didn't think it would hold many happy memories for Grey. Then she made herself quit thinking about it; the less concern she had for his welfare, the better off she would be.

Missy could go down the stairs quite gracefully now, and she went willingly because it meant going out-doors. But she still shivered while going through the interior. Brandy wanted her to go into the rooms on the first floor, but she knew how big a step it would be, and she had put it off. Finally, she decided she had to risk it on account of the weather; already rainy days kept them inside, and once the snow came, outdoor activity would be much more limited. She couldn't bear the thought of Missy spending most of the winter in one room.

Brandy warned Mrs. Bailey and Persia of her plan, and though they were both skeptical, they promised to act as if nothing out of the ordinary were occurring. And so after breakfast one morning, Brandy announced to Missy that they were going downstairs. Missy was wearing a calico dress, and she pulled it fretfully. Brandy never ceased to be amazed at how clearly the child could communicate when she wanted to, without uttering a single word. Missy was plainly pointing out that something was wrong because she wasn't dressed for going outdoors.

"We're not going outside, sweetheart. We're just going downstairs for a while." Softly spoken but a definite command.

Missy sat down abruptly and began to rock and flick her fingers. Panza whined worriedly and licked her face and cried louder because of the lack of response. Brandy's temper rose, and she had a sudden terrible urge to slap her, something she had never done to any child. Instead, she reached down and picked the child up, heavier now with more food and exercise, awkward again because of muscles so rigidly held.

She made her way downstairs carefully, carrying her burden and talking quietly. "You can't live in that room forever. There are all sorts of rooms in the house, rooms full of lovely things which belong to you because you are part of the family."

She put her down at the foot of the stairs, expecting her to sit and rock, but after a moment's hesitation and one quick look down the hall toward Grey's study, Missy put her arms around Brandy, hiding her face in her skirt. Brandy knew she was terrified of being tricked into another confrontation with Grey. "No, don't worry, he isn't here now," she assured her, thinking how miserable it was that that should always be good news to the child.

Missy pulled away and stood looking around. Brandy took her by the hand, and she walked willingly. They did not meet Mrs. Bailey, but Persia was dusting in the front parlor when they walked in. Her eyes grew wide in astonishment, but she managed to say quite calmly, "Good morning to you, Missy," before she hurried out on the pretext of another chore to do.

Missy surveyed the room and suddenly grew tense again. Brandy followed her gaze and saw the fire burning in the grate. She cradled the child against her. "I know you don't like it, love, but fire is only bad when it burns the wrong things." *Oh, no,* she thought wildly, *how else could I have said it, but that's ghastly, the wrong things—such as your mother, such as me.* She went on steadily. "It is a very good thing in your lamp, where it gives you light, or in a fireplace, where it gives you warmth. You really must get used to it. Soon your room will be so cold that even Panza's fur coat won't keep him warm enough."

Missy understood; she reached down and patted Panza as though to reassure him. Brandy breathed a sigh of relief and settled herself in a large chair with Missy in her lap, not holding her too tightly, letting her decide what she wanted to do. After a little while Missy got down and began wandering around the room, touching everything within reach. Brandy was so happy about it that she wouldn't have minded having to explain a few broken treasures to Grey (though telling Mrs. Bailey would be like bringing news of a death), but Missy was being very careful. Brandy took her upstairs again as soon as she showed signs of becoming restless. One room at a time was enough.

But she pressed her advantage about the fire, and she lighted a small one in the fireplace of Missy's room. She picked up a storybook and settled herself in a chair by the fire, pretending to be engrossed in the book, but aware of Missy's every move. At first the child shied away to the far side of the room, holding herself tautly but at least not rocking. But then Panza flopped down on the hearth with a wheeze of contentment, and that was too much for Missy. She came over and crawled into Brandy's lap.

Brandy began to read the story aloud as though nothing unusual had happened. She often read to Missy, but she doubted that Missy understood the words as anything other than separate units which she recognized. If she didn't play, what sense could a story make about others playing or doing a host of things she did not do? Brandy tried to choose stories about dogs, horses, and other things which were familiar to Missy, but she really didn't think the connection between fact and fiction was very clear. Streams of words couldn't make much sense in Missy's silent world, or so Brandy had reasoned. This time she wasn't so sure, for as she read, she became aware of a small but continuous motion of Missy's head against her breast. At first she wondered if it were some new means of shutting things out, but then a startling possibility struck her. She increased and then decreased the speed of her reading; the head followed the changes, followed them because Brandy was sure the eyes were reading the words.

She stopped reading abruptly, mumbling an excuse about resting her voice for a moment. The golden head stopped moving. Brandy's mind whirled; mixed with her elation was a good deal of apprehension. Missy could read, so God only knew what other hidden talents she possessed. It gave her an eerie sense of not knowing the child at all, despite all the time they'd spent together. She wondered if reading was a remembered skill of a precocious three-year-old or if Missy had somehow picked it up in the last two years. And she wondered if Missy had followed the words before while she sat on her lap. She didn't think so; the motion of the head was so noticeable. So why had she betrayed herself? Had the day been so full of rediscoveries that some of her self-control had slipped, or had she done it on purpose, letting Brandy know? Brandy thought in despair that she would never understand all the complexities of Missy's character.

As soon as she had the opportunity, she asked Mrs. Bailey if Missy had known how to read in the time before. The housekeeper looked thoughtful for a moment before she spoke. "Well, as I've told you, because of Jasmine, I never had much to do with Missy's upbringing, so I don't really know. But I do remember that Grey would hold Missy on his lap and read to her, pointing out words they had not read together before. She was very bright in those days, so maybe she learned a bit then. Why do you ask?"

When she had explained, Mrs. Bailey said sadly, "I still fear you see too much progress in Missy because you want it so badly, but I must admit there have been remarkable changes in the child since you came. None of the others managed to do a thing with her; they came and went like the tide, and I don't think she ever really saw any of them. Though I must admit some of them reported strange things." Her voice trailed away, and she looked apologetic.

"What kind of things, Mrs. Bailey?" Brandy asked, wishing her voice didn't sound so sharp.

"Oh, nothing much, little things left on the top of the stairs where one might trip over them, and other things disappearing, never to be found. Why, one poor lady lost a very precious—to her anyway—packet of letters from a particular gentleman friend. But there, child," Mrs. Bailey said, patting Brandy's hand, "I don't think they had anything to do with Missy, just careless women blaming others for their own foolishness."

The housekeeper's reassurances rang hollow comfort in Brandy's ears until she convinced herself that whatever those other women had done or had had done to them had nothing to do with her. She only wished she hadn't had to do so much self-convincing lately.

The changes in Missy were not the only ones at King's Inland, Brandy noticed. Rafe had taken to whistling happily as he worked, and Persia beamed all day long. Brandy guessed their new relationship was a delicate thing, and she didn't want to damage it with clumsy questions. She was flattered when Persia herself offered an explanation.

It was the day before Thanksgiving, and Brandy had Missy downstairs again. Each day they explored, and they had seen every room except for the music room, Grey's study, and Mrs. Bailey's apartment. The housekeeper had said they could come visiting anytime, but Brandy didn't know how she could explain to Missy; she wanted the child to develop the freedom to wander around the house, and it would be confusing to show her the housekeeper's place and then to tell her she could not go there at will. Brandy knew Mrs. Bailey would give up her privacy for the child's sake, but she thought she deserved a place of her own just as Grey's father had intended. As for Grey's study, it was certainly not a room Missy would enjoy. The music room, with Jasmine's picture dominating it, they would tackle when Brandy thought Missy ready.

They were in the dining room, and Persia was there, too, polishing everything in preparation for the morrow's festivities. They could hear Mrs. Bailey busily at work in the kitchen. Missy wandered around looking at the marvelous wall hangings and touching chair coverings shyly, glancing back often to make sure Brandy was still there.

Brandy asked Persia what she would be doing for the feast and was startled by the sudden flood of color in the girl's cheeks. "Well, I'll help here in the mornin', an' then I'll hurry home to be with my family. But, oh,

Brandy, this year's special, Rafe's comin' home with me!"

"Why, that's wonderful!" exclaimed Brandy.

"Ayuh, 'tis all round wonderful 'tween Rafe an' me now. He's still holdin' back somethin', I can feel it, but at least we know we care for each other, an' I reckon he'll get round to tellin' me what's so heavy on him when he has a mind to. I can wait. I was beginnin' to think I was goin' to have to wait my whole life, be an old maid before anythin's happened." She glanced shyly at Brandy. "I don't know quite how, but I know you had something to do with bringin' us together, startin' with the night o' the dance, an' I thank you for it."

Brandy laughed guiltily. "I'm glad it's working out. I don't fancy playing the meddling old maid myself."

"You'll never be an old maid! It isn't my business, but I know Mr. Raleigh is fond o' you, an' you seem so o' him. Even if he is a bit o' a will-o'-the-wisp, I wish the two o' you could get together. Accordin' to Mrs. Bailey, he ought to be comin' in tomorrow."

Brandy said gently, "Thank you, Persia, but we're just good friends." She knew Persia wanted everyone to be as happy as she was. She tried to shut down an inner voice wailing, "I want Grey, not Raleigh!" She looked around for Missy and saw her staring at them. Brandy suspected she had heard and understood everything they had said, and to her amazement, Missy's reaction looked like relief, eyes and face quiet. The only thing Brandy could make of it was that the child was glad she did not love Raleigh, another hard-to-fathom response. She dismissed it, thinking that Missy was probably jealous of her loving anyone except herself.

She was seldom away from the child for long now, but when she was she usually found on her return that Missy was very anxious, sometimes shivering in what could only be acute fear. Brandy worried about it but felt helpless to change it. It was so important for Missy to love another human being that her dependence on Brandy was certainly healthier than her former with-

drawn state, but the day would come when Brandy
would be leaving, Ruth arriving to take over the house.
Brandy hoped she would be equal to the task of making
it acceptable to the child. Then she thought ruefully:
*Acceptable to the child? How will I ever accept it
myself, I love her so*.

She had taken Missy to the dining room several times
for a specific purpose; she wanted the child to eat
Thanksgiving dinner with the rest of them. In houses of
the size and richness of King's Inland, it was not
unusual for the children to eat at different hours from
their parents or in the nursery for quite some years, but
Brandy thought it important that Missy share the feast
and learn to carry on normal tasks in the presence of
others, one more weapon against Ruth. She did not
think Missy could be any more nervous than she was
about the experiment.

Raleigh was a big help. He had ridden hard to arrive
on time for the midday meal. Even with her new
opinion of his character, Brandy could not resist his
high spirits and teasing ways, and apparently neither
could Missy.

Raleigh came to her room, picked her up, and swung
her around. "Well, pet, I hear you're going to eat with
us today just like a young lady. I know you can walk
there by yourself too, but Uncle Raleigh is claiming the
pleasure of carrying you." And so it was easily
accomplished.

But the meal was not a success. Missy was ill at ease,
not looking at anyone, eating little, shivering occasionally but trying her best to behave properly. Brandy sat
beside her, hugging her now and then, whispering
words of encouragement to her, thankful for Raleigh's
banter, which eased the strain.

After it was over, she told Missy how proud of her
she was, and as a reward she brought up some extra
food which Missy ate hungrily. At least it was another
step forward.

Raleigh stayed for a few days, and they rode and

walked during the day, Brandy making sure Missy went with them. She did not want a repetition of Raleigh's kiss; even the memory of it made the comparison of Grey's harder to bear. In the evenings, when she played the piano and they sang, Mrs. Bailey was with them, and so she was safe then, too.

Raleigh wasn't blind, but all he said was: "Running away or to, Golden Eyes?" And when she pretended not to understand, he shrugged and let it go.

On Sunday he left early because the sky had a new look, low and shrouded in heavy gray-white clouds, and the air had the unmistakable clean, sharp fragrance of coming snow. Brandy gave him some letters to post and asked him an additional favor, apologizing for putting him to so much trouble. Though Rafe served as messenger and supplier for King's Inland, she knew this task would be easier for Raleigh. She gave him a list of purchases to make for her and the money for them, asking that they be sent out with the next delivery, if he could find out when that would be. She laughed, looking at the sky, and said she would understand if the articles didn't arrive until spring.

He didn't want to accept the money, but she overrode him, thinking cynically that it would more likely be Grey than Raleigh who paid if she didn't. He brushed aside her misgivings about the delivery. "Don't worry, I'll get them to you in a few days. There are always ways; we don't get frozen in here as solidly as they do in the north. But, Brandy, you haven't been away from King's Inland since the day you arrived. I could at least arrange to take you to Union, if not to Wiscasset."

She answered him truthfully. "I haven't really thought about it, and the only reason I need anything now is for making Christmas presents. I always start much later than I should. I'm perfectly happy here, and I don't want to leave Missy too long."

He looked at her searchingly for a moment, nodded,

gave her a light good-bye kiss on the cheek and was gone.

The snow began at twilight, and later Brandy sat by the window holding Missy. She felt as excited as she always had by the first snowfall in the high mountain country of California. Memories flooded back, and she was strangely close to her father, to Pearl, and to all the varied characters she had known in her old life. For a moment she was so homesick for the West that her throat knotted and her vision blurred, but then Missy stirred, curling her body into a more comfortable position as she fell asleep, and the old images vanished, leaving nothing but the weight of love for the child she held. She did not think she could feel more than a mother to Missy even had she given birth to her; they had come so far from infant blankness together. She tried to banish Ruth from her mind; surely even so selfish a woman would be charmed by Missy once she really knew her. She put Missy and Panza to bed and sat for a long time watching, drawing peace from them.

It snowed all night, and morning saw a new world. The sun shone fitfully, offering moments of flashing brilliance as an extra gift. Brandy could hardly wait to be out, and after breakfast she hurriedly bundled herself and Missy into warm clothes.

Snow was no new thing to Missy, but she hadn't been out in it for a long time. She touched and tasted it and delighted Brandy with her explorations. But Panza was best of all to watch. He had never seen it before, and his antics were hysterical. He put his nose in it and gave a startled yelp. He tried to pick up his feet up and walk on top to no avail. Finally he sat down, his fat rump sinking into the snow, and yowled his outrage. Brandy was laughing so hard she hardly had the strength to pick him up, but when she did, he gave her face a grateful swipe with his tongue. She heard another sound and looked around at Missy.

Missy was smiling, not a tentative movement of the mouth, but a true smile, and the sound had been the rusty beginning of a laugh. As Brandy had guessed, Missy's face was unbelievably beautiful when she smiled. Her black eyes danced; her whole face curved into new planes of joy.

Brandy went to her and kissed her as Panza snuggled between them. She thought that laughing and crying after so long a time of denial must be similar to trying out a leg which had been broken and immobile for months. The sob in the woods and now this—they were fine beginnings.

They plowed through to the barn and found Rafe busily at work putting special shoes on the horses. The shoes had sharp cleats on them so the animals would not slip on the ice. A big old sleigh had been pulled out and stood in the middle of the floor, gleaming with evidence of Rafe's hard work.

He greeted them with the happy look he so often wore these days. "Yes, you see, the horse too must change his clothes for the winter." Missy smiled again and Rafe saw it. His eyes flew to Brandy, who nodded, but he went on as though nothing extraordinary had happened. "When the ice is on the top of the snow, then we will go on the sleigh."

Missy wandered around the barn while Brandy talked to Rafe. Brandy didn't want to pry, but she couldn't stand it anymore, so she asked, "Rafe, did all go well at the Cowperwaithes? Did you have a good time?"

His eyes held the same softness they had for Missy. "They are a good people, and it was good sharing such a feast with them. I think even they like me and do not mind that Persia and I may be together," he added with wonder.

"Of course they don't mind, you fool," Brandy admonished him. "You are a fine man and the only one who will make Persia happy, so why shouldn't they like you?"

"I do not think I yet believe it, but little by little it seems true. And the bad things of myself, these too I will tell her," he assured her anxiously.

"That's up to you, Rafe, but surely you know Persia well enough by now to know that whatever you have to tell her will make no difference in her love." She met his eyes steadily, not wanting to betray how much she knew. He nodded as though not trusting himself to speak, and Brandy headed Missy and Panza back to the house.

Raleigh was true to his word, and the things Brandy had ordered arrived by the end of the week. She was glad to start on the gifts, and she let Missy watch all the work except that on the child's own present, a wardrobe of clothes for the rag doll. For the Cowperwaithes she had got a bag of hard candies for the toddlers, bottles of scent for the girls and their mother, and hunting knives for Ben and his father; they were all so self-reliant that she couldn't think of anything to make that they hadn't made already. For Mrs. Bailey and for Dorothea Adams she planned ruffled aprons, and for Rafe a pair of mittens. Raleigh would receive handkerchiefs with finely rolled edges and his initials embroidered on them—a nice gift but not too personal. She decided on the same for the Adams men. She would knit a shawl for Pearl, though she thought ruefully that it would probably arrive in California quite a time after Christmas. Only with the choice of Grey's gift was she at a loss. She thought of making him a pair of mittens like Rafe's, a scarf, a shirt, but nothing seemed right, nothing seemed adequate. Then she made her decision and was satisfied, though she reflected sadly that he probably wouldn't even be at King's Inland for Christmas; he would probably be with Ruth.

She and Missy were outside at every opportunity, and when the snow crusted over, Rafe took them out in the sleigh. Brandy loved it all: the merry sound of the harness bells; the smooth slip of the runners carrying them through an enchanted kingdom of trees transformed into white castles, of distances changed in lost perspective, of bare patches on the evergreens making eerie black silhouettes against the snow. And Missy's cheeks were always bright from the cold air and her pleasure by the time they got home.

It kept snowing on and off, and by the week before Christmas there had been no word from Grey, and Brandy resigned herself to the fact that he would not be coming for the holiday; even if he wished to, the drifts would discourage him, and there was no reason for him to want to anyway, not with Ruth in town.

She couldn't help feeling a little lonesome with everyone's plans that Saturday, for Rafe was leaving early to spend the day at the Cowperwaithes, dropping Mrs. Bailey off at a neighborhood farm on the way, but she had never minded their absence before and knew she did now only because she was missing Grey. Outwardly she gave no sign of it, ordering everyone to scat because she had Christmas secrets to work on, and finally they were gone.

Brandy took Missy outside for a while, but it started to snow again as it had been threatening to do since early morning, so they were forced back indoors. They had lunch from the lavish spread Mrs. Bailey had left for them, and then they went up to Missy's room, and Brandy put some more logs on the fire, something Missy now accepted without fear.

The child fell asleep at once, exhausted by the romp in the cold. Brandy tried to work on Rafe's mittens, but her own eyes were intolerably heavy, and soon she was sleeping soundly in the chair by the fire.

A log breaking with a rumble in the fireplace and Panza's worried cry woke her. She sat up rubbing her eyes and looking around dazedly, feeling very muddle-headed. But then her pulse quickened. Missy wasn't in the room. Panza was, and Molly lay on the bed where Missy had been sleeping, but the child was gone.

Brandy stood frozen for a moment, trying to still panic with reasons for Missy's absence—perhaps she had gone to a room downstairs on her own. But no, she wouldn't go without Molly and Panza. Brandy didn't think she would go without her either.

She raced out of the room, checking her own room and the others on the second floor, calling Missy's name all the while, before she ran downstairs. The draft hit her immediately, frigid air sweeping in through the open front door, snow blowing in to melt in the hall.

She stared at the opening, trying to take it in. Missy outdoors, by herself in the falling snow, in a dress as light as the one Brandy herself was wearing. She grabbed her cloak from the rack in the hall; there was no time to change into sensible clothes and boots; a child would freeze to death so quickly.

The snow was deep and hampering, and Brandy cursed in desperation. It blinded her and was coming down hard enough to cover tracks as soon as they were made. She reached the barn, calling as loudly as she could, finding no one.

Brandy didn't pray often, but she did now, repeating over and over, "God, don't let her be dead, please, please keep her safe until I find her!"

She tried desperately to think of where Missy might have gone—Missy who did not seem to feel the cold but who would die of it anyway. She had a sudden image of the first happy day at the pond. It had remained Missy's favorite place. Brandy tried to run, struggling and falling in the deep drifts, sobbing in fear. If only someone else had been home today, if only, if only.

She was already tiring, and she forced herself to go more slowly down the trail, peering through the muffling curtain for any sign of the slight form. She lost track of time and distance as she plodded on. The world was becoming a bright mass of pain starting in her hands—gloves or at the very least mittens for a lady, she thought crazily—her feet, her uncovered face, and moving through her whole body.

She swayed dizzily as she caught sight of a dark spot at the side of the trail. But when she reached it, it was no more than a fir branch which had dropped its burden of snow. She sank down, deciding to rest for a while.

She knew it was dangerous, this peaceful sleepy feeling, but it was so much better than the earlier pain of the cold. She would rest just a little longer. Nothing mattered anymore anyway; Missy must be dead by now. *Missy, I love you, and there was so much hope, someday you would have left your private darkness and joined us in the sun. Ruth, damn her soul, will be glad. But Grey, your father, no, I don't think so, I think he loves you much more than I do.*

She curled herself tighter in her cloak. The shivering had stopped. She felt a comforting warmth spreading through her. No, she wouldn't move now; it was so nice here. The snow went on about its gentle business of covering her.

Someone was pulling at her, shaking her, picking her up. Her blood poured like fire, searing its way back into her frozen limbs. She screamed in protest.

"I know, I know, but it can't be helped. I've got to get you back." Grey's face was close to hers.

She remembered, and the shivering started again, adding agony. "Missy, Missy's dead, she's out here. I couldn't find her. Oh, Grey, I couldn't find her. My fault, my fault, I went to sleep." She thought she was shouting, but the words came out in a broken whisper. Grey had to bend closer to hear them.

"Brandy, Missy's fine, she's warm and safe at home. Can you hear me? Nothing's wrong with her."

She slipped from the jarring pain of being carried into darkness. She did not feel Grey's strong hands holding her fiercely against his own warmth; she did not hear him repeating her name over and over.

Icy fire brought her back. They were robbing her with it. Everything hurt, and she struggled to get away from the relentless hands.

"There, Brandy, the snow will start your blood again, then we'll make you warm." Grey's voice, then something held against her mouth, her head lifted. "Drink it slowly, Brandy." She gasped as the heat of the liquor cut her breathing for a moment. "There are two kinds of brandy in Maine," she said, and tried to smile, but the shivering had started again. "Missy?" came out through her chattering teeth.

Grey lifted her head again so that she could see her in the corner hugging herself and rocking. "Don't do that, Missy, I'll rock you," she said, and slipped back into the shadows.

She was watching her father gamble at the Belle Union. It was much too hot there. She tried to tell him she was going outside for air, but he didn't seem to hear her. Then she was with Pearl, who asked her if she was all right, but a customer called her, and she left. She was back in the high country. Winter had come early, and she was freezing. Again she tried to tell her father. He was setting Jed Mitchel's broken arm. He didn't look up; he just said, "Brandy doesn't freeze." Why were they out in the snow in the middle of nowhere? No one would explain. And then Missy was beside her, saying her name over and over. "Oh, Missy, that's wonderful. We've got to tell your father. He'll be so happy." But Missy disappeared, and so did her father and Jed. She ran through the snow calling their names. She ran into the sun's blazing heat and back into winter again and again, finding no one.

CHAPTER X

She felt flat and light as though her body weighed nothing at all, but she was awake; the West had gone back to where it belonged, and she knew where she was. Then, as she took in the scene in her bedroom, she wasn't sure she was as conscious as she thought. Grey was sitting beside the bed, watching her anxiously. Obviously she'd had her eyes open before in delirium and hadn't recognized him. Across from him, separated only by the bed, was Missy, curled up in a chair, fast asleep with Molly clasped against her. Brandy's eyes widened; Missy had on the dress Grey had sent, and it had been buttoned so crookedly that she must have put it on herself.

Brandy looked at Grey again and saw the relief dawn on his face as he realized she was back with the living. His smile answered her own, and the rhythm of her heart beat a curious tattoo.

He spoke softly so as not to wake Missy. "How are you feeling? May I get you anything?"

"No, thank you. I'm fine, really, just tired." She didn't have to make any effort to keep her voice low; her best effort was weak and faraway-sounding. "How long has it been?"

"Today is Monday, or rather tonight is. Who is Jed Mitchel?"

Brandy stared at him blankly for a moment, trying to

155

follow, finding her mind was working very slowly. He sounded jealous. She had an instant's temptation to make up a wild story to tease him, but she had more important things to talk about. "Jed Mitchel was a prospector my father and I knew. He must be at least eighty by now, but I bet he's still roaming the mother lode looking for his next fortune. He's made and lost several." She glanced at Missy again; the child was still sleeping soundly. "The dress, Grey, and her being in the same room with you, I don't understand."

"Neither do I. Persia's been staying with her, but even so she's been rather neglected the past few days, and she put the dress on herself and came in here, in spite of my presence. I'm not concerned about why she did so; both acts were so positive that nothing else matters. But I think it's because she was worried about you and wanted to please you. She ignores me completely, but I prefer that to screaming terror." His tone was matter-of-fact, but his face betrayed his intense love for his child as clearly as it had on the night he had carried her to her room. Knowing as she did now that, despite outward control, Grey's emotional reactions were fierce, she wondered how he could love so cold a woman as Ruth Collins. But then she chided herself wryly; for all she knew, Ruth was anything but cold when she was alone with Grey.

Though he still spoke quietly, there was an underlying note of urgency. "Brandy, I'm not sure you're strong enough to talk about it yet, but I want to know what happened, why you were out there, why you thought Missy was in danger. God, you nearly froze to death!" He covered his face with his hands for a moment, hiding his expression.

Brandy relived the wild panic which had sent her out into the snow. She fought for control so that she could make the story sound reasonable, but before she could begin, a movement from the chair drew her attention. Missy was staring at her, her small face drawn with worry.

Brandy held out her arms. "See, darling, I'm fine, just sleepy. Come here so I can hug you."

The beautiful smile appeared, and in the next instant, Brandy was cradling Missy in her arms. Missy burrowed against her warmth, sighing in contentment, a strange new sound for her, not once looking at Grey. The slight jostling against the bed and sharp squeaks told of Panza's attempts to join them. Grey went around and picked the puppy up and deposited him on the bed. "I'll talk to you later, but right now I'm going to go tell Margaret and Persia the good news and have them bring you something to eat." *And if I leave, Missy's joy will be complete*, rang in Brandy's mind as if Grey had said it aloud.

Missy's vigil must have been even more tiring than Grey's, for once assured that Brandy was safe, she relaxed again into sleep. When Persia came in, Brandy put a finger to her lips in warning against waking the child.

"Mrs. Bailey's bringin' your supper. She wouldn't let me do it, wanted to see for herself that you're all right. I'll just put Missy to bed. She's been terrible worried, poor mite." Persia's whisper sounded awfully loud to Brandy, but Missy didn't wake, not even when Persia picked her up, and Brandy was thankful that her anxiety had lessened enough to allow her to sleep so deeply.

Mrs. Bailey arrived next, bearing a heavily laden tray. "Well, my dear, you really are back with us. What a fright you gave us! This room has been a meeting hall, what with Grey and Missy insisting on staying and Persia and I in and out."

"There isn't any adequate way to thank you all for your care of me, Mrs. Bailey. I just hope you know how grateful I am. But I'm completely in the dark. How did Grey find me?"

"You were very lucky. Since it was snowing so hard, I had Burt Thomas bring me back from the farm a little earlier than I'd planned. I didn't want to be stuck there. When I arrived, the front door was wide open which seemed odd, though I thought a gust of wind might have pushed it if it hadn't been properly shut. But when I couldn't find you, I started to worry. Then I found Missy asleep in the music room all by herself, but of course, she couldn't tell me where you were."

"The music room! She's never gone in there." Brandy shut her eyes, remembering that she hadn't even checked it. What grief she could have spared herself!

"Well, that's where she was. And I had taken her back upstairs and was still looking for you when Grey came in. I told him about the open door, and he seemed to know instantly what had happened. He went out to find you. Lucky for you he did! Now you eat what you want and leave the rest. And then you go right back to sleep; you've had a difficult time."

After Mrs. Bailey left, Brandy picked at the food, but she wasn't hungry. A very disturbing question was forming in her mind. Why had Missy let her go out in the storm? The only reasonable answer seemed to be that Missy had opened the door and tricked her into going out on purpose. She must have heard her calling, yet she had given no sign of her whereabouts, had stayed in a room which, if she were as clever as Brandy thought she was, she had known would not be checked. Further evidence of the demon side?

Brandy clung to her knowledge that Missy had been truly worried about her recovery, so at least the good side was still operative. She turned restlessly, shutting her eyes tightly, wanting to sleep so that she would not have to think. But her mind refused to stop working. Missy had put on the velvet dress, and she had betrayed her ability to read, both actions connected with Grey. What was she trying to say? Maybe nothing at all, maybe just the good side trying to please Brandy or maybe a statement about her father, that he was guilty, innocent? What if Missy herself had lured her mother out to the barn? She moaned aloud in confusion, not hearing Grey come in.

He was beside the bed, asking urgently, "What's wrong? Are you in pain? Shall I get Margaret or Persia?"

She managed to smile weakly at him, touched by his concern. "No, I don't need anyone, but thank you. I'm just disgusted by my own stupidity. I could have saved myself and the rest of you a great deal of distress had I searched for Missy more thoroughly before I ran out of the house in panic." She wished she sounded more convincing; Grey was a hard man to fool.

"Tell me exactly what happened, Brandy." No room for refusal.

She related the events, hoping that even if they made her seem foolish, they would provide a logical explanation for the whole thing. But Grey's capacity for detail extended to everything, even to the behavior of his daughter. Brandy realized that someone must have given him even better reports of Missy's activities than she had.

His eyes never left her face; his voice was slow and deliberate. "But Missy doesn't go anywhere without you and you've never taken her into the music room, have you?"

Brandy shook her head and closed her eyes again so that she wouldn't have to look at him anymore. His voice went on inexorably. "Then she must have done it on purpose. She must have opened the door and hidden so that you would go out in the storm."

Her eyes flew open, and she met his, bird and snake. Her throat worked convulsively, but when she spoke, she had herself in mind. "I would like to believe she went to the music room because she wanted to do it on her own and that she fell asleep there—we were both very sleepy; we played out in the cold that morning. But I admit that sounds pretty farfetched, and I'm prepared to accept the idea that she did it on purpose, or at least part of her did.

"Grey, sometimes it seems as if Missy might be two different people, one good, one bad, and the more progress the real child, the good child, makes, the more the bad one tries to disrupt things."

She didn't have to wait long for his reaction. "So where in the hell does that leave you?" He was making an unsuccessful effort not to shout. "Apparently she has tried to kill you by a fall, by fire, by cold. What do you think she'll try next, so clever and inventive a child?"

"Stop it! She'll hear you! All those accidents or whatever they were . . . . well, I still have no proof Missy caused them. You are still just as likely a suspect save perhaps for this last episode." She watched him as she said the brutal words, but he did not flinch. "But if she did, then just the fact that I'm aware it's a possibility will help. Trouble is always easier to handle if you know where it's coming from.

"Can't you see, if it's true, it must be a good sign? It must mean that the sick part of Missy feels so threatened by the progress she's making that it feels moved to do something about it. My job is to make the good part stronger and stronger until it can take over completely."

Grey shook his head wearily. "I think you would judge it a good omen if Satan himself appeared." He stared blindly at a shadowed corner of the canopy above Brandy's head. "I want her to get well more than anything else. But I do not want anyone dying in the process. Yet, if you leave now, everything will go back to the way it was; she will cease to exist again. Perhaps you are right about being able to avoid further danger, but I can't give you any more chances. It is hard enough to let you stay now. If anything else happens, you will leave immediately. If you are still capable of leaving, if you are still alive," he added grimly, his ebony eyes once more focused on her.

She knew it was an ultimatum without recourse, and ultimatums usually made her angry, but this one was just. She reached out and took his hand. He looked startled; then he smiled ruefully and shook her hand firmly as if sealing a gentleman's agreement. Inwardly Brandy cursed her weakness; even touching his hands made her giddy. The controlled strength, the hard ridges of muscle or sinew, the calluses from reins and work, the long fingers with blunt nails—for a moment Brandy was lost in the sculptured beauty of them. She saw them younger, finer, carving the little boat for Mrs. Bailey; she saw them controlling Orpheus with ease, she saw them touching Ruth, and she dropped the one she had been holding for such an embarrassing length of time.

The hot blood rose in her face, and she forced herself to look at Grey, expecting him to be sardonically knowing and amused. But strangely he looked as if he had been caught out, too, stunned and unsure of what to do next.

Brandy took a deep breath and brought them back from the dangerous place. "I am certainly grateful for it, but I'm curious, how did you happen along at just the right moment to find me? How did you know where to look?"

This brought the reaction her earlier comment had failed to provoke; all the harsh lines were back in an instant, and she realized he had mistaken the reason for her question. "No, Grey, no. I'm not blaming you. Had you not come, I would be long dead. I'm just curious because your timing was so perfect for my need."

His defensiveness was replaced by a wry smile. "For once I was trying to do the right thing. Ruth wants me to spend Christmas with her, and she won't come here." Brandy knew she was the reason for that, but there was no rancor in Grey's statement. "I came out to deliver gifts and early wishes for a happy Christmas. And I knew of your walks with Missy into the woods and to the pond. It used to be my favorite place when I was a child. I suppose some instinct told me you had gone that way."

How ironic, Brandy thought, to owe thanks to Ruth for her life. "Then, please, don't delay because of me. I'm fine, and I'm sure Ruth must be anxious to have you back." She was satisfied with the cool reasonableness of her voice.

But Grey's eyes glinted and bored into hers as he asked with false sweetness, "Trying to get rid of me? Ruth will just have to celebrate Christmas a little later this year if she wants to be with me. Christmas Day will be soon enough to leave. Any objections? Will that interfere with your plans?"

Mutely she shook her head, ignoring his sarcasm, made much too happy by the prospect of having him at King's Inland for the holiday.

He was suddenly contrite. "You're tired, go to sleep now. I won't tease you further."

He turned back to look at her when he reached the door. "How very glad I am that you are safe."

She felt as if she had been given a special benediction, and she lay at peace, letting the unanswerable questions slip away at last. Her last thought as sleep found her was of the days ahead, with Grey.

Persia's entrance with a breakfast tray the next morning reminded Brandy of her first day at King's Inland; how long ago that seemed! "I'm not an invalid, you know," she protested. "I feel quite well this morning and can't wait to get out of bed." But to please Persia, she did as she was told and ate the meal ravenously, finding her appetite had returned with a vengeance.

Persia perched on the edge of the bed, and the absence of her normal chatter was very noticeable. Brandy glanced at her curiously and smiled to herself. Wherever Persia was, it wasn't in this room. Her eyes were soft with faraway dreaming, her mouth curved happily, and her skin glowed with a new radiance. She felt Brandy's gaze and turned. She hesitated, and then her smile widened, and she burst out: "Oh, we were goin' to keep it secret awhile longer, but I can't keep it from you a minute more. Rafe an' I are goin' to get married come spring! I'd like to have done with waitin' right now, but Rafe, my poor man, he had such a bad time afore, he's skittish 'bout takin' another wife."

Persia's eyes grew round, and she cried in dismay, "Jus' look what I've done, gone an' blathered half o' Rafe's shame." Her voice took on a firm, defiant note. "Only 'twasn't shame, 'twas only what any man would have to do. He was married to this Marianne woman, an' a right piece o' sin she was. She cheated poor Rafe, but he killed her more for th' child than for that."

Brandy had thought it would be difficult to appear sufficiently surprised at the retelling of the tale, but her gasp of "The child!" would have convinced anyone that she had never heard the story before.

Persia nodded. "They had a little boy. Rafe wanted to give him lots o' things, so he spent a good lot o' time in th' woods, huntin' an' trappin'. An' while he was gone, that woman took another man, a man who was supposed to be a friend to Rafe. But my man is a good man, an' I think he could have put up with that. It was comin' back to find his child ailin' an' left in the hands o' neighbors that pushed him too far. Th' child died in his arms, an' Rafe went lookin' for Marianne. He found her with her lover, an' he killed 'em both, an' I can't fault him for it."

"I can't either," murmured Brandy softly. Her faith in Persia had been justified; Rafe's confession had made no difference to the girl, save to make her love him more compassionately. A new thought struck her—how typical of human nature; the crime remained the same as when Mrs. Bailey had told it, but seen through Persia's lovingly prejudiced eyes and with all the details, all the venom was gone.

She congratulated Persia wholeheartedly and tried to ignore a sad pang of envy; Maine people seemed to take spring very seriously as a season for new beginnings— Persia and Rafe, Ruth and Grey, marriages to come at a time when she would be leaving King's Inland, Missy, Grey.

When she had finished her breakfast and Persia had left with the tray, Brandy got up. Her legs felt as if they belonged to the rag doll Molly, and she fumed impatiently over the time it took her to dress. She was appalled at the changes the short but violent illness had made in her appearance. Her face was pale, her eyes ringed by bruised shadows, and she had lost enough weight to make her dress hang loosely.

"No wonder everyone is making such a fuss," she said to her reflection. "You look quite horrid; not even the cats would associate with you."

There was a knock at her door, and Persia brought Missy and Panza in and then went off to do her chores. Brandy was content to rest in her favorite chair by the fire with Missy on her lap. Missy held Molly tightly against her, and Brandy still found it difficult to believe that there was a part of her so separate that it could abandon the treasured doll.

That afternoon Persia came to take Missy and Panza for a walk. Missy tugged at Brandy's hand, but then she went willingly with Persia after Brandy had explained it would be a few days before she could go out.

Brandy decided she had been upstairs long enough. She pinched her cheeks to give them some color and headed for the stairs. But she wasn't halfway down before she had to stop. "Damn!" she swore in vexation as she hung on to the banister. The stairs seemed to be moving of their own accord while the whole world rocked gently as if at sea. Perspiration stood out on her face and ran down her neck. She wondered giddily if this was how Missy had felt when she had first walked down the stairs. She shut her eyes and shook her head to clear it and yelped when Grey swung her up into his arms.

He gave her a little shake. "Do you have some overwhelming desire to break your neck? You looked as if you were going to finish your descent with one plunge from the top."

She was so thankful that he'd caught her before she'd done just that that she answered meekly, "I guess I overestimated my strength, but I got so bored up there!"

"Please, next time yell for assistance. Now, where to, miss?" he asked, causing her to giggle because he sounded just like a polite hansom driver. Her laughter helped her to ignore the disconcertingly intimate feeling of his heart beating against her.

He was carrying her when Mrs. Bailey met them. Her eyes went wide with surprise behind her spectacles. "Gracious!" she exclaimed, shocked by the impropriety of the scene.

"Just found an early Christmas present," explained Grey, wickedly straight-faced. "We'll be in the front parlor. Please bring Brandy some tea and something good to eat. We'll have to feed her up for a while. I know from firsthand experience, she's pretty bony right now." Brandy, for fear of being dropped, restrained herself from finding his ribs with her elbow.

When she was comfortably ensconced in the parlor, she apologized for troubling him further but asked if he had any books or sheets of Christmas music, and she was surprised by the wide selection he brought to her. But the inscription in *Christmas Carols New and Old* reminded her of why it should be so: "To my wife and my daughter, the music of my days, with all my love, Grey." The book had been printed in sixty-five, a time when Jasmine, Grey, and Missy were still a family, two years before the fire.

She looked up at Grey, suddenly aware that Christmas might be a bad time for him. Though she said nothing, he answered the expression on her face. He spoke gently, as though explaining something to a child. "Life is difficult enough without being haunted by the dead, particularly by someone else's dead. And Jasmine, for all her faults, would not have relished the role of a ghost. She was far too vital for that."

He left to work in his study as Mrs. Bailey brought in the tea tray. She glanced at the music. "Oh, it will be nice to have carols again! I do think Christmas music is the most fun of all." They chatted amiably until Mrs. Bailey said she had to get back to work, and Brandy was relieved when she left because she could not take her mind from Grey and Jasmine. In spite of what he had said, the music had ended for Grey when Jasmine died. Brandy was stunned by the emotions she felt; she was ragingly jealous of the love Jasmine had had from him and afraid that by her death she had killed his capacity to love anyone else. "But it's Ruth's problem, not mine," she said to the empty room, and forced herself to study the lines and notes until she began to hear the melodies in her mind.

By the time Persia came in with a pink-cheeked Missy and a slightly damp Panza, Brandy was feeling much more in spirit with the season. She hugged them both and chattered about festive plans.

She felt stronger each day, and by the time Friday brought Christmas Eve there was no denying that King's Inland was in tune with the season, ghosts or not. Grey and Rafe had brought in armloads of greenery, which, tied with red ribbons, filled the house with the clean fragrance of pine. They had cut a beautifully symmetrical tree, which stood in the music room bedecked with candles waiting to give light. Packages had been appearing as if by magic at its base, and Brandy had to restrain herself from behaving like a child and prowling through them to shake, weigh, and to guess their contents. Enticing smells drifted out of the kitchen, and Brandy worked frantically to lend a hand and to finish the gifts she was making. As she set the last stitches in Raleigh's handkerchiefs, she couldn't help breathing a sigh of relief that he was not there; she hoped he wasn't lonesome, but his presence would bring the awful tension between the brothers, would break the fragile peace of King's Inland.

Brandy donned her velvet dress for the festivities. She was ready well ahead of time and went to prepare Missy. The child had not dressed herself again since the episode of the blue dress, but when she saw Brandy, she ran to the wardrobe and pulled out her own velvet gown. Brandy was so pleased with this performance that her hands were unsteady as she helped Missy with the buttons, and she buttoned one wrong on a sleeve. Missy's hand immediately touched hers, and the child shook her head. Brandy laughed. "How right you are, and what a clumsy buttoner I am!" *And how observant you are,* she added silently.

She explained the plans for the evening as thoroughly as she could, hoping that knowing what was to come would make her less fearful. And at least Missy did not protest going downstairs, though she clutched Molly tightly and looked around every time Panza lagged.

Before supper they met in the parlor for holiday toasts from a bowl of hot spiced cider which Grey had laced liberally with spirits. A milder brew had been set aside for Missy, and Brandy thought she ought to share it with her since she already felt drunk with the excitement of the evening. But then she decided to hell with caution and drank the stronger punch, feeling the warmth explode and flow through her. She watched Missy carefully and had the absurd thought that she was the only adult in the room; the rest of them, even Grey, were acting as silly as five-year-olds at a first party. Missy was solemn and self-contained, valiantly holding her body still, only fixing her eyes on Brandy, ignoring the others completely.

Persia and Rafe were with them, dividing their time between what they called their two families. Christmas Day they would spend at the Cowperwaithe farm. The first toast was to the couple, for Persia had gone on spreading the news of their engagement.

"That one, my Persia, she is not to be trusted with the secret," Rafe complained in mock disgust, but the melodious way he said her name betrayed him. Brandy knew he must be relieved that Persia was so open; Marianne had had far too many secrets.

Grey raised his glass. "To Rafe, my most trusted friend, and to his lovely bride to be, may your years together be long, happy ones." If there was a double meaning in "most trusted," Brandy didn't care; Grey's wish for their happiness was sincere, and the toast made her want to weep for the couple's joy and Grey's lack of it.

But Mrs. Bailey's tart comment made her laugh instead. "I declare," she said, "I am getting old and blind—I didn't know. It's a sure sign of being in your dotage when you miss the signs of a couple courting. Grey, I may have to retire to my rocking chair for the rest of my days."

"Not on your life!" he exclaimed. "If you gave up, I am sure King's Inland would fall into ruin in no time at all."

Mrs. Bailey scolded him for being a flatterer, but her cheeks were bright with the compliment.

They toasted crops yet to be planted and colts yet to be born in the spring yet to come, and Brandy watched Missy lifting her glass to drink at each signal. At first she thought the child was just aping her elders, but the final toast convinced her that Missy was listening to every word and knew what was going on.

The solemnity of Grey's voice brought stillness to the room. "To my beautiful daughter, Missy, who has traveled so far in so short a time, and to Brandy, who made the journey possible and who, thank God, is still with us."

Tears blurred Brandy's vision, and in spite of herself, she could not stop the few that left warm, wet traces on her cheeks. Grey's eyes looked into hers as if no one else were in the room, and she turned away, meeting the same black intensity in Missy's. The young eyes were narrowed, aware, and focused on her as the child raised her glass with the others and gravely sipped her sweet cider. The good side was thankful for her safety.

Supper was lavish and gay, and even Missy ate well, though still she looked at no one but Brandy. Brandy was glad that the custom of keeping Christmas Eve rather than Christmas Day prevailed at King's Inland; she and her father had done likewise, finding the night a better harbor for miracles than full sun. As they left the table, she drew a deep breath and hoped her next plan would work as a small miracle and not a disaster.

The tree had been set up in the music room at her request. Grey had been doubtful but had complied. Brandy reasoned that Missy had made the first decision about the room by going there to cause harm; therefore, she must be shown that the room was a place for joy. One point more for the good side.

Rafe and Grey went ahead and shut the door behind them, leaving the ladies to wait outside, Missy pressed closer to Brandy, and Brandy could feel her trembling—from fear, anticipation, guilt, or old memories? Who ever knew what Missy was truly feeling?

When the men opened the door, there was a collective gasp of astonishment. The room was in darkness save for the pyramid of radiance from the many-candled tree. For an instant it seemed to Brandy the essence of the season, the sudden splendid light, but then Missy shattered the moment by sinking to the floor and beginning to rock and flick her fingers.

Ignoring the stiff agony in Grey's face, Brandy motioned everyone to go in as she sank to the floor beside Missy and drew her into her arms.

"It isn't the same, darling, it isn't. It's like the fire in your room, in the lamps, the good fires I've told you about. There are many flames, but they are for happiness, not sadness. If you'll just look at them, you'll see how beautiful they are." The rocking stopped; the fingers ceased to dance. Missy looked up at her and then slowly turned her gaze to the tree. A small sigh escaped, and she stood, waiting quietly for Brandy to get up. It was as if she had said, "If you say it is so, I will believe it." Brandy felt that no gift could exceed that of Missy's trust.

She smiled at the others to reassure them, but as Rafe lit the lamps in the room, her attention was on Missy. As incredible as it seemed, she was sure that the child did not remember her recent visit to the room. Her eyes were exploring everything with the peculiar intentness she only showed when seeing something for the first time. A barely perceptible jerk of the golden head told Brandy she had recognized the portrait of her mother and had been startled by it, conclusive and comforting proof that the good side shared nothing knowingly with the bad. It followed logically that the Missy she loved had no wish to harm her. The last miserable knot of doubt eased and disappeared.

Gay with the relief of it, she drew Missy against her, telling her of the music to come, of the rainbow packages to be opened. The others, who had been chattering with false brightness to cover Missy's reaction, relaxed— all save Grey, who looked withdrawn and thoughtful. He never missed anything; he had seen Missy's response to the room as clearly as she had, but the difference was that he did not see it as a cause for rejoicing.

She didn't want him to think about it anymore. She went to the piano, settling Missy at her side on the bench. She stroked the keys softly at first, wandering from one tune to another, watching Missy. Missy concentrated on the hands touching the keys, and Brandy, noting the absorption in her face, saw another way to teach her to communicate. She wondered what kind of ecstasy and terror Missy would ask from the piano if she knew how to play.

Mrs. Bailey, Rafe, Persia, and Grey gathered around to sing, but Missy's only acknowledgment of their presence was to press closer to Brandy. Brandy struck the chords for "Joy to the World!" and started to sing while the others joined in. The women had sweet hymn-trained voices, and even shy Rafe sang, his accent softening the words, but the biggest surprise was Grey's voice, deep and true on every note. Brandy pushed away the thought of all the music he and Jasmine must have made together.

They sang "Hark! The Herald Angels Sing," "It Came Upon the Midnight Clear," and many traditional English tunes. And when they sang, "O, Come, All Ye

Faithful," Grey sang the Latin words in perfect harmony. Brandy finished with "O Little Town of Bethlehem," a song which had been written the year before, but she faltered when no one else joined in, realizing that new music had not come to King's Inland after Jasmine's death. Grey said, "Please, go on," and so she finished the song, knowing she was singing not to praise the Lord, but to please Grey.

After the caroling, Grey read from the Gospel, according to St. Luke, and Brandy felt closer to the miracle than she ever had. She was thankful King's Inland was not a rigidly churchgoing household; she and her father had rarely had contact with organized churches, and warnings of doom and lists of rules made her feel embarrassed and uneasy rather than pious.

When the reading was finished, Grey smiled briefly. "Now I trust the Lord will forgive a secular ceremony," he said, gesturing toward the packages.

Brandy led Missy toward the tree, and after one hesitant pulling back and a long look at the tiny flames, the child went without resistance. Brandy settled down on the floor, the velvet circle of her dress rippling out around her, and drew Missy into her lap.

Grey read the names on the packages and handed them out. Brandy discovered that one of the nice things about being older was the pleasure she got from watching other people's joy. Rafe donned the mittens to show what a perfect fit they were, and Persia dabbed scent on her wrist and held it out to ask Rafe if he liked it. Even the redoubtable Mrs. Bailey was so pleased with her apron that she put it on. Brandy saw with amusement that the bright wrappings and ribbons fascinated Missy as much as the contents of the packages, but when she had finally got to the clothes for Molly, she knew immediately what they were, and dressed the doll in a new dress before she went to her next gift. Surely that was playing.

The one thing Brandy decided not to watch was Grey opening her gift to him. She was suddenly and uncom-

fortably aware that the gift was much too intimate. She
didn't look at him as he handed her her packages. One
was small and bore Hugh's unmistakable script. She felt
guilty because Hugh must have gone to much trouble
to get the gift to her on time while her presents for the
Adamses would be late. One of the other boxes was
large and heavy, and it was from Grey. These two she
saved for last.

She was touched by the gifts she received from the
household. Persia and the other Cowperwaithe girls
had made a many-colored quilt for her. It reflected the
same passionate love for brightness that she had seen in
the little touches such as the knots of colored yarn in
the oil wells of the lamps and the brilliant hooked rugs
on the polished wood floors in the Cowperwaithe home.
Mrs. Bailey gave her an intricately embroidered work
bag, and from Rafe she received finely braided leather
reins which she knew he had made.

She crowed aloud when she opened a package she
had not even noticed at first. The book was newly
published, and Pearl must have taken great pains to
send it to her. It was entitled *Eminent Women of the
Age* and contained, in addition to thick pages of text,
marvelous steel etchings of its heroines. On the flyleaf
was written: "To Brandy, to her unquenchable and
independent spirit, with love, Pearl." How like Pearl to
use a sly pun to send her such a book.

Brandy looked up to see Grey regarding her quizzically.
She handed him the book. He smiled and said, "I think
I would like to meet her; then I would have some idea
of what you'll be like in fifty years or so."

Brandy turned her attention to the box from Hugh;
Grey's remark had been so odd and personal that she
didn't know what to make of it. Tears stung her eyes as
she saw what Hugh had sent her. On a bed of purple
velvet lay a heart-shaped locket. Tiny blue forget-me-
nots enameled one side and on the other was engraved:
"To Brandy, my love, Hugh." It was a precious gift, but
it made her feel miserable and treacherous. *Oh, Hugh,*

she pleaded silently, as if he could hear and heed from so far away, *stop loving me, please, please, stop!* She kept her head bowed, not wanting Grey to see.

Her hands fumbled for the solid weight of the box from Grey. There was no use putting it off, and its bulk suggested something safe such as a set of books. She had noticed what he had given the others—puzzles, books, and a dress for Missy, and for his employees small personal gifts and bonus wages. Brandy thought she would not be able to bear it if her gift included money from him.

The first thing she saw when she opened the box was the candlelight reflecting on a glistening sea of heavy silk. She had never seen such a variety of ambers, browns, and golds; the material might have been woven into a shawl just for her. She picked it up and buried her face in it, loving the sensuous touch of it against her skin. "Oh, Grey, I . . ." Her voice trailed off as she caught sight of what had given the box such weight.

She knew what it was only because Chen Lee had one like it, and among all his possessions, it was his most treasured, the one inanimate object he vowed he would risk his life to save from destruction. It was a thousand or more years old, yet still patches of the original finish remained as evidence of the blues, reds, and greens which had decorated the pottery tomb horse. And the beast himself had lost none of his arrogant power to the ages. His muscular haunches held him as one foreleg forward, one up curved, he prepared to leap skyward.

Brandy touched it timidly but did not pick it up. "Grey, it's beautiful. It's the most beautiful thing I've ever seen. But I can't accept it—it's much too . . ." She looked up and saw her father's watch chain with the gold nugget in his hand.

She and Grey were alone. Even Missy ceased to exist. Grey watched her with amused tenderness, swinging the gift she had given him gently back and forth. "Too precious? Too valuable?" he asked softly.

She felt as she had that day on the steps before he had saved her, as if she were going to fall a great distance. But now she wanted to fall, she wanted to say, "Grey, don't marry Ruth. She'll never love you as I do." Instead, she felt the sudden urgent weight of Missy pressing against her, and the room slipped back into focus. Persia, Rafe, and Mrs. Bailey were staring in dazed silence.

Never had Brandy wished so much for the affectations of a gentlewoman, for a dishonest face. She managed to say, "Thank you. I shall take it with me when I leave King's Inland," quietly and with only the slightest tremor in her voice, not looking at Grey.

Grey said something in reply, but Brandy lost the words in the uneasy chatter which rose in the room and in Missy's need. At first she could not understand what had caused the shivering which gripped Missy like a chill, but then she realized how stupid she had been to speak of leaving. She held Missy close and crooned to her, ignoring everyone else. "Darling, I'm sorry to have said such a silly thing. I won't be leaving for a long while and not until you don't need me anymore. I promise." *Forgive the lie when the time comes,* she begged silently. Missy nestled against her, still and trusting. Brandy had to wait a moment before she could speak. "Missy and I are tired. We'll go upstairs now. Thank you all for the lovely Christmas, and Persia, please wish your family a Merry Christmas for me.

"Come, Missy, we'll collect our presents tomorrow; they're quite safe here now." Missy waited docilely to go up, insisting only on bringing Molly with her as usual. Brandy felt sneaky as she picked up the locket from Hugh, but she did not want anyone to read the inscription.

Grey watched them leave but did not protest their going.

As Brandy readied Missy for bed, she glanced out the window and saw that it was beginning to snow, and she was glad of it. Perhaps Grey would not be able to leave in the morning.

She was very tired by the time Missy was asleep, and she was in her own room, but her emotions were wide awake. "All right, wise one," she said, staring at the owl, "what does it all mean? He is marrying Ruth, yet he gives me gifts fit for a queen. Is it only gratitude for Missy's improvement? Is it only that?"

The owl stared back, solitary, silent.

CHAPTER XI

Christmas Day dawned with mocking brightness, and by late morning the snow proved to be neither refuge nor barricade. Grey was preparing to depart, and disaster arrived.

In Persia's absence Brandy was helping Mrs. Bailey in the kitchen when the front door slammed. Thinking Grey was leaving without saying good-bye, she flew into the hall only to stop short. Raleigh was there beaming at her, his smile quickly changing to a frown as he got a better look at her, and Ruth Collins stood beside him, her face distorted with hate she made no attempt to conceal.

"Why, Golden Eyes, what have they done to you? You look like a haunt!" Raleigh crossed to her swiftly, taking her in his arms, and she did not resist. She forgot her nasty suspicions of his character, taking comfort in his warm care of her, in the barrier he provided against the vengeance of Ruth.

She did not hear Grey come out of his study, but she suspected uneasily that Raleigh had, for when the icy voice cut the air and made her flinch, Raleigh did not start or put her out of his arms. It was she who stepped away.

"No wonder you did not wish to delay me, Brandy. You did indeed have other plans." Grey's eyes raked her insolently. He did not even notice that Ruth was there until he heard her gasp of outrage. He gave her one cold look which damned her for coming uninvited and froze her into silence for a moment. Brandy shared her silence, staring at Grey, helpless with anger, afraid of what she might say. Not so Raleigh; his carefree tone told that he was enjoying the situation.

"Shame on you, big brother, for jumping to such an unjust conclusion. Actually Ruth and I made the long cold journey, even to spending Christmas Eve in a strange farmhouse, on your account. Ruth threatened to make the trip alone if I was not willing to escort her. Such love this fair lady has for you to be so inconvenienced. You were, I believe, supposed to spend these days with her, and you are to be the honored guest at her New Year's Eve party. She couldn't help fearing some harm had befallen you."

Grey's voice lost none of its chill; if he felt guilty about his treatment of Ruth, he did not show it. "I would not have suspected you of such consideration for me, little brother." The emphasis was on "little." "I was going back today, but since you are both here, I will delay my departure for a few days, and we can go back together."

"That will not be necessary." Ruth had found her voice. "I will return with you today. I know what's been going on, and I will not spend one minute more than I must in this house with your whore. If you want me to stay, send her packing this instant!"

Brandy did not know whether or not Grey would have defended her; her anger rose so quickly that her own voice seemed separate from her, the words spoken by someone else. She moved to stand glaring down at Ruth. "You have a foul tongue, Miss Collins. I'm thankful that I can't see the muck in your mind. I too know what's been going on. Though I expect you use a more delicate word for yourself, you've been Grey's whore for years. Keep the title—there is no contest."

Ruth raised her hand to strike, and Brandy grabbed it fiercely, hissing, "I wouldn't do that if I were you. I'm much stronger than you are, and right now I'd welcome an excuse to teach you some manners."

Brandy released the hand, and Ruth shrank back. Grey's voice lashed out, "Enough!" as he stepped between them, pushing them roughly to get them out of each other's range. His breath came quickly as though he had been running, and his terrible anger seemed to include everyone, even himself. For an instant he looked blind with it, and Brandy stepped back and felt the renewed comfort of Raleigh's arms, just as Grey turned to say something to her. The sudden and queerly gentle expression was gone so quickly from his face that Brandy thought she must have imagined it. His eyes ignored her as he spoke to Raleigh. "We'll leave shortly. Will you be accompanying us?" It was a thinly veiled command, but Raleigh stood his ground with surprising firmness.

"No, you go right ahead. The only thing I have waiting for me in town is an empty house, and the only family I have is here. I think I'll just spend a few days at King's Inland for the sake of holiday cheer."

"All right. Do as you please," Grey said, his voice flat and empty. Though Brandy thought Raleigh's victory was deserved, she hated the idea of Grey losing any battle. She was, she decided, just as bad as all the lovesick, simpering misses for whom she had always had such disdain. How could she feel compassion for him when he was preparing to leave with the woman of his choice? She was a complete fool.

Grey barely gave Ruth time to freshen up and accept a cup of tea from Mrs. Bailey before they left. Brandy suspected that the housekeeper must have heard the whole disgraceful scene, but in no way did the older woman betray it. And Brandy, in the music room with Raleigh, was shocked at the jealousy that rose in her at the thought of Mrs. Bailey soothing Ruth's ruffled feathers, of Ruth preening. The housekeeper seemed so genuinely fond of Ruth, Ruth so deferential to Mrs. Bailey—Brandy had a hard time understanding it. She suppressed the cynical thought that perhaps the two didn't truly like each other at all but had simply made an early truce regarding which shares each would own of Grey and his possessions.

Raleigh and Ruth had come by sleigh, and Grey tied Orpheus in place of Casco to the back. As soon as Ruth left the house, Brandy went to the door to watch them depart. It made further shambles of her pride, but she couldn't help it. If Grey saw her, he made no sign.

"Poor Golden Eyes, you do have a bad case of it, don't you?" said Raleigh as he came up beside her. His voice was pleasant, but for an instant his eyes had a strange glitter which made him look disconcertingly like Grey. Brandy had the fleeting thought that perhaps all three members of the King family were mad—light and dark. "I asked you some time ago, before the recent war, why you are so thin and pale."

She watched the sleigh disappear before she spoke. Ignoring his remark about her feelings for Grey, she told him what had happened, emphasizing how much the fault lay with her for losing her head, but he was not taken in. "He is a very clever man, my brother, when it comes to getting his own way. And the second time must be easier."

Brandy was so overcome with fury and revulsion that she didn't know what she was doing until she felt the sting of her hand on Raleigh's cheek. She backed away, stunned to have done such a thing. "I'm sorry! I am no better than Ruth, and that is bad indeed. But Grey saved my life. Don't flaunt your disloyalty to him around me. I don't want to hear it." She turned on her heel and left him rubbing his jaw and staring after her.

When she brought Missy down with her for the midday Christmas dinner, she felt as if Grey had taken the holiday with him, leaving the house with nothing more than echoes of his presence. She had difficulty swallowing any of the tasty meal she had helped to prepare. Seeing Raleigh sitting at Grey's place in pale imitation made it worse. She was glad he and Mrs. Bailey had so much to talk about since it saved her the effort, and she was glad neither of them mentioned Ruth; it would please her mightily if she never heard that name again. Her misery was compounded because Missy was obviously aware of her tension; her smile had vanished, her body shook with slight, periodic tremors, her hands clenched now and then as if to prevent the forbidden finger flicking, and she reached out with jerky motions to touch Brandy every now and then as though to reassure herself. It was a heroic attempt at self-control, and Brandy had to fight the same battle to keep from breaking down and weeping.

She felt a little better when she took Missy and Panza out for a brief tramp in the snow before the early dark came down. It was the first time out since her illness, and she drew in the crisp air thankfully. Raleigh insisted on going with them, but he said little, being careful not to make her angry or to distress Missy, and so it was easy to ignore him. Seeing the barn made her wish Rafe was there to visit; disfigured and gnarled as he was, he seemed a gentle, protective force at King's Inland. She shivered suddenly as she remembered his Marianne, and she told Missy it was time to go in.

She excused herself early in the evening but remained awake long after Missy had been put to bed. Her life was becoming unbearably complicated. Raleigh had found his package from her, had opened it and thanked her, but then he had made a cryptic remark about waiting until the right moment to give her his gift. It gave her the uneasy certainty that she was going to have another problem on her hands fairly soon. Meanwhile, the locket from Hugh and an unfinished letter to him waited accusingly in Melissa King's writing box. She sat at the desk, took the letter out, and struggled with the words once more. How do you tell a fine man who has offered you the best of himself that you aren't interested, are in fact distressed by his persistence? She gave up, put the letter back in the box, and got up to pace impatiently around her room. She almost wished for one of Missy's eerie visits, but that wasn't even a possibility; the child had an uncanny knowledge of when it was safest to prowl.

No matter where she looked in her room, her eyes always came back to the pottery on her bureau. She felt as if through the carved and painted eyes, Grey watched her. If she were not such a weak fool, she would hide the figure. Then she snorted in disgust at herself; trying to banish Grey from her mind was like trying to lock the wind in a closet.

In desperation she settled down to read from the book Pearl had sent her, quickly deciding that by comparison with the courageous ladies of the text, she was absolutely spineless. "Olympia Brown, I hate you," she declared grimly as she closed the book.

For the next few days she played a child's game of hide-and-seek with Raleigh. In spite of his persistent efforts to see her alone, she managed to be chaperoned by Persia, Rafe, Mrs. Bailey, or, absurd thought, Missy. But she suspected he knew what she was doing and that for him it added just that much more spice to the chase.

He finally trapped her one night, and Mrs. Bailey served as his willing, though unwitting, ally. Missy was asleep, and Brandy was playing the piano for Raleigh and Mrs. Bailey when the older woman yawned and said, "It's rude of me, I'm sorry, it's all the Christmas excitement catching up with me. I can hardly keep my eyes open." She left the room swiftly, telling Raleigh to have a good time.

Brandy stood up abruptly, fully intending to follow Mrs. Bailey, but Raleigh's lazy insolence stopped her. "Running away again, Golden Eyes? You've been very busy avoiding me all week. Aren't you weary of it?"

Brandy planted her feet, and her chin went a shade higher. "What did you expect me to do, set the stage for whatever scene you plan to play?"

She expected him to be angry, but instead, he spoke gently. "No, of course not. I just prefer to make my proposal in private." He was at her side, holding a small open box out to her. In the box was a ring. "Will you marry me, Brandy Claybourne?"

She stared at the thing. She saw Raleigh's hand tremble a little, and all she felt was a rush of pity for him. He truly wanted the marriage, but for all the wrong reasons. She spoke to him in the same careful way she used with Missy. "Raleigh, you hardly know me, and maybe you know yourself even less. You don't love me; you just want me because you think I'm one of Grey's possessions. You're wrong; he's marrying Ruth of his own free will. He chose her, not me. You mustn't base your life on hurting him." She wondered again how much truth there was in the rumor that he had had an affair with Jasmine; that would certainly have been a pretty piece of vengeance.

Raleigh had a right to be angry for her blunt speaking, but he only looked thoughtful and his voice was mild. "Perhaps you're right. I always have liked getting the best of Grey, though I haven't done it very often," he added with a disarming grin. "But I think you're underestimating Grey's interest in you. I'll try not to slander him anymore, not in your hearing at least, but I warn you, he is not a gentleman. Be wary of him, Brandy. You're wrong about us, too; I think we would suit admirably. Just consider all the improvements you could make in my character," he teased. "Will you accept the ring, anyway, as a Christmas gift of friendship and for being kind to Missy? I got it for you. I would not give it to anyone else, so it will be a great waste if you don't take it."

Brandy was at a loss. She had braced herself for an angry battle, but now she felt as if she had purposely kicked Panza. She had to suppress a laugh; Raleigh would hate to be compared to a puppy. She looked at the ring, three flawless amethysts set in an ornately scrolled band of gold. It was beautiful, and she wanted to accept it for the reason given, but she still felt uneasy. Lavish gifts from both brothers. What would she say if she had to explain? Raleigh saw her hesitation and took her right hand gently, placing the ring on her third finger. It fit perfectly, and defiance rose in Brandy—it was no one's business but hers.

It burned with purple fire as she turned it on her finger. "It looks quite old. Wherever did you get it?"

Raleigh laughed easily. "I would make a fine pirate, and I know several fellows who would make a good crew. The ring came from an old salt who managed to collect a fair store of plunder during his sailing days. His chief delight is trading his treasures for someone else's and making a profit besides. We both had a good time dickering."

She was afraid to ask what he had traded for it. Instead, she reached up and gave him a light kiss of thanks and a firm good-night. As she fell asleep, she thought of how odd it was that when Grey was in the house she was always conscious of his movements, of when he retired to his room, yet she never heard Raleigh come or go from the one he used. She did not care whether he slept or not, and perhaps in time she would not care about Grey either.

Raleigh left the next morning, and Brandy saw him off with relief and cynical amusement. She was quite sure that having failed in his object at King's Inland, he would find ample consolation in town. Despite what he had said to Grey, she doubted very much that Raleigh's house was ever empty for long.

His leaving did raise one unpleasant thought—tomorrow night in town, Ruth and Grey would see the new year in together, while she would probably see it in alone or, at the very best, in the company of a bored Mrs. Bailey—so open and welcoming with Raleigh and Ruth Collins, so distant with her—and a sleeping child. An overwhelming pang of homesickness hit her as she recalled the riotous celebrations she had enjoyed in San Francisco. She lectured herself sternly for self-pity. Nothing would be the same, even if by magic she could spend the night there. Her father was dead, the city was more straightlaced now, and Pearl would probably be sleeping just as soundly as Missy by midnight.

By afternoon she was happy and at peace again as she bundled Missy and herself into warm clothes. Rafe saw them and insisted he had enough time to take them for a sleigh ride. The world seemed very empty and still save for the jingle of the harness and the muffled beat of hooves, but then Brandy caught sight of the rusty stealth of a fox moving in and out of cover and pointed him out. Missy squirmed in delight as the fox stopped in mid-trot to glare haughtily at them before he melted into the shadows of a snow-laden tree. Panza barked and tried to jump out of the sleigh, and Rafe took his hat off in salute. "That one is very sure of his cleverness. To him we are slow and stupid beasts."

When they got home, Brandy jumped down and Rafe handed Missy to her. She put the little girl down and then reached for Panza, turning to hand him to Missy, but Missy's eyes were focused far down the lane, and she paid no attention to the puppy. Rafe let out a hiss of surprise. Brandy saw the horseman and thought it was Raleigh returning until the sun turned Orpheus' coat to black satin.

She felt the blood pour out of her head, leaving her brain dry and dizzy, and she clutched the edge of the sleigh for support. Grey back, now, why, what about Ruth and the party? She looked around wildly for Missy and found her in the same spot regarding first her, then her father with no apparent signs of panic but rather with a calculating expression which unnerved Brandy even further.

"Aren't you trying to do too much too soon?" he asked, looking down at her, enjoying her discomfiture.

She was weary of allowing herself to be played with,

cat and mouse. She forgot anyone else was there, and her voice was waspish. "Why are you here? What about your darling Ruth and her party? Don't you belong somewhere else?" She stressed "belong" but Grey did not rise to the bait; her anger pleased him just as much as her first shocked reaction had.

His voice was easy, pleasant. "Surely you know by now I come and go as I please?" No explanation about Ruth. "Is my brother still here?"

"No. He left this morning. I'm surprised you didn't cross trails." An even more satisfied glint appeared in his eyes. Brandy turned away in disgust and took Missy into the house while the men went to stable the horses.

Mrs. Bailey met them in the hall, and her inquiry about the ride died as she saw Brandy's stormy face. Brandy forestalled any questions by snapping, "Grey's back," and continuing her march with Missy up the stairs.

It took Brandy several incredulous moments to recognize the child's reaction—Missy was gleeful, not indifferent or fearful about her father's return. Her movements were quick and light as she danced around her room picking things up at random, hugging Panza now and then, flitting as Rafe had once described it, "as a butterfly flower to flower," making Brandy's confusion absolute. The only reason for the child's joy might be that Grey's return represented a blow to Ruth, clearly an enemy in Missy's eyes. But as clever as Brandy thought her, she did not think her capable of such inverted thinking. She left her as soon as she could and took refuge in her own room, trying to bring order to the chaos in her mind, trying to slow the frantic beating of her heart. Grey's influence on her emotions was something she had never encountered before, diametrically different from the effects of Hugh and Raleigh. And never had she resented another human being as much.

She wanted to have supper with Missy or take her downstairs as a shield. But then she was so chagrined to have thought that way, her defiance flooded back. With so little effort, Grey had her completely cowed. "Not anymore, Grey King, not anymore," she muttered to herself.

There was a soft knock on her door, and Persia came in timidly in response to her harsh permission. "Mrs. Bailey said you seemed upset, an' I see she was right. She wanted me to check on you. Do you need anythin'?"

Brandy felt like saying, "Yes, Grey's head on a platter, please," but instead, she relaxed and smiled at Persia, whose concern for her was genuine. "No, really, I just had a bad temper tantrum. I seemed to have had quite a few since my silly illness." She patted the bed. "Come, sit down and talk to me if you have time. I've hardly seen you all this week."

The ready warmth colored Persia's cheeks. "I'm like to be sent packin' if I don't behave myself. I keep findin' th' best reasons in th' world for goin' out to check on things to th' barn."

Brandy laughed and hugged her, her own tension easing. "Seems to me the best reason in the world spends most of his time in the barn. I'm surprised you can make yourself spend a minute in the house. I'm so happy for both of you!"

Persia's smile died abruptly. She looked away as though afraid of meeting Brandy's eyes, and she spoke in a rush, words tumbling over each other. "Oh, I want you to be happy, too, an' I know you haven't been lately. Mr. Raleigh, he had somethin' to do with it, didn't he? He was walkin' around with love in his eye, an' you were runnin' an' hidin'. But it's Mr. King—*funny*, thought Brandy, *it shows even in the way people speak of him; Raleigh is the diminutive, "Mr. Raleigh," Grey is the only "Mr. King"*—who frets you, isn't it? Do you love him?" Her eyes went wide with surprise at her own audacity.

But Brandy wasn't offended. It was a relief to tell someone. She nodded slowly. "Yes, I guess I do, if that's what this awful, helpless, churning feeling is."

The worst thing of all was that Persia, try as she might, could provide no comfort. She loved Brandy and loathed Ruth, but Grey had, after all, chosen Ruth, and Brandy knew another though unspoken factor bothered her—Ruth and Grey were of equal station. In Persia's mind for Grey to marry one of his employees would be odd indeed. Brandy realized how differently the West had set her mind. When she had been growing up, society had had few levels beyond honest and dishonest, and sometimes it had been difficult to tell which was which. When high society had begun in San Francisco, Brandy, her father, Pearl, and others like them had dismissed it as artificial. The East, she reflected grimly, had had much more time to put things in order.

When she went down to supper, her pride surfaced over everything else. Her head was up, chin out, her back was straight, and she was ready to take on anyone who thought that mere social position made one superior. Mrs. Bailey blinked in surprise, and Grey grinned to himself—obviously they both noticed her new demeanor. But before the meal had progressed very far, she was suffering new doubts. Grey was openly making an effort to charm her, speaking gently, smiling often, questioning her with what seemed like genuine interest about Missy, about music, books, teaching, and a myriad range of subjects. Brandy felt herself thawing and couldn't do anything about it.

Grey excused himself and returned with a bottle of wine and three glasses. Brandy was awed by the idea that the precious liquor had come all the way from France to this isolated spot in Maine and wondered why Grey thought the occasion special enough to warrant it. Her pride dissolved under his smile, and the world seemed to explode into the bright colored sparks of Chen Lee's fireworks.

Grey handed Brandy her glass, and as she reached out to take it, the amethyst ring caught the candlelight. Had she not taken it quickly, Grey would have dropped the glass. As it was, some of the ruby liquid sloshed over the edge. She knew it was the ring. She looked up at him, wanting to know why it had disturbed him so, willing to explain why Raleigh had given it to her. But his expression stopped her. The black eyes bored into her ruthlessly, saying they found her beneath contempt. She feared him at that moment more than she ever had before. She gathered the tattered vestiges of her pride and rose unsteadily.

"You will have to forgive me. I am suddenly very tired." She kept herself from running to the door, and she didn't care what Mrs. Bailey thought. Let Grey explain in his own devious way.

She lay awake with her heart pounding until she thought she would suffocate in the sound. Then fear gave way to anger. If Grey wanted to know about the ring, let him ask. Damn him for his arrogant judging, for doing as he pleased and denying her the same right. She slept peacefully after that.

The next day brought an overcast sky and air rich with the snow scent. Brandy heard Grey leave his room, and she cherished the hope that he had decided to go back to Wiscasset and had started early to avoid the storm. She did not inquire about his whereabouts, and no information was volunteered by Mrs. Bailey or Persia, who were both behaving with nerve-racking caution, tiptoeing about and not mentioning Grey. Finally, she stole out to the barn and noted with satisfaction that Orpheus was gone. Rafe was nowhere in sight either, and that was a relief because he usually saw her thoughts far too clearly.

She spent the day happily with Missy and found that the prospect of a quiet New Year's Eve no longer dismayed her after the past twenty-four hours of tension.

The first snow did not fall until dusk. She was standing idly by her window watching it when she caught sight of him—a moving shadow at first in the dim curtain of snow, then starkly defined—Orpheus stumbling with weariness, Grey still arrogantly upright. She saw the movement of his head and knew he was seeing her silhouetted by the light from her room. She jerked back out of sight and then suffered the rushing blood, bitterly aware of how much her childish action must have amused him. But there was at least some satisfaction in the conviction that she was the demon he had spent the day outriding.

She dressed carefully for the evening, choosing a simply cut brown dress with a soft full skirt and cream lace trimming on the bodice and sleeves. She pulled her hair into a tight chignon, hoping the total effect would make her appear severely proper. But looking in the mirror, she wasn't so sure; already tendrils of hair were escaping, curling willfully, destroying any semblance of neatness. She sighed and made a face at her image.

She heard Grey going to and from his room, and she waited until he was gone before she ventured across the hall to Missy's room. And then she was late going down because of Missy's behavior. The child was so restless and twitchy, so impish, that Brandy thought she would never go to sleep.

When she finally arrived at the table, her faint hope that Grey's temper of the night before might have eased was lost in one quick glance at him. The harshness in his face added years to his age. He made no attempt to carry on a conversation, and Brandy heard herself and Mrs. Bailey go from nervous chatter to a silence that matched his. It frightened her further to realize that Mrs. Bailey, the formidable Mrs. Bailey, was just as apprehensive as she was. And they seemed to have no wills of their own, for though she knew they would both like nothing better than to escape to their respective quarters, neither of them protested when Grey announced after dinner that they would go to the music room, and Brandy did not refuse his command that she play; she hoped it would save her from thinking.

But only Pearl's training made it possible for her to find the right notes, for Grey's unblinking stare never left her, and she could feel it as strongly as if he were running his hands over her. As she played, the ring winked like a malevolent eye, and she wished she had not been so defiant as to wear it.

She strove fiercely to lose herself in the sound, and she felt the first wave of success, the beginning of the ascent into a universe created entirely by music.

He did not even have to raise his voice; low and even, without effort it shattered her refuge. "Jasmine used to do that, too, hide in her music. Especially after I came home from Gettysburg. I think it made her feel pure again. Is that what it does for you, Brandy?"

Her hands came off the keys curved rigidly as she swung around to face him. She gasped when she saw Mrs. Bailey was gone. He smiled pleasantly and nodded. The glitter in his eyes made Brandy shiver. "Poor old woman, she was too tired to see the new year in. But you're not too tired, are you?"

She was shaking so hard it was difficult to stand. "I don't know what you're talking about, but I've heard enough." She started for the door, but Grey moved in long strides to bar her way. "It's much much too early to end the last night of eighteen hundred and sixty-nine, my dear." "My dear" was a threat.

Scorching anger rose in Brandy. "Get out of my way!"

His answer was to reach out and grab her so suddenly that she had no time to evade him. There was no gentleness in him, his hands were biting into her shoulders, her face was pressed so hard against the weave of his coat that she could feel a button digging into her cheek, and it was difficult to breath. It was hard to get any space, but she managed to kick him in the shins, and she tried to bring her knee up, but this was nothing like the other time. He was not drunk. He simply stepped back easily, holding her away from him. She had never seen a face so devoid of pity, so filled with grim intent. Terror exploded in her, and she fought frantically, kicking, biting, trying to get her hands up to claw his face, screaming for Mrs. Bailey. He seemed to feel none of it. He captured her flailing arms, pinioning her two wrists easily with one hand. He lifted her, and she jerked her body desperately to no avail. Her strength drained as quickly as it had come. The world was spinning crazily, and she shut her eyes.

She lay passively in his arms as he carried her. "Grey, no, please, no," she pleaded, and was disgusted by her whimpering. She opened her eyes to look at him; he gave no sign he heard her. His face was so savage that she closed her eyes again and felt a merciful numbness beginning.

She knew only vaguely when he no longer carried her, when he put her down, when she felt the pins being pulled from her hair, his hands on her clothing. Beneath the canopy of her own bed his face was contorted with lust and fury. He snarled something about Raleigh, Jasmine, Missy; none of it made sense except that when she started to struggle again, he said very clearly, "Lie still or I will kill you." She believed him; she thought he might kill her anyway. Nothing mattered anymore; this was the man she loved, this insane, evil man. *Oh, Missy, poor Missy, what things have you seen?*

She lay motionless, hearing the cloth rip as if it were someone else's body which was being stripped. The numbness spread, putting a barrier between her body and Grey's rough hands. The words ran over her, harmless as drops of rain—"bitch, whore, you too, just like her, the same, the same"—they had nothing to do with her. She lay unresisting when the weight of his body covered her own. But then her senses came alive, and she screamed before the darkness.

She hurt; she was bruised and torn but the unbearable pain had ceased. Someone was holding her, cradling, rocking her gently. He was crying. Why? The broken words dropped into strange patterns.

"Oh, my God, Brandy, my darling. I am mad! I didn't know. I was told you'd been with Raleigh, like Jasmine. His ring, my great-grandmother's ring. I couldn't bear it. It was worse than knowing about her, worse than knowing Raleigh is probably Missy's father." The sobs tore at his throat, making the rest of his words unintelligible.

"The devil doesn't cry," she said flatly. She turned her head away and tried to ease her body out of his hold. His arms tightened compulsively; then he let her go.

"Brandy, I think I ought to go for Margaret or someone." The desperate note in his voice grated.

"No. I am all right. There is nothing anyone can do, nothing that needs doing. You've done it all." Her voice rose frantically at the end. Hugh, gentle Hugh, why did I leave you?

She started to shiver, and it was worse than the time in the snow. Now there was no comfort in Grey's presence. He covered her with blankets, but when he took her hands and tried to warm them in her own, she pulled away, screaming, "Get out! Get out!"

He backed away, old, hunched, nothing like Grey. Pity stirred briefly in Brandy, and she strangled it with her will. Her shivering stopped; the numbness began to creep through her again. She lay staring with empty eyes at the shadows beyond Grey.

"Brandy, don't do that, don't go away like Missy! I love you. What I did tonight is unforgivable. There will never be enough I can do for you to make up for it. But I love you! Can you hear me? Ruth was no answer, and that's finished. I wanted to strangle her for calling you a whore, for saying such vile things to you. I had to take her back to town. I owed her at least that much. But I wanted to marry you. I know it isn't possible now, but I'll do whatever you want. I'll take you back to Hugh Adams. I'll explain. He won't love you any less for what I've done. Brandy, goddamn it, answer me!"

In contrast with his painful rush of words, her speech was slow and slurred, as if she had been drugged. "You love me? As you loved Jasmine and Missy? No, thank you, your love is a very destructive thing from what

I've seen of it. Explain, give me back to Hugh? And what choice would he have? He is too kind. I will stay here until you find someone else for Missy. I won't leave her to your tender mercies. Then I will make my own plans. Now, get out!"

She saw his face clearly again. If it was revenge she wanted, it was hers. Yet she felt no joy in her victory or in her sudden knowledge that of the grief this night, the greater share was Grey's. She closed her eyes against his image. She heard him blow out the lamp and leave the room. She drifted in the emptiness, wanting sleep, filling the void with anger when oblivion would not come.

Her bed was an intolerable place to be. The room was in darkness save for the ember glow from the hearth. She pulled her body out of bed as though it were a heavy, aged thing. She put more wood on the fire, fighting unreasoning terror of what might happen if it went out completely. The added wood caught, and she sighed with relief.

She curled up in the patterned chair, and before she wrapped the blanket around herself, she saw by the firelight the dark places on her body which were not shadows. Grey was a strong man.

Think about it, Brandy, face it and be free. Things hidden in the mind fester and cannot be healed. Would you have me face this too, Father? Could you face it yourself? Yes, Brandy, yes.

She let the thoughts come, dealing with them one by one. Where to go? Aunt Beatrice? No, never there. Somehow the old woman would know, would glory in it. To Pearl, back to California? Perhaps, but even as she considered it, she realized that of everyone, Pearl would be the most hurt by what had happened. Pearl's dealings with men were honest and businesslike. Grey's behavior would shock her deeply. She believed in a woman's ability to choose her own destiny and manage her own life. She had instilled this in Brandy, and she would never feel free of blame because she would sense how violent the death of dreaming had been. To the Adamses then, as Grey had suggested, to the home they offered her? That was more difficult. Hugh would take her back, that she knew, but she would never know how much pity would corrupt his love because he would have to be told; she could not bear to live with a lie hovering over her like some dark bird. Though she longed for his healing gentleness, she admitted to herself that what had happened would not make her love him any more than she did. And worse yet, how could he avoid thinking it was at least partially her fault? Desperate for order in the chaos, she decided she would go back to the Adamses and stay there only until, with their help, she could find another job. She could simply say that her task at King's Inland had been as hopeless as everyone had said.

Indeed, it was like touching a wound. Brandy was now convinced Grey had murdered his wife—his admission that he had taken her because he thought she, as Jasmine, had been Raleigh's mistress added to the evidence against him. She shuddered; she knew only too well the cruelty of which he was capable. She faced the act squarely. Nothing could erase the revulsion she felt. Nothing could be more physically demeaning than rape. But there was something apart from her body which was essentially herself, inviolate as long as she kept it so. Her greatest danger had been in being so ready to give that essence into Grey's keeping. She had been so wrong; the bleakness stretched into infinity.

But Missy, Missy still needed her, more now than ever for protection as much as for teaching. She had no right and no place to take the child, but she would stay until she was in safe hands. She knew Grey would accept her verdict on Missy's new companion; she would not allow any woman to come unless she was older and stronger than she was.

She was too exhausted to think anymore and too uncomfortable to sleep in the chair, but she had achieved a small corner of quiet in her mind. As she got up to go back to bed, she saw that it was snowing heavily, renewing the white purity of the landscape. "Much, much too late and only the first day of the new year," she moaned bitterly.

CHAPTER XII

She woke and remembered. She lay with fists clenched at her sides, heart pounding, sweat clammy on her skin. She knew what had wakened her; Grey was outside her door. If he came in, she would scream the house down. But he did not try the door, and she heard a scratchy sound, then his footsteps fading toward the staircase. The snow had stopped. Dim light filtered through the windows; it could not be much after dawn.

She got up and saw the envelope he had pushed under the door. Her hands shook as she opened it:

DEAREST BRANDY,

I will be well on my way by the time you read this. [How little he knew of her consciousness of his movements in the house.] I will do my best to find a replacement for you, though such a person does not exist, for there is only one Brandy. An adequate substitute is the only possibility. I will send word to Margaret regarding my return. In any case, if I cannot accomplish this in a fortnight, I will make arrangements for your passage to wherever you wish to go. Persia and Margaret can surely take care of Missy until a new teacher is hired. You are as important as Missy.

After last night, I know it is impossible for you to believe that I had nothing to do with the strange "accidents" which have befallen you at King's Inland.

*But I swear to you that I had no knowledge of them and
beg you to take care while I am gone. I have never used
another human being as cruelly as I have you, nor have
I ever loved another as I love you.*

GREY

As she stared at the words, she remembered her
dream. In it, Missy had come and stood beside her bed
and whispered softly, "Don't go away, Brandy, Papa
needs you. Don't go away." For a moment she hated
them both for demanding so much, for taking so much.
But then she felt only pity for the tragedy which
continued to ruin their lives.

The full import of things which Grey had said the
night before began to hit her. He believed Missy was
Raleigh's child! It couldn't be, it just couldn't; Missy's
eyes were her father's. Yes, they were, and Raleigh's
eyes were Grey's. Raleigh, did you betray him so? And,
Jasmine, you started this and left the child to suffer.
No, whatever you did, you did not deserve to die by
fire.

The ring, what had Grey said? Brandy fought to
make her mind recall in spite of the terror of the
memory. Grey had recognized it; it had been his great-
grandmother's. Something Raleigh had inherited to give
to the woman of his choice? Then he had lied about its
origin on purpose, leaving it with her like his brand,
taunting Grey with it. She pulled it off of her finger
frantically. But Grey should have asked her about it. "I
was told you had been with Raleigh, like Jasmine." The
words came back with chilling clarity. Told? Who had
told him? Raleigh himself? No, the change in Grey had
come after he had seen the ring, so someone must have
added to his anger by telling tales after that. Rafe,
Persia—such dear friends? It was more likely that something had been innocently said by one of them and
wrongly taken by Grey.

She tried to quit thinking about any of it because she
was still too stunned by Grey's attack to see anything

very clearly, but one thing she saw very well—Grey doubted he was Missy's father, and yet he had spared no expense in his care of her. Of course, there were many reasons which might explain that, among them a way to torture Raleigh, who could never claim his child, or perhaps an apology for killing Missy's mother. But Brandy didn't believe it; she believed he loved Missy, and she was appalled at the treachery of her mind which, despite what Grey had done to her, made her think kindly of him.

Missy still slept, and it was still early when Brandy went down to the kitchen. Persia had the day off, and Mrs. Bailey was not yet in evidence, and Brandy was doubly thankful for that when she saw the note addressed to Mrs. Bailey in Grey's script. She opened it with no guilt:

DEAR MARGARET,

Please allow Brandy to sleep as late as possible. She suffered a chill last night and needs rest. She is not fully recovered from her illness, but you know how stubborn she is, so please do not be obvious in your cosseting.

GREY

Damn his attention to details, thought Brandy, struggling against tears as she shredded the letter. And then the phrase "suffered a chill last night" swung her mood around like the wind, and she had to fight against hysterical laughter.

She was still taking deep breaths and clutching a cup of tea as though it were a lifeline when Mrs. Bailey came in, stopping in surprise when she saw her. "I thought you would sleep late today." She peered closer and snorted, "And it looks as if you ought to have done. But happy eighteen seventy anyway, and may it be a good year for King's Inland."

Brandy toasted her with her cup and managed to keep the bitterness out of her voice as she returned the good wishes. She had the sudden horrible suspicion that the housekeeper's concern for her well-being came from having heard some noise of the struggle with Grey. But then she thrust the thought away; even though she had been intimidated somewhat by Grey's behavior, Mrs. Bailey, a woman, for all that would have had to have come to her defense had she heard her screaming. Brandy's smile relaxed into a more natural line. If the older woman noticed the absence of the ring, she made no mention of it. They had a quiet breakfast together, and then Brandy took a tray up to Missy.

It was the final blow of too many. Missy knew what had happened. She sat rocking furiously, flicking her fingers with mad rhythm. The tray crashed to the floor, and Brandy buried her face in her hands, unable to check the choking sobs.

There was not even the prelude of a tentative touch, only the hurtling weight of Missy's body and the desperate tugging of her hands. Brandy sank down on the floor amid the ruins of the breakfast and submitted in awe to the tiny hands patting her, smoothing her hair, touching her tear wet cheeks, comforting her as if she were the frightened child. She gathered Missy into her arms.

"Little love, it's all right. I'm safe; I'm with you. Forget whatever you heard, whatever you saw." Missy stiffened in her arms, and Brandy saw her blunder— apparently trying to forget what she had seen and heard had caused Missy's illness. "No, you're right, and I'm wrong. We can never really forget things, can we? But we have to learn to live with the bad things we've seen and still be happy." Missy relaxed enough so that Brandy knew she was somewhat comforted, though obviously her burden was still too great for any child to bear.

When she went to get another meal for Missy, she met Mrs. Bailey and offered her own clumsiness as an excuse. The housekeeper nodded. "You might not believe it, but I can still remember when I was young enough to feel a little shaky on New Year's Day." Brandy smiled dutifully, doubting that Mrs. Bailey had any New Year's Eve memories quite like hers.

Though she was happy to see Persia the next day, she found it galling to hear tales of the fun she and Rafe had had at the Cowperwaithes' farm. She felt like snapping, "Oh, I had a fine time, too. I was raped," but Persia's glowing face killed the notion. She avoided Rafe because she was terrified that he would see that something was terribly wrong.

But she could not avoid Missy, and that was hardest of all. The constant, though subtle, expressions of love from the child made her imminent desertion seem indefensible on any grounds, and her guilt was constant. She considered countless ways to break the news and discarded each in turn as too cruel.

And Hugh was as unavoidable as Missy because Brandy knew that if she were going back to the Adamses' house, she must write to Hugh first, and winter mails were slow enough without adding her own delay. She decided to finish her letter about the locket, add her homecoming, and trust Rafe to find a way to get it sent. But she let a week pass with no word of Grey's return before she sat herself down to complete the letter.

Missy had been fed, and Brandy had time enough to write before supper. She opened the writing box, thinking how soon the glories and, she hoped, the terrors of King's Inland would be nothing more than memories. She took out the partially finished letter, and the locket gleamed from the corner of the back of the box. She picked it up and found that the chain had slipped under the back panel. Annoyed, she tugged, not caring if the chain broke. There was a click, and the chain was free and unbroken, but Brandy didn't notice. The locket slipped forgotten from her hand.

The sound had come from the panel swinging open to expose a drawer which ran the length of the box. Brandy pulled the little gold nob, and the drawer opened easily, revealing a stack of thin sheets of paper covered in fine script. She took them out thinking they were some old record of events kept by Melissa King, too long removed to harm anyone. But she froze when she deciphered the date on the top sheet. It was August 2, 1867. The last words on the page were: "I've got to get Melissa away from here. I hear her now c..." Trailing away, not finished, hastily thrust back in the secret drawer.

Brandy knew it was the date of Jasmine's death. She closed her eyes, denying the words, wishing she had never found the writing, knowing the pages might provide the final proof of Grey's guilt, still, after all, wanting him to be innocent. And she knew her only, frail right to read them came from having loved him. It was enough.

She rearranged the pages chronologically; the earliest date, October 10, 1862, was on the bottom of the stack, and she made that the first page, continuing to 1867. There were long spaces of time when nothing had been recorded; Jasmine had used these pages as a confessional, not as a journal of daily life. From the first entry onward, Brandy knew why Jasmine had hidden them— such a tale of infidelity was not the sort of record one shares. She read grimly, feeling ill as the story unfolded:

October 10, 1862
I married the wrong brother. I know that now. Raleigh is charming, young, and carefree. Grey is a great brooding devil in comparison. I don't even miss him. I would not weep if he was killed in the war. So many men are dying, why can't he be one of them? How dare he go off to fight my people, leaving me trapped up here with these sour-faced Yankees. Raleigh was right not to go; I respect his principles and love his company.

November 15, 1862
Raleigh and I went for a long ride today. I am never

frightened with him. I am a good horsewoman, but with Grey not even that is enough.

December 27, 1862
Raleigh brought me some beautiful violet silk for a new dress. I wonder how he got it; such things are hard to come by with this Godforsaken war on. I am going to have it made up specially to please him. I am still as slender as I was when I was seventeen, and Raleigh notices it. His hands are so gentle. If Grey comes home, I will not be able to bear him touching me.

March 3, 1863
I have not heard from Grey for some time now, and I have not written to him. Maybe news will come soon in my favor.

June 18, 1863
I wish there was some marvelous ball to go to. How I would love to dress up and dance with Raleigh. But at least he came in time for supper tonight. I think the old witch knows we are lovers. How I hate her! She loves Raleigh and fears I'll harm him.

September 7, 1863
No, no! Grey is coming home. He was wounded at Gettysburg and contracted a fever afterward. Oh, God, what shall I do? Raleigh will not take me away. He says we'll manage. How?

September 15, 1863
Grey came home today. He was sent by ship to Wiscasset and brought by cart here. He is too much of a wreck to even ride a horse. I should feel sorry for him, but I don't. He repulses me. His shoulder is still a great oozing wound, and he is yellow and shrunken with fever. Maybe he will die anyway. But his eyes are just the same, black and mocking and something else now. I think he suspects. If he knew, I think he would kill me.

October 13, 1863
Raleigh comes often to get me out of the house. I would go mad without him.

October 29, 1863
Grey is going to live. He is too arrogant to die. I wish I had the courage to poison him. Mrs. Bailey fusses over him. She has no more courage than I. I know she'd like to see him dead, too. Then Raleigh would inherit. I love my Raleigh. I desire him every minute of my day.

November 20, 1863
I feel sick, unclean. I did not think he was strong enough yet, but he was. He came into my bedroom tonight and took me brutally. He never treated me this way before, as though I were a slave, nothing, something to be used. I hate him. Raleigh, my love, please take me away.

January 25, 1864
I have prayed it wasn't so, but it is no use, it is true. I am with child. Grey's or Raleigh's, I don't know. But I will tell Raleigh it is his, and he will take me away.

February 3, 1864
There is no hope. Raleigh can do nothing. He is too dependent on Grey, for his job, for his money. And he says Grey would hunt us down and kill us both no matter where we go. I believe it. Maybe I will die in childbirth, and it will be finished.

April 17, 1864
I will not die. I have discovered the ultimate power over Grey. He is mad about the idea of being a father. He is being so kind and attentive, I want to laugh in his face. The fool. Mrs. Bailey is in a rage of jealousy, one more to come between the fortune and her favorite.

August 14, 1864
The child was born a week ago, a girl named Melissa for Grey's, and Raleigh's, great-grandmother. Grey is wild with joy. He doesn't even care that it is not a boy. He looks young again; almost I remember why I married him. I will never have another child. It is not true that you forget the pain. I remember every horrible hour of it.

April 20, 1865
The war is over. If it had gone on a little longer, I know Grey would have been well enough to rejoin his regiment. He has not had an attack of the fever for months now, and his shoulder is no longer as stiff. My God, even Mrs. Lincoln has lost her husband, but I have no more chance of losing mine. I wonder what has happened to my family, but I don't care. Even though they were right about my marriage, I will never forgive them for the spiteful way they behaved. Days pass so swiftly with the baby to look after, it is hard to spend much time with Raleigh, but Melissa is my joy, so I do not mind.

August 7, 1865
Melissa is a year old today, a beautiful and clever child. Every day she learns something new. She crawls all over the place and hoists herself up and stands for a minute. If I hold her by the hands, she walks quite well. She is Raleigh's gift of love to me; I must go on believing that. Grey plays the proud father until it sickens me. Sometimes I am tempted to tell him. After the birth of the child, I forbade him my bed, and he has not troubled me. The child is enough. But I know he goes to other women. They can have him. I still have Raleigh, if only for stolen hours.

March 10, 1866
Melissa (I will not call her Missy as Grey does) walks with great ease now and picks up new words every day. She adores Grey and that makes me jealous except that

she has enough love for everyone. And Grey has the means to give her a good life.

August 7, 1866
To think that Melissa is two years old today! She knows more than four hundred words, and I am sure that must be a record for such an infant. Raleigh gave her a rocking horse. It must be hateful for him to see us as a family and to know the child is his. I am sure he believes she is.

January 5, 1867
We gave a New Year's Eve ball. People came from miles away with sleigh bells announcing their arrival. Five couples stayed the night, and the house was alive with music and people. I know why Grey agreed—to show off Melissa—but I don't care. It had been so long since I had been to a party. I danced and danced and hardly at all with Grey, thank God. Everyone said how beautiful I looked, even that spiteful Ruth Collins. Raleigh danced with her twice, and I hated her, but I know he didn't whisper the same things to her that he did to me. Melissa was seen by all before she went to bed. She was wonderful, chattering away and smiling her lovely smile. Everyone was enchanted by her.

April 9, 1867
Grey hates leaving Melissa even for a day, but he is involved in so many new ventures that he is gone for longer periods now. What delight, more time with Raleigh! If only that old hag wasn't here, watching every move I make. She has been in this house for so long, it seems impossible to get rid of her. But I will keep trying. It helps that she isn't very nice to Melissa. Perhaps Grey will notice.

June 24, 1867
The weather is unseasonably hot. Everyone is short-tempered. I don't pay much heed to servants, but Grey

*has a new stableman, and he frightens me. His name is
Raphael Joly. The last name doesn't fit at all. His face is
horribly scarred, hard, and leathery, with eyes which
seem to look right through me. Grey found him at the
docks. What a way to pick a groom! Our dislike is
mutual. But Melissa took to him right off, and he has
already taken her out on several rides, holding her
before him. She has no fears and loves it, so I must
bear the awful man for her sake.*

August 2, 1867
*God forgive me, I've ruined everything for Melissa. I
told Grey, I didn't mean to, but I did. Back tonight,
drunk, started talking about making love to me again.
He grabbed at me, ripped my dress, I ran for my room,
but he got there before I could lock the door. Said he
wanted me, wanted another child. I couldn't credit I
was the one screaming the words, but I was. I told him
he couldn't have me and he didn't have a child at all,
Melissa is Raleigh's. I thought he would kill me, but he
just went dead still. I know where he's gone, gone to kill
Raleigh first. I've got to get Melissa away from here. I
hear her c . . .*

Brandy's eyes ached from reading the furtively small
script. She willed her stunned mind to impose some
rational order on the jumble of impressions. The out-
standing revelation was of Jasmine's character, and for
the first time, Brandy had a true picture of her: beautiful, willful, vain, educated enough to write well, totally
lacking in compassion for her husband and capable of
feeling justified in her infidelity, fearful of people who
saw through her too clearly, and yet with all this,
capable of deep love for her child and wild passion for
Raleigh. And now Brandy knew that Grey had not just
accepted vile rumors about his wife and brother but
had been told in the cruelest terms that he had been
betrayed and that the child he loved so much was not
his. Oh, Grey, it was enough to drive a man to murder!

In her mind, Brandy saw Grey coming home, his great strong frame diminished by pain and fever. The image closed her throat. And then she saw him fighting fiercely to live, growing stronger and then joyful with the birth of the child, bearing his wife's coldness, still loving her for a long time because Missy was his delight and Jasmine was her mother. And she saw his world destroyed again and his harsh right to revenge. She forced herself to picture him murdering Jasmine but could not, and she realized with a surge of joy that she could not because the picture was false. He had gone after Raleigh, but he had not killed him. And if he had wanted to kill Jasmine, he would have done it cleanly, probably with his bare hands. Brandy knew him well enough to believe him perfectly capable of that, whatever the consequences. She also knew him well enough to know that he would never burn down a stableful of prize animals to accomplish the death of one worthless human being.

Then who had started the fire? "I've got to get Melissa away from here. I hear her c..." Calling? Crying? Why so late at night? Had Missy heard the fury between Grey and Jasmine? Perhaps Jasmine had caused her own death, taking Missy and going to the stables and inadvertently tipping over a lantern. Or perhaps one of the horses had kicked her, and she had fallen unconscious, spilling oil and flame into the hay. It did not satisfy Brandy. Jasmine had been a good horsewoman, albeit more timid than Grey would have liked, so she had probably been a careful one, too. Anyone who had been around stables knew the danger of fire.

Brandy felt as if some important information were prowling around in her mind, staying just out of her grasp. She searched through the pages again, and this time the phrases leaped at her with stunning force: "I think the old witch knows we are lovers"; "She'd like to see him dead, too. Then Raleigh would inherit"; "Mrs. Bailey is in a rage of jealousy, one more to come between the fortune and her favorite."

Competent Margaret Bailey who had run King's Inland for so many years? Yes, Mrs. Bailey whose face was alight with love every time Raleigh arrived, never when Grey came home. Mrs. Bailey who remembered and tried to speak casually of Grey's always making the distinction between the "woman who takes good care of me and my real mother." Mrs. Bailey who was constantly fondling the treasures of the house as though they were living things; Mrs. Bailey who had nearly had heart failure when she had lost her hold on the piece of jade. Mrs. Bailey who got along well with Ruth Collins because Ruth had no intention of having children, because Ruth would let her continue her rule, because Ruth hated Missy as much as Mrs. Bailey did. Margaret Bailey who had little to do with Missy, not because she was too old, but because she loathed the child.

Brandy was terrified. She felt as if the bottom had just dropped out of the world, leaving her falling slowly after it. She tried to attribute the words to Jasmine's spite, but she did not succeed because the attempts on her own life were flashing before her. The futile but frightening attempts at smothering, the cut girth, the fire, all things a woman could do with stealth and little strength. And had the house burned, Mrs. Bailey had had an easy way out through the back, and Raleigh had not been there to worry about. It had been worth it to her to risk the loss of the house on the chance of killing all three—Brandy, Missy, Grey. And the day in the snow, not too difficult if Margaret Bailey had come home early and gotten Missy out, hiding her in her own apartment if not the music room; she would have been sure that Brandy would take the bait. But Missy, why hadn't she struggled? Too terrified probably, or too sleepy; Brandy remembered the drugged feeling she'd had. A careful dose in something they'd eaten? Had Mrs. Bailey lured Jasmine out—"I hear her c . . ."—to kill her before she could tell much and endanger Raleigh? Perhaps she had known that Grey had ridden off after an argument but had not realized the full extent of his knowledge. Why hadn't she killed Missy then? Because no matter how much she hated her, there was a chance that Missy was the child of her beloved Raleigh.

"But why me? Why should she want to kill me?" Brandy asked aloud, and had the answer—because she was making progress with Missy and the child might soon tell what she'd seen that night. And the half-told tale of Rafe's crime—the child left out, no mention of the fact that Rafe had found his wife with her lover, that fitted the sly, malicious way. Make Brandy distrust everyone. She saw the pattern with Grey too. No doubt with a great show of innocent concern, Mrs. Bailey had planted the suggestion that Brandy and Raleigh were involved with each other, and no doubt Brandy had been pictured as the improper one. And Ruth had been told by someone that Brandy and Grey were carrying on. Make everyone distrust Brandy. With grim amusement, Brandy admitted to herself that her usual lack of decorum had undoubtedly made the housekeeper's job easier. But she reflected with no amusement at all that Mrs. Bailey must have heard her struggle with Grey and ignored it. Another way to make her leave. Another way to destroy lives.

Her longing for Grey was so intense that she sobbed. Even with Jasmine's account, she did not think anyone else would believe her. She wanted to spirit Missy away, but she could imagine how insane Rafe or the Cowperwaithes would think her story; they had all known and trusted Margaret Bailey for too long. And they would not want to face Grey's anger if he came home to find that his daughter had been kidnapped by her governess.

She had never felt so cornered. She buried her face in her hands and then froze as she heard a faint sound at her door. It seemed an age before she made herself move, but then she went swiftly to the door and opened it. There was no one in the hall, and Missy's door was closed.

Stop it this instant! If you can behave normally until

Grey gets home, everything will be all right. No one else knows the diary exists. She drew a deep breath, and the world refocused. She was late for supper, and she hurried to freshen up, trying to erase all evidence of tears, and go downstairs; no sense in doing anything out of the ordinary.

Mrs. Bailey greeted her pleasantly, and Brandy realized how difficult it was going to be to maintain her air of innocence; even the older woman's smile gave her gooseflesh. She wished the weather had been severe enough to keep Persia from going home except that it might delay Grey's return. She was afraid to ask if Mrs. Bailey had heard from him since even that now sounded suspicious, but the housekeepr volunteered the information.

"I received word from Grey today. Poor man, he seems to be having difficulty completing some chore, but he said to expect him night after tomorrow."

Not so long to wait. *Why has she told me? Is it because Rafe picked up the letter for her and she is afraid he might have mentioned it? Or is it just to test my reaction?* The questions were shouting in Brandy's brain, and she felt the creeping paralysis of fear triumphant. She forced herself to look straight at Mrs. Bailey, wondering if she ought to provide herself with extra protection by telling her she could be leaving soon, deciding not to because it could be used as another weapon against Missy's sanity. Instead, she said noncommittally, "Oh, so soon? He certainly doesn't seem to mind the rigors of winter travel."

The bright-blue eyes watching her from behind their spectacles seemed more intense than usual.

She excused herself as soon as the meal was finished, saying that Missy had been very restless and she hoped she wasn't coming down with anything. Mrs. Bailey expressed her concern, and Brandy hated her.

She tried to compose herself before she went into Missy's room; the last thing the child needed was to know that she was afraid. But she had no intention of letting Missy sleep alone. She didn't think Mrs. Bailey would attempt anything—why should she when there was no reason to suspect that Brandy knew?—but she wasn't going to take any chances. She had thought of moving Missy in with her because her door had a latch on it while Missy's did not. But she feared the change would upset the child and warn the housekeeper. On the other hand, if she stayed with Missy while she slept and then just neglected to leave until early morning, the child might never know, and if Mrs. Bailey checked on her, it would appear that nothing was out of the ordinary save for Brandy's worry that Missy might be sickening for something. She devoutly hoped that Missy would not be in one of her wakeful moods for the next two nights.

She put on her night rail and took down her hair in her own room and went back to the child. Missy stirred but did not awaken, and even Panza went back to sleep after one lazy wag of his tail. Brandy spent the night awake in the chair by the fire and slipped back to her room at sunrise, feeling a little foolish and very tired besides. There had been no sound of anyone prowling, no creaking boards or doors softly opened, and Brandy thought the vigil had probably been a waste. She still could not believe that Mrs. Bailey would try anything violent so close to Grey's homecoming, but if she did, Brandy was certain it would be by stealth at night since face to face she was easily stronger than the older woman. The important thing was not to leave Missy unprotected.

By the time she went downstairs Persia was there, and Brandy was so glad to see her that she nearly blurted out a plea for her to stay the night. But she stopped herself in time; she had no adequate reason to give Persia, and it would warn Mrs. Bailey that something was afoot.

Persia eyed her with concern. "You're lookin' peaky again. Is somethin' wrong?"

"No," Brandy assured her. "I just need more fresh air. I'll take Missy for a walk this afternoon."

"That's a splendid idea. You do look pale and tired." Brandy had not seen Mrs. Bailey come in, and she barely restrained herself from jumping like a startled rabbit at the sound of her voice. She wondered if she imagined the sarcasm underlying the cheerful tones.

The day passed with agonizing slowness, but a long walk helped and served a useful purpose besides—Brandy wanted Missy to be tired enough to sleep the whole night through again. On their way home, she saw Rafe in the distance and waved to him but continued toward the house, curbing her desire to run to him and beg him to take them both away.

She could hardly bear it when Persia called her happy good-night and left at dusk. She felt utterly forsaken by all save the evil force at King's Inland. Then her chin went up, and she thought: *Come on, Brandy, just one more night, and then Grey will be here.* She even managed to chat naturally with Mrs. Bailey during dinner, and the housekeeper made no protest when she again excused herself right after.

She checked on Missy and saw with satisfaction that she was sleeping soundly. Then she went to her own room and changed into what she now considered her disguise, since the last thing she intended to do was to sleep. She looked longingly at her bed, knowing that if she lay on it even for a minute, she would probably sleep for a week. She decided to take the book from Pearl and the letter to Hugh with her to keep her occupied and awake. The letter would be particularly useful for that, she thought ruefully, for now that she knew so much about Grey's past and present motives, now that she knew her love was justified, it was going to be doubly difficult to write to Hugh. She opened the writing box to take out the fragment she already had written.

Her mouth was instantly dry; her voice echoed oddly

in her ears. "Very stupid, very untidy, Mrs. Bailey, or do you want me to *know* you've read them?"

The locket lay on top of Hugh's letter, not under where it had been, and she knew she had put the papers back and closed the panel carefully though now it was slightly awry and the corner of one of the thin sheets protruded through the crack, probably from being crammed half in half out of the drawer behind. Perhaps Persia had surprised Mrs. Bailey in her reading, and she had had to put everything back quickly. But how had she known? Brandy remembered the sound at her door, the sound she had discounted as the product of overnight nerves. She had been late, and the housekeeper had come to see what she was up to.

Her skin prickled as if ants were walking in legions over her, but she did not seem to be able to move or think at all. Then she heard the sharp echo of a self-given command. "Move, damn it, move, get to Missy!"

Even as she wrenched open her door, she heard the front door slamming shut. She grabbed up the trailing skirt of her night dress and ran, slipping and sliding on the stairs, cursing in desperation as she stopped to open the heavy door. She made it outside in time to see Mrs. Bailey dragging Missy into the barn. "I'm coming, Missy!" she screamed as she saw the door close.

She ran through the snow to the door and swung it open, stopping dead. The bar had been left off on purpose, of course. She was doing everything according to Mrs. Bailey's plan. The barn and the stable wings were in complete darkness, but the horses were stamping and nickering nervously. She was in there somewhere, waiting for her. But all of Brandy's caution left her when she heard Missy crying, and she headed for the sound, stumbling over things she couldn't see.

The sobbing was coming from one of the empty box stalls. Brandy called as she came, "It's all right, darling, I'll be there in a minute." She found the entrance to the stall, and in the next instant, Missy was in her arms.

The double door slammed shut behind them, and she heard both bolts go home. The housekeeper's voice was muffled by the heavy doors, but its eerie quality came through. "Nicely done, Mrs. Bailey, an end to all of this, a beginning for my Raleigh, my own Raleigh. He liked people to think I was his mother, oh, yes, he did, not like the other one. She should have died, useless woman, but not him, that was mean; he should have lived to make pretty Margaret into Mrs. King, into Raleigh's mother. Oh, this is much better than burning the house down; that was a silly thing to think of." It was as if she were crooning to a separate part of herself, to pretty Margaret whose plans for becoming mistress of King's Inland had been blighted by the random chance of the master's death by disease. Light and dark, not in Ruth or Rafe or Raleigh, not in Grey or Missy, but in Margaret Bailey.

Brandy's flesh crawled, but she made her voice strong. "Mrs. Bailey, you can't get away with this. Let us out!"

The laugh cackled hysterically. "No, I can't do that. I have you right where I want you. That damned Jasmine, she left things for you to read. And I didn't tell you the truth—Grey will be home late tonight, not tomorrow night, late enough to find you both in ashes. And who will believe he didn't do it? It happened once before, you know. I wish he'd died then too. They'll get rid of him, and my Raleigh will have everything."

"You *are* mad! Grey will know you did it. He'll kill you for it. Or Rafe will come." Keep her talking, please God, let one of them arrive in time.

The ugly laughter assaulted her ears again. "Rafe won't be out on a night like this, last time was a lot more risky. And Grey might think Missy did it, but I don't care if he knows the truth; it would be better if he kills me. The loyal housekeeper murdered, the governess and his child burned to death. Bad boy to do all that. He'll be hung for it, and Raleigh will be king. Oh, clever, pretty Margaret."

The voice became querulous. "It's all your fault; you

were making Missy well again. I *promised* her nothing would happen to her father if she kept still about how her mother died. But she won't keep her part of the bargain. It's only fair she should pay."

The key to Missy's terrible silence, the blinding revelation that the child had given up the world not because she feared her father, but because she loved him enough to destroy herself to keep him safe. What little hope Brandy had died in that knowledge; anyone insane enough to so abuse a child was capable of any evil. Keep her talking.

"What about Raleigh? You know what this will mean to him."

"He'll hate Grey for it, not me. It's sad, but he wouldn't like it if he knew I killed Jasmine, and now Missy might tell him."

"Mrs. Bailey . . . Margaret . . . what if we promise not to tell about tonight? Will you let us go?" There was no answer. "Margaret, are you still there?" Brandy tried to keep the rising panic out of her voice. No response. Margaret Bailey was too clever to be delayed by such a simple ruse.

She made her voice steady. "Stay here, darling. I'm going to see if I can get the door open." She hugged Missy convulsively and moved the short pace to the door. She threw her weight against it again and again; she tore the ends of her fingers trying to pry open a crack so she could lift the bolts. It was no use; the stall had been built of the finest wood to hold even the most unmanageable horse; her puny strength didn't even make it creak. She slumped against the door, panting, and then held her breath and tried to hear any noises from outside. There was silence, and then a horse screamed and others answered. She heard a crash and another scream which sounded human. She hoped viciously that Mrs. Bailey had had her skull caved in by a pair of hooves. It wouldn't do them any good, though, for the noise of the terrified animals was increasing, accompanied by the sound of crashing timber and a strange roaring. Brandy caught the first odor of smoke. So this is the way it's going to be, she thought, such a horrid, wasteful way to die. She ceased to be afraid; all she felt was overwhelming sorrow for what Grey must now bear and for Missy who had just found life again and was now to lose it forever.

She went back and cradled her. She expected she would be in such shock by now that she wouldn't know what was happening, but Missy was renewing her contact with the world with a vengeance. Her body, completely pliable and responsive, pressed against Brandy, her hands touched and soothed with an eloquence which said clearly, *Don't worry about me; I fear for you*.

Brandy made no attempt to lie to her. "Missy," she said, "we aren't dead until we both stop breathing. Maybe we'll have a better chance when the fire reaches us, maybe the door will burn enough for us to get it open. Maybe not. But we have to try to stay alive. Your father needs us." She choked on the last words; smoke was beginning to fill the stall.

She took Missy's hand. "Come on, we're going to get close to the door so I'll know if I can open it." Brandy had to shout because suddenly the roar was all around them. She shoved Missy to the floor. "Better to breathe there, stay down!" she gasped, and knew Missy understood, for her hands told her the child was staying put.

She began to push and claw frantically at the door, and she thought it might be giving way a little, perhaps from the flames on the other side, when she heard the creaking above her and looked up into the hellish glow of the first flames eating the beams. She saw a section begin to sag, and she threw herself on Missy. She managed to say clearly, "I love you, Missy," and she heard Missy say her first word after the long silence, "Brandy," before the world caved in.

CHAPTER XIII

Sounds. "Brandy, love, can you hear me?" a man's voice kept repeating, and a strangely pitched child's voice begged insistently, "Wake, please, Papa needs, don't leave," abbreviating the connections, speaking only the heart words.

Brandy opened her eyes slowly. She was lying on her stomach. The snow was cold beneath the material against her skin, and she wrinkled her nose against the sour, scorched smell of the air. How odd to be lying naked outdoors—well, not entirely, something covered her back. Her head was cradled in someone's lap. They would fire her from Greenfield Academy for this. She started to laugh, but pain exploded in her rib cage and rippled along her back and legs, and the sound came out as a whimper. A confusion of hands were stroking her head, two large, two small. "Missy?" she croaked.

The man's voice again, Grey's, curiously husky. "Don't try to talk or move, sweetheart. Missy's fine. You protected her; the fire didn't touch her. But you've got some burns, and I think you've broken a couple of ribs. Rafe has gone to get a big blanket so we can carry you in safely."

Despite the pain, she worked desperately to turn her head enough to look up, and she saw the tear streaks on his soot-stained face. "Even the devil cries sometimes," he said, and then his voice broke, and his hard body

217

trembled. "Brandy, Brandy, I came so close to losing you tonight."

"But we found Missy! Grey, she's home again. She always loved you."

"Yes," said Missy, and kissed Brandy on the cheek. "Now you Mama?"

Grey's voice answered for her, hesitant, humble. "She will be if she wants to. Bad things have happened to her at King's Inland, and she may want to leave." But then he ruffled Brandy's hair and said to Missy, "But the fire cut her hair so short, if she leaves right away, someone might think she's a boy and kidnap her for a sailor."

Missy giggled, a melodious child's sound, and observed wisely, "No, there's girl under coat."

Brandy gasped and would have managed to laugh this time if she hadn't caught sight of Grey's hands and arms. He had been holding her as if completely unaware of the burns he'd got. "Grey, your poor hands!"

"It's not serious. Looks worse than it is," he said briefly.

Everything rushed back. "Mrs. Bailey? The horses?"

Grey's voice was steady. "Margaret is dead. We got Pete, Polly, one of the colts, and Lady out. We can talk about it later, when you're better."

Rafe appeared with the blanket, and when they slid her onto it and lifted her, she could see the glow of the still-burning stables. She shut her eyes and concentrated on keeping silent. Rafe and Grey were being as gentle as they could; crying out would only make it harder for them. She found it curiously easy to keep still; anything was better than death.

She drifted in and out of consciousness, but she was aware in flashes of Rafe and Grey taking care of her, putting something which smelled strongly of tea on her burns, salving her torn hands, binding her ribs. She tried to say something about how many things Maine men knew how to do, but she lost the words and slept instead.

Missy was often present and so was Persia when Brandy opened her eyes, but Grey seemed to be forever there, his own hands bandaged, his face weary but peaceful, the old harshness gone as if it had never been.

Finally, after what seemed an eternity of drifting, Brandy wakened fully. Her body hurt in a thousand places, but she was clearheaded. It was evening, and Grey was sleeping exhaustedly, hunched in the chair beside her bed, but he felt her gaze and opened his eyes.

"Go to bed right now," she commanded.

She watched the dawning of his smile in wonder, no longer a brief twisting of the lips but a full acknowledgment of joy flowing to light the midnight eyes. "Now I know you will be all right, bossy Brandy." Tenderness had replaced the mockery in his voice, and Brandy resigned herself to spending the rest of her life feeling weak-kneed and fluttery every time he smiled or spoke to her.

His expression sobered as he asked, "Do you want to talk about it now?"

"No. I want you to get some sleep first." What she really wanted was for him never to have to read Jasmine's hateful words, but since they existed, she did not feel she had the right to keep them from him.

He went and got Persia and then hovered until Persia shooed him away, assuring him that Brandy's fever had broken and that she was perfectly capable of taking care of her. He kissed Brandy before he left, not at all embarrassed by Persia's presence.

Persia looked so pleased about the whole thing that Brandy laughed, and Persia said, "Well, I do like things to work out, an' I never could abide that Collins woman."

She was as competent as she claimed, bringing Brandy a light meal, fluffing pillows and deftly rearranging the bed clothes to make her more comfortable. She chattered away, and Brandy was content to listen to her account of Missy's amazing talents. "Why, she's just as bright as a button, always was, just took you to know it." She hesitated and then went on. "That wicked, wicked woman, it's still past believin'. Did you reckon it was her?"

"Not until it was almost too late."

"Why ever didn't you come to Rafe or me as soon as you knew?"

"Because, as you said, it was past believing." There was no accusation in Brandy's voice, but Persia said contritely, "You're right. We'd known her for so long it would've been a goodly fish to swallow."

When Brandy woke again, it was morning, and Missy came to visit her. Brandy thought the child's voice the best music she had ever heard. Her inflections were close to normal now, her sentences were filling out, and Brandy was amused by this proof that Missy had been doing a lot of practicing. She found to her relief that Missy could talk about "bad Mrs. Bailey" and the fire with no qualms; she had been through so much before that the terrifying way her silence had ended seemed to have left no additional scars.

"Darling, I know everything you did was to protect your father, but why didn't you just tell him about Mrs. Bailey?" Brandy asked.

Missy looked at her, obviously surprised an adult could be so foolish. "I saw what she did to Mama. She said would do to Papa if I told." Brandy saw the terrible logic of it; Margaret Bailey had killed Jasmine, had destroyed the security of Missy's world; how was the child to know that Grey was strong enough to prevent the same thing from happening to himself? Missy's voice went steadily on. "She was bad. She came at nighttime to your room. I watched. I was afraid for you."

Brandy swallowed the lump in her throat at the thought of this tiny child staying awake, helpless, but still trying to protect someone she loved. "Missy," she asked gently, "that day when I went out in the snow, were you in the music room?"

Missy shook her head. "No, I went to sleep in my room. You were there. When I woke up, Papa was there." Brandy's suspicions were confirmed—undoubtedly they had both eaten something which had contained a sleeping draft. Had Missy not been drugged when Mrs. Bailey picked her up, she might have screamed in terror. And Brandy was sure that Missy had been taken to Mrs. Bailey's quarters, a truly safe hiding place, not the music room. No wonder the housekeeper had so kindly prepared that nice meal with many of their favorite dishes. What an evil woman to risk poisoning a child with too much of some drug, probably laudanum, so easily obtainable for the headache.

"You are the bravest person I know, Missy, but now you don't have to be so brave anymore; you've got your father to be brave for you."

Missy twisted a thread on her dress and asked anxiously, "Will you stay? He can be brave for you, too."

Brandy smiled at her. "Your father and I have many things to talk about, but I expect I'll be here for a very long time."

Grey appeared at the door, and Missy ran to him, squeaking excitedly as he lifted her in his arms. "She *will* stay. I told you!"

Grey's eyes met Brandy's, and Missy said, "Put me down now. I will go to my room so you can talk grown-up." She bustled out with Panza at her heels.

Grey shook his head in mock despair. "Heaven help me! I've got two females giving me orders." His expression was suddenly as anxious and appealing as Missy's had been. "Did she get it right? Did you say you would stay?" His voice grew ragged. "Brandy, I'd be lying if I claimed I was a better man than Hugh Adams. I'm not. I am ruthless, arrogant, and cruel, you know that better than anyone." He swallowed audibly before he could continue. "But I swear I'll spend the rest of my life trying to make up for what I did to you."

Brandy couldn't bear it. "You will not, Grey King! We'll mark that off as a bad beginning, and we'll make a

new one together. I love you as you are; and I don't
want you to be like Hugh Adams. You are the only man
I know who could survive such tragedies as you've had
as well. And I discovered long ago that it makes me
absolutely miserable when you're humble!"

He was beside the bed, trying to temper his urgent
strength as he held her. "Damn your broken ribs," he
groaned, and cut off her laugh with a long kiss for which
she thought breathing well lost.

She would have been content to let the moment spin
out forever, but she still feared Jasmine's power to
destroy them. She pulled away a little and said, "I want
to talk about it now." He nodded.

She began by repeating all the signs which had led
her to believe that Missy's reaction to him was not
caused by hatred and fear as everyone assumed. "And of
course, the stronger my love for you became, the less
able I was to believe you were responsible for your
wife's death, your child's silence, or any of the things
which happened to me." She stated it as a simple fact,
but it didn't strike Grey as simple, and she had to look
away from his fierce joy before she could go on. "Then I
found something and through me, Margaret Bailey did,
too. She even talked about them in the barn, along with
all the other crazy things she said." Brandy related
snatches of Mrs. Bailey's mad monologue, putting the
time off, but then her voice faltered. "Grey, I . . . maybe
I should have burned them. I don't know. But I think
you have the right to read them. Will you bring me the
writing box from the desk, please?"

Grey had listened in stunned silence to Brandy's
account of Mrs. Bailey's mad speech, and he was puzzled by her request, but he complied and set the box
on the bed within Brandy's reach. But she didn't touch
it. "Was it always kept in this room, or was it in
Jasmine's room before?"

He understood. "No, it was kept in here. I didn't
know that Jasmine ever used it, and I guess Margaret
didn't either because she knew of the secret drawer;

she showed it to Raleigh and me once. It was something to amuse two restless boys on a rainy afternoon.
We even used it for a while for hiding special treasures
until its novelty wore off."

Brandy had tripped it accidentally with the locket
chain, but now she saw how it worked. Grey opened
the box and pulled out one of the small drawers,
reached into the empty space and pushed something at
the back. The panel under the writing surface clicked
open. Grey's hands were steady as he straightened the
sheets, and his face was very still as he read. Brandy
watched anxiously, afraid she would see pain flash in his
face, confirming Jasmine's eternal ability to hurt him,
but his expression did not alter, and when he was
finished, he rose and put the sheets into the fire and
returned to her, meeting her eyes squarely.

"There wasn't much in those that I didn't know
except for Margaret's treachery, but that blindness was
enough; it nearly cost you your life, nearly ruined
Missy forever. I knew Raleigh was Margaret's favorite,
but I didn't know he was her obsession, didn't know
how much she hated me or how jealous she was of my
love for my mother. Pitiful woman, she was wrong
about my father; he would never have married her,
even had he lost my mother. He adored my mother,
who, frail as she was, was always full of laughter and
love for him. And I never saw that Margaret's attach-
ment to King's Inland, to the house itself, was a sickness. And Jasmine was right about my intentions that
night." His voice did not falter. "I did want to kill
Raleigh, but the distance between us was enough to
blunt my rage. I realized that killing my brother would
accomplish nothing except perhaps to separate me from
Missy for the rest of my life. I turned back and found
the stable in flames, Jasmine dead. I knew I hadn't
done it; I thought it was an accident. But then the
change in Missy was so devastating I felt I was to blame
because I had started the whole disaster by quarreling
with Jasmine. Perhaps I was a little mad with guilt. And

then, God forgive me, when things started happening to you, I truly believed they were Missy's doing, and I was helpless against it; I couldn't bear the idea of putting her away. And I thought if anyone could change her, you could. I risked your life for it. For that I will never forgive myself. As for the rest of it, the affair between Jasmine and Raleigh, that had nothing to do with you and will have nothing to do with our life together."

Brandy knew he believed it, and she wanted to believe it with him, but she had to be sure all the ghosts had been exorcised. "My darling, I am a strong-willed woman; I stayed in spite of your protests. The risk was mine and worth it; any risk will always be worth it because I love you so. But I must ask—what about Raleigh, now that you know so much, do you blame him? And what of Missy, seeing it written, knowing it may very well be true, does that make you love her less?"

He winced at the harshness of the questions, but he understood her need. "I blame Raleigh for committing adultery with my wife. But he was young, foolish, and jealous of me; all dangerous things to be with a woman like Jasmine. He and Jasmine paid much too heavy a price—Jasmine with her death; Raleigh by a loss of self-respect and knowing that though Missy may be his child, he will never be more than an uncle to her. I don't blame him for Margaret's crimes; it would destroy him completely to know he was the twisted root of them. I will tell him that she was mad, nothing more. As for Missy, I will never know whether or not I am her father by blood, but in every other way I am, and nothing on earth could make me love her any more than I do.

"There, love, don't cry," he said, brushing the tears from her cheeks.

"For joy," she managed to whisper before he kissed her again.

Neither of them heard Missy when she stopped at

the door, peeked in, and proceeded down the hall, explaining things to Panza. "Grown-ups talk funny ways, but it's all right, now she'll stay." Word perfect, she sang one of Brandy's songs as she skipped down the stairs.

ABOUT THE AUTHOR

THE LATEST BOOKS IN THE BANTAM BESTSELLING TRADITION

DON'T MISS
THESE CURRENT
Bantam Bestsellers

☐ 05097	**THE SISTERS** Robert Littel (A Bantam Hardcover Book)	**$16.95**
☐ 25416	**THE DEFECTION OF A. J. LEWINTER** Robert Littel	**$3.95**
☐ 25432	**THE OCTOBER CIRCLE** Robert Littel	**$3.95**
☐ 23667	**NURSES STORY** Carol Gino	**$3.95**
☐ 25135	**THE DANCING DODO** John Gardner	**$2.95**
☐ 25139	**THE WEREWOLF TRACE** John Gardner	**$3.50**
☐ 25262	**AMERICAN FLYER** Steven Smith	**$2.95**
☐ 25055	**THE CEREMONIES** T. E. D. Klein	**$3.95**
☐ 25074	**RETRIEVAL** Colin Dunne	**$2.95**
☐ 25378	**MY SCIENCE PROJECT** Mike McQuay	**$2.95**
☐ 24978	**GUILTY PARTIES** Dana Clarins	**$3.50**
☐ 24257	**WOMAN IN THE WINDOW** Dana Clarins	**$3.50**
☐ 23952	**DANCER WITH ONE LEG** Stephen Dobyns	**$3.50**
☐ 24184	**THE WARLORD** Malcolm Bosse	**$3.95**
☐ 22848	**FLOWER OF THE PACIFIC** Lana McGraw Boldt	**$3.95**
☐ 23920	**VOICE OF THE HEART** Barbara Taylor Bradford	**$4.50**
☐ 25053	**THE VALLEY OF HORSES** Jean M. Auel	**$4.95**
☐ 25042	**CLAN OF THE CAVE BEAR** Jean M. Auel	**$4.95**

Prices and availability subject to change without notice.

Buy them at your local bookstore or use this handy coupon for ordering:

Bantam Books, Inc., Dept. FB, 414 East Golf Road, Des Plaines, Ill. 60016

Please send me the books I have checked above. I am enclosing $_____
(please add $1.50 to cover postage and handling). Send check or money order
—no cash or C.O.D.'s please.

Mr/Mrs/Miss_____

Address_____

City_____ State/Zip_____

FB—2/86

Please allow four to six weeks for delivery. This offer expires 8/86.